Heir of Lightning

SATURN GUO

This is a work of fiction. Names, characters, places, and incidents either are the product of the author's imagination or are used fictitiously. Any resemblance to actual persons, living or dead, events, or locales is entirely coincidental.

Copyright © 2022 by Hanjia S. Guo

All rights reserved. No part of this book may be reproduced or used in any manner without written permission of the copyright owner except for the use of quotations in a book review. For more information, address: guo.saturn@gmail.com.

First paperback edition, 2022

Book design by Bandrei

ISBN 979-8-9869656-0-4 (paperback)

Prologue

IT WAS SUPPOSED to be a beautiful day.

A beautiful day for the Kingdoms, where people across the world reveled in celebration of the Winter Solstice. A beautiful day in nature, where snow fell from the sky, covering the world gently in a blanket of pale white. A beautiful day for that woman expecting the birth of her twins.

The man strode through swathes of darkness as easily as a serpent slipping through water, a predator in search of prey, his mouth twisting into a grimace. Joy would morph into sorrow, light into darkness, and beauty into tragedy. Today, that woman would pay, a child would be stolen, and a world would begin to change.

Faintly, he wondered what he would do with the child once she was old enough to be manipulated by his words. Once she was old enough to understand the necessary evil required to save the world.

First, however, he would steal the child and make them all pay.

* * *

The barely-audible sound of snow tapping on the windows was strangely haunting.

Gray clouds hung over the sky like a vast curtain, broken only by the dull-orange light of the sunset. The sky's gloomy visage sharply contrasted the din of wild celebration echoing inside the palace. The Great Hall was filled with people feasting, dancing manically, and shouting raucously, inebriated or nearly so.

Piercing through the ruckus, a baby's cry rang through the elaborately decorated hallways. A woman sat propped up on a bed of silk and cotton. In her arms lay two babies, their tiny forms swaddled tightly, their shrieks fading into contented quiet as their mother cooed words of comfort into their ears. Even as young as they were, their eyes had already opened. The boy stared sleepily up at the queen, his eyes fluttering blearily before falling shut. Not quite asleep, but quiet and content. The girl, meanwhile, was squirming in her blankets, letting loose a cry of what the woman could only say was indignance—at what, she didn't know. A fist escaped the blankets and wildly flailed, managing to strike the woman's arm before she swaddled it back up. A sigh of happiness escaped her. As the woman clutched her children closer to her chest, she smiled. Two children, born on the Solstice. It was a perfect, beautiful day, but for one problem.

The pact.

An agreement made with a sorcerer of terror from so long ago, still unfulfilled even after generations of growing complacency. Although she tried to urge herself that it was impossible for *him* to still be alive, she could already feel the sorcerer's overwhelming presence approaching. She could feel that unearthly darkness, feel those creeping tendrils and slithering shadows and haunting nightmares, and from within the darkness the woman sensed the spirit of endless hatred, the ghost of a lost people, and then—

"Did you miss me?"

The voice wasn't what one would expect from a being of pure darkness.

It was smooth as honey, deep and entrancing, drawing her in and holding her close. His voice seemed to summon ringing echoes, indescribable tones of chaos that followed his words. His body blurred slightly at the edges, as if years of living in shadows had taken even his physical form away. If the woman looked very closely, she could just make out his eyes beneath the cowl of his hood. Even suffocated by the darkness, they shone a clear and beautiful gold.

"*I missed you... After all, I have been waiting patiently for my turn... Finally, the child shall be mine.*"

As he hissed those words, he leaned in, the shadows beneath the cowl covering his face revealing nothing more than a white streak of a smile. The woman knew the face and the lovely smile behind the cowl. They played like a broken record through her head, forging her stunningly deadly nightmares. They stared at each other, the face of beauty staring into the man of shadow, before he leaned back and tilted his head up, just the slightest bit.

"*You are... unwilling. No surprise there. But a promise is a promise, after all. Now, give me the child. I tire of repeating my words.*"

"Please. Not my children. Anything else. You can have anything else," she begged. The words she so desperately whispered stung her pride, but pleading was the only choice she had. Childbirth had stripped her of her strength and magic.

"*Begging will serve no use here.*" A pause. "*We made a deal. I've been waiting patiently. You promised me the child.*" As he spoke—well, no one really knew whether he spoke aloud, for the demonic echoes that trailed his words seemed to suggest otherwise—the woman felt her arms gently lift one of the children. The girl. In spite of herself, the woman felt a horrible sense of relief that he hadn't taken the firstborn. The man stood still as the woman, with obvious great effort, sat up in order to place the girl into the man's arms.

"Why the girl? Why not the firstborn?"

He looked at the woman with seeming incredulity, then threw his head back and laughed. His hair was curly and messy, and, exposed to the light, his stunning golden eyes only seemed to shine brighter. Around him writhed shadows, swirling in unorganized spires of darkness, almost as if his body had been consumed by the darkness.

"*You know me. You know my past, and you know of the future I will create. The girl will become my tool. I will manipulate her just as I would have manipulated myself. She will be mine, as a firstborn will never be.*"

"No," the woman said. "She'll never be yours."

The man let out a low laugh that was both enthralling and haunting, spidery fingers reaching out from the sleeve of his cloak to gently touch the girl's cheek. Far from crying or thrashing away, the daughter seemed to curl into the man's touch.

"She will. She will grow up to hate me, but when she understands why she was given to me, she will hate you more – and then, well. She'll be joining me soon."

"No."

"Think about it."

The woman let out a shuddering breath and clutched her son closer to her chest.

"Her name," she murmured. "At least let me name her. Please."

"Her name is not ours to decide."

"What do you–"

"Look out of the window."

The snow was beginning to slow. It fell, still, but lightly. The last rays of the sun shone atop the snow covering the castle grounds, nearly blinding the woman with glimmering brilliance as she squinted at what the sun illuminated.

Blooming amid a wasteland of ice and snow was a single blood-red rose.

"A rose? In the midst of winter?"

"Almost as if magic itself is celebrating the birth of your twins. A pity, I must say, that I cannot have both."

"Her name?"

"Rose."

"Fitting," the woman murmured. As she looked back out of the window, the sun completely vanished from the horizon, leaving the world outside in complete, suffocating darkness.

When she looked back, the man was gone.

* * *

It had been *decades*.

Decades of careful scheming, planning, researching, creating, and waiting. Now, with the girl finally in his arms, he could begin the first chapter of a revolution.

He cradled the sleeping child, staring down at her in amazement. This tiny thing, so small and so fragile, could be destroyed with a twitch of his finger—and yet she held so much life, so much magic within her.

Withdrawing blood from her barely took a few seconds. Carefully, he disinfected and bandaged the cut on her arm before gently laying her in the small, blanket-lined basket beside him. The knife had seemed more ritualistic. Fitting. Besides, his Darkness would've hurt more. For now, her role was finished.

The blood was still warm as he dipped a brush into the vial.

Painstakingly, the Dark Sorcerer drew a large hexagonal symbol on the ground. He felt a strange urge to laugh. It was a cliché way to create a homunculus, but the most effective nonetheless. Staring down at the intricate design painted on the stone floor, the man turned and plucked five vials of beautiful, golden liquid from the walls. *The blood of a raiju, phoenix, griffin, nymph, and mermaid. The blood of your enemy's child. Combine them, infuse it with your magic and blood, and create your homunculus.*

The man withdrew the knife from his belt and slashed diagonally over his wrists, ignoring the brief spark of pain. Scarlet blood spilled out of the cuts, splattering over the hexagonal symbol of gold and red blood. Slowly, steadily, it began to glow. Gathering his magic within his palms, the Dark Sorcerer took a deep breath before feeding it to the hexagon. It absorbed it greedily, shining with a luminescent black light that slowly took the form of a small child. Letting out a shaking breath, the Dark Sorcerer dropped his hands and stared up into the flickering form of his homunculus.

It was still incomplete.

The final sacrifice was still required. To create the form of a human required the materials to do so: a body, a soul, and a heart, a sacrifice from another. The Dark Sorcerer had tranquilized the sacrifice so that they wouldn't feel pain. As an orphan, they wouldn't be missed. Even so, he felt just a touch of sickening nausea as he placed the human child onto the circle.

There was a final flash of light before it faded away, the blood and sacrifice consumed, leaving behind only the figure of a small boy. He took after his creator's appearance. A perfect human, imbedded with its creator's will, bound to the Dark Sorcerer by blood. A smile bloomed on the man's face, a slash of white in pure darkness.

"Hello, Prince..."

Chapter One

"ARE YOU STILL THERE?"

"Yes, Rhysand. Don't you worry."

"Can you... hold me?"

"Okay."

"I'm sorry. I'm... so sorry."

"Don't you worry, Rhysand."

"You'll... be joining me... soon, right?"

"Yeah. Yeah, I will. Rest easy."

* * *

As Rose slowly drifted into awareness, the first things she registered were the tears on her face and the distinct feeling that she had forgotten something. Sitting up, Rose wiped her face, staring at the faint reflection of her face on the clock across from her, straining to remember what she had been dreaming about. There had been suffocating darkness and a little boy with swollen veins, but even as she strained to remember what it was, the dream faded from her mind like water between her fingers. Sighing, Rose allowed herself to stretch for a few seconds before scrambling out of bed.

As she made her bed, she surveyed her surroundings with a forlorn eye. It was a dull space, a small attic adorned only by the few belongings she owned: a picture of herself with Katherine as a child, a warm, pastel blue sweater that Master had given her on a particularly cold day, and a small bag of candies from a few weeks ago that she had somehow preserved until now. The bed, a straw pallet with a thick but suspiciously itchy blanket, fit its surroundings. Even though it looked shabby, Rose's main complaint was how small it was – she had, after all, been using it for all fifteen years of her life. With the corners folded in and tucked underneath the mattress, it was tiny, only a foot longer than Rose's height and about three feet across. She was just about to make her way to the bathroom when, suddenly, she heard footsteps outside. The door to her room was thrust open, slamming against the wall with a loud crash. Rose flinched.

"Rose!" Master, in his foul-faced glory, stormed into the room. There was a split-second of silence as Master took in her disheveled hair and appearance before he sighed.

"I thought I told you there were two meetings today?" he asked.

Oh, shit. That's what she had forgotten. Rose's mouth opened and closed as Master shut his eyes and pressed a hand to his forehead.

"I—" Rose began, her mouth dry.

"Rose. They arrive in three hours! Breakfast should be *ready* by now!" The last words were hissed with a ferocity that sent Rose scrambling back toward the wall, her back pressed against its cold surface. Master glared at Rose, who averted her gaze to stare at the ground, before sighing once again and stalking out of her room. Being late was bad, very, very, bad, and Rose cursed her forgetfulness as she ducked into the bathroom. The mirror hanging on the wall was cracked on its left side, but functional, and the bathroom itself was clean, if not a bit cramped. Letting out a sigh, she dragged a small hickory comb through her hopelessly tangled hair. She eventually gave up, securing her hair behind her back in a high ponytail that would keep it out of her face. It wasn't going to be a good day. She had already screwed up. If she managed to piss him off again, there would be consequences. Fear welled within her, and Rose grimaced, taking a deep breath and shoving it down. Fear made you clumsy, fear made you stumble, fear made you weak.

I will not be afraid.

She slowly backed out of the bathroom, running her hands through her hair one final time before exiting her room. After running past a laundry room and wine cellar, Rose turned a sharp right and entered the kitchen.

"Morning, Rose!"

"Hey, Katherine. Do you have Master's breakfast? I'm late," Rose said, stopping to catch her breath at the doorway of the kitchen.

"You forgot about the meeting?" Katherine asked, exasperated. "Wait a few seconds. Take this food while you're at it too."

"Thanks, Katherine," Rose said gratefully, straightening up and accepting the slightly charred, buttered bread. Rose watched as Katherine carefully removed the tray of bread from the oven, placing it and a cup of some sort of light alcohol onto a tray on the table. The tray in question, mahogany brown in color, was laden with dishes Master was fond of: rice covered in toppings such as pickled lettuce and salted pork, fried bacon, a small crystal bowl on the side filled with smoked salmon, freshly baked bread with butter and marmalade, and a plate covered in ornately cut fruit.

"Okay, you can take it now. You're serving him today at the library, right?"

"Yeah. Pain in the ass. Which books do you want?"

"I'll write you a note later. You should hurry," Katherine urged. Carefully picking up the tray, Rose couldn't help but glance back at Katherine one last time before walking out of the kitchen. Watching her cook was soothing and familiar. After all, every movement was intricately familiar to Rose. They *had* grown up together, indentured to Master since birth, and even though Katherine was only a year older than Rose, she had always felt like an older sister. She was much more level-headed, even as a child: the steel to Rose's fire. Katherine was so focused that she didn't even glance at Rose, carefully adorning an intricately made pastry with some sort of frosting.

"Good luck today, Rose," Katherine said.

"Thanks," Rose said. When she eventually reached the door, Rose carefully balanced the tray on her knee before opening the door, wincing as the tray tilted.

With a creak, the door opened.

"Master, your breakfast," Rose muttered quietly, placing the tray on the table in front of him before casting her eyes toward the floor and curtsying. She was dressed in the common servant garb, a comfortable cotton shirt with sleeves that ended just beneath the shoulders, breeches that ended below the knee, and a black cloak slung around her body. Embroidered on the back was Master's symbol.

"You're late," Master hissed. He looked over the tray on the table, and Rose's heart pounded in her chest as he contemplated her with narrowed eyes. After a minute of silence, he turned away and dismissed her with a flick of his hand.

"Clean the library, prepare it for the client, then ask Katherine what she needs. You're dismissed." Rose couldn't help but let out a sigh of relief as she exited the lounge, making a left turn and breaking into a run as she ascended the staircase and opened the heavy doors to the library.

The library was enormous. With over ten thousand books, Rose stopped and admired the sight of the high-rising shelves before shaking herself out of her stupor and turning her attention toward the table in the center. Across it was sprawled several books and maps: *The Five Sorcerers, A History of Royal Sabotage,* and a map of the Six Kingdoms. Rose tilted her head and stared at the intricate lines and borders, fingers grazing the Lightning Kingdom to their east before she shook her head and picked up the scroll. Scooping a few books into her arms, Rose grabbed one of the stools and shelved them. The table was used for all of the meetings Master held, some with clients, others with the occasional friend or visitor, most of them with "the Council." Tucking a few books into her alcove, Rose cast one last look at the library, making sure everything was perfect, before backing out and closing the door carefully. If she made a single mistake today, she was dead.

* * *

"Katherine!" Rose shouted into the kitchen. Katherine looked toward her and then smiled.

"Master sent you? Yes, I needed someone to head to the Market anyway," Katherine told her, winking. The Market was Rose's favorite place. When the previous cook, a stern man named Ashter, had left Master's abode, Katherine had taken his place. Rose had snuck into Katherine's room that night to tell her about how *lucky* she was that she could go to the Market regularly. As a child, Ashter had taken her there on multiple occasions. Even then, she had been enamored.

"If you really love it that much, I can send you there instead of going by myself."

"Wait, Katherine, you can't! You've never been to the Market, you have to see! It's amazing!"

"I've never liked crowds, Rose. You can go tomorrow. I have a list of things you need to pick up."

"Rose! Hello?" Katherine asked, peering into Rose's eyes.

"Yeah, sorry. I zoned out. Go on?"

"I'm going to need some saffron and cinnamon bark. Vanilla beans and cocoa if you can find that, and some of the oysters I heard were shipped in this morning—and some bambam berries. Master wants them for today's second meeting. If you can find them, some mint leaves would be good too. See if you can stop by the butcher and get some fresh veal."

"*Bambam* berries? Where'd you expect me to find *that*? It's way out of season!" Rose asked with incredulity in her voice. Katherine laughed.

"Take as long as you need," Katherine said, taking out a large cloth bag and a heavy bag of coins and tossing them at Rose. The coins *clinked* together merrily as she caught the bag. Grinning broadly, Rose ducked out through the kitchen door and skipped toward the direction of the market.

* * *

"Dragon eggs for sale! Dragon eggs for sale!" someone was shouting. Rose ignored him, pushing past his cart and crashing into a group of white-robed priests. They turned around, interrupted, and glared at her. Averting her eyes, Rose pushed past the large group of people listening to the priests and darted away.

The Market was a dusty, sweaty mess of people, mostly lowborns. Highborns—nobles, mages, knights, and successful merchants—would never lower themselves to the level of shopping at the Market. Fights often broke out on the roads in front of vendors, most going unchecked and only ending when one party was knocked out. Or dead! Rose was only safe from thieves because of the servant's emblem on the back and front of her cloak. Even so, Rose couldn't help but glance behind herself furtively as she pulled out a handful of gold coins, counting out thirteen for a single small bottle of red threads: saffron, an extremely rare spice that was exceedingly hard to find and harvest. Tucking it inside the worn bag clipped to her side, Rose squinted at the vendor next to her that carried an array of pretty necklaces and accessories made from acclaimed dragon bone.

"Is this real dragon bone?" Rose asked the vendor. He turned from his client and narrowed his eyes.

"I don't serve Nulls," he said. He sounded bored. As Rose seethed, the man *spat* at her before turning back to his customer.

After purchasing a quarter of a pound of cinnamon, cocoa, and vanilla beans, Rose walked toward the butcher's shop. He was one of the few that owned a real store. He lived above his shop and kept the animals in the back. Rose opened the door, wrinkling her nose at the scent of blood.

"What's needed today?" he grunted. Despite always being splattered with blood and currently holding a rather unpleasant-looking knife, he had a jolly deposition and treated Rose well enough, although that was probably due to the amount of money she spent on behalf of Master.

"Veal, apparently."

The butcher grimaced.

"Veal? I'm afraid I was going to wait a few hours to slaughter one, but since it's you, I'll do it now. Come back in half an hour."

Rose nodded. Half an hour was, hopefully, enough time to find some bambam berries.

After about twenty minutes of searching, Rose finally found a cart with a few baskets of pink-red berries. They were a bit larger than a coin, juicy with a tiny pit in the center, and mostly out of season. Handing over the last of the coins in the pouch, Rose strapped the cloth bag filled with berries onto her belt.

Just as she turned around, preparing to head back toward the butcher, she nearly bumped into the person behind her. Ducking her head, she muttered an apology and slowly backed away.

But when she saw the crest on the man's chest, Rose froze.

A slave trader.

Slave traders were required to identify themselves with an officially distributed badge, or they'd be arrested if they were transporting humans. The man glared at her, and Rose had to stop herself from glaring back. Slave traders were synonymous in her mind to scum of the earth. They were known for being cruel and uncaring for the people they transported, and some even kidnapped people, especially orphans, instead of buying or contracting slaves legally. Slave traders ran rampant in the Earth Kingdom, which, unlike the Lightning Kingdom, had no excess military power to enforce laws. Rose would, if she could, spit in his face and walk away. But she was Null. Magicless. Powerless. If he really did get mad, she wouldn't have any way to defend herself.

So Rose forced herself to avert her eyes, apologize politely, and walk past him.

* * *

"Rose!" Rose grimaced and turned toward Master. "I was looking for you. Where were you?"

"At the Market. Katherine sent me there," Rose responded. Master nodded.

"The guest pushed ahead the trade deal. It's in twenty minutes. All I need is basic refreshments and wine. *Don't be late.*"

Nodding, Rose clutched the bag of food and ran toward the kitchen. *Twenty minutes? He's crazy.* Bursting into the kitchen, Rose let out a sigh of relief when she saw the tray of refreshments already prepared.

"Rose? You're back? Put the food on the table and take the tray. Here, take these sausages. I'm sure you're hungry."

Rose accepted the food gratefully, which she devoured within seconds before wiping her hands on a nearby towel. After splashing her face with cold water, she made her way to the library.

Rose hurriedly set the table with champagne, pastries, and fruit. Glancing at the clock, Rose swore and slipped into an alcove hidden in the wall. The main entrance of the library opened, and inside walked a man in a cloak with a deep cowl that covered his face.

But on the man's cloak was a badge.

It was the slave trader from the market.

Chapter Two

EVEN AS THE slave trader's unpleasant voice echoed through the library, Rose smiled as she opened the book in her hands. She had been working *The History of the Six Kingdoms* in her free time. Serving Master's guests was *exhausting*, but the moments in between retrieving refreshments and meals were moments Rose used for her favorite pastime: reading.

"So, you say you have an offer of a slave for me?" the man asked.

"Yes," Master replied. Rose bit the inside of her cheek so hard she tasted blood and tuned out the conversation, focusing her attention on the *History of the Six Kingdoms*.

The book began with the creation of humans. That alone had taken up a third of the book, which had explained dozens of the most prevalent theories, from an all-powerful god up above to the creation of an ancient artifact to evolution from primal animals. After a long period of hunting and gathering, humans had then developed farming, thereafter developing domestication, weapons, and forming small civilizations.

"I'm not taking *it!*" the man shouted. Surprised, Rose jumped and grimaced. Master began to talk in a slow and soothing voice, likely working his magic with his words. Master was unusually well-spoken, even for a noble. Whenever he worked—which seemed to be *always*—it was with words. As his personal servant, Rose had grown up listening in to his endless conversations and bargains. Even in her earliest memories, she could remember his meetings with clients always ending up in his favor.

As time progressed, a ruler united the small civilizations into what historians deemed the Great Kingdom. Agriculture developed quickly and people began to specialize. The Great Kingdom lasted for six centuries until it fell to a rebellion, starting the Three Great Wars: the first being the efforts of the Kingdom to subdue the rebels, the second being the Kingdom's fall and the rebels' internal war, and the third being when unknown and uncontrollable forces of magic began to slaughter humans at random.

"Rose!" Master commanded. Rose snapped out of her reverie and exited the alcove, refilling the flutes of champagne before removing the plates and returning to the kitchen. When she returned, the two were examining a packet of papers. She served the beautifully plated opera cake to them carefully, trying her hardest not to draw attention, before returning to the alcove.

From the chaos eventually rose three kingdoms, which lay in fragile and tense peace for a century. However, magic continued to kill citizens without reason, and all pretense of peace was eventually shattered by the slow onset of the Great Famine that swept over the land and destroyed all life. The kingdoms, desperate for food, fought each other until they were all in ruin.

"Two thousand and twenty."

"No," the man said icily. Rose frowned. Even for Master, two thousand and twenty coins wasn't a reasonable number of coins to receive for a slave. Rose closed her eyes.

As the world descended into madness, with no explanation, six sisters gained the first traces of magic. Each gained control over Six Elements: Light, Fire, Air, Water, Earth, and Lightning. They subdued the conflict quickly, used their magic to restore prosperity and stability to the land, and split the land into Six Kingdoms, the same that still stood now. The kingdoms stood in peace for two centuries but for minor and brief conflicts, until, without warning, the Light Kingdom fell. From its ashes arose the aloof and cruel Dark Sorcerer, and with him, a terrible reign of darkness that lasted nearly a hundred years.

In front of Rose, the two men had seemed to reach a deal. Master shook hands with the slave trader, and he stalked out of the room.

"Who'd you sell?" Rose asked as she left the alcove. Master glanced at her, frowned, and shook his head. She was dismissed. Rose seethed.

"Who'd you sell?" Rose demanded again. "How could you sell one of us to *them*? None of us have done anything wrong!"

Master ignored her.

"Hey. *Look at me!* Tell me who you sold!" Rose shouted. Master paused, perfectly still, and twitched a finger. There was a blinding flash of pain across her cheek. Rose cried out and fell to the floor, scrabbling back away from Master, who turned around and stared down at her.

"You dare question me?" Master's voice was a low, dangerous rumble. "Know your place, *girl*. You're an orphan. A *Null*. You have no place in this world. You are *nothing*. Leave me, before I take out the whip."

Rose shrank away. Looked down. Bit her lip.

He was right.

Of the entire population of humans in the world, it was calculated that about 2.5% of people had absolutely no magic. Their lack of magical signature made them shockingly obvious to even the weakest of magic-users and gave them the nickname Nulls.

I am nothing.

Some Nulls, born into well-off families, could dodge the worst discrimination and live normal lives. With the influence that came with being a noble, they could go to school and even attain higher education. The vast majority of Nulls, though, lived harsh lives. Most infamously, the majority of schools in the Six Kingdoms universally turned away Null children. They often could not find employment. Most Nulls fell into poverty.

I am nothing at all.

Rose had no family. She was a servant, indebted to Master from birth, unable to escape the life she had been born into.

Nothing.

Ducking her head to hide her tears, Rose nodded and crept away.

It had been awhile since Master had said something so harsh and yet true.

The rest of the day was a blur of activity and movement. By the end of the day, Rose was exhausted. She collapsed into bed, her body heavy as though laden with weights, but even in her dreams, that word echoed: *nothing*.

* * *

"You remember all I have told you?"

"Yes."

"She will arrive tomorrow morning."

"Understood,"

"Oh, and, Prince?"

"Yes?"

"Please do not deviate from the plan."

"Understood."

"You will watch from the shadows. You *will not* get involved, no matter who dies and who lives, no matter how tempting it will doubtlessly be. The only thing you cannot do is let her die. Do not get involved otherwise."

"Understood."

* * *

Rose was awoken by a hand clapping over her mouth.

A muffled cry escaped from her mouth as Rose thrashed, biting down on the hand and tasting blood. The man holding her cursed and dropped her. Rose hit the ground with a *thud* and scrambled to her feet, sprinting for the door. Panic raced through her veins, adrenaline blocking out the pain of falling to the floor.

"Use your magic!" *That voice sounded familiar.*

"All right, all right!"

Rose went still.

The second voice belonged to Master.

Rose had been one of Master's servants since the beginning of her memory. He treated her coldly, and they despised each other – even so, there were moments of kindness that had made her think... she hadn't expected to be *sold* to a *slave trader*. He had never treated her cruelly. She had felt, after all, that she had been... needed. Wanted, even, because Katherine—*Katherine*, oh god, she couldn't even say goodbye. And now, she was being sold. Even though she had dreamed of escaping Master's home, she hadn't wanted it to be this way.

Immediately, Rose felt herself restrained by invisible magic, and even as she struggled and thrashed with all her might, she was carried effortlessly down flights of stairs until a door opened and she felt the cool night breeze on her skin. Rose opened her mouth to scream for help, but a cloth was tied over her mouth that rendered her mute.

It was strange that she felt betrayed. She had *never* trusted him, and yet ... Rose bit her cheek until she tasted blood. The adrenaline that had raced through her veins was now fading away, leaving her ears buzzing and hands trembling.

"Get moving! We're going to the shipment location in the Howling Deserts!" someone yelled. *A shipment location in the Howling Deserts.*

A shipment.

Rose had just become a slave.

Had it really been a few hours ago when she was in the Market? Was it just this morning that she had talked and laughed with Katherine?

Rose hunched over herself, buried her face in the cloak that still smelled like home, and wept.

* * *

At some point, Rose must've fallen asleep, because when she opened her eyes, the sun was shining through the open door.

"Get up and out of the wagon," the man in front of the door growled. Rose groaned, stumbling out of the wagon, one hand still clutching Master's black cloak.

"Put your hands behind your back!" the man ordered. Rose tossed on the cloak out of habit before allowing the man to shackle her wrists together. She was marched with two or three other people—*slaves*—toward the back of a wagon. When the door was opened, Rose nearly threw up from the stench of piss, blood, and shit that was now wafting from the wagon.

Um, no.

"Get in the wagon!" the man shouted, gesturing into the wagon.

Rose ran.

She barely made it ten feet before she was tackled to the ground, her shackled arms screaming in pain as one of the guards wrenched them back and pinned her down with a knee to the neck. Rose bucked and thrashed before turning her head and biting the man's arm. He cursed, loosening his grip, and Rose managed to roll away and scramble to her feet.

"Get back here, bitch!" the man yelled. He raised his hands, prepared to use magic, but as she rolled under what she was sure was an incoming blow, someone kicked her in the stomach. The point of a knife was pressed against her neck, and Rose stopped moving.

They're going to kill me. Rose squeezed her eyes shut.

"Eren, Angle, stop. We shouldn't harm the merchandise," a voice said from above her. There was a pause, and the pressure on the knife lightened. Rose tilted her head, staring up at the silver-haired boy who had spoken, and spat at him. He stepped back, averting his eyes, and walked away.

"If she really doesn't want to get into the wagon, I guess we won't make her," the man above her said with a harsh laugh. "Slave. We're in the Howling Deserts. We're more than three *thousand* miles away from the nearest village. If you escaped, you'd die."

"Fuck you," Rose spat, pushing herself up to her feet.

"She's going to make a shitty slave," he said. "Just put her in a cage. We can load her in the empty space in the supply wagons. I recommend you comply."

Rose's lips curled into a sneer. She turned around to run, only to feel a fist strike the side of her head. She fell to the ground, landing on her shoulder, crying out in pain before she was kicked in the side and everything went dark.

* * *

Rose woke up in a cage.

The cage was surrounded by crates that smelled of salt and briny seaweed, just out of reach of Rose's unshackled hands. It was just big enough for her to sit and stretch in. Clenching her fists around the bars, Rose attempted to bend them apart, then shook them vigorously. The cage bars wouldn't budge.

Rose sat back and stared up at the dull wooden ceiling, clenching and unclenching her trembling fists. Rain was falling, pounding on the wagon with a steady *pitter patter,* and there was the sound of horses' hooves and men shouting just audible beyond the rain. A lantern hung from the ceiling, swinging with the wagon's movement, sending shadows swooping in and out of vision. The sounds around her were peaceful enough that as Rose closed her eyes, she felt the anger diminish and her hands stop trembling.

The door to the wagon opened.

Rose opened her eyes to stare at the boy who had stepped inside. His hair was silver, and Rose registered that he was the same boy that had saved her life earlier. Letting out a heavy sigh, he sank down to the ground of the wagon, knees pulled up to his chest as he pulled a piece of wood and a small knife out of his pocket and began to whittle. His hands were thin, fingers long and graceful, but his hands were shaky. Trembling. He had to be around Rose's age, maybe younger.

"How the hell are you in this business, anyway?" she couldn't help asking. Her voice was dull and scratchy, and the boy looked up at her, eyes widened slightly with surprise. For a moment, it looked like he was about to speak. He looked back down and made another cut with the knife.

"Hey. Hello? I know you can hear me."

No response. Was she being ignored?

"Okay. Well, what's your name? Where am I being shipped to?"

"Please, uh, stay quiet. I can't really talk to slaves."

"You can pull that smug façade on me all you want, but please at least tell me where we're going."

"I will knock you out if I have to," he warned. He didn't even look up from his carving.

"So you're just gonna ignore me? You're literally as old as me. Have so many years in a slave camp taken away your compassion? Where's your humanity?" Rose spat. The boy stiffened but stayed silent. Rose seethed. What little resemblance of inner peace she had just collected had been shattered by the appearance of whoever this smug bastard was.

"You're a *monster*," she spat, and the boy leapt to his feet.

"Shut up," he snarled. Rose flinched. "You couldn't even begin to imagine half of the shit I was put through. You have *no* right—"

He stopped. Swallowed. Sat down.

Rose felt unbidden tears well up in the corners of her eyes. *I just want to go back home.*

Maybe it was because of the tears that the boy's harsh, angry face softened.

"My name is Ezra."

* * *

They traveled.

The conditions were, surprisingly, not horrible. She was fed twice a day with a small meal of a few strips of tough, dried beef jerky, a piece of hard bread, and a handful of some dried vegetables that smelled like seaweed. Every few nights, in order to prevent muscle deterioration, slaves would be brought out in small groups by guards and allowed to walk around and stretch their legs.

From what Rose had seen in her brief time outside, the caravan of slave traders was composed of five wagons, three of which were filled with slaves, two of which held supplies and herself. When they stopped for camp, the group of about twenty men would take out bedrolls and sleep on the desert floor. Ezra was the only exception. He slept in her supply wagon at night, most likely to guard the supplies and supervise Rose.

It had been nearly a week since Rose had been sold, and they still seemed to be no closer to reaching their destination.

The night air was surprisingly cool on her skin as Rose stepped outside, surrounded by two or three guards. She didn't bother trying to escape. She had tried twice already and had been knocked out both times. Rose made eye contact with another slave before glancing away, gnawing on her lips. The little girl's eyes had been so dead and empty of hope.

Rose glanced up at the moons, one appearing barely smaller than a fingertip, the other as big as someone's head. Both were full. They illuminated the earth with a pale, skeletal, light that allowed Rose to see the tiny, dark gray mass on the horizon. Rose frowned, glanced between the sky and the mass, and turned toward the guards.

"Guard!" Rose said. "I swear I'm not trying to escape. Just look at the horizon. Do you see the—"

She was backhanded across the face. Rose held back her cry of pain, grimacing and spitting a small mouthful of blood out onto the ground.

"I'm serious. This is for your own good, look—" Rose insisted, but was cut off by another blow.

Whatever that dark gray mass was, it wasn't good.

* * *

It was two days later, during dinner, when the gray mass caught up to them.

"I tried to warn you," Rose told Ezra when he burst into the wagon in the middle of the day, chest heaving and eyes wide with fear. "What is it? Are we in danger?"

"Yes. Shut up," Ezra growled. Rose shook her head and stayed silent. The beat of the horse's hooves slowly sped up until they were galloping across the desert floor, and Rose's cage was rattling so badly that she wanted to punch something. The caravan was trying to outrun whatever was chasing them.

It must be pretty bad, then.

"You guys won't be able to outrun it. I hope it kills all of you, honestly," Rose taunted, only half joking.

"That'd probably be a good thing," Ezra said, his voice so low that Rose could barely hear him. Rose snapped her head up and looked at him, and his eyes were hollow.

There was a tense second of silence before someone outside screamed. The sound was filled with desperation and pain, and after a few seconds, the scream stopped. The horses stopped galloping, the wagons stopped moving, and everything went still.

Ezra cursed. There was a tinkle as he withdrew a ring of keys from his pocket and unlocked Rose's cage.

"If you're in danger, run," he hissed. Rose only stared as he stepped outside the wagon.

A few seconds later, chaos erupted.

Chapter Three

ROSE STEPPED out of the wagon and felt her blood freeze.

The supply wagon she had been stored in had been on the very edge of the caravan, allowing her a grotesquely perfect view of what the gray mass had been. As she watched, eyes wide with horror, the scent of blood filled the air.

Wild werewolves.

Sentient and intelligent, wild werewolves were originally human werewolves who had, usually intentionally, forgone their human forms. Rose felt her hands grow clammy. There were at least two dozen of them, so many that they outnumbered the traders. They ripped through flesh and bone, slaves and traders alike, spilling so much blood that the air seemed to be filled with bloody mist.

Would this be how it ended?

* * *

She didn't have a name.

She was the sky and the sea, the land and the waters. She was fog and mist, sun and light, shadows and darkness. She was a nightmare embodied in a daydream's body. She was fire and ice, ember and smoke, wind and breeze.

She was everything and nothing.

A lithe body of lean muscle and strength. Midnight fur and glowing amber eyes, hooked claws on the ends of large paws, she was a werewolf. Feared by all. Opposed by none.

There was one thing she wanted. One thing she desired.

The hunt.

There was one law that all obeyed: the nature of prey was to run. *Especially when faced by a predator.*

The adrenaline of chasing that prey through the desert sands, hot wind through silky fur—that was her drug, her lifeblood.

She had been hunting for decades, hunted down many fearsome foes.

But the sweet-scented prey that lurked in the corners of her consciousness was something that smelled so succulent that she felt more uncontrolled than she had since she first turned.

Senses coated with lust, she put her nose in the air and began to stalk her prey.

* * *

Rose was huddled in a ball at the corner of the wagon, praying to whatever god was up there, when the door of the wagon was opened.

Opened?

"Rose! Get away from here! The werewolf—" Ezra was cut off. Rose looked up, saw him standing in the doorway, and furrowed her brows in confusion.

Ezra didn't scream. He merely let out a wet, gurgling noise as blood bubbled from his lips.

Rose jumped up, paling as Ezra collapsed to the floor, blood blooming from four gashes on his back. *Claw marks*. A werewolf stepped into the door, her steps silent and graceful, ebony black paws stained with red, muzzle covered in blood, teeth bared at Rose.

She nearly fell to her knees.

Do not feel fear, Rose told herself. *Lock your emotions away. Do not fear*. She pushed her fear down, deep, praying the werewolf couldn't hear the wild beating of her heart.

"What is your name?" *What was she doing? Asking for a werewolf's name.*

Rose could vaguely remember what she had seen once in a book. *What werewolves enjoy is not the kill but the thrill of the hunt.*

The werewolf stopped, as if confused. The werewolf's expression was emotionless. Stone cold. Void of mercy as it stared down at Rose. It tilted its head, and Rose stared deep into those amber-gold eyes and wondered, vaguely, who it had been before it had turned into a monster.

It didn't matter.

* * *

The thrill of the hunt. Yes, that was what she lived for.

But this girl, yes, this sweet-scented prey, was different. There was no tangy scent of fear from her.

Hunting the human would not be a thrill if she didn't beg, didn't cry out, didn't scream in pain.

"What is your name?" the girl spoke.

She needed no name. She simply *was*.

"You do not have one. The greatest of predators need no name. They merely hunt."

Indeed. But what was this human doing, trying to talk to her?

"Would you like to play a game? Would you like to hunt with me?"

But the human was prey. What could she hunt?

"The other humans think I'm crazy. They don't understand the thrill of being hunted. You see? I, too, am like you. I crave the thrill of the hunt."

Impossible. That weak human, like her? She growled with anger.

"No? Perhaps, not like you? Either way, we can play a game together."

Games. She vaguely remembered them from her past life, activities played for fun by humans.

"For we are predator and prey, both in love with the hunt. So why don't we play a game, you and I? You, the predator, and I, the prey. Whoever kills the other wins the game."

A game with a predetermined winner.

"For, despite being prey, I can kill, too."

Oh?

"Here are the rules: you may stalk me for a turn of the moon. You may bring as many comrades with you as you wish, but if I kill you, your comrades will not pursue me. They will allow me to leave."

Interesting rules. Fair.

"Would you like to play?"

Yes. Yes, she wanted to. The werewolf felt a thrill race through her that she hadn't felt in a long, long time. Most of her prey cowered beneath her, begging for mercy, filling the air with the stench of piss and tears. This one was special.

Standing up, she stalked over to the human, baring her teeth, searching for a sign of fear. There was none. Gray eyes stared into gold as the werewolf and the human silently made a pact.

The werewolf backed out of the wagon, and the screams outside stopped.

***

Rose waited ten seconds before she allowed the fear to surface.

Her knees weakened, and adrenaline shot through her. Rose collapsed to the ground, her breathing speeding up, her hands shaking. *I'm safe. I'm safe. I'm safe.*

"Rose. Please... help..."

Ezra.

Rose stood up and turned toward the boy on the ground, bleeding out from the claw marks on his back.

"Please... help... me..."

Fucking monsters.

Both of them were monsters. Both of them were the *same*. Ezra, who had turned his back on his fellow humans, capturing and trading them as merchandise, killing so many month by month. The werewolf, who had turned its back on society, was consumed by primal instinct, killing. *Monsters.*

Staring down at the boy on the ground, Rose was about to turn her back on him when she heard him whisper.

"If you're going to leave me to die... hold my hand. Please."

"You couldn't even begin to imagine half of the shit I was put through. You have no right–"

Rose flinched as those words reappeared in her head. Ezra was a *child*. Probably born into this life. He hadn't *chosen* this.

She couldn't let him die.

"Medical supplies. Are there medical supplies in the wagon?" Rose asked, stumbling toward the stacks of boxes and barrels and tilting her head to read the labels. There was no response. Rose swore, moving aside barrels and crates until she found a box labeled *medical supplies* and tore it open. Withdrawing two rolls of bandages, antibiotic cream, and other medical supplies, Rose dropped to her knees next to Ezra and examined the wound.

"Will I... turn?" Ezra asked. His voice was trembling.

"No. You were slashed, not bitten. If you had been turned, you would be rampaging by now. Shut up."

Ezra went quiet as Rose took his shirt in her hands and ripped it in half, peeling it off his back gingerly. Ripping off a section of her cloak, Rose dipped it into a barrel of water and gingerly washed Ezra's back free of blood. Once it was clean, it didn't seem nearly as bad. The claw marks were deep and oozing blood, but once she applied pressure to them with another segment of her clock, it stopped. Rose slowly patched Ezra up. He had fallen unconscious, allowing Rose to stitch his wounds shut, lather them with antibiotic cream, and painstakingly haul him into a sitting position so she could bandage it. As she worked, Rose couldn't help but observe his torso. Nearly every inch of him was covered in scars, although most looked like accidental wounds.

Rose tucked the remaining medical supplies into her cloak pocket, wrapping it around herself before retreating into the cage. Outside, Rose could hear men shouting.

Burying her head in her arms, Rose felt the adrenaline that had surged through her fade away.

She was tired.

Before she fell asleep, Rose rummaged through the crates until she found a blanket and spread it over Ezra's unconscious body. Her last thought before she fell asleep was, *I hope he survives.*

* * *

Am I... finally... dead?

Ezra opened his eyes.

The swaying of the wagon confused him. Was the werewolf attack just a dream, or was hell just a supply wagon?

Ezra tried to sit up, only to feel an explosion of pain emanating from his back that sent spots filling his vision. *Not a dream, then. Fuck.*

Blinking his eyes clear, Ezra slowly pushed himself up into a sitting position, knocking loose the blanket that someone had placed over him. Looking around himself, Ezra saw the slave—Rose—in the cage. She was asleep, head resting on the bars of her cage, a cloak wrapped around herself.

Not hell, then. So I'm alive?

Sighing, Ezra pushed himself to his feet, a hand braced against the wall. Pain exploded across his back and Ezra clenched his teeth, slowly shuffling toward the wagon door. He reached out to open it and made to step outside, his breath catching as he stepped forward. He barely lasted a few seconds before the weight of his body caused his hand to slip forward. There was a sickening falling sensation and Ezra fell to the ground on his side, biting back a scream.

"You idiot," Rose's voice said from the cage. Ezra shifted slightly on the floor, turning his head to look at her.

"What do you want?" Ezra asked. Rose shook her head and opened the door of her cage, stretching her legs before standing up and walking toward him. Her face was tired but dead-set.

"What are you doing?" Ezra said, hoping she couldn't hear the tremor in his voice. Rose stopped, her brow furrowed with confusion.

"I won't hurt you. If I hadn't bandaged you, you'd be dead," Rose replied. She shut the wagon door, bent down, and carefully lifted Ezra into the air. She carried him to a corner of the wagon, then grabbed the blanket and threw it over him.

"What do you want with me?" Ezra asked, wrapping the blanket around himself.

"I want nothing. I couldn't just let you die. Here, take some medicine. It should help with the pain."

She tossed a bottle of pills at Ezra, who examined the label before pouring two pills into his hand and swallowing them dry. Wordlessly, Rose withdrew some food from her pocket and the cup of water inside the cage and put them at Ezra's side.

"Why are you being so kind to me?" Ezra asked, through a mouthful of dry bread.

"Why should I need a reason? You were going to die, so I helped you. I couldn't leave you to die."

There was a small period of silence before Ezra spoke.

"How'd you get away from the werewolf? Is the rest of the camp okay? How many people died?"

"Not enough to stop the trade, apparently. I made some bullshit promise that she could hunt me in a month. Some predator and prey thriller bullshit. Fortunately, in a month, I won't be in the caravan anymore. Hopefully, wherever I'm going, they'll be able to protect me."

Ezra couldn't help but stare at Rose as she closed her eyes and tapped her hands. Anyone else he had known would've left him to die.

"Rose?"

"Yeah?"

"Thank you."

* * *

"Here's a wood block. Uh, here's a knife. Don't stab me."

Rose laughed as she took the knife. The handle was made of wood that was shaped to Ezra's hand, with a blade that was about one and a half inches long.

"How do I...?"

"Oh. Yeah. Uh—"

"Man, you're a terrible teacher," Rose commented teasingly. Ezra blushed and looked away.

"Uhm–"

"Oh, don't mind me. Probably just your personality. I know the basics, I had a friend who carved at my old home. Toward the direction of the grain, right?"

Ezra nodded. Rose clumsily carved off a shaving of the wood, barely avoiding slicing her finger.

"Here, let me show you," Ezra murmured, withdrawing his half-finished project and a larger knife from his pocket.

"What is it?"

"Uh, a crow. It's not finished yet and it's not that good, but—"

"Hey, hey, none of that self-deprecating bullshit," Rose scolded. "C'mon, show me how you do it."

A comfortable silence fell over the pair as Rose watched Ezra work from inside her cage. It was the second day since Ezra had been injured, and Rose was amazed to see his wounds were healing almost abnormally fast.

"Hey, Ezra?"

"Yeah?"

"Where am I going?"

Ezra let out a barely audible sigh, before leaning back against the wall, carefully placing the carving onto the ground and running a hand through his silver hair. The sky outside was darkening and the men outside were shouting, preparing to stop for the night.

"The Salt Mines."

Rose was silent.

"So, uh, I'm sure you've heard of them. It's a place where slaves mine salt—"

"Obviously," Rose broke in. Her voice cracked.

"Let me talk," Ezra said gently. "Uh, it's a super cruel place. Located on the edge of the Earth Kingdom, near the Lightning Kingdom border."

"We're still in the Earth Kingdom?" Rose broke in. Ezra gave her a look and she closed her mouth.

"Dozens of people die there every day. You work from dawn to dusk, sleep in a building with all of the other slaves, and do it again. We're one of the many slave caravans who ship slaves to them bimonthly. This slave caravan cares a lot less about its workers than its earnings. What usually happens is they find orphan boys and train them to be a part of their caravan, in exchange for food and shelter. It'd be a great deal if it weren't for, y'know, the slavery part."

Rose snorted.

"In order to maximize profit, the guy who owns runs caravan likes to sell workers who cause trouble to the Salt Mines too. It's the reason why we pick up new workers every rotation."

"Why are you in this camp in the first place?"

"Um," Ezra said, pausing. "I was one of the orphan boys they found. I grew up here." He was, Rose noticed, avoiding her gaze.

There was a period of comfortable silence as they ate their food.

"Do you think I can survive?" Rose asked.

"Depends if you have the will to survive the first few weeks. After that, as you get stronger, it gets easier."

"And you just stay there... until you die?"

"Nah. After enough years, they let you out."

Rose's eyes darted to the door, and her eyes widened. She held a finger to her lips. Ezra scooted away quickly, picking up his whittling, pretending to be absorbed in his work. The door opened, and two men walked inside. They surveyed Ezra and Rose before grabbing a barrel of water and walking out of the wagon.

"Close call," Rose murmured. She tucked the block of wood and knife into her pocket, leaning against the side of the cage, watching Ezra carve until she drifted away into slumber.

* * *

When Rose woke up, Ezra was gone.

"Ezra?" Rose asked, looking around herself. "Ezra. Hey, Ezra?"

Silence.

Did he leave? Is he working? Isn't he excused from work because of his injury?

The air outside was dead silent. It was probably late at night. Maybe Rose could check if he was outside.

But when she pushed at the cage, it was locked.

Rose felt her heart drop.

"Ezra. No, no, no. I thought—"

I thought I could trust him.

Rose pushed at the door, shaking the bars, her hands trembling. *He left, he left, he left.*

He's just like Master.

I should've known.

The door to the wagon opened, and Rose looked up and saw someone step inside. He didn't look friendly. He wore the same expression as the drunkards that swaggered along the streets of the Market, leering and pawing at pretty girls.

The man smiled as he withdrew Ezra's ring of keys.

* * *

"No. Let me go!" Ezra hissed from outside. He could feel his wound reopening, warm blood soaking his bandages as he struggled against the arms holding him back. "What are you guys doing?"

"She's quite a pretty one, isn't she? You've been keeping her to yourself," one of the men whispered. He opened the door and smiled.

"No, no, no. Don't you dare. You can take any of the other slaves, but not her. *Don't you dare—*"

One of the men clapped a hand over his mouth.

Ezra could hear the cage door rattling and keys tinkling.

"Stay the fuck away from me," Rose growled from inside. The man laughed. The cage door creaked as it opened.

Ezra erupted.

His magic flowed from him in waves of power, blending in with the darkness of the night. The men around him screamed and fell to the ground, bleeding from shallow but undoubtedly painful wounds. Ezra shook free of their limp grasps and stepped into the doorway of the wagon.

"Don't look, Rose," Ezra murmured. His silhouette was dark

against the night, but if he stepped inside the wagon, she would see him. See his magic. Rose stared up at him, eyes shining with tears, and closed her eyes.

There was a cry of pain and a wet *thud*. The man dropped to the ground.

Dead.

* * *

Rose opened her eyes to the crimson blood.

It was everywhere. On the walls, on the wooden floor, on her clothes. And, standing above it all, was Ezra. His fingers and hands were covered with blood.

"Ezra?" Rose whispered.

His face was emotionless. Stone cold.

A shiver crawled through her body as she realized just who Ezra looked so much like. *Ebony black fur, paws covered in blood, emotionless, stone-cold eyes void of mercy.*

Monster.

Rose turned away from him.

A group of men burst through the wagon doors, alerted by the screams, taking in the blood on the walls and the corpse of the shattered man on the ground before turning to Rose.

"Did she do this?" one of them asked.

"No way. We checked her for weapons, and she's a Null."

Rose watched as they turned to Ezra, who had just *ended a life.*

"Was it you?" one of the guards asked him.

Even in the dim light of the wagon, Rose could see the horror unfolding on their faces.

He had just killed someone. He had, very possibly, saved her life.

He didn't even fight as they dragged him away.

Chapter Four

ROSE COULDN'T HELP but feel slight awe at the enormous, barred iron gates that stretched high above her. The doors slammed shut behind them, just barely missing the last slave in the line.

Even from the surface, the Salt Mines looked grotesque.

About one hundred slaves were pushing wagons of dirty rock salt toward a huge wooden building in the distance, probably a storage area. They were watched closely by guards. Meanwhile, small, shaded wooded areas were constructed above gaping holes in the ground that Rose estimated were designed to be large enough for a wagon. *The entrances to the mines.* The holes were spaced far apart, and Rose knew that they were connected by the vast underground tunnels from which people dug salt. Meanwhile, on the very edge of the Salt Mines stood a relatively small assortment of wooden buildings—the abode of the slaves, perhaps.

One of the guards backhanded her across the cheek. Rose's head snapped to the side from the force of the blow, and she could taste blood in her mouth. As she looked back at the guard, she could see Ezra from the corner of her eye staring at her, his gaze filled with concern and pleading.

He killed someone.

Rose looked away.

"Eyes forward," the guard snapped. Rose grimaced and looked forward. They were being led into one of the several shafts, being led deeper and deeper into the tunnels until the air was filled with an earthy, musty smell. Even with the sparse lanterns that hung from the ceiling,

"There are a few basic rules you must follow in the Salt Mines," the guard who had led them in said. He sounded exhausted. "First, you must wake up at the first bell and be here by the second bell. The third bell indicates when you can go back to the lodge. Second, never stop digging. That is all."

As he spoke, a few guards walked in between the line of slaves, releasing the chains that bound them together, leaving only a pair of thick, heavy manacles on each wrist, linked together by a two-foot chain. A pickaxe was placed in her hands, and she looked at the wall in front of her, solid stone with slabs and specks of gray-white that indicated large chunks of salt buried deep within the stone walls.

The pickaxe was heavy in her hands as she raised it above her head and drove it into the stone wall. The heavy *thud* that sounded dully through the muffling cave walls were echoed hundreds of times around her by slaves, each with their own pickaxes: some next to her, some barely distantly echoing from the very deepest reaches of the cave.

It felt almost like an execution.

* * *

Rose's hands *ached*.

Even with the calluses that had gradually formed from years of work for Master, her hands were bleeding, staining her cloak with red. Her face was covered in dirt and gray powder stained her clothes.

The slaves were led from the mining shafts into the wooden houses. There were about twenty of them, lined up side by side. Looking around herself, Rose wriggled through the crowd into one of the relatively less occupied, smaller lodging areas. The ground was covered in small mats, barely softer than the floor.

Where do I go?

"Rose. Here!" Ezra hissed. Rose looked behind her and saw Ezra in one of the corners, hand placed protectively on the mat next to him.

He killed someone.

Rose was about to turn away when she saw six or seven men stalk into the lodging. Even in the large space that could probably hold fifty slaves, they seemed to take up the whole room. They scanned through the inhabitants, a leering smile on their faces, and one of the men grabbed a young woman by her hair and yanked her "out of their spot."

There are no laws. They could kill me tonight, Rose realized as she watched the group of men surround the woman. She screamed. *They didn't even check us for weapons, just clapped on magic-restricting chains onto people who weren't Nulls.* She glanced at Ezra, whose eyes were pleading. *And Ezra. He killed someone, but—*

Sighing and cutting off her train of thought, Rose walked toward Ezra's corner, blocking out the sounds of the woman screaming. He watched her as she sat down on a mat, his face twisting with some strange emotion before taking the wooden block and knife out of his pocket. His hands were covered with blood.

"Are you injured?" Rose asked, moving toward him. He looked at her, surprised, and then looked down at his hands.

"No, uh, it's from today. The mines. I cut my hand on a sharp piece of rock just as the bell rang. It's stopped bleeding, mostly."

Rose sighed and pried the carving from his hands.

"You're going to stain your carving. Here, let me bind it up," Rose said. "I'm not going to waste bandages on a wound this small though." He nodded, watching her cautiously as she tore a strip of fabric from the bottom of her cloak and wrapped Ezra's hand. He flexed it, nodding his head nervously at Rose before resuming his work. There was silence between them as food was distributed. It was a small bowl of some type of grainy mush that was tasteless and felt like mud. She handed the bowl to Ezra and watched as he crept into the center and placed their bowls on the quickly growing stack. A large man turned around and crashed into him. Ezra ducked his head, his lips moving in an apology, and the man spat in his face and turned away. Ezra looked down at the ground.

Was this really the same boy who had killed someone?

Ezra returned to the mat next to her, avoiding her eyes, picking up the carving and carefully shaving off a small piece. It was a small carving, as big as his palm. The bottom half of the crow looked finished. At the very bottom point stretched the crow's tail, on which the shape of feathers were marked carefully into the wood. Rose could see a beautiful outline of wings, on which two rows of feathers were etched, and above it stretched the vague shape of the crow's head.

"Are you, uh, scared of me?" Ezra asked. Rose tore her eyes away from the half-formed crow, looking into Ezra's golden eyes. Immediately, he glanced away, avoiding eye contact and staying very, very still. His hands were trembling. Hunched up against the wall, he almost looked like a child.

"I think I should be. The fact that your magic was powerful enough to kill so easily, and..." *your expression afterward...*

Rose looked from her hands to Ezra. His eyes were filled with a hopeless sadness as he looked back down at his carving, as if expecting and accepting her response. *Stone cold, emotionless eyes.*

"Why did you... *look like that*? After you..."

"I left."

"Huh?"

"I left. I wasn't there. I was gone."

"Huh?"

"Gone. I, uh, didn't even realize what was happening. It was like I blacked out. The last thing I remembered before waking up in the slave wagon was your face."

Disassociation.

Stone cold, emotionless eyes. Hollow. "Gone." That made far more sense.

"Y'know, I can't help but not be scared of you. I mean, look at you. You can't even form a sentence without saying uh," Rose murmured. Ezra snapped his head up and stared at her with shining eyes. "You're just a boy. A kid. Probably younger than me. And... whatever you've done, you must've had no choice."

Ezra looked so heartbreakingly happy that Rose wanted to embrace him.

"You're not...?" he asked, his voice cracking as if in disbelief. "He wasn't the only thing I've killed. I've done so much bad-"

Rose cut him off with a wave of her hand.

"Hey. It's okay. It's not like you had a choice. It was for survival, right?"

Ezra slowly nodded.

"Then it's okay. It's okay."

Ezra ducked his head and picked up his carving. His silver-white hair had grown over the course of the trip into messy bangs that nearly covered his eyes. Even so, she could see tears falling onto the mat below him.

* * *

Rose grimaced as a throb of pain lanced through her hands. Sighing, allowed herself to stop for half a second before raising the pickaxe and striking at the stone that buried a nearly exposed rock of salt. A piece of rock as large as her finger chipped off, and Rose raised the pickaxe again. After a few more minutes, she brought her pickaxe down on the area on top of the piece of rock salt, causing it to fall to the ground with a thud. Sighing, Rose knelt down and picked it up, examining its gray-stained surface as she tossed it into the wagon behind her. Her legs felt weak beneath her and her arms ached, but she managed to ignore how absolutely *tired* she was by focusing on the pain in her hands. The manacles were scraping at the skin on her wrists, causing throbbing pain whenever she raised her pickaxe, and her hands were bleeding so freely that the handle of the pickaxe was stained red.

Just as she had picked up her pickaxe, there was a shrill scream from beside her. Rose whirled around and watched as a guard reared his whip back, striking again and again, mercilessly. The old woman on the ground who had probably fallen due to exhaustion was screaming for mercy, and Rose stepped forward, a hand outstretched—but what could she do? A guard glared at her, raising his whip. The taste of bile filled her mouth, and Rose turned her face away, back toward the stone wall in front of her.

She hated them.

Hated them all, for the leering looks they sent the younger women, for the cruelty with which they treated the weak, for the way they seemed to delight in the pain of others.

Tightening her fists along the handle of the pickaxe, Rose ducked her head and continued to dig.

* * *

Rose scratched the tally into the wood of the room they were in. They had just finished a third set yesterday. It was the sixteenth day of their stay at the Salt Mines.

Sitting down on her mat, Rose stretched and massaged her sore fingers. Her hands, surprisingly, had stopped bleeding a few days ago, leaving only a lingering soreness to contend with. She was interrupted by a soft nudge at her side.

"What's up?" she asked Ezra.

Ezra shrugged his shoulders, focused entirely on his carvings.

"You don't know? Then why'd you—"

"I want a shoulder massage," Ezra clarified. Rose blinked at him and then sighed, scooting toward him and kneading his shoulders.

The small slave lodging was almost entirely filled with people. Two mats next to them, two children were crying loudly, being shushed by a thin, pale woman. The smell of blood and pus permeated the air, and there was the sound of women weeping. Last week, six bodies had been found in this lodging alone, and seven slaves had newly arrived.

How many slaves would survive until next week? How many lives did this endless cycle waste each year?

Suddenly, breaking through the haze of thoughts came the shrill, desperate cry of a girl.

A *girl*.

She was barely tall enough to reach Rose's shoulders. Two guards were yanking at her arm, dragging her toward the direction of the door, and there was a predatory gleam in their eyes. The girl couldn't be more than eight or nine years old.

She's just a child.

"What are you doing?" Rose shouted. The entirety of the building seemed to turn their heads and look at her.

"Rose, *no*," Ezra hissed. "Sit back down. Apologize."

Apologize? To them?

"Stop that! Don't touch her!" Rose shouted at the guards, standing up and stalking toward the little girl. "She's a child, goddammit! What do you want with a child?" The guards seemed almost shocked as they glanced at each other.

"What do you think you're doing?" one of the guards asked. "Shut up. You're a slave. I have better playthings to use right now. Move aside and let us take the girl. This is your last warning." Rose moved in front of the girl, sheltering her as much as she could with her chained hands. The guards glanced at each other again. One of them tugged at the other's arm, and he snarled as he glanced back at Rose.

The whip cracked above her and struck her against her chest.

Ow.

The desperate cry of the little girl and Ezra's shout seemed to be muffled behind a thick layer of pain. Forcing her eyes open, Rose looked up at the guard above her, who raised his arm, again, only for a taller man beside him to catch his arm. He whispered into his ear, and the man put down his arm.

"Don't defy me, girl. You'll face worse consequences next time."

Rose felt her eyes drift shut as the men walked away.

* * *

Ezra ignored the crying of the little girl as he stumbled toward Rose, and hoisted her into his arms. The whip had struck her across her chest, opening a wound that was now leaking blood. *Fucking bullwhips.* He carried her carefully toward their mats, his hands trembling as he realized that he had never, ever, treated a wound before. Usually, he just left his wounds open to the air.

"Rose. Rose! What should I do?" Ezra asked. Rose opened her eyes, her eyes bleary. "What should I do? Tell me what to do. I'll help—"

"Medical supplies... in my cloak..." Rose whispered. "How bad?"

"Um, bad?"

"Is the wound gaping?"

"No. Just bleeding. A lot."

"No stitches. Just... use a cloth. Absorb blood, apply pressure until the bleeding stops. Clean off the blood around it. Use the bandages. Butterfly bandages. Use antiseptic."

"A cloth. I need a clean cloth. Please!" Ezra shouted. There was silence before a nearly clean corner of a blue cloak was shoved into his hands. Ezra pressed down on Rose's wound, causing her to cry out in pain, but the bleeding eventually stopped. Ezra dipped the cloth in their water, wiping away the dried blood before smearing on antiseptic and wrapping it in bandages. It was clumsy work, but the sterile white of the bandage made the wound look better.

"Rose?"

There was no response.

Please be okay.

* * *

Where was she?

There was a vague feeling of intense pain that swept over her, again and again, and she curled away from it. Her vision was black and blurry.

Where was she?

Slowly, she felt herself drift further and further away from the pain. She was cocooned in darkness, soft and comforting.

She was in a room. She recognized the room. It was the kitchen floor of Master's house. Why was she here?

Her eyes began to close.

Rose looked down at her hands. They were small, chubby, the hands of a small child.

She drifted into unconsciousness.

There was a wonderful flash of light and a stunning burst of power. Rose felt herself thrusting open a door of beautiful, indescribable, power.

Between her fingers swirled a ball of pure lightning, which she made dance along the tips of her fingers, giggling in excitement as it jumped playfully from one hand to another. It almost seemed alive. Rose summoned a gust of wind that carried the sparks of electricity from one end of the room to another.

Then, a cloak of darkness suffocated the magic.

An iron grip of darkness pinned her to the ground. There was a burst of invisible magic and blinding, piercing, scorching pain. She had never felt anything like it, as if fire was burning and water suffocating, blades cutting and electricity surging through her body. Pain. Pure pain.

Screaming, she blacked out.

When she woke up, her beautiful magic was trapped behind gates of solid darkness.

The world felt empty without it. She was empty. The magic was part of her, the magic was *her. How would she live without it?*

The despair within her was overwhelming. Rose sat down on the ground, her arms wrapped around her knees, suffocated by grief. Darkness began to surround her, but from within, she heard a voice. It was shouting her name.

Rose. Rose.

Rose!

She tried fighting toward it, but the darkness around her thickened. Tired, she slumped to the ground in despair.

Rose!

Rose looked up, startled.

There was a different voice within the darkness. His voice was husky, rough, and a pair of strange eyes were looking at her, gleaming.

* * *

"Rose! Wake up!" Ezra shouted. Rose's eyes flew open, and she shot up from the mat before letting out a cry of pain and collapsing back down.

"Rose!" Ezra shouted, shaking her shoulder urgently.

"He locked it away. Please, give it back, give it back, *give it back*," she sobbed. Against all reason, he felt his heart throb with sympathy for her. He clutched her close to his chest, the camp silent around him.

"Locked what away?" he asked. His voice was reserved and cautious, even harsh, there was an undertone of kindness. Gentleness.

"A glowing pool of power, of light, of infinity. Something magnificent... something beyond human measures, a pool of infinity, a pool of intertwined light and darkness. It was mine. It was mine. *Why'd he take it?* Please, give it back."

Ezra ran his spidery-thin fingers through her hair, breathing shallow.

Her hair was not the hesitant darkness of dawn, or the impenetrable darkness of a world without light, but the darkness of the sky at night.

"It's going to be okay, Rose," Ezra murmured. He lifted her head into his lap, stroking her hair, and her sobbing calmed.

"It's going to be okay. Here, you can have my crow," Ezra whispered. He felt stupid - . What would a crow do to help her? But Rose took the crow in her hands and ran her fingers over the grove of its wings. Slowly, her breathing calmed.

"Ezra?" she asked.

"Yeah?"

"How do I get it back? The magic?"

Ezra's heart clenched. *It was his fault.*

He didn't respond.

* * *

It couldn't scent the girl.

The path of her scent had stopped in front of a large building made of stone and iron. The werewolves had studied from a distance for nearly a week. They hadn't found a settlement of humans this large in years, decades, even, and the gathering of werewolves it had summoned was so large it might be over a hundred. They had waited until the full moon, just like her prey had agreed.

But tonight was the night.

As the iron gates swung open, the werewolf turned her head to the rising moon and let out a piercing howl. The werewolves sprinted across the desert sand, so fast they looked like brown and black streaks. The first werewolves reached the guards in front of the door, tearing through their throats and spraying blood onto the stone walls. They stormed through the gates, slaughtering the guards who manned them, leaving the rest of the werewolves free to storm the Salt Mines.

Bells began to toll above them. Of warning, and of death.

* * *

Bells tolled above the slaves. Rose's eyes were bleary with pain, but even she looked around herself in panic. As the slaves murmured in half-asleep terror, the door to the lodge shattered.

Standing in front of the door was a werewolf.

Adrenaline rushed through Ezra as he picked Rose up, sprinting for the door as the werewolves flooded into the lodge. Slaves everywhere were screaming, but Ezra ignored them and sprinted out of the lodge. He set Rose down, looping one of her arms over his shoulders, half-carrying her as they made their way toward the center of the camp. Around them, guards and slaves alike were torn to shreds by claws and teeth.

"Ezra. Use your magic. Save them."

"I can't. The chains."

Rose grimaced as her legs buckled beneath her. They stood in the center of the chaos, the eye in the storm, and it seemed like the werewolves were almost *ignoring them.*

Suddenly, from behind them, they heard a howl of triumph. As one, they turned.

The werewolf that stalked toward them looked familiar, golden eyes and ebony fur, and as the werewolf bunched its muscles and prepared to leap at them, time itself seemed to slow. The werewolf's paws left the ground, front legs outstretched, claws razor-sharp and gleaming in what little light remained. Rose's face was a mix of pain and naked fear.

It was as if the Gods themselves had slowed down time for him. As if they were finally offering a chance for Ezra to choose, to do something right.

Behind them, the last light of the glowing sun vanished behind the walls of the Salt Mines, leaving behind a murky darkness.

Droplets of blood arched across the air in a graceful curve, gleaming dark red in the dimming light, as, with a wet thud, the werewolf's claws sank into Ezra's back.

* * *

When the werewolf bunched its muscles and leapt at Rose, she knew that it was the end.

Staring up at the sky, Rose took in everything around her one last time—the screaming, the scent of blood, the faint hints of the sun's light still barely visible in the sky, the wooden crow in her hand, her arm around Ezra's warm shoulders.

It wasn't a bad place to die.

Rose closed her eyes and smiled.

There was an impact, and she winced—but it was warm, a pair of arms wrapped around her, pushing her back onto the floor. As she fell, she opened her eyes.

A pair of claws were buried in Ezra's back.

He stood above her, arms spread as if shielding her, and Rose realized what had happened. *He had protected her. Pushed her out of the way.*

"Rose..."

"Ezra. Ezra! No, no, no, no!" Rose murmured, her voice breaking.

"You better get out. Out... of here. Survive."

"No, don't talk like that! *Ezra!*"

Ezra broke off in a wet cough as the werewolf's claws sank deeper into his flesh, foamy blood bubbling out from the corner of his mouth. The werewolf regarded the two of them, yanking out her claws from his body.

He fell into Rose's arms, his back staining her arms and hands in blood.

* * *

Ezra reached up with a shaking hand, reaching toward her hair. It was soft. Beautiful. He let his arm fall. He was tired. So, so, tired.

"Ezra. *Ezra.* Hey, don't close your eyes. *Ezra!*" Rose shouted. Ezra looked up into her eyes, remembering the sway of the wagon, the soft feeling of the wood beneath his fingers, tender fingers bandaging his wounds. He remembered light, laughter, beauty.

"Thank you... for everything..."

His eyes shut. The last thing he felt before the world faded to smoke and dust was a cold drop of water, rolling down his face. As if he were the one crying.

I'm sorry, Rose. I'm sorry.

* * *

Rose stared, motionless, as Ezra slid from her arms onto the ground.

Her hands were covered with blood. There was a silence in her head, a silence so loud that it rang through her ears, muffling the sounds of destruction that surrounded her.

"No. Ezra, Ezra! Ezra! Get up!" The werewolf stared at her, muscles tensing, preparing to strike.

"You... you killed him," Rose numbly stated. She pushed herself up, her body throbbing with pain.

"He was beautiful. He didn't deserve death," Rose murmured. She stared into those eyes and wondered, vaguely, how she had ever likened Ezra to that soullessness.

The werewolf stayed silent, regarding Rose with a gleam in its eye. Rose didn't care. Ezra. A caretaker, a companion, a *friend*. In this desert of life, he had been the one source of water, a cool oasis in a fiery hell. The glow of fire in the depths of night.

He was gone.

"And you *killed him.*"

The werewolf cocked its head, curiosity in her eyes. Did it feel it, too? The pulse of power, of anger, of deadly beauty deep within her, beating against gates of darkness. *Her magic.*

"Why? What did he do to deserve death?"

Everything around her faded into a blur of sound and color and noise and anguish.

"*Why?*" she whispered.

With a crack and the sound of creaking, those gates of darkness cracked open, letting loose fourteen years of anguish and rage and loneliness that had been trapped within it. From within, it flowed magic that rushed through her body, filling her every pore with otherworldly power. The werewolf whined, ears pressed back to its head, stark fear clear in each line of its body.

Tilting her head up toward the sky, Rose roared, and it was the battle cry of a god.

Magic burst through her.

Magic.

The power sweeping through her—it was infinite.

She erupted, and the werewolf faded into mere particles of matter. The guards around her were struck down with bolts of lightning. And yet there were still more, rushing at her, even as she glowed with power. And the werewolves, too—they stopped, perfectly still, staring at her magic with hunger in their eyes.

Ezra.

"Stop her!" the guards shouted. Rose looked around with eyes blurred by tears.

Ezra.

They ran at her, weapons outstretched. Her body was trembling with power, and they fell before her like a line of dominoes.

Ezra.

Rose could feel a red haze overwhelm her. Rage. If one were to put their ear to her chest, they would hear a thrum of sorrow.

The guards were shouting, working to close the doors that would lock her in. Rose began to run, eyes wet with tears, but she wouldn't make it in time. With a shout, she thrust a hand out toward the wall, which shattered beneath her power. It broke into thousands of shards of iron. Rose sprinted through the debris. She escaped, looked back at the guards, and twitched her foot, summoning a wall of ice that rose far above the gates. She turned her back, running, farther and farther away, and as the first few guards broke through the wall of ice, she turned around and contemplated the Salt Mines. *Cyclic rot.*

She outstretched her hand, and the haze of rage enveloped her. She stretched out her hand, her fingers curving sideways, her first finger and thumb enveloping the small figure of the Salt Mines in the distance.

With a twist of her hand, she brought that hell crashing down into rubble and stone.

And she ran.

She ran, and ran, and ran, her bare feet sore and bloody from the coarse desert sand. The rage faded, slowly, until all that was left was exhaustion, weighing her down until she couldn't move.

She sank to her knees.

Ezra.

She fell.

Chapter Five

ROSE OPENED HER EYES.

The ceiling above her was stone, lit up with a warm light by numerous lanterns. Beneath her were silky sheets, and she was half-covered by a thin blanket. She didn't move, examining the world around her. The world seemed just a bit clearer, just a bit sharper. The smell of sand and freshness was in the air, and she could hear the slight desert breeze blowing through an open window.

Magic.

Rose stood up, flexing her arms and moving around with amazement. She was moving with a fluid gracefulness that she hadn't noticed in magic-users until she now experienced it. Her wrists were free of manacles. Had they shattered when she awakened her magic? There were bandages wrapped around the soles of her feet and wrists.

But when she caught a glimpse of herself in the mirror, she froze.

Rose stared at her chest, running a finger along the white bandages wrapped around her stomach and chest. Slowly, Rose unwound the bandages on her wrists, revealing bruised, bleeding skin from the manacles. Gingerly she touched them, and almost physically felt all the memories return.

Ezra.

Her hands shook as they dropped to her side. She glanced toward her cloak, then ran toward it, rifling through the pockets until she felt grooved wood beneath her fingers. Pulling out the wooden crow, Rose stared at, her hands trembling.

I didn't even get to say goodbye.

Sinking to her knees, Rose bent over, gasping as a sharp pain manifested in her chest. There was so much pain. A sudden wave of it that rushed toward her, overwhelmed her.

Ezra.

Ezra.

Ezra.

His silky silver hair. His soft, nimble hands. His hesitant laugh.

Ezra.

This grief. This pain. When she thought about it, it felt absurd. Just another dying kid. Yet, her heart *ached*. Ezra—*her Ezra*—was gone.

"Hello?" a woman's voice said. Rose ignored her. Faintly, she heard a thud and footsteps. Warm arms closed around her, and Rose wept.

* * *

"We are one step closer to our goal," the Dark Sorcerer murmured. "Finally, after all of this time."

"There is no *we*," the Dark Prince hissed. The Dark Sorcerer turned toward him, his face flashing with annoyance.

"Do you think I somehow wanted to do this? That I somehow take pleasure from it? There is no cost too great to pay for the world I wish to create!" his last words were nearly shouted.

"These—these *crimes*—you can't justify them with an end!" the Dark Prince shouted back. There was a second of silence. "You're doing the same thing to her that was done to you. You've become a *monster*."

The Dark Sorcerer turned his back on him. His shoulders were shaking.

* * *

"Who are you?" Rose asked, glancing up and around her as she ate. They were within a stone cave that was so different from the Salt Mines it was jarring. The room was well lit with large, warm lanterns, and the floor was carpeted with a shaggy cloth. A small fireplace was lit on the side of the wall. The small table she was seated in front of was covered in food: slices of sourdough bread, a plate of ruby red fruit that she didn't recognize, oranges, and salt-cured pork.

"My name's Blossom. My husband's name is Halt. Eat, you're far too thin for your age," Blossom scolded. She had black hair, dark skin, and green eyes, and looked trustworthy enough. Fidgeting with the crow in her hand, Rose surveyed the plate in front of her, then took a piece of bread and wolfed it down. Once she had had her fill of oranges, salt pork, and dough, she gingerly picked up a few of the strange bright ruby red slices of fruit. Whatever it was, they tasted tangy and mildly sweet.

"Halt found you about ten miles north from here. How did you escape from the Salt Mines?"

"Ah..." Rose hesitated. "The mines were attacked by werewolves. A lot of them. I didn't know there could be so many at once. The doors were open, and I managed to slip out before anyone noticed. I hope they didn't chase me."

"Don't worry. They'll assume you were killed. How did you get away from the werewolves? You have a good amount of magic. They're normally attracted to it."

"You can tell I have magic?" Rose asked, looking up sharply.

"Yeah. Halt taught me how to sense it."

"He taught you? Does he know how to use magic?"

"He became a mage in the Lightning Kingdom. Attended the Academy."

The Academy—a school of magic so famed that every book Rose had perused about magic mentioned it in length.

"A mage? The Academy? Isn't it super hard to get an apprenticeship? And if he's a mage, why is he here?"

"He was released from duty. Mages in the Lightning Kingdom usually serve for ten years before they're first offered release. You can ask him more about the Academy later, when he gets back."

"Where is he?"

"Tinkering in his workshop with his toys. He loves building things."

There was silence. Rose tore off a piece of bread and shoved it into her mouth.

"Do you have anywhere to go?" Blossom eventually asked. "Anywhere you'd like us to take you?"

"I don't have... I..." Rose clenched her fist, crushing the piece of bread in her hand, staring down at the table. "I don't have parents or relatives. I served a man as a servant in the Earth Kingdom until I was sold to the Salt Mines."

Blossom's face was filled with pity. Grabbing Rose's clenched fist, Blossom gently spread the tense fingers and smiled as Rose glanced up at her.

"When I undressed you, I saw your scars." Rose jerked away from her grasp. Strangely, she felt betrayed

"I'm sorry, I really am. The clothes you were in were *filthy*, I couldn't stand leaving you in them."

Rose looked away.

"How old are you?"

"Fifteen, I think. I don't know what my birthday is."

"You're fifteen. And ... there's *so much*—" Blossom stopped, glanced at Rose's blank face, and paused. "We're letting you stay,"

What?

Her face must've shown the shock she felt, because Blossom sighed.

"What did you think we were going to do? Dump you at an orphanage? The world has done too much damage to you already. Halt..." she trailed off.

"Halt?"

Blossom smiled at her.

"Would you like a tour of the house?" Blossom asked. The subject change was not subtle. Starting, Rose opened her mouth to ask a question – what was Halt like? Why were they really keeping her around? Who in their right minds would want her to stay?

"Come, Rose," Blossom said gently. "If you want to know, you should ask him."

Rose frowned, but nodded.

The house was beautiful. Blossom took her through the many

rooms, explaining, as she led her through, that Halt had used his magic to build this house into the side of a mountain. Although the hallways were lit only by swinging lanterns, most of the rooms had large windows that let in swaths of sunlight. There was a kitchen connected to the room in which they had eaten, located in the center of the house. From the kitchen, the house split into two sections: an east and west wing. The very farthest corner of the east wing held Halt and Blossom's room as well as three storage areas, an expansive room which held punching bags, mats, training dummies, and dozens of weapons, as well as a few locked doors. The west wing merely held a few extra rooms, as well as a locked room that was Halt's workshop. Rose tugged at Blossom's sleeve, stopping in front of the door to listen. There were a few seconds of silence before she heard something explode. Blossom had to stifle a laugh as Rose jumped away from the door, heart pounding.

"He has interesting experiments," Blossom explained. "Here, let's go back to the dining room-"

"What's this?" Rose gestured toward a pair of large wooden doors, marking the very end of the west wing.

"The library." The words shot through her like lightning.

"Can... may I go in?"

"Of course."

The darkness of the library compared to the well-lit hallway seemed intimidating, but Rose walked farther inside. The floor of the library had two dimly glowing fires, four squishy armchairs, and a narrow staircase. The room was circular in shape, stretching three floors tall with walls covered in shelves and shelves of books. It was beautiful. She had just entered a tower of parchment and ink.

"How many?"

"Nearly ten thousand, although that was two years ago. Considering how many books he manages to collect every year, I'd estimate there's a bit more now."

"Ten *thousand*? I've never—" Rose paused. "Can I... read these?"

"Of course."

Rose stared up at the tower and laughed, running her fingers along the spines of the dusty books, tilting her head to read the covers. She recognized almost none of them.

"How is this organized? Why do you have so many books? How—"

"Hey, hey, slow down," Blossom said, laughing. "From what I know, It's nonfiction at the bottom, folklore and myths in the middle, and fiction at the top. Of course, you can ask Halt about subcategories. Halt loves books just as much as you seem to, he had already collected nearly four hundred by the time he became a mage and got a place to live in. He used his earnings to buy all of this, over time. Take this lantern to see the titles. It's pretty dark up there."

Rose ascended the stairs, sprinting up the steps, a grin spreading over her face. The staircase was designed so that most books could be easily reached from the steps and leveled out at the top of the library. By the time Rose reached the top, she had found five books—*five*—merely from skimming the titles as she ran.

"I'll leave you to it," Blossom called from below. Rose leaned over the railing and gave her a thumbs up. "I'll be in the workshop, the kitchen, or my room if you need anything. Be careful, okay?"

Rose nodded.

The top of the staircase formed a flat circle that covered the entire perimeter of the library, guaranteeing access to the books at the very top. As she walked along the circle she noticed a groove in the wall, so subtle that she probably wouldn't have noticed it if not for its similarity to the fake bookshelf that hid her alcove in Master's library. Curious, Rose pushed at the wall. It swung open, and Rose had to duck slightly to enter the alcove within.

She was thoroughly disappointed at the lack of a secret within. It was a small room, well lit, containing three or four of the most comfortable couches she had ever seen. Rose placed her books on a singular bookshelf built in the left wall that contained only five or six books before sitting down on a couch with a story named *An Immaculate Conception* that was at least two inches thick. It was well-loved, as if read through dozens of times, but in good shape.

It was a feeling she hadn't felt in what felt like years. Utter safety, kindness, warmth, the feeling of smooth leather beneath her fingers, the scent of wood, paper, and ink. Halt and Blossom had shown her a kindness she had never experienced before. Were they planning something?

If so, why let her explore their house? Why allow her so much happiness?

I'm safe. After all this time. Safe.

But Ezra wasn't.

Letting out a choked breath, Rose curled onto herself and flipped open the book, pushing those thoughts away and losing herself within another world.

* * *

Tick, tock. Tick, tock. Tick, tock.

Turning over, Rose pressed her face against the pillow and groaned. She pushed herself up on her elbow and glanced at the clock in the corner. By the light of the moon, she could read the time—*two in the morning*—and she sighed, burrowing herself deeper into the blankets.

She couldn't sleep.

Tick, tock. Tick, tock. Tick, tock.

Falling back onto the bed, she shut her eyes. *Ezra should be here right now, don't you think?* They were heavy, but her body remained tense. There was the sound of scratching in the corner. Rose jerked, her heart pounding, adrenaline rushing through her. She sighed, falling back onto the bed.

Tick, tock. Tick, tock. Tick, tock.

Rose sat up in bed, grabbing one of her pillows and throwing it at the wall. It fell to the ground with a pathetic *thud*, and Rose groaned.

Tick, tock. Tick, tock.

The sound of the clock was steady and continuous, like a heartbeat. She just wished it was quieter, like the rest of the house. Sighing, Rose closed her eyes—*you let Ezra die*—and then opened them again.

Taking one of the lanterns off the walls, Rose got out of bed, teeth chattering with cold as she put on a pair of soft, fluffy, loose pants and a sweatshirt. Opening the door, Rose walked down the long hallway, her bare feet cold against the stone ground, and walked toward the library. She crept inside. The walk up the stairs was quiet and slow, but comforting, especially as the scent of ink and paper thickened. The alcove door was shut—*had she shut it?*—and she pushed it open.

The problem was, someone was already sitting there.

The man sitting in the seat Rose had occupied was holding up *An Immaculate Conception,* brow furrowed in confusion. Slowly, Rose backed away, surprised. This was *Halt's* alcove? She lifted up the lantern, trying to get a closer look at his face, still cautious; mostly because he bore a strange resemblance to Master: dangerous-looking eyes, a chiseled jaw, hollow cheeks, and a short, scruffy, brown beard. Rose, very honestly, couldn't decide if his stare was a glare. She backed out of the room, staring at *An Immaculate Conception* longingly.

"Take the damn book," Halt growled. He tossed it at her. Rose flinched, ducking as it sailed past her head and hit the railing, barely avoiding falling past the staircase down three floors. Rose picked it up, checking for damaged pages, and gave Halt a vaguely reproachful glance.

"Use the room while I'm not here. Take your books," Halt said. He stumped toward the bookshelf, looked at the five huge tomes, looked at Rose and sighed. "Take your damn book and leave."

Rose nodded, darting out of the alcove. She was almost at the stairs when she heard Halt say something and paused to listen.

"*An Immaculate Conception,* huh? She's got good taste, at least."

As she reached the bottom of the stairs and settled into one of the armchairs by the fire, Now, *An Immaculate Conception's* worn state made sense. Exactly how many times had Halt himself read the book?

Flipping open the book to her marked page, Rose frowned as she looked down on the text. Why would someone as successful and powerful as Halt read a book about an imprisoned, demonized angel?

Chapter Six

HER DAYS BECAME A ROUTINE.

Rose finally drifted to sleep at five and found herself waking at nine in the morning. She would eat with Blossom and sometimes even learned to cook with her, then spend most of her hours in the library. However, no matter how hard she tried, and how tired she was, she *couldn't* sleep until late at night.

"Azriel's shoulders shook. He knelt on the floor, hands trembling, tears streaming down his face and his chest aching with pain. His bids for freedom had been thwarted, his beautiful white wings covered with soot, his hands shackled to the floor. Why was he doomed to this fate? Was it any fault of his that his conception was as sinfully immaculate it was? Was he really such an abomination?"

Rose sighed, putting down the book. It was three in the morning and her head was *aching*. The comfortable alcove seemed to close in around her, cornering her. Sighing, Rose shook off the paranoia and dove back into the book, occasionally pausing the slow stroking motion of the bandages along her wrists. Her feet had completely healed, but her wrists and the whip mark along her chest and stomach were still tender. Blossom had told her they would take at least a few more weeks to heal.

"Hello, Azriel." The man's voice was smooth as honey, and Azriel looked up into those ebony eyes and felt rage rush through him.

"Gabriel. What do you want?"

"You better quiet your tone around me, or he dies," the man said. Azriel felt his heart stop. Gabriel gestured toward someone beside him, and there was a cry of pain as a struggling body was tugged into vision. The guard pressed his body against the bars, revealing the gag in his mouth, the tears running down his cheeks, and the wild panic in his eyes.

"Michael. No! Let him go!" Azriel screamed.

Rose gulped.

"Give us your power," Gabriel snarled. Azriel jolted back, and Michael shook his head.

"No."

"In that case..."

The silver flash of the dagger was so fast Azriel barely saw it. It cut into Michael's back, so deep that Azriel could see the point of it piercing through his stomach. The dagger was yanked out with a thud, and Michael collapsed onto the ground. His gag was cut off, and his mouth worked before he spoke.

Rose felt her mouth go dry. *Ezra, Ezra, Ezra.*

"Michael. Michael, no. Don't go."

"Hey. Hey, Azriel, it's okay. Don't cry."

"Don't cry, Rose. Don't cry."

"Ezra?" Rose whirled around, dropping the book. She could've sworn she heard his voice, but where was he? She licked her lips, her hands trembling, and she could feel warm, sticky blood on her fingers. She blinked, and then she saw him—*she saw him, in her arms*—and his lips were bubbling with blood and his back was covered–

There was a touch on her back, and Rose whirled around, heart pounding.

"Don't touch him! *Don't touch him!*" She blinked again and Ezra wavered out of sight. He reached out toward Rose and whispered, "*Don't cry, don't cry, I'm sorry, I'm sorry.*"

There was someone shouting her name, but Rose darted away from them, curling into herself. *Ezra was dead. Ezra was dead. Ezra was dead.* Her chest, her chest, her chest—*Let me breathe, let me breathe, let me breathe.* Someone gently grasped her hand and Rose squeezed it tightly, letting it ground her.

If only she'd had the magic before Ezra died. If only she had trained, had unlocked this power sooner. If only she could protect him.

Around her, she could see other slaves dying—a little girl, the very one she had protected. An old man. An injured woman. *If only I could protect them all.*

"Rose!"

She slowly resurfaced. The world around her seemed to be underwater, but she could see again. Breathe again.

She was in the alcove. Safe.

"What are you doing here?" Halt asked. Rose grimaced. Of course, it had to be him. He made to grab her wrist.

"Don't touch me," Rose snapped, voice hoarse. Had she been screaming? Her entire body was shaking. "Sorry. Did I wake you up?" Halt stared at her, his gaze inscrutable.

"How did you find this door? I thought I designed it well enough so that neither you nor Blossom would be able to find it."

"I've used them before," Rose growled. "Please go away."

"This is my alcove you're in," Halt snarled, taking a step toward her. Rose flinched back –he was right. She was living in their house, she reminded herself, and had no place being so rude. Bracing a hand against the wall, she pushed herself to her feet. The world was slightly spinning around her, and she blinked a few times, swaying.

"I'm sorry. I'll go now," Rose murmured. She leaned against the wall as she walked toward the door, glancing toward *An Immaculate Conception* on the ground before deciding it wasn't worth the effort to pick it up.

"Sit down," he snapped. Rose glanced back at him, then slowly made her way back toward the nearest chair. Sitting down gratefully, Rose drew her knees up to her chest and let out a shaking breath.

"Are you okay?" Halt asked. His face was as emotionless as ever, but as Rose glanced toward him, she caught a glimpse of some unfathomable emotion in his eyes before she turned away. Her body, which had just barely began to calm, trembled harder.

"I'm fine. It's okay. Give me a second. I'll go soon," Rose said. He stared at her, and she shrank away, into the seat, the barely-subsided panic rising as he leaned closer toward her.

"Maybe ... move away, please?" Rose choked out. Halt moved away soundlessly.

"Are you ready to leave?" Halt finally asked. Rose looked down at her knees. She didn't want to move at all, but making Halt angry really seemed like a bad idea. Rose nodded, pushing herself to her feet. White flashed across her vision, but when she cleared out the lightheadedness, she found that her dizziness had stopped. Bending down, Rose picked up the book with still-shaking hands before slowly walking out of the alcove. The shadows along the wall seemed to leap at her as she walked out of the well-lit library, and by the time she reached her room, her shaking had gotten worse.

What was happening to her?

Rose lay in bed, staring up at the dark ceiling, her hands clenched in fists as she tried to stop the trembling. She was so, so scared.

If only I could protect myself.

She managed to drift asleep.

* * *

"You should've protected me!"

Rose flinched, whirling around and meeting a pair of golden eyes. Ezra. Her mouth opened, and she tried to say something, anything, but the words died halfway out. Taking a step toward Ezra, then another, Rose stopped in front of him, tears pooling in her eyes as she reached forward to touch his cheek.

It was cold and clammy.

"You should've saved me!" Ezra shouted at her. As Rose watched, his skin blackened and his skin rotted, but his eyes remained the same, filled with agony and hurt.

"Why didn't you save me?" Rose opened her mouth. She had wanted to, had wanted to so badly, but her magic hadn't awakened in time. She had been injured. She had wanted to—

"I trusted you. I thought you would save me," Ezra whispered. "It hurts so much, Rose. Please."

Tears began to drip down Rose's cheeks.

"Save me."

Rose whirled around, away from Ezra. There was another voice, another pair of agonized eyes, and Rose saw the little girl with dead green eyes. She reached toward Rose with tiny hands that were tight with tension, clawing with jagged fingernails at Rose's flesh, whispering, over and over again, why didn't you save me? Why aren't you saving me? Rose cried out in pain, thrashed away, but she felt another cold body behind her. She looked backward.

Another slave.

They surrounded her, their zombified bodies and pain-filled eyes encompassing her existence. Rose screamed, cried out, thrashed, apologized, but they only dug deeper into her flesh.

Rose sat up, chest heaving, a throbbing pain in her neck pervading her existence. Sitting up slowly, Rose wiped the tears from her face, and looked down.

Blood, everywhere.

Rose stared down at her hands, her fingertips that were smeared with blood, and then stared up at the clock—six in the morning. Clumsily, Rose stumbled out of bed, yanking on a pair of sweatpants before walking into the bathroom and pulling off her shirt, revealing her neck and six or seven deep scratches down its front. Choking down a sob, Rose watched as blood dripped down into the sink. The scratches hurt, and Rose's fingers tightened so much along the rim of the sink that her knuckles began to ache.

"Help," Rose whispered. "Please." Of course, no one responded.

Rose stumbled out of the bathroom. She had no medical supplies, but there might be some in the storage rooms. As she opened the door into the kitchen, she left behind bloody fingerprints on the doorknob. In the darkness, she tripped over the chairs, collapsing on the ground, smearing blood on the wooden floors - and even though she was in the safest place she had ever lived in, it felt like she was back at Master's house, on nights after whippings, in so much pain that she couldn't sleep. She had once tried to sneak out, take medicine from the servant's quarters, but had tipped over a pan and woken up Master.

He hadn't been happy.

But it wouldn't happen now, right? Halt and Blossom both were on the other side of the house. They wouldn't wake up. She could lay here for a little, rest, and then clean everything up. She was so tired. Maybe she could just sleep. Rose's eyes began to shut.

"Rose!" Rose's eyes opened slightly, and she saw a tiny light in the hallway. Was that Halt? Had she woken him up? Was he mad? She could tell him he could go back to sleep. He would be okay with that, right?

"What the hell are you doing?" Halt asked as he stalked into the kitchen. Rose opened her mouth to reply, but the thought of talking made her feel like choking. He stalked around the kitchen, back facing her as he methodically lit the lanterns until the kitchen was brightly lit before slamming down the candle on the table.

"If you're just going to make trouble, I might as well send you away," Halt snarled, still facing away from her as he bent down and threw away the used matches. Unbidden tears slid down Rose's cheeks as she flinched. The tears slid down, into the cuts on her neck, and she shrank into herself. She was so tired, and it hurt so much.

"Help. Please," Rose whispered. Summoning a small gust of wind that blew toward the candle, Halt either ignored her or didn't hear her. The candle refused to be extinguished. Waves of pain throbbed through her neck, from the saltwater tears and the wood rubbing against it and Rose cried in earnest.

"What the hell did you even want? Food? Just sleep, for god's sake," Halt snarled. The candle finally went out, and he finally—*finally*—turned around.

Halt froze.

Rose watched as he stared at her, shrinking into herself, curling into a ball. Had he seen the bloodstains? He was mad. He had to be mad. Rose pushed herself into a half sitting position, trying to move away from him, only for her arm to give out and for her to fall back to the floor with a cry of pain. Why was she so tired? Why couldn't her body just move?

"You can just go back to sleep... I'm sorry... I'll clean the blood up," Rose mumbled. She'd clean it all up tomorrow. She'd just sleep, now. But instead of moving towards her, Halt took a step back, slowly, as if disbelieving.

And then Rose saw his eyes.

Remorse, horror, and concern.

He wasn't mad?

Halt bent down. When he grasped Rose's shoulders, his hands were gentle. He wasn't mad. Gently, his hands just barely squeezing her shoulders, he pushed Rose into a sitting position before reaching forward hesitantly and wiping away her tears.

"Were you... looking for bandages?"

Rose nodded.

"What happened? Was it..." Halt's gaze darted down to her bloodied fingers, and his mouth curled into a frown. "Let's get you cleaned up."

As Rose tried to push herself to her feet, Halt pushed her back down gently. He scooped her into his arms, holding Rose as if she weighed nothing, one arm underneath her knees and the other supporting her shoulders. His warmth enveloped her and he began walking toward the direction of the storage rooms, and Rose drifted into sleep—feeling, inexplicably, safe.

* * *

As Halt carried her into his room, he could feel his heart break. The girl weighed barely ninety pounds, so thin he could probably carry her with a single arm. The scratches along her neck were brutal, still oozing out blood, and as Halt lay her on the bed, he realized that he felt guilty. Storming into the kitchen, threatening to send her away, yelling at her just to go sleep instead of "causing trouble." He had treated her like trash. His heart was heavy as he grabbed a wet towel and began to wipe the blood from her fingers and face.

As he carefully bandaged her neck, he noticed the bandages on her wrist and recalled Blossom's words. *She has a lot of scars, Halt. We have to let her stay.*

Curiosity overwhelming, Halt unwrapped the bandages. His breath caught in his throat, and he stepped backward, away from the half-bandaged girl, his left hand creeping unbidden to his right wrist, hidden by his long sleeves.

Manacle marks, ones that he knew all too well.

Usually, Halt enjoyed the silence and darkness of his room. Usually, Halt loved reading by the dim light of a barely swinging lantern. Today, however, the demon within him that he thought he'd banished forever crept forward, as if summoned by its invisible kin that slowly consumed the unconscious girl before him.

* * *

When she came to, the sun was shining.

Where am I?

"You're awake. Don't worry, you're just in my room," A deep voice told her. "Your bedsheets were stained with blood, so Blossom's washing them."

Rose frowned. A *deep* voice? Why would she be in Halt's room? She lay there, confused, before she remembered.

"Oh, fucking hell," Rose murmured as she sat up. Glancing down at her hands, anywhere but at Halt, Rose noticed that they were free of blood. She reached her hand toward her neck, running a finger along the rough surface of the bandage, and let out a deep sigh.

"How are you feeling now? Are you okay?" Halt asked. Rose turned her attention toward Halt, feeling her cheeks warm as she stared at him.

"I'm okay now. I'm sorry for the trouble I caused-"

"Stop apologizing," Halt said gently. "I asked if you were okay. Really. If you were okay, you wouldn't be clawing at yourself in your sleep."

"It was just a dream," Rose replied. "It was nothing. It won't happen again." Halt sighed.

"That's not what I was asking," Halt stopped, sighed. "I—"

"Man, you're bad at this," Rose blurted. Silence. She stared at Halt, who stared at her, and she huffed a half-hearted laugh. Halt stared at her and Rose sighed, reaching up to run her fingers along her bandaged wrists. There was a small period of silence before Rose began to talk.

"I really appreciate how you guys are taking me in like this," Rose murmured. Halt barely dipped his head. Rose took this as acceptance and a signal to continue. "But... I don't think I can stay here." Halt frowned.

"If you're talking about what I said in the kitchen… I'm sorry, kid. I just—"

"No, no, that's okay. It wasn't that. I know that staying here is probably the best idea. But—"

"I know."

"You do?"

"You want more, don't you?"

Rose nodded.

"What do you want?" Halt asked. "What are you looking for? Can't you just find it here?"

"I can't."

"What is it?"

"Justice."

Halt stared at her, as if disbelieving.

"No, no, no," Rose corrected herself. "Justice isn't the way to describe it. I don't want to be some hero, or walk the thorny path of a martyr. I just want to be able to do things about everything I've seen, y'know? I want to be able to protect myself and the people around me."

Cautiously, Halt nodded.

"I couldn't really do anything before this magic. I was a Null—"

"Excuse me?" Halt bit out. "Is this a joke?"

"Uh, no? Yeah, I was a Null until recently. Until Ezra."

Halt leaned back just slightly, eyes wide.

"I couldn't do *anything*. But then…"

Then, I awakened this magic.

"I can do *anything* with this magic," Rose breathed. The realization struck her like lightning. "I could become a Mage. Like you, at the Academy."

"*No.*"

Halt's utterance made her jump.

"That place is *living hell*," Halt growled. "It isn't worth it. None of it is worth it."

"And what am I going to do? Stay here, in this beautiful place, ignoring all the shit I've seen? That I could fix? Think about it all. Think about what I could do-"

"It's too much," Halt snapped. "The Academy. It *breaks* students,

Rose." Rose *knew* that. She had read about it in what seemed like every book she had touched. Despite being the most pretigious magical institution in the world, it was notorious and feared for being harsh and selective. But.

"There is no cost too great to pay if I can save even one person!" Rose retorted.

Contemplating, Halt sat back, stared at her, and sighed.

"You're a lowborn. Hell, not even a lowborn. You awakened your magic barely a week ago. The extent of your education is basic arithmetic and the ability to read. You've never touched a weapon in your life. Hell—" Sighing deeply, Halt seemed to be trying to calm himself down. "You have *no chance*—"

"So you're just going to lock me here?"

"Become a knight. A soldier."

"You and I both know that I can't become a knight. Look at me."

There was silence. Pushing herself to her feet, Rose walked toward *An Immaculate Conception*, picking up the book, running her fingers along the pages.

"Azriel escapes his cell," Rose murmured. Halt nodded. "He wanted freedom. He saw things, outside of his cell, that he never would've dreamed of. At first, it was trees, the sun, the moon, rainbows. But he also found friendship and love. He found *Michael*. Would he have been as happy as he was if he had stayed inside? If he had been afraid of his own power? If he had been afraid of the world around him?"

"Michael *dies*," Halt spat out.

"Michael and Azriel *both* would've happily done it all over again, if only for him to die again!" Rose shouted. "Don't you understand? I *need* this. I want to be able to *do something* about this goddamn world! Ezra gave his *life* for me. I need to pay him back."

Halt stared at her, his fists clenching and unclenching, and Rose glared back. As she stared at him, Halt seemed to *disappear*. Rose turned around and ducked underneath his first punch, but the next caught her across the cheek, causing her to fall to the ground. Ignoring the pain from her chest and neck, Rose rolled to the side. Halt's next punch just hit the floor next to her, creating a barely visible dent on the stone floor. Rose jumped up and away from him, retreating to the other side of the room, a hand pressed to her chest as she glared at Halt.

"You see? This is only *one* of many things you're going to have to deal with for the entirety of a year. The Academy isn't something you can just go to on a whim. It's suffering and exhaustion and—"

Halt swore and ducked as Rose picked up one of the heavy candlesticks, shook out the candle, and threw it at him with all of her strength. It struck the wall three inches from his head with a dull thud and fell to the ground, unharmed.

"I don't care," Rose snarled. She stared at Halt, nervous but prepared to stand her ground. To her surprise, Halt merely picked up the candlestick and examined it before walking over to Rose. She stared at him, then at the candlestick as Halt calmly placed it onto the nightstand behind her.

"You've got balls, that's for sure," Halt murmured. "As *utterly* foolish as this suggestion is, I can't stop you. You're your own person. If you expect me to help, I have three conditions."

"What?"

"I'm going to train you. We only have three months, but—"

"Um, what?" Rose broke in.

"In three months, I'll go to the Lightning Kingdom to collect supplies. I'll go a few weeks later than I usually do so you arrive on the day of the Academy's opening. In those two months, I'll train you."

"In what?"

"As much physical conditioning as I can. How to fight. Most importantly, basic control over your magic. That's usually taught to you at a very young age," Halt growled. "If you know what's good for you, you'd go through a few academic things, too. Basic arithmetic. Research-—"

"Wait a second. You're *training* me?"

Exasperated, he stared at Rose before throwing his hands up.

"You're clearly dead set on going. I'd like to use my experience to help you."

"Three conditions?"

"One. Don't complain, just do what I tell you to. Two. Don't bother me outside of training. Three. Stay out of the goddamn alcove at night."

Rose nodded.

"Studying?"

"I'll compile a list of things you should learn to even have a *chance* of understanding *anything* in the Academy's academics. I'll give it to you after we train tomorrow."

"We're training tomorrow? I'm still—"

"Yes, yes, you're still hurt. I'll go easy on you."

Rose stared at him. Their eyes met, and Halt looked away, seating himself on the stone floor, fiddling with his hands.

"I'll... I'll go now?" Rose hadn't meant for it to sound like a question. When there was no response, she turned toward the door.

"One more thing," Halt murmured. Rose turned back to face him. She was tossed a pair of plain, black gloves, made of a soft pliable cloth.

"In case the dreams come back," Halt explained. Rose stared at the gloves, noting that they were only a little large for her and couldn't possibly fit on Halt or Blossom.

"Who'd this belong to?" Rose asked.

"I used them for stuff when I was younger," Halt replied. "You can go now. Be outside at seven tomorrow, or I'm not training you.

Rose walked out of the room, and the door slammed behind her. Unmoving, Rose stared at the door, trying to fathom the man within before deciding that he was simply too complex.

The Academy.

* * *

The desert wind was *miserable.*

Glaring at the dark sky, the sand beneath her feet, and the wind blowing around her, Rose tucked her hands into her pockets and shivered. She was wearing a thick cloak, a thin, short-sleeved shirt, and long pants. Beside the entrance stood a large wagon. The wind was howling so loudly that she only barely heard the door open behind her, and she could barely stop herself from glaring at Halt as he walked out of the door.

"I'm glad to see you're early," Halt said. "You're coming with me to retrieve food."

"What?" Rose asked. "But I thought—"

"Oh, trust me, this is training," Halt cut in. "It's two miles away. I'll be taking a wagon there, of course, but you're going to run there. It's a perfect conditioning exercise."

Rule one: don't complain. Just do what I tell you to.

"I'll be a lot slower than you. I might get lost. What are we going to do about that? And what do you mean by retrieving food?"

"We're going to a grove of trees and cacti near a small oasis. There are dates and prickly pears there. I'll be spending at least a few days there. I harvest and dry them. As for following me, just follow the magic. You'll know what I mean."

Without waiting for a response, Halt turned and jogged toward the side of the mountain. Rose followed him as he climbed, eventually turning a corner and reaching a small stable built upon a large clearing covered in grass. In the shade of a few trees, two horses stood, peacefully grazing.

"Where'd you guys get this grass?" Rose asked.

"We planted it. It's a pain in the ass to keep it alive, but the horses are worth the effort."

Patiently, Halt led the horses down the short climb and attached them to the wagon. Before he climbed on, he passed Rose a water bottle.

"Ration it properly, until you get there," Halt said. "You can refill it there."

Rose barely had time to nod before Halt nonchalantly swung onto one of the horses and sped off into the distance, spraying her with desert sand. Tossing her cloak onto the ground in front of the door, Rose jogged after the wagon that was already disappearing beyond the horizon. As Rose ran after him, she noticed the thin, deep rivet carved into the sand by magic, forming a straight line that followed Halt's path. Glancing back at the mountain, Rose clenched her fists, took a deep breath, and broke into a jog. The motion made her chest ache, but not unbearably so. As she quickly discovered, inhaling the desert sand was inevitable. It burned her throat, resulting in pain that worsened every time she took a breath. She lasted fifteen minutes before she gave in, slowing slightly to take a swig from her water bottle before continuing to run. Ahead of her, there was no trace of Halt, only the deep trail within the sand.

If it had been a flat plain, Rose might've been able to make two miles in a light jog, although that was already generous. However, along the unwieldy, high-rising dunes of the desert, Rose had barely made it through three quarters of a mile before she had to slow into a complete walk. She alternated between slow walking and a pathetic jog, but the deadly noon sun was already rising, nearly overhead as she slowed to a complete walk. Each step became an effort, and her bottle was empty. Sandpaper seemed to be rubbing against her throat with every step she took, and her lips began to crack. The sand shimmered before her eyes, and her goal went from *a few more dunes* to *one more dune* to just a single step, one after another. Just as she was prepared to sink to her knees, Rose heard a faint *shick, shick*.

Magic.

As she crested the dune, she saw a small oasis in the distance, surrounded by trees and cacti. Nearing the oasis, Rose barely acknowledged Halt as he stepped toward her. She didn't even bother to take off her shoes as she stepped into the water, waded in until she was submerged up to her waist, and proceeded to let herself fall, face-first, into the water.

* * *

Halt was harvesting the fruit with such high efficiency that it was almost fun to watch. Slicing through the large bunches of dates that hung from the palm-like trees, Halt floated toward the wagon before slicing them off the bunches, letting each one fall into the half-full wagon gently before tossing away the branches of the bunches.

"Did you dig those irrigation channels?" Rose asked, pointing toward the channels that wound from the oasis to the trees. The oasis itself was fed by several small springs that bubbled from within the ground into the pool.

"Yeah, when I first found this place. That season was particularly rainy, which is how the trees grew in the first place. They were barely as high as my leg, but I decided it would be worth the effort and spent a few days planning and digging them."

Rose didn't respond, instead choosing to take another bite of the bread that Halt had given her. She was sitting on one of the larger stones, her bare feet still dipped in the icy cold water, watching as Halt worked. Across from her, on the other side of the oasis, the horses were sprawled in the shade, drinking water and eating from a hay bale.

"Do you wanna feed the horses?" Halt asked. Rose glanced at him, then looked back toward the horses. They were *huge*, and could probably trample her.

"Oh, don't worry about them being big. These two are very gentle. I named them Monte and Cristo, after the book. There's carrots and sugar cubes in the pouch in the front. Only give each one one of each though. Break the carrots into smaller pieces so they don't choke."

"What do you normally feed them?" Rose asked as she grabbed the pouch from the driver's seat.

"They graze a lot during the day, so we only feed them at night, if it's needed. Usually hay and some of the treats you see here. They've been running a lot today, so I brought a hay bale. We keep salt blocks in their fields too," Halt said. Rose waded through the oasis, approaching the horses cautiously, holding out a broken off piece of a carrot as if it were a peace offering. One of the horses, a dappled gray stallion, merely rolled onto his back in the shade and ignored her. Stifling a laugh, Rose watched as he flopped around on the floor before laying still on his side, against the tree. She was so taken with him that she had forgotten the other, a dark chestnut mare that was nudging her nose into Rose's hand.

"The gray one is Monte, and the chestnut is Cristo," Halt told her. Rose relinquished the piece of carrot and laughed as Cristo shoved her enormous nose against Rose's shoulder, nearly knocking her over. Reaching forward, Rose hesitated, then stroked Cristo's nose. Her fur was matted by desert sand but still felt pleasant and silky. The mare's eyes were large and gentle as she bent down toward the hay bale and gently tore off a piece of hay. Rose felt, suddenly, warmth near the hand holding the pouch, and looked down to see Monte nudging at the pouch. Remembering Halt's instructions, Rose gently pushed his nose away. Monte snorted, raised his head, and shoved it against Rose, knocking her to the ground, sending pain lancing down her chest. Monte stopped, stepped back, and then whinnied and danced slightly where he stood as if agitated, maybe even worried. Cristo, gentle as she was, headbutted Monte in the side, as if scolding him.

Staring at the two horses in astonishment, Rose laughed.

* * *

"Hey. Hey, Monte, stop," Halt snapped from across the oasis. Rose had been knocked to the ground by a single forceful push of his head. Squinting at Rose, Halt observed a slight shaking motion in her shoulders. Was she panicking again? Wading through the oasis, Halt was halfway there and ready to scold Monte before he stopped and stared in amazement.

Because for the first time since he had seen her, Rose was laughing.

* * *

"Here. The list of things I want you to learn before we leave," Halt said. Rose looked up at him from her seat at the kitchen table. As she had predicted, he had made her run back to their mountainside home. Everything ached, and even though she had switched into clean clothes, she felt as though she could feel sand against her skin.

"I hope the run hasn't tired you out too much, because that, and more, is going to happen every day. You're expected to learn all of this at the same time."

Rose nodded. Halt threw a small roll of parchment at her, and Rose unwrapped it. It held about twenty items: arithmetic, algebra and geometry, basic geography, knowledge of a long list of weapons and how they were used, how magic works, a vague understanding of history, the governments of the six nations, and so on, as well as about thirty textbooks Halt had suggested.

"Duly noted," Rose groaned. "And I'm supposed to finish all of this in three months?"

"Yes. The math will be tough, but it's the most important of all. The

Academy will be covering only the most advanced algebra and calculus, so if you don't understand algebra and geometry, you're screwed."

"Got it. What order should I take it in? Should I cram in everything from one subject at a time and move on to the next, or do several at once?"

"Keep the studies of math in the background every day. No excuses. I suggest sprinkling in whatever you find fun in between cramming things that aren't so fun."

"Okay."

"I'd expect you to complain more about this."

"Learning's fun."

"You'll think differently by next year."

It took a week for Rose to be able to make it back to the mountain before nightfall, and another week before she could make it there before late afternoon. After harvesting enough fruits, Halt would bring a few baskets of fruit, fly to the oasis, and sit in the shade, drying the fruit. The prickly pears' hard outer thorns were removed and they were cut into thin slices, while the dates had their pits removed. They were then placed on clean palm leaves that he plucked from above to dry on. Rose's short break was usually taken in total silence, with her eating lunch and some fruit before resting and preparing for the run back home. It was only on the day that Rose reached the oasis in less than two hours that Halt finally spoke.

"Are your studies going well?"

"Yes. I've finished arithmetic and basic geology. I've started geography, weapons, and algebra."

"Good. It's time to teach you how to fight."

Almost instinctively, Rose reached a hand to press against the wounds on her chest. Her wrists were still bandaged due to being sensitive and raw, but her neck had completely healed and her chest barely ached anymore.

"I'm assuming your wounds are healed enough for you to fight."

"Yes."

"Good. Another thing: place studying magic above everything else for now, it should only take you a couple of days. After that, I'll start teaching you magic as well."

Rose nodded.

"Ready?"

"What?"

Halt threw himself at Rose, his first punch sailing past her head as she jumped to the side, his second striking the water of the oasis as Rose dived into its depths. Thrashing away from him within the water, she realized her mistake. Water slows you down. Nimbly ducking under the next blow, Rose swept her arm along the surface of the water, sending it spraying into Halt's face as she turned tail and ran. Even as she ran through the water, she could hear Halt behind her, and a kick hit her on the side, sending her into the water with a splash. Spluttering, Rose resurfaced, prepared for the next blow.

"At least you have enough reaction time to dodge, even if you don't know how to do so effectively yet," Halt commented. "You're moving too much. That first attack could've been avoided by just ducking, which would've let you move to the side instead of into the water."

Rose nodded.

"And while you did a good job trying to spray that water into my face, a better option would've been the dirt beneath it. Of course, that would take longer, but it'd be much more effective. You don't even know how to throw a punch, do you?"

She nodded, again.

"I won't teach you, for now. You need to learn how to evade."

And with that, without even letting Rose get out of the water, Halt threw himself at her, a deadly machine of movement and speed. He was so fast that, despite her trying her best to move less, the only option she had was to move entirely to a different location. She barely lasted five seconds before a sweeping blow swept her feet from beneath her, sending her sprawling to the ground.

Sighing, Rose pushed herself to her feet and readied herself for the next attack.

* * *

"Magic is collected within you in what may feel like a body of water," Halt explained. "Close your eyes, search for that water within your conscious, and when you find it, extract a tiny piece of it and expel it. Gently."

"Why?"

"To learn control."

Rose nodded and closed her eyes. There was now no trace of those pitch-black gates that had locked away her magic, of throbbing magic locked behind that barrier. Instead, she saw a small body of magic, cool to the touch, and Rose scooped up a tiny piece of magic and released it into the world.

Electricity sparked within her clasped hands, burning her skin. Rose opened her eyes and recoiled in pain. Halt merely watched as the electricity sparked and melted away.

"There are two types of magic. Do you remember this?" Halt asked.

"Yeah," Rose said. "First, you Manipulate the body of your element around you. This requires less mana but more skill, as you are manipulating what is around you and not creating it, so you don't have innate control. Second, you Manifest your element by using your mana to create it. This requires much more mana but is easier for beginners to pull off."

"Exactly," Halt said. "The thing textbooks don't tell you is that, in order to balance out the disadvantages lightning has in terms of Manipulation, lightning users have evolved to generate more lightning while Manifesting. The difference is pretty much undocumented, but it's scientifically proven. When you use the same amount of magic to Manifest, for example, as a water user, you'd create much more lightning than they do water. As you can tell, this causes Lightning magic to be very destructive when you first start. Your job is to control it. That is all I want you to learn before you go."

"My textbook never told me that," Rose remarked, sucking on her burned fingers.

"For you, the most reliable textbooks were written at least a few decades ago. Textbooks nowadays take this sorta stuff as a given. You're one of the few people who didn't grow up with magic. For most, it's as natural as breathing."

"Then why does the Academy exist? Why train for years to master something that normally comes naturally?"

"The Academy..." Halt paused. "...teaches you not only how to fight, not only how to use your magic, but to push beyond ordinary human limits. Any human limit to your stamina must be broken. You become not only adept at using magic, but capable of using it subconsciously."

Rose sighed in awe.

"But to get to that extent," Halt said, "You've gotta learn to do what everyone else can naturally do first. Get to it."

Glancing down at her hands, Rose sighed before closing her eyes and delving back into her consciousness. Her magic, she now saw, was agitated, writhing slightly at the touch. Carefully, with no small hint of trepidation, Rose attempted to extract a piece of it. It writhed, and Rose could tell even before she released it that it would backfire. She opened her eyes.

"So?" Halt said impatiently. "Where's the lightning? Are you scared?"

"No," Rose said. She closed her eyes and remembered Halt's words: *extract a tiny piece of it and expel it*. "Halt? Could you tell me what your magic looks like?"

"What?"

"My magic looks like it's agitated and writhing, which I think might be because of lightning. What about yours?"

"It's—" Halt hesitated, brow furrowing. He shut his eyes briefly. "It's almost like the magic is curling into itself. If I look closely, I can feel it flowing. Why?" In response, Rose shut her eyes and delved back into her conscience. Halt's affinity – Wind – would obviously be different from hers. Tearing a piece of it away from the whole made more sense with something *curling into itself*, but with something agitated and writhing, maybe the right approach would be to *sooth it*. Rose visualized her magic, and instead of extracting a piece, imagined a single droplet of magic flowing down a funnel into her outstretched hands. *Stop, there*, she commanded, and she opened her eyes to find lightning flaring to life a few inches above her cupped hands. It was beautiful. She smiled, triumphant, and glanced over at Halt for approval. There—just barely, Rose could see a hint of a smile on his lips.

"Nice job," he said. Rose grinned. "Now try shaping it."

* * *

As important as the subjects she was studying all were, Rose found that she was most enamored with history and studies of magic. She had always been interested in magical theory, but had never delved too deeply into studying it, seeing as such information had had limited usefulness to her until now. History, however, was different. Halt's library had rare books about history that Rose had never heard of until now: first-person accounts of the enormous trading cities of the late Great Kingdom era, the Water Kingdom's formation and the details of the minor war that had given them control over a strip of land on the Main Continent, and even a first-person account of the Dark Era from an individual who had worked for the Dark Sorcerer.

On the morning of the day he took over the Fire Kingdom, the Dark Sorcerer gathered his inner circle in the Council Room. He rose from his seat for the first time, and walked amongst us to the covered boxes in the back of the room. They had been there for a while. When he uncovered them, he laughed, because our loved ones were behind the bars, and we were helpless. I had joined him because... because he had promised to keep them safe. Because he said he would win. I believed him and wanted my daughter safe. She was behind the bars. Emaciated, otherwise unharmed. And then he told us to fight. That the winner would receive a piece of his power, and the others, along with their families, would be killed. He sat back as we did it. I won, and he dispatched me immediately to the Fire Kingdom. I led the armies while he stayed back, that coward, and was captured. I haven't seen my daughter since.

"Rose!" Blossom called from the floor of the library. Rose looked up from the book, shuddering a little at the brutality portrayed in it, and exited the library, returning the book to the shelf as she did so.

* * *

It was nearly a month later when Halt decided, on a seeming whim, that she was ready for a weapon. Although Rose had improved, she hadn't expected to be introduced to weapons that quickly. As of now, she could only evade his attacks, her own punches being too weak to allow her to do much damage.

"Why a weapon? I'm obviously not prepared," Rose asked him as she followed him toward his weaponry rooms.

"Because even though you're poor at hand-to-hand, I'm teaching you how to survive. With your stature, you can't beat your opponent to death. Your best bet is to learn how to fight with weapons," Halt told her. Withdrawing a key from his pocket, Halt opened one of the few doors with locks. Rose's mouth fell open. "Careful, a lot of things here are very dangerous. Don't knock anything over. Take your pick."

The room was small, only just tall enough for Halt to fit inside and about seven feet wide. However, the walls were lined with shining, polished weapons that sat on notches on the walls.

"Take your pick," Halt repeated dryly. "If I were you, I'd choose a pair of daggers. Agility and speed are well-paired with them."

Stepping into the room, Rose stared up at the walls of weapons in amazement. The most plentiful weapon in the room were swords and daggers, ranging from short to immensely long, as well as an impressive collection of other weapons: battle-axes, recurve and longbows, six or seven quivers of arrows leaned carefully against the wall, and spears. Of course, there were also a few exotic weapons: a nagatina, a scythe, a pair of deadly-looking whips, and two daggers attached by a chain.

Axes and spears were out of the question, as were the more unique weapons. While having something as flashy as a scythe would be fun, it would only result in ineptitude. As Rose looked up at the wall, a pair of daggers caught her eye.

"I like these," Rose told him. Halt watched as she slowly unsheathed one of the daggers. Smoothing a finger along the shagreen grip, Rose realized exactly how light the blades were – she could barely feel their weight in her hands.

"Those blades are nice," Halt remarked. "Made from a lighter metal than most other daggers, but they're far harder to throw because of that. I wouldn't recommend throwing them. Here's how you hold them."

Gently, Halt rearranged Rose's clumsy grip.

"Slash... like this," Halt showed her. Rose imitated his movement, the deadly blade slashing against the air and examined the dagger closely. It shone in the dim light of the lanterns above, and while the dagger was perfectly, absolutely plain, it was a beautiful blade.

"They're kinda pretty, right?" Halt said. Rose tilted her head, glanced back at him, and then back at the dagger.

"Yeah. They're deadly. What weapons do you use?"

"During my first year, a broadsword. I switched to a single ax in my second year, then began using a pair of battleaxes."

"Aren't those *heavy*?" Rose asked. "I could barely lift one with both arms last time I tried."

"That's the point. Although I might be slower than someone who uses daggers, like you, if I hit you, you're almost certainly dead, even if you try to parry."

Slowly, Rose nodded. She imagined trying to block a blow from a battleax with the daggers in her hand and shuddered.

The next few hours were spent in Halt's room, where he taught her how to care for the blades. It was much more complex than Rose had ever imagined. Halt taught her how to oil and maintain the leather of the sheath and grip, how to sharpen her daggers with a whetstone, and how to polish the blade itself. As she admired the gleaming length of the blade, flipping it in her hand and marveling at how the light shone off its metal, Halt watched her. Although she might've been imagining it, there was, just barely, a hint of sadness in his eyes.

* * *

The day before the journey to the Lightning Region, Halt showed her how he fought with his battle axes. He was deadly lethal, hefting the heavy axes as if they weighed next to nothing, axes spinning and slashing at an invisible opponent as he occasionally pretended to parry an invisible opponent or duck from a blow.

"The Academy is a very hard place. It's not too late to turn back." Halt told her. His axes were sheathed on his back and he was sitting on the desert sand, staring down at his hands. They were calloused and rough.

"I know you're not the type to give up, but there's no shame in staying here, now. You've become strong enough that you'd even be useful. You could work with me and help take care of the house. With your help, we could probably get and care for more livestock."

Rose lowered herself onto the ground next to Halt, one hand absentmindedly stabbing the ground with her dagger as she stared up into the beautiful blue sky.

"I would like that."

"Does that mean you'll stay?"

"Do you really think my conscience will allow me to? Everything I've been avoiding will come back if I do."

Halt sighed.

"You're a lowborn. Some highborns at the Lightning Region have been training since birth to become a mage."

"I don't care."

"If you want to succeed, you'll barely have time to sleep. You'll feel like the walking dead."

"I'm already like that. Besides, isn't there a curfew?"

"You won't be able to keep up with training, studies, and magic with just the time they give you before curfew. No one actually checks the barracks themselves after curfew, only the hallways and libraries. They expect a few students to be ballsy enough to sneak out."

"And you think I can pull that off? I've read the books. Their curfew is strict."

"That's where my secret comes in. After dinner, the first thing you do is go to the barracks and train. Practice with someone who's smart enough to not need time to do homework, or train by yourself. Everyone will be doing homework, but you'll have to put in that work later if you want to keep up."

"So when will I do homework?"

"Before curfew is called, go to the fourth floor into the flag tower. It's the highest point in the Academy, and the staircase is pretty clearly labeled. It has a few tables in it, and on one of them, you'll see a few carvings.

"Of?"

"Initials. I had a few friends up there with me, *Violet Eneria* and another kid we didn't know. Mine are there too. Just *H*. Directly above the table should be a trapdoor."

"What if the table moved?"

"Oh, that happened to me once. I got a friend to stick the table to the wood with Earth Magic."

Rose grinned.

"How'd you find it?"

"It's usually a secret among the Royal Family."

Rose choked. "You want me to invade the Royal Family's secret study?"

"It wasn't so secret when I found it, even if it was completely by accident. If the prince is in your year, he probably won't care as long as you don't tell anyone else."

"The Prince *is* my age," Rose said. "He'll probably be in my year. If he gets mad–"

"It won't matter. Complaining to a teacher will just mean you both get expelled."

There was a comfortable silence, interrupted only by the *shick, shick* of Rose thrusting her knife into the sand.

"Thank you."

"It's just a secret, I didn't even—"

"You know what I mean, you dumbass," Rose said. The *shick, shick* sound stopped as her hand froze in midair and she sucked in a breath. Then, as she glanced up at Halt, she saw a sight that nearly made her drop her dagger in stunned surprise.

Halt was smiling.

* * *

"Rose?"

Rose looked up from her prickly pear slices. Man, she would miss those. Blossom was standing above her, her mouth curved in a lovely smile.

"So, Halt told you about the secret study?"

"Yeah."

"He's never told anyone that. Well, he told me that he would never tell anyone. You've gotten to him, you know. I think he's going to miss you."

"Really? I've been a pain in the ass."

"Don't swear," Blossom chided gently.

"Halt does all the time!" Rose protested. Blossom smiled again, shaking her head. In a startling contrast to Halt, her smiles were easily earned, gentle, openly beautiful and happy instead of grudgingly reluctant.

"Halt leaves at the crack of dawn tomorrow. Try to get some sleep tonight after you pack your supplies."

Walking toward her room in what she had learned was the northern wing, Rose entered silently and picked up the leather backpack sitting on her bed. There were already several supplies she needed stacked in a small pile on a pillow, probably by Halt: a bottle of oil and two whetstones, quills and ink, a stack of notebooks and loose parchment, a first aid kit, a compass, and a pair of small glass containers Halt told her would be useful later on, filled with salt and pepper. Hands smoothing along the daggers clipped to her waist, a habit she had picked up in the short time she'd been training with them, Rose realized that she'd need extra weapons.

Sprinting to the opposite wing of the house, Rose knocked on the door of Halt's workshop, then opened the door when she heard a gruff *"Come in."* Upon seeing her, Halt carefully placed the tiny mechanical bird he was making onto the workbench before wiping his hands on his pants.

"I need extra weapons," Rose explained. "Just one dagger that's similar to the pair I have, and a few throwing knives. I only have one right now."

Following Halt into the locked weapons room, Rose watched as Halt looked over his daggers before choosing one a long dagger similar to the two she owned, albeit noticeably heavier. Reaching toward the topmost corner of the wall, Halt retrieved a plethora of throwing knives, from which Rose chose four. Thanking Halt, she ran back along the length of the mountain home into her room, sweating. As she pulled off her sweater, she caught a glimpse of the whip scar along her chest in the mirror.

There was almost unbearable silence as Rose pulled off her shirt, revealing the scar in its whole. It marred her pale skin, as did the ring of scars along her wrists, slightly raised and still strange to the touch.

Are you watching me, Ezra? Can you see me? Am I making the right choice?

Silence.

I need a sign, Ezra. Anything. Convince me to stay.

Nothing.

I want to protect people like I couldn't protect you, but do you think it's worth it?

A gentle breeze stirred the curtains, and Rose sighed.

Your death was my fault. I just want to—

There was a knock at the door.

"Rose, are you alright?" It was Halt. Forcefully ripping herself away from her thoughts, Rose shouted a *yes* at him. There was a silence that somehow made Rose think Halt was unconvinced.

"I'll be in the alcove if you need anything."

* * *

The sun was rising, marking the beginning of a new day. A new era.

The golden-red ball of flames rose up from its bed of color-tinted clouds, the sky a canvas splattered with tens of thousands of hues of red, blue, purple, black, orange, and salmon pink.

Ripping her attention away from the gorgeous desert sunrise, Rose turned her attention to beautiful, dappled-gray Monte. Although she knew how gentle Monte was, Rose had never ridden a horse.

"Don't be afraid, he knows the way. I usually ride him to the Lightning Kingdom, you won't even have to steer."

Gulping, Rose stepped onto Halt's hand and hoisted herself up, swinging a leg over onto the horse's back. Her mane was soft, and Rose clutched it in her fingers as Halt walked away and swung onto Cristo's back.

"Rose! Halt!" Blossom cried, running out from the house. She was holding a familiar cloak in her hands. As Rose looked down at herself, she realized she was wearing one Blossom had made her. "You forgot your cloak! The one from your old home!"

Home?

"I don't want it."

"What? But—" Blossom quited as Halt glanced at her. Rose, after a split-second of hesitation, jumped awkwardly off the horse and ran toward Blossom, running into her embrace.

"That wasn't my home, Blossom." Even without looking at her, Rose could almost see Blossom's gentle smile in her mind eye.

"Thank you, Rose."

"You're saying thank you to *me?*" Rose pulled away and smiled. "Blossom. Thank you. So much. For everything."

As if knowing how uncomfortable this closeness made her, Blossom smiled and motioned toward the horse with a hand.

"Come back here a Mage, Rose," Blossom told her, hoisting her onto the horse. "And remember. No matter what, you'll always have a place here."

As the horse began to gallop beneath her, the mare's gait smoother than she had expected, Rose's eyes tilted toward the rising sun, gleaming with light.

Blossom stood at the door of the house, a hand on the frame, watching the two horses gallop into the distance, disappearing into the horizon.

Rose did not look back once.

Chapter Seven

"HOW OFTEN DO YOU DO THIS?" Rose asked, rubbing her aching legs and buttocks.

"A few times a month, for long hunting journeys and the like," Halt replied.

"That's crazy," Rose breathed. "My ass hurts." Halt didn't respond.

They had stopped by an oasis forty miles away. The sky was already dark, and the wind had just begun to pick up, blowing back her sweaty hair and cooling her brow. As she lay half-submerged in the cool water of the oasis, Halt lit a small campfire, checked the horses' halters, and picketed them to a shady spot near the oasis.

"Normally, you shouldn't light fire in this environment. There's coyotes and even a few werewolves, as I'm sure you know, and some nasty critters like venomous snakes, scorpions, and insects. Luckily for you, you have me here. I've set up a magical barrier of wind," Halt told her. Rose nodded, watching as he heaved two large rocks near the campfire for them to sit on.

"Why are we stopping again? It's not like either of us will sleep," Rose asked Halt.

"The horses need rest," Halt replied dryly. "If you like, we can go for a run. We both know you love that." Was that a joke?

"You're right. Still seems like a waste of time to me," Rose murmured, tilting her head at a coyote stalking around the barrier. Halt hadn't even looked in its direction. Cocking her wrist back, Rose made to throw her blade at the coyote but changed its trajectory at the last moment. It stuck to a tree trunk, a rarity, given how little she had practiced with it. She walked over, grabbed the knife, then yanked it from the wood. As she made to sit back down, she heard yelping and a howl.

When she glanced back, startled, there was only a smear of blood where the coyote once stood.

"Werewolves," Halt groaned. "We're unlucky. It's a full moon."

"Didn't we pass a village?" Rose asked, whipping her head back to stare at Halt. "That was barely an hour ago, they're going to be in danger." Halt cursed, a filthy slew of words that Rose had never heard used in conjunction.

"I can get us there in ten minutes, if I fly," he said. Rose nodded.

Rose felt herself lifted into the air, the wind channeling to carry her body, and even the extreme distance between herself and the ground wasn't enough to stifle the panic she felt. *You cannot let them die.*

They saw the village in the distance. It was unharmed, but as they flew, Rose saw a small group of werewolves closing in on the houses.

"Faster, Halt!" Rose shouted. "There are werewolves down there. Look!" Halt sped up, the wind whipping at Rose's cheeks, until they reached the village square. People began to gather around them, murmuring, and Rose pushed herself to her feet and shouted.

"Get into your houses, *now*! We came because we saw werewolves. Get into your houses, now, now, now!"

The people around them evidently knew what to do. Gathering up their children, they ducked into their homes and their lights went out. Within a matter of seconds, only one woman was left in the center of the square.

"Madam, what are you doing? You have to go—"

"My son."

"What—?"

"My son. He said he'd visit a friend's house. It's on the very edge of town. He's not here. I don't know—"

"Madam, we'll find your son. Prioritize your own safety first," Halt cut in.

The women had just disappeared into her house when Rose heard a shrill scream.

Sprinting toward it, Rose pulled out her daggers as she turned the corner. The scent of blood flooded her nostrils, and Rose met the eyes of a young boy.

"Leave him alone!" *Where had Halt gone?* The werewolf, dark gray with white markings, met Rose's furious stare with hunger in its blue eyes.

Werewolves are attracted to magic.

"I know you can understand me. Drop the boy and let him walk over here, and I'll drop my weapons."

Slowly, the werewolf withdrew from the boy. Rose dropped her weapons, letting them clatter to the floor as she scooped him into her arms. He was crying, snot dripping from his nose as he curled into Rose's arms. The wound on his side was shallow. He would survive.

"You're safe now," Rose murmured. "Stay still. I'll kill the werewolf."

Moving away from the boy, Rose held her arms high in surrender as she approached the werewolf. Hunger shone in its blue eyes, and as Rose watched, it bunched up its muscles and launched itself at her.

Now.

Jumping to the side, Rose pulled out the extra dagger and throwing knife from her sheathe, hurling the knife at the werewolf as it landed on the ground, growling. It yelped as the knife dug into its side, but the knife barely sunk into its thick, furry hide. Its yelp was of anger, not pain. Rose stepped to the side as the werewolf threw itself at her. This one was small compared to the one she had killed with magic. She could do this. She could save him.

As the werewolf flew past her, Rose thrust the dagger down into its neck.

It hit the ground with a thud, spraying blood on her fingers, and the dagger hit the stone ground with a resolute finality as the werewolf thrashed on the ground and became still. Rose stood above the body, her chest heaving, triumph coursing through her.

There was a deadly growl.

Another one?

Whirling toward the direction of the growl, Rose found herself staring at the little boy. As she watched, his pupils narrowed and fur began to grow from his skin. His fingertips morphed into claws, and in this state of half-boy half-wolf, it was already trying to kill her. Stumbling toward her, the little wolf-boy clawed at her leg.

"Rose! Where are you?" *Halt.*

The boy seemed to be fighting it, even as he leapt on top of her, half the size of the adult she had just slain. His eyes were filled with tears, and he seemed to be begging her, *please save me, please save me.*

But if Rose left this boy alive, this village would be slaughtered.

The transformation of a werewolf at full moon could only be prevented through expensive medicines. Once a person was a werewolf, there was nothing stopping them from killing an entire village of helpless people. As Rose watched, the werewolf transformed entirely back into a little boy, sitting on Rose's chest, tears leaking from normal eyes.

He won't transform.

But that was impossible.

Maybe he can afford medicine.

If he could, he wouldn't be living here.

You can't kill a child.

Even as Rose thought this, claws raked down Rose's arm, a shallow but stinging wound.

You can't kill him.

I have to. In order to save the rest of the village.

Unsheathing the knife from her side, Rose stood up, sending the little wolf tumbling to the ground. He remained there, staring up at her, and Rose's hand clenched around the knife in her hand.

"Rose! *Don't kill him!*" Halt shouted. Rose whirled around, nearly collapsing to the ground in relief when she saw him. *"Rose!"*

A gust of wind pushed her away, onto the ground, and the small werewolf clawed at the floor where she was. He was so small that Halt could yank him into the air with wind magic.

"We don't have to kill him. I can buy enough medicine to last him until next time I come around," Halt explained. "We don't have to kill him."

Slowly, Rose sheathed her knife.

"Are you sure it's going to be safe?" Rose asked. Halt nodded.

"The wound on his side is bleeding pretty badly, I'll go wrap it up. You go explain to his mother what happened. The rest of the werewolves are dead."

Picking up the pair of daggers she had dropped on the ground, Rose slowly walked back toward the village. As she explained the little boy's situation to his widowed mother, there were tears and worry, then relief and gratefulness when Rose explained what Halt was going to do.

"Thank you," the woman had said. "For saving my son. I..." she dissolved into tears as she took in his newly changed eyes and bite wound. She cradled him in her arms anyway.

Rose inclined her head before walking out, barely making it to the edge of the village before sinking onto the floor, burying her face in her hands.

She did not cry, and that scared her.

"Would you have done it?"

It was Halt. Rose stared at him, into those stony eyes that hid so much kindness, and smiled sadly.

They both knew her response.

* * *

The capital of the Lightning Kingdom was *beautiful*.

The streets were littered with shops, vendors, people shouting in a mix of their native languages and the common language. There were vendors dedicated entirely to exotic animals, most of which somehow didn't use cages at all, apothecaries, magical trinkets and spells, and so, so, many books. There were strange-looking foods, devices similar to the ones Halt built, and small homes above the shops.

The most beautiful thing, though, was the palace in the distance, sitting on a hill. It had glowing spires and glittering towers, a flag on the top of the highest spire waving in the wind. It glittered like a gemstone in the light of the rising sun, its silvery surface reflecting the colors of the sky. The inside of the inn Halt led Rose into was a startling contrast, filled with the scent of alcohol and sweat. Its one saving grace was that it was relatively empty, being that it was only seven in the morning.

"It's beautiful, isn't it?" he asked her.

"Yeah. And the palace. Is it visible from everywhere in the city?"

"Nearly, yeah. I've actually been inside. It's magnificent."

"You've *been inside?* What'd it look like? Did you see the queen? What about the Five Sorcer—"

"Eat. If you become an apprentice, you get to go inside."

Rose stared up at the shining castle through the grimy window as they ate in silence and wondered, briefly, what it would be like to be a princess. It was a laughable thought. Turning her attention toward the thick stew that was the day's special, Rose grimaced as she pulled out a lumpy piece of meat that felt like rubber.

"Yes, this is safe," Halt told her. Glancing at him, Rose held out the piece of meat. "One of the better inns, trust me." If this was one of the better inns, Rose prayed to the Gods that she would never visit a bad one.

After squeezing their way through the crowd within the inn, Halt led her to one of the rooms. Surprisingly, it was actually quite comfortable. The mattresses, while itchy and hard, were free of bedbugs and, best of all, two steaming-warm tubs of hot water had been laid out in the bathroom. After the two of them both took a hot bath, washing away the grime and dirt, Halt led her out of the inn into the depths of the marketplace.

"The Academy's enrollment is in two days, so we'll start traveling there tomorrow. It's nearby. I'll show you where I buy my favorite trinkets today. When you become a Mage, you can pay me back by buying out these vendors." Rose couldn't decide whether or not he was joking or not.

Everyone in that section of the market seemed to be familiar with Halt. They greeted him with eager smiles and an almost greedy gleam in their eyes. The stalls were fascinating, filled with trays of wires, hinges, screws, and tools that she had never seen before. It was strange to see Halt's enormous hands so delicately pick through the gleaming parts. As Halt picked out pieces at a stall, often taking an hour at each, Rose found herself drifting further and further away before coming back when he shouted. The first stall she found that caught her attention was a live animal vendor, in which there was a large cage holding six or seven tiny pink foxes.

"They replenish mana. They're popular because they naturally like humans. They feed off our life energy, although the effect is so small you can't feel it. The happier and healthier they are, the more they replenish." *That explains the good condition the cage is in.* "You can take one out and play with it if you'd like."

Rose nodded. The man opened the cage, removing one of the small pink foxes, laughing as it scuttled from her hand up onto her shoulder. It ducked into her hair, perching on her neck, radiating comforting warmth. Reaching up into her hair, Rose gently removed the fox, watching as it curled up in the center of her palms, barely larger than one of her hands.

"Do you want one?" Halt asked from behind her. Rose stared down at the fox, moving one hand from beneath it to stroke along its silky soft fur. It blinked up at her with large, innocent eyes.

"I don't think I could take care of a pet," Rose said, grinning. "It's really cute, though."

Grudgingly, she placed it back in its cage and followed Halt to the next stall. A table filled with pastries and sweets caught her attention, and Rose found herself marveling over the intricately formed cakes and buns. They reminded her of what Katherine would make for Master and his guests. Strangest of all was the chocolate. Although she had seen and bought it several times for Master, she had never tasted it and was, quite frankly, confused as to how these strangely-shaped brown lumps could taste so good.

"Hey, Halt, can you buy some chocolate? For me to try, I mean."

"You've never had chocolate before?" Halt looked, for some reason, horrified.

"Yeah."

Before long, a small pouch of it was shoved into her hands, and Rose popped one into her mouth to discover she was in absolute heaven. The chocolate was soft, melting in her mouth, rich and sweet with a hint of bitterness.

"Ah, right, one more thing," Halt said. "Have you ever tasted coffee?"

Tilting her head, Rose had to think for a second before remembering what coffee was: an aromatic-smelling, dark-brown drink that Master only ever occasionally drank.

"I've never had it."

"I drink it all the time. It keeps you awake. The Academy serves low-quality coffee. I recommend you try it."

"Wait, what do you mean, it keeps you awake?"

"You'll see."

It was just after sunset when Rose and Halt finally made their way back to the inn. She had received a few more gifts: a large, cylindrical container enchanted to keep liquids warm and a set of black-gold fountain pens with two different colors of ink.

"Is that all the time we have for the Market? I want to see more," Rose asked. Halt had thankfully refrained from ordering any sort of stew for dinner. They were instead dipping slices of bread into oil.

"Don't worry. We haven't even visited the Black Market yet."

Rose choked on the water she was drinking. After some spluttering and gasping, she managed to speak.

"The Black Market?"

"We're avoiding the bad parts, don't worry. I want poisons, illegal but functional medicine, and dangerous weapons and machines."

"It's the Black Market. All of it is terrible."

"It's really not! You should see it, it's honestly amazing."

Shaking her head, Rose looked back down at the slices of bread they were eating for dinner. Despite her reservations, she felt *really* curious.

* * *

"Keep close," Halt told her. Drunkards were stumbling across the streets of the near empty Market, which were relatively quiet except for the bawdy singing and shouting. As he neared the end of the street, Halt turned into a small, mostly-empty pub.

"Are you sure this is safe?" Rose asked Halt. He held a finger to his lips and whispered into the bartender's ear. A few seconds later, a large painting was drawn aside, revealing a tall tunnel.

"I don't think—"

Halt sighed and yanked her down the tunnel. It sloped downward at a steep angle, causing her to almost fall on several occasions, but Halt merely lifted her back up every time. The scent of alcohol was slowly replaced with the scent of blood and a strange bitterness, and when they finally reached the bottom, there was a door blocking their entrance. Halt motioned for Rose to stand back, then bent down and sprinted at the door, hitting it with his shoulder. It flew open with a loud *crack*, and Rose winced. That must've hurt.

"That entrance is pretty old, but it's the closest one to the inn I like. I've used it for so long I know how to open it. Welcome, Rose, to the Black Market."

Rose didn't know where to look first. As she stared around her, astonished, Halt reached behind her and pulled her hood up, over her head. People were *everywhere*, hoods obscuring faces, selling small boxes, drugs, weapons, what looked like small vials of liquid, and dirty, matted animals.

"This is the upper section of the Black Market. I've never descended lower than the second floor, and I recommend you to do the same. Shit gets bad down there."

Halt first stopped at a few stalls covered in beautiful-looking weapons. Everyone Halt visited seemed to be familiar with him, as if he were a yearly customer that made a large enough impact on their sales that they remembered him. He bought a pair of ordinary-looking swords that, when Rose touched them, shocked her with electricity, as well as a strange-looking brooch that gleamed turquoise-blue even in the semi-darkness. It was fascinating to watch his silent interactions and how at home he seemed to be, weaving between other silent buyers from stall to stall. And then they arrived at what Halt called his favorite stall, and Rose's heart stopped with glee.

Intricate devices were laid out over the tables: a small, mechanical dragon, a pair of cuffs that could be fed oil and would shoot out plumes of fire over three feet long, and a thin pair of armbands that Halt instructed her to put on and attach her daggers to. It was designed so that the knife in the sheath would press flat against the underarm, and when Rose rolled her sleeves back down, their slim outline was barely visible against the loose cloth. They were designed so that as Rose flicked her wrist to the side, the blade would be propelled into her hand.

"Our merchant here mass-produces these," Halt whispered to her. "I have a pair too. They take a while to get used to, but believe me, they're worth it." Despite her protests, Halt bought a pair for Rose, as well as a few other trinkets for himself.

They spent the better part of the night buying little trinkets, and even a few mysterious square boxes that Halt seemed more nervous about buying. Most interesting were the magical devices Halt had instructed her never to touch: a book that lunged at Rose when she neared their stall, a cursed necklace that killed whoever put it on, and a strange pair of white devices that could be inserted into someone's ear and would proceed to literally deafen them. Even as she explored and laughed, the ever-looming deadline of the Academy's entrance day continued to hover over her shoulder.

* * *

The Academy wasn't in the city. At the break of dawn, Halt and Rose traveled westward, toward the large trading port of Sekja. It was unremarkable aside from the bustling port, surrounded by small shacks and houses, known, mostly, for the school it held—the Academy. Rose gulped. The Academy was three stories high at its lowest, covered in spires and towers; at the topmost center of it all, a flag waved in the wind. It was intimidating. A promise of a hard and yet possibly rewarding future.

Halt and Rose turned their horses toward the entrance.

"Good luck, Rose," Halt told her. He spread out his arms, and Rose nearly fell to the ground in surprise before cautiously entering his embrace. It was warm, comforting, and made her nervous anticipation melt away. He pulled away far too quickly. Without a second word, he mounted Cristo.

"Oh yeah. Rose?" he said as he turned Cristo toward the direction they rode from.

"Yeah?"

"You better become the best goddamn Mage this kingdom's ever seen. I believe in you."

Rose nodded, her throat tight. She lifted her hand to wave goodbye, but Halt was already riding away into the distance. Turning away, Rose put her hand on the handle and yanked it wouldn't budge. Frowning, Rose yanked and pulled until the door opened.

What little remained of her breath vanished. Of course, she had known that the Academy was beautiful, but this was breathtakingly stunning. She was in a hallway perhaps twenty feet long, with a floor of smooth black marble and numerous torches mounted on the walls. The circular atrium at the end of the hallway seemed to grow larger and larger as she approached it, the sheer *size* of it overwhelming she stepped fully into the enormous room that was illuminated with stunning sunlight. A jagged iron staircase was set at the center of that atrium, and as Rose looked up, her mouth opened with awe, for, constructed surely by magic, was a ceiling of glass that seemed to be infused with living, glowing, elements.

It was only after a good few minutes of admiring the atrium's beauty when she finally heard the loud chatter of people around her. She glanced toward the crowd about ten feet away from her and slowly approached it, growing self-conscious of the dust and mud staining her plain cloak and clothes. Just as she had reached the back of the crowd, her vision obscured by the heads of the people in front of her, the others suddenly grew silent.

"First years!" a man shouted. Pushing her way into the front of the crowd, Rose finally saw who had quieted the crowd: an intimidating man who was glaring at the students as if they had killed his mother. The insignia on his sleeve was blood red, suiting his deposition, and Rose realized what it implied just as everyone around her did.

"Is that Master Mekhi?" someone whispered.

Master Mekhi, the head of the Academy.

"Quiet!" the man shouted. "No more fun and games, no more whispering like children. You are at the *Academy*, for god's sake! If you're looking to have tea parties and chat with friends, feel free to attend the

War School." A few students laughed, and you could *visibly* see him swell with rage.

"Oh, and you guys think this is funny—" He sighed, calming himself, before continuing. "Now that the gates have been shut, I'll start with what your year will be like. You'll be, firstly, introduced to the basics of fighting, physical prowess, and the use of magic before you choose a specific element to specialize in."

Whispers of excitement were cut off by the man's next words.

"Silence! Please *let me speak*. The rest of the time here will be spent on a mixture of magical control and more physical battle. You'll start specializing in weapons as well. Of course, you will be dedicating time to studying the basics of academics. If you don't pass the exams, you won't be able to become one of the twenty-five apprentices, no matter how good you are at fighting."

More whispers, and then a mumbled question.

"How are you going to have enough time to do everything before curfew? Well, you'll just have to be quick, I guess."

Glancing around herself, Rose saw only about ten or fifteen people like her, covered in dust and mud. The highborns—nobles, successful merchants, and the like—were dressed in wastefully elaborate riding clothes, as if trying to give a best impression, and a concerningly decent number of them possessed weapons. A harsh laugh from Master Mekhi yanked her attention back toward him.

"How do I recommend you guys train? Well, all you need is hours and hours of repetition, repetition, repetition. By the end of these nine months, *if you're still here*, all you will think about is how to fight and how to use your magic."

Another mumbled question. With the people crowding in front of her, Rose could barely hear him. She felt someone behind her stir and then shove their way through the crowd, causing her to tumble to the ground, barely missing a highborn boy that stood before her.

"Sorry," Rose said, standing up quickly, face warming. She froze. Stunning eyes, one green and one blue, glared condescendingly down upon her, and the boy scowled.

Highborns. So goddamn annoying.

"What the hell's your problem?" Rose snapped at him.

"What do you mean, what's my problem?" His voice was tinged with anger—and surprise.

"Oh, y'know, I *accidentally almost bump into you,* and—y'know what? Forget it!" Rose said, annoyed. She drew herself up to her full height, which wasn't very tall and nearly half a head shorter than him, and returned his condescending glare as best she could. Staring at her with condescending astonishment, his mouth curled in a snarl and he turned away. Observing his stature, demeanor, the boy was very obviously a highborn, and yet he seemed a little different from the rest. He held himself as if he were far above everyone in the room, not just the lowborns, and had a stern stoicism that reminded her of Halt. Most interestingly was the plethora of weapons he held: a sword on his back, at least four daggers on his belt, and what Rose could barely distinguish as some sort of chain, coiled in a neat circle and attached to his belt. She was just preparing to look away when she saw the tiny streak of fresh blood staining the back of his shirt. *What the hell?* Shaking herself free of her thoughts, Rose turned her attention back toward Master Mekhi.

"No, we do not care which element you chose to specialize in, you can try to learn Fire magic with a Water affinity for all we care. It won't work though!"

"When will there be breaks?" someone shouted.

Master Mekhi looked incredulously in the person's direction.

"Breaks? Who said there'd be any breaks?" Master Mekhi shook his head and snorted. "Maybe you should've attended the War Academy instead. With how huge it is, you guys would have a better chance."

"Where will we be sleeping? Can we choose who we room with?"

"Where do you think you are? A castle? You will be staying in the barracks."

Rose couldn't help but grin at the gasps of horror and shock she heard among the highborns. It couldn't be *that* bad.

"Yes, barracks. If you can't survive barracks for a year, you have no business trying to be a Mage."

A murmured question.

"Yes, you can go wherever you want in the Academy as long as the doors aren't locked. We check hallways and rooms before curfew, which is at eleven."

"Can we enter the other gender's barracks?"

"*No*. If you do, you're expelled."

"What about hazing?"

"We used to allow it until someone died. If you get caught hazing, you're expelled."

The students began clamoring for an explanation, but Master Mekhi merely sighed, turned on his heel, and walked away.

* * *

Rose and the rest of the girls were led by a silent servant into the barracks. From end to end, there were about seventy beds, each five feet apart, around which could be drawn a thick curtain. On the other side of the room stood several fireplaces and a few armchairs around each one, with a door to the washrooms located opposite from the entrance. The girls filed in, some looking almost comically displaced. Unsure of where to sleep, Rose found herself standing in the center of the barracks until a group of lowborns in a corner caught her eye. Hurrying over, Rose set her belongings down in the bed in the corner. It had a single foot-long shelf built into the wall beside the bed and a small trunk underneath the bed. As she was folding her sweaters and placing them on the shelf, Rose briefly wondered why Halt had instructed her not to bring any unnecessary clothes before shaking aside the thought of placing her small pouch of chocolates on the shelf before placing the rest of her belongings into the now half-filled trunk. Just as she sat down on the bed, someone approached her.

"What's in the pouch?"

Glancing toward the direction of the voice, Rose couldn't decide whether she was a bully or a potential friend, given the fact that she looked like a highborn but had willingly approached her. Although her expensive-looking clothes were spotless and her brown hair was elegantly tied back, Rose could also see small scars flecking her hands and calluses on her palms as she reached her hand forward. Rose shook, cautiously, and watched as the girl sat down on the bed next to Rose's.

"The rumors about the Academy weren't exaggerated, huh? It all sounds so brutal. I probably should've become a knight, like my dad," she remarked. The two bags on the ground had to belong to her. As she rolled over onto her stomach, facing Rose, Rose noticed with no small amount of interest the beautiful jeweled sword on her back.

"Nice sword," Rose said. "I've never seen one so pretty."

"Yeah, it's nice. Which weapon do you use? I don't see any on you. But it's okay if you don't use one, most students here don't either, which I don't get. There's no way someone could become used to a weapon in nine months if they haven't trained," she said. She spoke very fast, bouncing slightly on her feet. Rose watched, amused, as she continued to ramble for a few more seconds before turning to Rose. "So, do you have a weapon?"

"Ah, I have daggers." Rose flicked her wrists, covered by long sleeves, and the girl watched as Rose's perfectly plain daggers popped out into her hands with no small amount of glee.

"Woah, those sheaths are cool! Lemme see the dagger." She jumped up, startling Rose, and gently took the dagger. "Woah! It's light. I can see why you'd like using these, considering how short you are."

"I'm not *that* short," Rose protested, then sighed as the girl patted her head.

"Anyway, you haven't answered my first question. What's in the pouch?"

"Chocolate."

"Oh, you gotta give me some," she begged. Rose shrugged, reached up toward the pouch, opened it, and handed her two pieces.

"Not much of a talker, huh?"

"Not really. It's just... aren't you a highborn?"

"Ah, well, not really. When I was a kid, my dad gained a lot of prestige as a knight—I can tell you the whole story later, it's long. But, yeah, now I'm here, and I have cool clothes and this amazing sword. I mean, look at it! Oh yeah, I'm Ash, thanks for asking," Ash paused, drawing her sword in a fluid motion, and flipped the blade around, handing it to Rose hilt-first. It was beautiful. The blade was about one and a half feet long, slightly thinner than the usual but ordinary otherwise. The hilt and grip, on the other hand, was a work of art. It was warm in her palm and felt like it was molded to her hand, made of blue-gray leather that perfectly matched the metal of the pommel and hilt. The cross was shaped in a pair of symmetrical dragon wings that, despite looking intricate and fragile, felt quite sturdy to the touch, and the pommel had an intricate metal carving of two entwining dragon heads which clutched a beautiful blue jewel in their mouths.

"It is very beautiful. I've never seen anything like it. Where'd you get it?" Rose asked, handing it back to Ash carefully.

"My father had it custom ordered for me when he came back from the campaign."

"How old were you?"

"Eight."

Rose smiled ruefully.

"You used that sword while you were *eight*?"

"Well, it was a little heavy for me then, so I used an ordinary smaller one. I actually began using it when I was ten."

"That's amazing," Rose said. Ash smiled at the compliment, nose scrunching as she did so.

"What's your name? How old are you? Where are you from? Have you measured your height? I doubt you're five feet."

"I'm Rose," Rose paused, hesitated, and then: "I was a slave. Hope you don't mind. I'm fifteen. I am in fact five feet one."

"Rather you than *them*," Ash said, wrinkling her nose at the group of highborn girls.

"What do you have against them?" Rose asked.

"*Everything*," Ash said. "I just hate their bullshit logic of noble highborn blood. Some really don't like my father, even though he's a better fighter than most of them."

The words noble highborn blood were said in a sarcastic, lilting tone that made Rose smile. Given her father's background, her disdain was unsurprising. Only a few lowborns managed to claw their way into becoming a knight, let alone a mage, and they faced countless discrimination and hardship as they did so.

"It seems kind of lonely. There must be some lowborns who don't accept you, and highborns definitely don't either."

Ash wrinkled her nose in agreement.

"Yeah, but other knights do respect us. That part's fun. My father's so obviously a good knight they can't *not* respect us. That's what my father said I should become."

Their conversation was interrupted by a cautious greeting from two other girls: Cascade, a quiet girl who retreated back to her bed as soon as she said her name, and Celeste.

As the highborns finally began to settle in, Rose realized exactly how much clothing some of them had brought. One girl with chestnut hair had *three* trunks. Rose couldn't imagine owning that many belongings, let alone clothes. Just as people were starting to realize their trunks couldn't fit underneath the bed, a servant entered the room unnoticed by most people. Rose nudged Ash, pointing at the clothes she was holding, and Ash laughed.

"Hand all of your clothes over, students. Including the ones you're wearing now."

Rose watched in amusement as shouts of protest filled the room, and Ash doubled over in laughter.

"I'm kidding. That type of action is not yet necessary."

The woman held up the clothes she had been holding: a gray short-sleeved tunic, sturdy leather boots that rose three inches above the ankle, and long black pants and a cloak.

"The Masters don't particularly care what you wear at night, or after your studies, but during studies, you will be wearing this uniform. We don't tolerate indulgence. There will be nothing here that matters beyond your training."

Each student was given two sets of the uniform, instructed to switch between them every day and throw the dirty uniform into the large laundry basket in the washrooms. Rose was pleased. The clothes were decently comfortable and loose enough that she knew they would be decent in battle, although she wished she had something to cover her wrists. The sweaters Halt had instructed her to pack could be used for colder weather, especially when she was studying.

Staring at the sea of highborns and lowborns alike changing into the plain uniform, Rose realized that there may be a hint of more equality here than she had first imagined.

Chapter Eight

ROSE WOKE up at seven in the morning and already felt tired.

Not wanting to risk going to the study for no reason, Rose had merely drawn her curtains and stared at the ceiling until about three in the morning before finally falling asleep. Rose made her way, exhausted, down to the atrium, spotting within seconds the drinks table and praying to the Gods that coffee was as effective at its job as Halt claimed. As she took a seat at a table in the corner, she observed the mostly empty atrium around her. The disgustingly confident, strange-eyed boy from the day before was reading at a table in the corner across from her, and a pair of dark-skinned lowborn twins who had ignored Ash's attempts at friendship were cautiously poking at a food Rose recognized as leeks.

Rose was, thankfully, unconcerned about seating arrangements. Over dinner, Rose and Ash had already formed a small group—Cascade, Celeste, Ash, Venus, River, and herself. Just as she thought this, someone sat down across from her.

"Good morning. Did you sleep well?" River asked her. He was, by far, the most polite student she had met. Picking up a fork and knife, he sliced into the thick ham and carefully popped a slice into his mouth. Rose nodded, and he continued to eat in comfortable silence, a welcome change to the chaos of last night, when the rest of the table had watched in mild horror as Ash and Venus flirted like a pair of lovers.

"Is the food good?"

"Yeah. There's not much to choose from, but it's all very good."

Rose stood up, downing the rest of the coffee and sighing in relief as it began to kick in before walking toward the wall of the room lined by carts of food, each one dedicated to one type of food. Grabbing two large slices of ham, two boiled eggs, a slice of bread, and some raw carrots, Rose sat down with a second cup of coffee and began to wolf down her food. Schedules had been posted on a bulletin board in the barracks, and Rose had written it down on a piece of paper before heading out. As she ate, Rose read it over.

Studies: 8:00-12:30
    Library, second floor
    Lunch: 12:30-1:00
    Physical Studies: 1:00-3:00
    Training fields
    Magical Studies: 3:00-6:00
    Training fields
    Dinner: 6:00-6:30

"Did you catch the schedule?" Rose asked River. He looked up from his food, chewed, swallowed, and then spoke.

"Yeah. It's kind of intimidating, don't you think?"

"Yeah. Three hours on physical studies seems..."

"Overkill?"

"Yeah."

"What're you two lovebirds doing alone so early in the morning?" Ash's voice asked from behind her. Rose sighed as she swung into the chair beside her but couldn't help but crack a smile.

"I'm sorry, but we're not you and Venus. You two already went to heaven together, I'm sure," River remarked passively. Choking on her sip of coffee, Rose laughed at the shocked expression on Ash's face.

"Don't worry, I didn't think he had it in him either. Good job, River," Rose said, patting Ash's shoulder and giving him a thumbs up. Ash seemed to splutter for a second before coughing, turning red, and moving toward the carts. The rest of the students were filing into the atrium just as Rose and River stood up to leave, heading up the stairs toward the library.

When she walked in, Rose's jaw dropped. Libraries as beautiful and maze-like at this one would never cease to amaze her. This had to take up the entire second floor of the castle. She hadn't seen any other rooms except for the library. At the center of it all stood an enormous classroom-like assortment of chairs and desks in perfectly straight rows. Choosing a seat at the side of the second row, Rose dropped her near-empty backpack beneath the desk and placed her notebooks and quill on the desk and the ink bottle in the small hollow in the desk.

She now had half an hour to explore the library.

She was deep within the labyrinth of books when she saw the boy with the strange eyes in the distance. *I probably shouldn't have snapped at him.* Approaching him, she tapped his shoulder to get his attention. He turned around, his stare hardening into a glare when he met her eyes, and Rose steeled herself.

"I'm sorry for snapping at you yesterday. You had a right to be mad, I—"

"I don't need filthy slaves telling me what I can and can't do," he said, his eyes honing in on the scars on her wrist. Rose jerked back, her fists clenching, taking a deep breath before she spoke.

"I'm sorry I didn't have the same privilege as you and had to work to even get here," she snarled.

"Well, that's a bummer. What do you want me to do? Apologize and kiss your feet? Don't make me laugh."

And, with that, he stalked off. Rose stood there, absolutely astonished. Just as she made to pursue him, she felt a hand on her shoulder and turned around.

"Don't even bother with that prick." Rose glanced back toward his retreating figure, seething with anger before sighing.

"I guess you're right."

"You like books too?" Ash's loud voice pierced through the library, and Rose couldn't help but feel a twinge of annoyance.

"Yeah."

"What do you like to read? Here, I'll show you some of my favorites. Have you read *The King and his Ivory Princess*?"

"Oh, that one's amazing."

"'Come, my princess, come upon this horse, and we shall endure this hellhole together!'" Ash shouted dramatically, quoting the book. She pointed at the rows of desks and chairs, and Rose doubled over with laughter. All previous annoyance she had felt melted away as Ash introduced her to five or six more books, all of which Rose had never heard of.

"I wonder how many books there are in here?" Rose asked as Ash flipped open a book.

"Over six-hundred *thousand*," a soft voice said from the front of the library. Starting, Rose ripped her gaze from the books and realized that more students had filed in. She made her way through the bookshelves and sat down on her chair.

"Class will start in three minutes, but servants will be passing out textbooks now. Please take good care of them. These will be the most fundamental aspects of your studies, although you will soon learn that you will have to study much more than this to pass." Servants holding stacks and stacks of books emerged from some hidden alcove in the back, and Rose almost wanted to help them. The books looked so unbearably heavy. There were four enormous textbooks, at least three inches long, as well as a thinner, two-inch-thick book that Rose flipped open and discovered was a math workbook.

"Beyond this, you will receive other books that will be issued when they are needed. Those will be handed out after the textbooks. If you have not, please take out your supplies and anything you need to take notes. You will need to do so." Rose carefully screwed open her ink bottle, careful not to spill the ink, and dipped her fountain pen within it.

"My name is Master Dara. As I'm sure you know by now, fighting is not the only thing you have to excel in order to become a Mage. Being someone of such importance and influence, you must be knowledgeable in order to make good decisions, both politically and battle-wise." Rose saw several students glance at each other exasperatedly and briefly wondered why.

"So what are the basics of this knowledge? In this Academy, we teach Science, so that you know how the world around you works; Mathematics, so that you understand the complicated subject of numbers and calculation; Law, so that you can enact justice efficiently; War Tactics, an obvious choice; History, so we don't repeat our previous mistakes; and Literature, so you can learn from fiction as well as reality. Do you all have your textbooks and papers?"

Murmurs of assent filled the classroom.

"Now then. Shall we begin?"

*　*　*

Rose was four and a half hours into the Academy and already felt overwhelmed.

"God, we're so dead," Ash moaned. Rose didn't even bother to reply. Halt had been correct. Instead of teaching them the basics, the Academy taught based on the assumption that everyone was a highborn and had had fourteen years of education before this point. That was untrue for Rose, as well as for many of the other lowborns. Instead of explaining what the criminal, property, trading, and foreign laws of the Lightning Kingdom were, Master Dara had skipped automatically to how the government enforced them. Although Rose knew more about basic History, she felt almost equally as lost. There were references made in the lecture to battles and dates she'd never heard of.

That was only Law and History, which were, relatively, the more manageable topics. Science and Math were *completely* beyond understanding. She barely understood anything that was said, from the equations to the example problems and had been forced to hurriedly copy everything down to cram in later. While Literacy was *easier*, it was by no means close to being *at all* easy. They had been assigned to read an ancient book by some philosopher she hadn't heard of, among other books, and had four or five questions to answer, in paragraphs, about them. War Tactics was by far the easiest. It was, mostly, *understandable*!

Rose felt no little amount of ire at that. Although there were about ten books seemingly *everyone* had read but her and a few lowborns, it was generally doable.

Even so, she was absolutely screwed. They had so much homework Rose could barely figure out what to start.

"I can't comprehend *anything*," Rose muttered. "All of it seems impossible." They were sitting at their normal lunch table, and Rose was writing down everything she needed to learn in a notebook with her right hand while mindlessly shoving food into her mouth with her left.

"What do you think you have to learn?"

"Anything that isn't the basics of algebra and geometry in math. Basically, all of quantum physics, if I want to understand magical science at all—" Ash interrupted her by choking on her food in shock. Rose smacked her back until she could breathe and motioned for her to continue. "I need to eventually read all of the books Master Dara listed. War Tactics should be fine, but there are some things I need to catch up on. And I didn't even live in the Lightning Kingdom until yesterday. I don't know any laws."

"What?" Ash asked. "You"

"Yes, I'm serious. Let me eat—"

The class was louder than during studies, as if the delicious meal had revitalized them. When they filed into the training fields half an hour later, most of the students were outright talking, far at odds with the near silence and whispering before the studies. As the class saw the weaponry on the side of the training field, they grew even more excited, conversations reaching a fevered pitch.

It was almost funny when they all fell absolutely silent.

A man, slender but muscular, stepped out of the weaponry, wearing a shining suit of armor, two swords strapped to his back. He looked over the students and his stare seemed to sharpen into a harsh glare. Everyone collectively gulped.

"Ah, finally listening, huh?" the knight spoke. Rose winced—was he always that loud? "That much is good, at least. Welcome to Physical Studies. You have come out of wonderland, kids. No more reading books in front of fireplaces."

Wonderland? Their last class had been anything but heaven. As

Rose glanced at Ash, their eyes met, and Ash widened her eyes comically, causing Rose to smirk. Just as she glanced back toward the knight, she heard whispers and a snicker from the front of the crowd.

"Oh, you find this funny?" The knight's voice had somehow gotten louder to the point where Rose resisted the urge to cover her ears and hide in a corner. "Come over here, boy."

A highborn boy, still managing to look pompous despite wearing the same clothes as everyone around him, swaggered up to the knight. It was obvious that he felt somewhat cowed by the knight's glare, but brash stupidity had outweighed any of his common sense, urging him to continue speaking.

"You're not a mage. I don't see why I have to respect you."

There was a blur of motion, and before any of them could even react, the tip of the knight's sword was mere inches from the boy's throat. He stiffened, throat bobbing as he swallowed.

"Go on," the knight said, softly. "Try to push me away. I'll let you draw that sword of yours."

Rose watched, unable to look away, as the boy pushed with all his might at the knight's sword. He didn't budge – not even an inch, body rippling with lithe muscle.

"The day one of you can move my sword," Sir Damien said, "maybe I'll consider hearing you out. As of now... have we made clear the expectations of this class?"

Silence.

"Wonderful. My name is Sir Damian, and my job is to turn you all sorry lot into presentable warriors. Let's start with a simple warm-up, shall we?"

* * *

After a mere hour of the onslaught that was Sir Damian's warm-up, Rose was on the ground, doubled over, dry-retching. Across the field, students were falling one by one like flies. Sir Damian's simple warm-up had been running six miles, and that would've been doable. Exhausting, but doable. However, after each mile, Sir Damian had set up an obstacle course that, despite being relatively simple, had completely destroyed

Rose's stamina. After a balance beam, three rope climbs, and sprinting through a gauntlet of flying obstacles such as knives, enormous logs, and stones until they managed to do it without getting hit. Rose's body was covered in bruises, tiny cuts, and what felt like a bruised rib from a log ramming into her after the fifth mile. The only people she had done better than were the lowborns who had never held a weapon in their lives.

"Rose, are you okay?" Ash asked. "Need help getting up?"

"Nah, it's good. Trust me, you don't even want to get near me right now, I probably smell like a swamp monster."

Her panting had abated slightly, and Rose was leaning against one of the walls of the Academy with Ash, River, and Celeste, far from the crowd that was now watching the six or seven people still remaining—mostly lowborns, although there about two highborns mixed in. As she pushed back her damp, sweaty hair, she caught a glimpse of the strange-eyed boy in the corner of her peripheral vision, let out a *tch*, and looked away.

Rose simply couldn't fathom how the highborns were so effortlessly capable. How long had they been training become Mages? Most noticeably talented was the boy with the strange eyes and his group of friends, who Ash had told her was Emma Eneria Lasica, a highly ranked noble, a pair of brutal boys who seemed to find companionship in each other because of their shared love of hitting people, and a kindly dark-skinned boy who didn't share the same deposition as most of his highborn friends. These were, of course, the best of the best, predicted to be the most obvious choice for apprenticeship. That was only those who obviously excelled. Most of the highborn students barely looked ruffled, while Rose and a few other lowborns undoubtedly looked like they just crawled out from a gutter. Even Ash and River weren't that far behind. They had finished only a little behind an average highborn student, while Rose herself had barely finished her third obstacle course without collapsing.

It struck Rose then that she was one of the worst students there.

"Here, take some water," River's voice said from above her. Rose gave him a pained grin and accepted the cup of water with trembling hands, causing drops of water to slosh out of the cup.

"Do you want me to—" River started, then blushed and looked away. Rose reflected that by offering to feed her water, he might've thought he crossed some invisible line.

"No, I can do it by myself. Thank you, though," Rose said and then downed the cup of water. Her ribs weren't as badly bruised as she had first thought, and although taking a deep breath, running, or laughing felt like someone was inserting a knife into her lower left chest, it was mostly ignorable if she didn't move. It was just her luck that as she began to feel nearly normal again, Sir Damian's voice filled the room.

"Stand up, shrimps. I'm going to have to interrupt your tea party. It's time for your next exercise. You're going to be sparring, and I don't care whether you're injured or not."

Rose couldn't help but groan as she stood up, walking with Ash toward the large six-inch circles of dirt, now transformed into nearly solid ground by countless feet that had doubtlessly sparred upon it over the years. Ash's eyes were filled with childish excitement. The first years awkwardly filed into a row behind the circles, a little off the field as Sir Damian announced pairings.

Rose was guiltily relieved when her first match was with one of the few highborns who didn't know how to hold a weapon. Rose defeated her within a few seconds. Her second opponent was more challenging, one of the dark-skinned twins who Rose now knew was named Kitsun, who pulled out two plain swords. Reaching forward, Rose offered a hand, and Kitsun barely glanced twice at the scars on her wrist before shaking it with a nod. Unsheathing her daggers, Rose stepped back as Kitsun swung down at her, the tip of her sword barely grazing her front, parrying her next side strike with her right dagger. Their blades trembled as they pushed against each other only for Rose's dagger to skid to the side from Kitsun's force. Cursing, Rose barely dodged underneath her attack. She was surprisingly strong, probably impossible for Rose to parry with her inferior strength and smaller blade, and so Rose could only dodge.

That wouldn't be a problem. She was used to dodging. It was the act of moving forward into Kitsun's range and putting herself into danger that made her mind go blank with terror. Ducking underneath the pair of side swings, Rose hurtled toward Kitsun, deflecting her downwards swing with her right dagger as she slashed with her left, hitting something just as she was knocked back from the force of her deflection. Kitsun and Rose both stopped, and Rose glanced down at her dagger to see droplets of blood dripping down its edge. Although Kitsun's blows were heavy, she paused almost as much as Rose between each attack, considering what to do next, as if just as new to fighting as Rose was. That gave her a chance. If it were anyone else, she'd be dead.

Giving Kitsun a nod, Rose flew back into battle. Kitsun's dual swords reminded her of what fighting against battleaxes must feel like. A single direct hit to her body would mean instant death, and parrying was such a huge risk that Rose only dared to deflect or dodge. Weaving between attacks, Rose could only score shallow slashes on Kitsun's arms or sides, never deep enough to actually be deadly. *I can never win like this.* Just as she thought that, she made a mistake: lunging beneath two sweeping blows, Rose had closed into attack before she saw from her peripheral vision a blade rushing toward her, and against all common sense, Rose felt terror within her and jumped backward. Kitsun's sword struck her right dagger and it flew out of her hand, out of the circle.

"Goddammit," Rose cursed, angry at herself for not having her extra dagger on her and for making that mistake. She could've easily attacked and then dodged to the side without getting hit. Kitsun looked almost guilty, but she continued her attack, pressing forward, slowly forcing Rose back until she was standing on the very edge of the line.

"Just step out, please. I don't want to hurt you," Kitsun said, raising her sword. When Rose didn't respond, she struck, slashing down with her right arm, the left sword hanging by her side: a simple execution. Rose ducked and rolled to the side, stopping in front of Kitsun's loose hand, her mind stuttering as she heard the whistling of the sword behind her. Rose simply froze as now-familiar terror entered her veins, and she jerked as the very tip of her down-striking sword struck her right shoulder with shockingly resounding pain that throbbed through her. But she had an opening. As she rose to her feet, Rose slashed with her dagger along Kitsun's left hand. Her sword dropped to the ground with a clatter as Kitsun pulled away quickly, and Rose kicked the sword out of the ring before quickly backing away. Warm liquid was soaking the fabric of her sleeve, and Rose cursed as she clutched the wound with her left hand, dagger in her right. The wound on Kitsun's hand was deep, and Rose realized, far too late, that she could've ended the battle right there if she had aimed for her wrist.

But I have a chance now, right?

Withdrawing two throwing knives, Rose hurled them at Kitsun, one after another, as she rushed at Rose. Kitsun dodged both of them, but as she did, Rose lunged at her, another throwing knife and dagger in her hand, meeting Kitsun's strike with her crossed blades. They stood absolutely still, arms trembling, before Rose remembered Halt's words. She had just been introduced to the daggers, and he had told her, *Don't be too dependent on your blades. If you can knock someone out with a punch, drop your daggers and do that.*

Rose's daggers clattered to the ground. Kitsun's blade, free from the blocking pressure of the two knives, fell downward in a deadly arc. But Rose was already gone, too close to Kitsun for her blade to hit Rose. She threw her shoulder and back into her punch, as Halt taught her, landing it straight at Kitsun's stomach before rearing her knee up into her groin. Kitsun stumbled back, coughed, and dodged Rose's next attack. She stepped back again as Rose attacked, obviously not as familiar to hand-to-hand combat, and her next punch caught Rose in the jaw. As Rose tumbled to the ground, she pointed at Kitsun's feet.

She had stepped out of the circle.

Rubbing her sore jaw, Rose picked up her various weapons and held out a hand for Kitsun to shake. She was gratified to see the respect instead of hate in Kitsun's eyes and hoped her own eyes reflected the same sentiment.

The highborn boy with brown hair and tan skin she had been put up against next used only one sword, and yet Rose knew from the very beginning that he was better than she was. He was comfortable with his sword, as if it were an extension of his arm, and moved between attacks with a fluidity Rose simply could not keep up with. It was now that Rose's lack of experience became clear, and Rose had to surrender within ten minutes.

The next two battles were almost worse. She was paired against a highborn named Dawn and the strange-eyed boy. Neither bothered to use their weapons. Rose had thought that someone as small as Dawn would have manageable power and had been proven wrong within a few seconds. Her first punch dug into Rose's stomach, knocking the breath out of her and sending her flying a few feet back, and Rose barely ducked underneath Dawn's next kick. Rose barely lasted two minutes before she felt the cold metal of a dagger pressed against her neck. She wasn't even surprised. What astonished her was Dawn's respect. She bowed to Rose before moving on to her next victim and had shook her hand before the battle despite her scars.

And then, the boy with the strange eyes.

Rose had barely gotten into position before he was moving, abnormally fast, a fist coming at her face, and Rose could only duck as quickly as she could. Even so, the punch smashed into her left shoulder with a *crack* that she threw off. The adrenaline flooding through her veins allowed her to only distantly feel the pain. She grabbed the boy's retreating fist, grabbed his collar, and flipped him over her shoulder onto the ground. He shot up to his feet, hitting Rose's jaw, and Rose felt herself tumbling backward several feet, out of the circle. The crack was *definitely* her collarbone. It throbbed with pain and was turning bright red, probably fractured.

"*Goddammit*," Rose swore. "I should've brought medical supplies." The boy, obviously, ignored her.

"Holy shit, Rose, are you okay?" Rose turned around, clutching her left shoulder with her right hand as it throbbed with pain, and gave Ash a pained grin.

"Only a slash on my right shoulder and what's probably a broken collarbone. Are there healers?"

"If something's broken, yeah. They're over there."

Stumbling toward the small stand in the distance, Rose observed the small group of students gathered in front of the tent.

"No, you can't get treatment if it's not severe!" one of the healers was shouting.

"I'll fucking get you fired," one of the highborns spat.

"Try it. I dare you. I think you guys have forgotten we're Healers. We're ranked above you. Here, girl, that shoulder looks bad." She gestured at Rose, who carefully pushed her way to the front of the crowd, gritting her teeth as someone jostled her roughly.

"Broken collarbone. That looks pretty bad. How'd you get it?"

"Someone punched me so hard that it broke."

The healer nodded, unsurprised, moving her hands over Rose's shoulder. Rose felt a split-second of itching warmth before the pain slowly melted away and vanished.

"I'm not healing your other wounds. Just be careful not to get them infected." Rose nodded and retreated, leaving the healers to deal with the rest of the students.

Rose was eventually put in the second group with Kitsun and River, the only people below her being the six or seven students who had never held a weapon in their lives. It was disconcerting how much experience everyone around her had with combat. While Rose had barely spent a month learning daggers and three months fighting, Ash, for example, had eight years of experience with fighting. Rose had to consciously think about every attack and action, which was why she'd done okay with Kitsun, who had to do the same. Most of the highborns and even a few of the lowborns were fluid with their actions, one attack melting into another without thought. Ash herself, skilled as she was, had been placed in the fourth group, only below the boy with the strange eyes and his group of friends. Glancing at Ash's wristwatch, Rose noted that it was 2:56. Class was, finally, approaching its end.

As the students gathered back at the training field for Sir Damien's final words, they were surprised to hear that his voice had softened. Just a bit more tender, or as tender Rose imagined his voice could ever be. Maybe he felt pity for the students.

"Let that be a taste of the Academy. Fortunately for you shrimps, you will be focusing more on combat more than anything else for the rest of the year. While stamina and brute strength is important, mages should focus more on magic and actual combat." There were audible sighs of relief, and his gaze darkened. "Don't misunderstand me. You will be running, but a little less than you did today. The rest of the year, a few other knights and I will be training you based on the level of competence you have shown me today. Those of you who can wield a weapon properly will be introduced to many other ones." He surveyed the crowd of sweaty, tired students before turning away. "Stay here. Master Eliot, the teacher for magic, will be here in a few minutes."

***

Master Eliot was a tall, slightly chubby man who was dressed in a black robe outlined in sky blue, indicating the Water Element.

"Welcome to the Magic Studies class." He glanced over the group of students, as if marking each face, before continuing. "Those who do not possess Elemental Crystals may follow me. Those who do stay here and begin to warm up." Standing up, Rose followed Master Eliot into the building along with about fifteen other students, most of the lowborn. The room was located on the third floor of the Academy behind a locked door.

Master Eliot led the small crowd into the classroom. Although it was small, unassuming, barely noticeable in comparison to the other beautiful places Rose had seen, there was an intake of breath from the students. For, on the platform, were five round crystal bowls, placed in a semicircle that left an empty space in the center. Each bowl held a beautiful mass of energy: one of scarlet, crimson, orange energy that flicked and danced almost as if it was burning, a leaf-shaped mass of calm, pulsing, bright green energy, a pool of sky blue energy with waves of crashing blue, a coil of silver energy that whirled and coiled around and around violently, as if it was a gust of wind on a windy day, and a circle of purple-blue energy in which a jagged knife of lightning occasionally flashed, before disappearing back into the circle of energy. The energies were ever-changing, dancing and destroying, and Rose found herself staring at them, entranced.

"This—" Master Eliot waved an arm toward the semicircle of bowls, "—is Elemental Energy. It is pure magical essence, and we channel it to create Elemental Crystals. Although most highborns with magic receive an Elemental Crystal at a very young age, you guys don't have any. Do you know how they work?"

Rose nodded, but many other students shook their heads.

"An Elemental Crystal is currently the most effective way to test for someone's elemental affinity. Once again, although you may have practiced magic in the past and don't know why this would be needed, most receive theirs at a very young age. You are largely receiving one as a courtesy, as it is traditional for a mage to own one." He paused, glancing around the students as if checking for understanding, and then continued.

"As you walk up to the five bowls, I will give you an empty Elemental Crystal that will float above your dominant hand's palm. Stand in the center of the bowls, and hold your hand above the bowls, palm down, and wait for the crystal to absorb your element. If nothing happens... you have no magic, or nearly none." His voice softened. "You'll have no chance becoming a mage."

Whispering amongst themselves with excitement and nerves, the students arranged themselves in a line that wound around the classroom, each performing the ceremony, taking from about two seconds to a full minute. Rose noticed that water and earth seemed to be the most common, although she wasn't sure if that was because lowborns specifically had it more. Two people had no spark, no magic at all. They rushed out of the classroom, tears leaking from downcast eyes. Before long, Ash was standing in front of the bowls. Observing her face as she accepted the crystal, Rose noticed that Ash looked confident, as if sure of the outcome, and she smiled as there was a flash of red energy.

"Fire," Rose breathed. Ash grinned, and Rose gave her a thumbs up.

"You're next," someone behind her said. Rose jumped and walked forward, her hands trembling with nerves. The Elemental Crystal was a beautiful, teardrop shape with a string through the hole embedded on the top.

There was a silent ringing in her head as she poised her hand over the bowls and waited.

Thirty seconds passed.

A minute.

As Rose watched, the energy in the bowls seemed to get more and more frazzled and seemed to glow brighter and brighter. People snickered, and Rose felt tears burn at the corners of her eyes. This *couldn't* be right. She had controlled lightning countless times. This *couldn't be right.*

Two.

Rose began to turn away, but then she caught the gaze of Master Eliot, who shook his head.

So Rose stayed.

There was an explosion of light. Rose, as well as everyone in the room, screwed their eyes shut and turned away as light filled the room.

When she opened her eyes, her crystal was filled with beautiful, flashing, swirling, lightning.

* * *

Magic was one thing in this Academy that Rose *loved*, even though it came with a side of pain.

Halt had been right. The days of meditation and learning control had helped. The hours of practice allowed her to focus on her magic with almost no effort, and, by the end of the class, sparks were dancing across her hands and one of the targets across the field was smoldering in ruin. It was safe and extremely gratifying to say that she wasn't below average at magic. Shaking herself out of watching their amazing magic, Rose reached into the exhausted mana pool, searching for more magic, causing the dim aching pain that had formed when she first reached her limit to worsen and spike across her body. She winced, vision flashing, and stopped as she dimly heard Master Eliot speak.

"Students!" Master Eliot called. "I have assessed your use of magic through the three hours you have just spent demonstrating your power. Most of you, even the highborns, are lacking stamina. You will find a sheet of paper with that assessment on your beds. Unfortunately, because of how valuable Mages are to the kingdom, I am the only mage currently available to teach you. While that number will change soon, for now, you will have to work on improvement on your own. Is this clear?"

Rose, along with several other students, nodded, but a boy shouted from the crowd, unhappy.

"Why would we need stamina? If we just kill our opponent automatically, we shouldn't care about how long we last."

Master Eliot's gaze hardened, and Rose sighed. Students needed to stop challenging the Masters. Hadn't they learned from Sir Damian?

"You. Kid. Come up here." Rose watched in mild trepidation as he approached the front of the silent classroom.

"There are five knights running at you, and you've been disarmed. You have to kill them with magic. Try."

The boy blanched, then opened his mouth.

"Don't protest. I've been in that exact situation before. Now, what do you do? Remember, the targets try to simulate a real human being. It's only when they're completely destroyed and start rebuilding themselves that they represent a human being killed. What do you do?"

The boy held out his hands, lightning flashing from his fingers, and three targets were brought to smoldering ruin before he dropped to his knees, panting.

"Two more seconds before they kill you."

"I... just need..."

"And, you're dead."

Dead silence.

"Does anyone who thinks stamina is unimportant want to demonstrate?" As he glared out at the crowd of students, they looked away, avoiding his eyes—but, as Rose noticed, the boy with the strange eyes was staring at him, almost as if he was bored. *Stupid, arrogant, highborn bastard. He can't be that much better than us.*

"All right, Princeling. Come up."

Princeling?

The boy stood up, brushing off his pants as if the ground had dirtied them before making his way through the crowd toward the front of the crowd. Enough time had passed so that the servants that had been bustling among the targets during the last demonstration had cleared over half of them, leaving about forty left on the field. The boy glared intently towards the direction of the five targets. *So, only five. There's no justification for his arrogance. He's just normal, like us, although a bit better at fighting.*

The five targets burst into flame, and Rose sat back, satisfied. He was just an arrogant bastard—but even as she thought that, five more targets burst into flame. *You've gotta be kidding me.* Methodically, target by target burst into flame until all the targets on the field were burning, smoldering, and charring into a dead black within seconds. Several students cried out, and Rose ignored them. She had learned from experience that the fire wouldn't spread. She continued staring at the boy in astonishment.

Dead silence.

The boy was panting, his legs shaking, but still standing, even after all of that magic.

"Good job. And this is why stamina is important. He just took out a platoon of an army, and, after an hour, he could do it again. Do we have any objections?"

Absolute, dead silence.

"Good. Class is dismissed."

Rose frowned, watching as the smoldering targets receded back into clean red and white. As she made her way back into the atrium, she bitterly acknowledged why so many students would, inevitably, resign, even as a highborn. As a lowborn, she, River, and the other students were fighting an uphill battle that had only just started. Among the table, as Rose shoved down her food, only Ash and Venus were chattering lively. Only they would make light of this situation.

"How'd it feel being the slowest runner? I wouldn't know," Ash taunted. It was true. She'd done excellently during physical conditioning and had placed in the fourth group, and while she was worse than Rose at magic, it was doubtless her skill with a sword made up for that.

"Oh, it was fun. I was slow enough that on my second lap I actually got to flirt with a pretty girl who was on her last lap. She was in a good enough mood to not slap me until we reached the obstacle course," Venus said, leaning back in his chair and raising his fork back flippantly. Wincing at his half-open mouth, where Rose caught a glimpse of half-chewed food, Rose sighed and looked away.

"And who was it?"

"That girl. The small one. She hits *hard*. Look, I still have a bruise." So that's where the mark on his cheek was from. As he pointed at Dawn, Ash laughed so hard she spat out her mouthful food onto the table. Grinning and handing Ash a tissue, Rose pushed aside her plate and leaned back to watch the banter.

"You have absolutely no chance with Dawn. She's a Mage's daughter and frigid as ice, and that's a good thing."

"Can't help but try."

"She's definitely one of the front runners for the apprenticeships," River commented.

"Yeah. It's unfair, don't you think? That they don't have to work hard at all for what they have," Venus said. Rose examined Dawn, once again noting how small she was, probably at least a few inches shorter than Rose. Despite that, though, she looked like she could crush Rose's skull with her hands. She had changed into a different short-sleeved shirt at some point, revealing sinewy and toned arms, all bulging muscles and veins; as Rose watched, Dawn stretched and revealed the hint of clearly defined abs against warm brown skin. *Goddamn*, Rose thought, before shaking herself out of her stupor. That at least explained how hard she had hit.

"I don't think they don't work hard," Rose said. They stared at her, confused. "I mean, look at Dawn. Look at how small she is. It's not natural. I wouldn't be surprised if it was because of some illness. *I'm taller and probably would be stronger if she hadn't trained as much as she did.* I mean, look at her *arms*."

"Oh my god, Rose, we *get* that you—" Ash said, and Rose flushed a dark red.

"Not to mention," Rose interrupted hastily, "that breaking limits must be a lot more painful for her. I don't think it's fair to say they haven't worked hard. What *is* unfair is that they got the opportunity to train before us." Everyone at the table nodded in agreement, staring in silence at

"Her, Emma, and the Prince. Already front runners to become three of the Five," Celeste murmured.

"Five...?"

"How do you not know this, Venus?" Ash said, shaking her head. "The *Five*!"

"I come from a faraway land, my princess," Venus flirted.

"You're from the Fire Kingdom, Venus," Rose said, exasperated. River grinned at her.

"The Five Sorcerers are the most powerful sorcerers of each element, Venus. They're rechosen once every ten years through an intense arena battle," Ash explained.

"We haven't even become apprentices yet," Venus said. "How can they be in the running for the Five?"

"They're highborns, and one of them is the Prince. Anyway, they must, naturally, have an advantage in terms of their magical capacity against us, although it isn't as vastly different as you would imagine. We can catch up. Of course, we haven't even talked about their political influence," Rose said.

"It really is unfair. In the last five different rotations of Mages, we've only had one lowborn," Celeste said.

"We still have four more years to catch up to the highborns," Venus protested. The rest of the table exchanged a grim glance.

"That's only if we become apprentices. And, well…" Rose trailed off into silence. They all knew what she was suggesting, how the odds were stacked against them so immensely there was nowhere to turn. Glancing toward Ash, Rose saw a brief flash of feral excitement flash through her face.

A small part of Rose hoped Ash wouldn't become a Mage.

Not for nefarious purposes. Life without Ash would be dull, she was one of Rose's only friends. But her childish excitement for fighting didn't belong here.

It didn't belong in this cruelty-ridden world.

Rose only hoped that Ash would grow out of it before it truly began to hurt her.

Chapter Nine

"YOU'RE NOT GOING to go to the library?" Ash asked Rose. Rose shook her head.

"I'm studying after curfew, I have to train." Rose's muscles ached. She couldn't believe that she was willingly going back to the training field. After taking a thirty-minute break, bandaging her deeper wounds and warming up in the barracks while her stomach settled, Rose grabbed the piece of paper sitting on her shelf and made her way outside. The silence outside, broken only by the sound of heavy panting and weapons smacking against dummies, startled her. Most students were training individually, some hacking away at dummies with their weapons, others destroying—or, at least trying to destroy—magical targets. As she walked toward the armory, Rose read through the long block of writing on the piece of paper:

Work on the power of your attacks instead of their frequency. That may allow you to do more with the abysmal stamina you possess. To do so, simply create more potent lightning. It won't feel good because you'll need more magic, but even someone new would be able to destroy a target in two or three hits. An easy way to visualize this is gathering up power within your palm until it forms a destructive sphere. This will, unfortunately, take more time to do at the beginning. Work on your stamina. This can only be achieved through brute force. By forcing yourself to do more magic despite the pain, you can slowly extend your stamina. This is something all mages do. Other things you must work on that you may do after you extend your stamina significantly (when your lightning is more powerful)l include more variance in your attack patterns and how frequently and quickly you can create them. After about a month, where you will be quickly introduced to summoning lightning, how to manipulate it so that you can form shapes and actual attacks and how to withstand basic electricity so you can hold it and achieve finer control. Fortunately, your control is barely average and your manipulation is just advanced enough that you can practice with it now without burning your skin off. You have a lot of work to do. I see potential. Good luck.

Rose frowned at the piece of paper. That was a lot to work on. She spent the next half hour practicing building up lightning in her palm only for it to slowly melt away after she lost control, over and over again until she was finally able to sustain it long enough to thrust it into the target. It certainly drained much more magic but felt much more satisfying to land. Instead of about eleven bolts, it only took six for the target to begin to repair itself. However, even after destroying only two targets, Rose could feel herself reaching her limit. It hurt. Pain from magic exhaustion was unlike anything she had experienced. It felt as if her body was slowly being crushed by some overwhelming pressure, her bones aching and her senses dulling. Clenching her teeth, Rose dug deep into her magic, forcing out as much mana as she could, pain building. It fizzled away as Rose collapsed to her knees and Rose opened her eyes, panting as the pain slowly receded back into an ache, and Rose pushed herself back to her feet and tried again. It took her half an hour to create two more attacks.

After taking a break from magic to throw herself and her daggers at her dummy, chaining attacks together smoothly mostly because it was easier when the opponent was a lifeless piece of metal, Rose stopped, panting, and sighed. The foundations of her skill were fine, and Rose was usually decent at evading, Halt had made sure of that, but she'd panic or freeze when faced with danger and end up misstepping or acting rashly as a result. Merely dodging could not win her a battle. *I should probably wait until Ash comes out, then spar with her. The more experience I have with combat, the less I'll panic and freeze up.* Sliding her daggers back into her sheath, Rose collapsed down on the floor, leaning against the dummy. She had been putting off running for a while, but she needed to do it.

Standing up, Rose jogged along the track. She made it four miles before she was bent over double, retching, trying not to puke. As she cooled down, she resumed practicing her magic. Her magic had barely begun to remanifest, and Rose barely made it through a single target before she was at her limit. The exhaustion from running was replaced by pain, but even through the haze of light flashing beneath her eyelids, Rose noticed that she had to push just a little less for another attack after she reached her limit. Doubled over on her knees, Rose knelt, blinking rapidly in a futile attempt to clear her spotty vision.

"Here, Rose, you look pretty wrecked. I got you some water," Ash said from behind her. Rose jumped, face warming as she pushed herself to her feet. She accepted the cup of water without speaking, a spark of warm gratitude blossoming in her chest.

"Thanks. I really needed it."

"Yeah, I bet. You really should start on your homework. We only have a few hours until curfew."

"Nah, it's fine." Rose stood up, waving aside Ash's questions as she did so. "Hey, you're going to the armory, right? Grab a sword for me." Ash nodded. Halt had briefly introduced her to the sword, teaching her basic movements and drills before focusing his attention on the daggers. While Rose preferred the smaller blades, the sword was undoubtedly a more powerful weapon. She spent the rest of the hour and a half alternating between strength-building exercises using the equipment, drilling with her sword against a dummy, and pushing her magic to its limit, over and over again until pain seemed to her merely like a constant. Ash had gathered with a group of other students, mostly the other children of knights, and they spent the rest of their time dueling. Rose couldn't help but watch during her short breaks. They seemed to duel with an unspoken code of honor. Ash was, undoubtedly, one of the best fighters within the group. As she battled, her eyes would shine with joy, finding happiness within a dance of death. Rose didn't understand her, but she couldn't deny that it was fun to watch her fight.

Finally, ten minutes before curfew, Rose entered the atrium, legs shaking, retrieving her backpack from the barracks and quickly changing into a sweater and sweatpants. Hurrying up the stairs and toward the library, Rose walked up to the second floor. Looking around her at the deserted library, Rose roamed the shelves, picking out about ten books she thought would help with her homework and stuffing most of them into her backpack. Hurrying outside, Rose sprinted up the staircase, then took the right staircase up to the fourth floor. She entered the flag tower which was covered in small circular tables, on one of which Rose could see carvings. *UA. NU. AZ,* and, of course, Halt and the initials VE. Rose hoisted herself haphazardly onto the table and saw the grooves of the trapdoor. It looked nearly identical to the ceiling tile but for, as Rose now saw, a small latch. She yanked on it, trying to open it, but it was stuck shut.

Rose cursed. Below, she could hear the sounds of servants calling curfew. She yanked on the trapdoor again. Still nothing. *Come on, Halt!*

Just as Rose heard servants coming up the stairs, she flicked her wrist, sending the dagger springing free, and wrenched the trapdoor open. sighing in relief, Rose scrambled up the rope ladder that swung down and shut it just as the servants walked in.

"Did you hear something?" one of them said. Rose's heart was pounding so loud she was sure they could hear it.

"I certainly didn't see anything," the other responded. They laughed, extinguished the fires, and walked away. Rose let out a breath of relief and struck a match. Before long, she had lit several candles around the room that emitted a dim light.

The room was small, cozy, barely twenty feet wide, a tiny, ordinary alcove amid the splendor and beauty of the Academy. Dust filled the room, so Rose opened the window. Even in the darkness, the view was breathtaking. The mountains were barely visible in the distance, the small village stood beneath the castle like an assortment of child's blocks. There was a river that she could barely see in the distance, curving between the mountains like a smooth, dark blue snake. Two desks stood on either end of the room, covered in moth-eaten paper, and Rose swept them off into the waste bin below, wincing as the dust stuck to her sweater, and quietly dragged one of the chairs to the desk. It was tall, large and padded, and Rose brushed off the dust and sank down on its cushioned surface with glee. After so much exercise, sitting down felt indulgent. Taking out the books in her bag and placing them on the bookshelf next to the desk, Rose took out her notebook and looked down at her page of homework.

- Write a four paragraph essay about the values of the five constant factors in both battle and politics (two days)
- Finish math problems 1-43 from page 1-4 (tomorrow)
- Write an three paragraph essay explaining the role of the Water Kingdom in the Dark Sorcerer's rise.
- Diagram the science of magic (two elements, you can choose) (tomorrow)
- Read The Examination (finish it in five days) (more question essays due soon)
- Other stuff: more algebra, all of the laws, the books (listed below), quantum physics, more geography.

Letting out a mumbled string of curses, Rose took a swig of her coffee and began.

She decided to start with the simplest of the five, the three-paragraph essay. History was hard, but manageable. All she needed were some reliable books, which she had taken from the library. Just as she dipped her fountain pen in ink and flipped open a book, she heard the creaking sound of the trapdoor from behind her.

A pair of green and blue eyes were the first thing she saw as the boy climbed up and shut the door silently behind him.

The Prince.

Everything clicked into place.

His deposition, the expensive clothing, the beautiful sword, his unjustified hatred for Rose. And, most of all, his prodigious nature. A member of a Royal Family had control over all Five Elements. Even with only his specialty element, Fire, he was more powerful than all of the students here. Most infuriating was the surprise in his face. Rose clenched her fist, her nails digging into her skin.

"You keep on getting in my way," the Prince finally growled. "Just like every—"

"Shut up. Let me study."

The boy's eyes lit with surprise, but he turned away and shook his head.

"If you disturb me, you're dead."

Rose glared at his back as he retreated to the other side of the small room, lifting a chair into the air and placing it gently in front of the desk. Occasionally, he picked up his fountain pen, scribbling down notes, the scratch of the nib the only sound in the entire room besides for the whistling of the wind. Of all the people to come to the study, it had to be *him*. He excelled physically and magically, and if his dedication to the two was any indicator, he probably had no problem with the academics either. So why was he here?

Sighing, Rose turned toward her books and glanced toward the clock. It was 11:30, and as she chugged down the rest of her coffee, Rose picked up her quill and began to write.

* * *

After tackling the more manageable essays, Rose started her math work. The foreign numbers and letters seemed to jump out at her, and Rose shut her eyes and sighed. *Math*. It had never been a thing she had cared to read about at Master's house, and now she was paying for it.

"Why are you still up here?" the boy asked. His voice was gravelly, rough, as if he hadn't had enough water, a jarring opposite from Ezra's smooth, beautiful honey. If only he were here instead of this highborn prick.

"I've only done half of the homework," Rose replied, annoyance creeping into her voice.

"Lowborns," the boy muttered. "Why do any of you even bother to try?" Something about the lilting jeer in his tone just *pissed her off*. Rose couldn't help herself. She threw the book in her hand at the Prince, who turned and caught it in his palm.

I just threw a book at the Crown Prince of the Lightning Kingdom.

"You—" the prince started, then shook his head and tossed the book back at her. "I could execute you for that."

"Go ahead and get expelled. That'd almost be worth it."

"I—" he started, speechless, and then looked away. Rose observed him further. His hair was midnight black, the closest shade to Rose's that she had ever seen, and although he was taller than her, he seemed very small when hunched up against the chair. Frowning, Rose turned her attention back to math. Painstakingly, she worked through the problems, using example problems from a book as guidance. As she worked, she found herself comprehending more and more of the material. Even so, by the time she finished the math problems, it was already one in the morning.

The science homework was actually pretty easy. She had found the diagram they were supposed to draw in a book she'd picked up at the library and copied the intricate lines down in twenty minutes, making a few changes to adjust to recent discoveries. Understanding it was another matter. After half an hour of staring at the diagram blankly, Rose resolved to ask Ash tomorrow.

Taking out the issued version of the *Examination,* Rose smoothed a hand over the leather cover, opening it to the first page and beginning to read. This was easy. Surprisingly, despite the dull synopsis, Rose found it fun to ponder over the lines of mind-bending philosophy. Before she knew it, it was nearly two-thirty, and the Prince was still there. Even though her conscience was screaming at her to go to sleep, a childish part of Rose refused to allow him to stay later than she did. So Rose pulled out a quantum physics textbook only to realize that if she wanted to have a chance at understanding this, she had to get better at math. Making a note to get more textbooks from the library, Rose finally settled on one of the history books Master Dara had recommended and began to read. It was a good choice. She skimmed the book, too tired to truly read in depth, flipping rapidly between speculation regarding the true power of the first six possessors of magic and the motivations of the Dark Sorcerer. Had the Six truly been so powerful as to tame nature itself, as the folktales said, or had magic evolved in power over time to what it was now? Had the Dark Sorcerer destroyed the Light Kingdom in a move of cruel strategic intelligence, seeing as Light was his Dark's most potent enemy? Had the Six's power been what unified the nations, or was it something else? How had the Dark Sorcerer destroyed the Light Kingdom so thoroughly that even its magic had disappeared? Rose read until it was three in the morning before finally giving in and returning to the barracks. Dropping her bag on the ground beside her bed, Rose crept into the bathrooms, sinking herself gratefully in one of the steaming hot baths and sighing as it soothed her aching muscles. After thoroughly washing off the sweat and blood covering her body, Rose rebandaged the cut on her shoulder before creeping back into her bed.

She had so little of a chance here that it was sickening.

The Prince, whatever his name was, was right. There was no logical reason for her to keep trying, there was no hope for her within this den of beasts. If she knew what was good for her, she'd leave, right now.

But then again, she was already too far in to leave.

Rose fell asleep within minutes. She was too tired to think, or even dream.

Chapter Ten

THE FIRST THING she registered when she woke up was dull, aching pain.

As she pushed herself up from bed, she nearly shouted in pain; every single muscle in her body seemed to ache and throb with agony. Sitting up painfully, Rose reached underneath her bed, pulling out the small trunk she had been given for belongings. She pulled out the first aid kit, massaging a relaxing oil over legs, arms, and what she could reach of her back. It helped, a little. The barracks were silent. She could see maybe a few other girls awake. After brushing her teeth and changing into her uniform, she still had fifty minutes until breakfast started. *I might as well read The Examination.*

Rose reached into her bag. It wasn't there. Heart falling, she realized she probably left it in the alcove. Jogging up the stairs to the fourth level, Rose opened the trapdoor and ascended into the study. The window was still open, and Rose shivered with cold, goosebumps rising on her skin, and Rose walked toward the window and closed in.

The view was even more beautiful in the morning, but Rose's focus on the boy who was asleep, head resting on his crossed arms and a bottle of ink dangerously close to his arm.

Should I wake him up? Will he be mad?

Walking over, Rose carefully moved the bottle of ink and screwed on the cap before tapping him softly with a hand. When he didn't move, Rose shook him gently.

"Wake up. It's six twenty," she told him.

He awoke jaggedly, eyes flying open, jumping up from his desk and pulling out a dagger concealed at his side, eyes wide with carnal fear. Rose's daggers popped out of her sheath and she jumped backward, crouched in a fighting stance, but when he saw her, he sighed and relaxed back into his chair.

"Sorry," he muttered. "Bad dream."

Rose didn't respond. Cautiously sliding her daggers back into their sheaths, Rose retrieved her bag, crept down the stairs and back toward her room, where she read until breakfast.

* * *

The week only got worse.

Her lack of experience in combat somehow only seemed to get worse as time passed. It made no sense. The exhaustion caused by sleeping only a few hours a day only made it worse. Eventually, it got so bad Rose was publicly called out by Sir Damian on Friday of the first week.

"You there. Lowborn," Sir Damian snapped. Rose flinched, lowering her raised daggers, watching from the corner of her eye as her opponent lowered her sword from against Rose's neck. He was glaring at her, and most of the students around him, including the Prince and Emma, had stopped to watch.

"Why'd you back so far away from that last blow?" he called.

"I..." *It's obvious,* Rose reflected bitterly. "I didn't want to get hit."

"And do you think not getting hit is more important than winning?"

Obviously. Rose nodded, and Sir Damian threw his hands up into the air.

"You might as well just leave," Sir Damian said. He contemplated her for a split-second more before walking away. Rose stared at him as he retreated, feeling tears well up in her eyes, and stabbed her daggers into the dirt.

I don't understand what I'm doing wrong.

It was obvious she was definitely doing something wrong. Over the course of five days, among twenty-five sparring matches, Rose had only won three. Rose had spent hours each day drilling against the wooden dummies, going through drills that were gradually becoming more complex, but it hadn't helped. Rose looked up only to see condescending stares from those around her, as if she had said something wrong.

Rose didn't understand.

"I'm sure you'll improve soon," Ash told her over dinner. Picking at her plate of mashed potatoes and carrots, Rose was silent as she mentally went over every single battle she had participated in in her head. Each one was usually caused by a single, simple mistake, usually caused by fear. Fear made her freeze up, made her misstep, made her make simple mistakes.

And Rose didn't know what to do about it.

"Look at poor baby Rose! Too afraid to get hurt!" People jeered from the hallways as she walked back to the barracks. Rose knew that they'd forget about this by the next day, but she still simply didn't understand. She was working so much harder than all of them, and yet they were still so far ahead, lording their tutorship over her as if they had earned it themselves.

"Take more risks," the Prince said. His voice was curt, sharp, as if this answer was supposed to be obvious.

"Why should I take more risks? It's life or death!"

The prince merely shook his head and looked away. Slamming her book shut, Rose glanced up at the clock—*3 am*—and stood up, kicking open the latch and nearly tumbling down the trapdoor. Glaring at the trapdoor, the stupid, arrogant prince who was above it, and the stupid Academy below her, Rose stormed down the staircase and into the barracks.

* * *

Rose was training alone when the first magical limit broke.

It had been faltering for a while. In the last two weeks of training, Rose had gradually pushed her limits from about twenty-one attacks to thirty. Today, as Rose stood her ground against the agony flashing through her, something shattered within her and Rose's vision went black.

When she woke up, the first thing she noticed was that she had more mana. At first, it didn't make sense to her. Unless she had been knocked out for more than an hour, there was no way her magic could've been regenerated so much. But as Rose delved into her magic, she sensed the extra depth her pool of mana had gained. She had enough mana to destroy another target. *The Academy teaches you to push beyond ordinary human limits*, Halt had said.

Rose decided it wasn't the day to push more. What mattered, though was that *she still had more mana left*. She had finally decreased the number of attacks to destroy a single target from six to five, so she still had enough mana for about two more attacks.

Vary your attacks.

Barely able to repress an eager grin, Rose stopped training and went back inside, grabbing her usual supplies before heading toward the library. There, she grabbed as many books about famous lightning users as possible: Audra, Beowulf the Mighty, and even a collection of stories about a so-called god of lightning. That night, when she had finished her homework, she went through the books, one by one by one, taking notes on their strategy and how they utilized their lightning. Her good mood, caused by the fascinating topic of researching magic that was a welcome change to the dullness of homework, was quickly shattered by the Prince.

"You do realize you're never going to get to that level, right? You have the magical reserves of a peasant. Be realistic." he asked, frowning down at Rose's notes. She jumped, glaring at him as he looked over his shoulder and smirked condescendingly at her list of notes.

"You realize you're never going to be likable if you keep on holding your gold-bought tutoring over people, right?" Rose bit back, slamming the book about *Ogrim the Mighty* shut. The Prince flinched back before sighing.

"It doesn't matter—"

"And if you keep on avoiding the fact that you hold your royal status over us commoners like we aren't even worth anything. Honestly-"

"You really aren't worth much, if I'm going to be honest," the Prince bit back. "The fact that you guys have any *hope* at all to become a Mage when you're so far behind is shocking."

Rose snatched up her notes before dumping her textbooks into her bag, storming out of the alcove for the second time that week. Distracting herself from the words of the prince, Rose stared down at her notes. The scale of most attacks from these legendary mages were on a scale she couldn't imagine, but some stood out to her: using lightning to enhance her speed, although that seemed to be very painful, as well as coating parts of her blades with lightning to electrocute someone. Yawning, Rose was just about to enter the barracks when she heard a scream. Hurriedly shoving her notes into her pocket, Rose sprinted toward the direction of the scream, which lasted for barely three seconds before it was cut off. Peeking into a small room from which she could hear muffled thumps, Rose saw a sight that made her blood freeze.

There was just something so intrinsically *wrong* about it.

Dawn was being forced to the ground by the pair of twin boys who accompanied the Prince. Her arms had been tied together with a strange silver rope, and tears were leaking out of her eyes as one of the boys leered over her with carnal hunger in his eyes. Each of the boys had to weigh twice as much as her and were nearly two heads higher, and, even as Rose's instincts told her she wouldn't win this fight, Rose felt rage bubbling within her. *They don't even know I'm here.*

The two lightning balls that crashed into the pair of boys, one from each hand, gave Rose enough time to cut Dawn free of the rope. Rose cursed as, when she touched the rope, her magic cut off completely. Anti-magic material. It was illegal in the Lightning Kingdom, so how the hell had they gotten their hands on it? The electricity was slowly fizzling away, and as Dawn remained, still, on the ground, Rose pulled out her daggers.

"Run, Dawn! Go get a teacher!" Rose shouted.

"Aw, look, the lowborn's trying to be a hero," one of them snarled.

Their first attack, performed by the twin on the right with a broadsword, nearly knocked Rose back onto the floor. And, as they kept on attacking, Rose realized she couldn't win this. She couldn't even stall this battle, not like this.

Take risks.

Ducking underneath the sword, Rose cursed as the other twin's fist barreled into her, sending her hurtling to the ground. She rolled to the side as the sword embedded itself into the wood where her head had been – *were they trying to kill her?* – and barely managed to leap to her feet to avoid the next attack.

Take risks.

Rose cried out in pain as the sword struck her side. The gash was already bleeding freely, soaking her tunic with warm blood, and, *holy hell*, she couldn't die here. Not like this. She couldn't leave Dawn alone with them.

Take risks.

So, the next time the sword came her way, Rose ducked underneath it, striking it with her left dagger, pushing it farther to the left. Even as she saw him raising his sword, preparing to thrust downward, Rose darted closer to him, slashing along the length of his forearms before jumping away. The fear that usually overwhelmed her when she saw a blade approaching her was gone. Clearheaded and strangely confident, Rose jumped behind him as he stabbed down avoiding his attack. And she could see his next attack from the way he was standing, his feet shifted toward the left, and Rose already knew how to counterattack, how to dodge.

A kick struck her side and Rose tumbled back, smashing against the wall roughly, coughing and biting back a cry of pain as the other twin kicked her again, again, again. Something cracked in her ribs, and Rose screamed. *At least Dawn's gone by now. If I could just...* Light flared above her and Rose's eyes flew open. A plume of fire formed above her, and Rose scrambled away only to be kicked back down by one of the twins. Closing her eyes, Rose prepared for the pain.

Everything went still.

Opening her eyes, Rose stared up at the twin who had been kicking her, his foot still raised, his mouth open and gaping with shock. His body was completely covered in ice. As Rose and Dawn watched, he screamed insults and furious threats at them before falling silent. A plume of water washed over the fire, putting it out, and as Rose watched, it morphed into ice in midair, avoiding the ground, before slowly dissipating into gas. Glancing at Dawn, Rose stared in awe as she lowered her hand, letting out a shaky sigh. *Dawn's the daughter of a mage. Of course, she'd be able to fight back with her magic.*

"Are you okay?" Rose asked, pushing herself up to her feet. Her previously bruised ribs, which had just barely begun to heal, were now aching worse than before. Biting her lip to hold back the cry of pain, Rose clutched at the bleeding wound in her side and stared down at the blood.

There was far too much of it.

Ignoring the dots in her vision, Rose stumbled toward the direction of the door. If she could just reach the barracks and bandage her wounds, she'd probably be fine.

"Get back here," Dawn said. Rose glanced back at her, confused. "Just let me heal you," she said gently. Rose sank down to the floor, bracing a hand against the wall, and Dawn knelt down beside her. As Rose watched, she drew moisture from the air and settled it against Rose's wound. It glowed a gentle, bright blue, and the cut began to heal. Dawn knew *healing magic*. Dawn had really nice hands. Just how good was she at magic, and how had Rose not noticed before?

"I'm sorry I don't have enough skill to fully heal your ribs. I've never dealt with bones before. It's not like I don't want to use magic for you or anything—I still have a lot left—it's just that I don't know how." *Does that mean she still has magic left? Even after all of this?*

"It's okay. Thanks for healing the gash. It was nasty."

They sat in silence for a few seconds before Dawn spoke.

"What're we going to do about them?" Dawn asked, nodding her head toward the twins. *The Prince's friends.*

Rose had a visit to make.

"Come with me," Rose said. "The ice will stay, I'm assuming?"

"Yes."

Leading her up to the flag tower, Rose noted Dawn's own bruises and peppered cuts, littered on the length of her arms. If Dawn would let her, Rose would try and bandage them for her.

"I'm going to trust you won't tell anyone about this." When Dawn nodded, Rose pushed open the trapdoor and climbed up the rope ladder. The Prince looked surprised as he glanced back at the trapdoor, his eyebrows raising as Dawn followed Rose into the study. There was recognition in his eyes as he looked at Dawn, and he nodded at her, showing the first sign of blatant respect Rose had ever seen from him.

"Rose, what—" Dawn began. Rose slapped him. The Prince's eyebrows rose, and the study was suddenly lit by a bright plume of fire. Rose barely had time to dodge to the side. But even as the plume railed back, ready to strike Rose again, it was extinguished by an elegant wave of water that froze and evaporated. As Rose stared between the Prince and Dawn, she registered that the Prince had paused his attack because he was, at least in some way, showing her respect.

Strange.

"Why'd you come in here and slap me?" the Prince finally asked. Rose merely motioned him toward the trapdoor. He obliged, following Rose down the flag tower into the classroom where the pair of twins were still encased in ice.

"What is the meaning of this?" the Prince asked. He almost looked angry. Did he truly care for these friends and not know of their faults, or did he want to keep them around for their powers? Rose merely stayed silent, watching as he glanced between the fragments of silver rope on the ground and the handprint-shaped bruises on Dawn's arms.

His face whitened.

So he wasn't quite a monster.

"Unfreeze them," the Prince commanded. Rose opened her mouth to protest, but Dawn obliged before the words escaped her mouth.

"You two. We shall go to the barracks together and have a talk," he growled. Rose watched as their faces whitened and they finally looked remorseful—not at what they had done, but the prospect of getting in trouble.

Rose felt disgusted.

"Are you okay?" she asked. The Prince and the twins were already gone, and when Rose turned toward Dawn, she saw her on the ground, hands shaking, tears leaking from her beautiful brown eyes.

"Hey. Hey, it's okay," Rose murmured. *What had Blossom done when Rose cried?*

Carefully approaching Dawn, Rose knelt down, hesitated, and then embraced her. Dawn shook, sobbing, and Rose felt her own gaze harden as she rubbed soothing circles on Dawn's back. Not yet a hero of justice, but she had finally protected someone. It felt warm, as if she had finally achieved something important, and Rose clamped down on that feeling, shutting it away. This was only one of many, a beginning to a long road of justice.

* * *

That morning, whispers and rumors spread over the student body as the Prince's pair of twins walked into the atrium covered in cuts and bruises. There were, of course, the three or four deep slashes Rose had given them on their arms, but their faces were also painted with a gruesome combination of blue, green, and black. The Prince's work. It was really quite satisfying to see.

And then there was the other problem.

Although Rose had expected tension when she invited Dawn to sit with them, the silence at the table as the rest of the lowborns stared between the politely eating Dawn and Rose was deafening. Just as Rose wanted to shout at someone, Venus spoke.

"Just to be clear, Rose, you're not some mage scout who's going to execute us with Dawn if we say something wrong, right?" He smiled at her, and Rose burst into laughter, which she quickly stifled when Venus took that as permission to wink at Dawn, who glanced at him, primly placed her fork down, and slapped him, open-palmed, across the cheek. She had held back, Rose noticed.

"Aw, c'mon, beautiful, don't be like that! You gotta at least give me a chance!" Venus whined, rubbing his cheek and sitting back.

"I'll give you a chance when you learn to swallow your food before you speak, and—" Dawn raised her fork to daintily point at River. "I'd honestly rather have that one. He has manners." Rose glanced at River, who had been staring down at his plate for the past two minutes and was now turning slightly red. *He's smitten. Me too, honestly.* And with that, as Venus began shouting reasons why he was the superior man and River turned a deeper and deeper shade of red, the table resumed its merriments.

Chapter Eleven

BY THE GODS, *he's trying to kill us.* Sir Damian seemed to be in a particularly bad mood today.

The class had been set to spar within a gauntlet of death. Twelve feet in length and width, the small sparring fields were filled with death traps, manned by servants with basic control over magic. Being in the proximity of the edges of the fields caused plumes of fire to erupt. Certain areas within the arena would cause honing daggers to fly toward the target. To top it all off, if you weren't sparring, you were doing brutal sets of high-intensity exercises that made Rose's body feel like jelly.

Ignoring the pain in her ankle from a bad step into a pitfall from the last match, Rose focused on her opponent: a tall, lankly, highborn boy who was holding a pair of daggers.

This would be interesting.

Lunging forward, Rose attacked, her movements barely stuttering, and realized just how fun it was to fight against someone with a similar weapon. They feigned and parried, darting between each other, one striking like an asp only to find their opponent already elsewhere. It only took her a few minutes to realize that the boy's weakness was his predictable stepping patterns. He tended to retreat to his right, for example, when an attack approached from any other direction. When he spotted an opening, he'd consistently lunge forward to the right to target his opponent's flank. Maybe there was a reason he favored his right so strongly—a past injury, perhaps. Nonetheless, Rose decided that her most reliable approach would be to bait him into the traps and use them to her advantage. The dagger traps especially would give her an advantage, as she had memorized their locations in her first match. Furrowing her brow, Rose began to carefully guide the boy toward the nearest trap.

A whistle of wind filled the arena. It had begun.

Blocking the boy's blow to keep him in place, Rose saw, from behind him, the first dagger. The whistle of wind behind her told her another dagger was flying toward her, guided by the winds, just as she had predicted. As Rose lunged toward him, the dagger followed her. Lashing out behind her with her dagger, Rose struck it with one of her blades, causing it to fall to the floor. The boy saw the flying dagger, realized what was happening, and—*there*—glanced behind him. Another dagger was flying toward her, this time from her right, but Rose tackled the boy to the floor. The dagger barely skimmed over her head, and Rose didn't even look at it, knowing it had to take a few seconds to stop, turn in the air, and gather enough velocity to hurl itself back at her. Wrestling with him on the floor, Rose eventually ended up on top of him, barely inches away from triggering the fire. She held her blade to his neck. The trap dagger fell to the ground, less than a foot from hitting her.

"Good. You're learning." Rose's head shot up in surprise as she met the gaze of Sir Damian, who was—*smiling*? Offering a weak smile in return, Rose stood up, rubbed her ankle, and continued to run.

She wasn't perfect, but, yes—she was learning.

* * *

"Unfortunately for you, only six students have left our ranks since the beginning of the year," Master Mekhi growled. "Our attendance rate this year was disturbingly high. Even now, two months into the

Academy and a week before you chose your factions, there are still a hundred and six people here."

Rose didn't like the sound of this at all. She did feel some small amount of satisfaction in the fact that so many people had managed to survive for this long, but that would only mean it would be harder to make it into the final few.

"In order to weed out over twenty of you at once, we have decided to set up a very long survival test in order to test your resolve."

Oh, no.

"And, luckily for you all, many of the older and even a few retired Mages have been allotted free time. Many of them have agreed to help us. That means Lightning Phasing is now an option."

Oh no. Without enough mages to perform Lightning Phasing, or the act of teleporting someone or the user through Lightning, the Academy would be limited to what was nearby. However, in this, nearly anywhere within the Lightning Kingdom would hypothetically be available. Exchanging a wide-eyed stare with Ash, Rose turned back toward Master Mekhi.

"The test is going to start tomorrow morning. It will be a challenge of survival. In a forest." At that, some of the students let out protests of outrage. Rose reflected, with no small amount of amusement, that highborns would not be well-equipped to survive in a forest.

"*Quiet!*" Master Mekhi roared. "You may bring anything you have with you. Keep in mind that you will receive a small number of supplies other than what you have with you. Remember that your aim is to survive. You will *all* be here at seven in the morning tomorrow, or you're automatically expelled."

As he walked away, the student body burst into chaos.

* * *

"I'm assuming that, if we can, we're teaming up, right?" Rose asked Ash. She nodded.

"Hey, Dawn, do you—" Rose started. Dawn shook her head, and Rose sighed. It would be comforting to have someone as powerful as

Dawn with them, although Rose admitted they would likely hold her back.

"What about you guys?" Rose asked, waving her fork at Celeste, Venus, and River.

"Personally, as someone who's lived in the wilderness, I don't think large groups are recommended," River murmured. "Rose and Ash can be in a group and I'll go with Celeste and Venus." Rose barely held back her relieved sigh. River was right.

"What supplies do you have, Ash?" Rose asked.

"I have a sword-"

"For survival," Rose reminded her. Ash scrunched up her face, shoving a bite of food into her mouth and chewing rapidly.

"I don't have much," Ash finally admitted. "I didn't think we'd need to have anything to survive with. In this case, I think the only applicable things I have are a backpack and a water bottle."

"That's good. Two less things we'll need. I have a backpack, compass, and a first-aid kit. Oh, and seasoning. Is that why—anyway. Do you have any warm clothes?" Halt had known about this, Rose realized. He had prepared her for it.

"Yeah."

"Even if it rains?"

"I think so, yeah."

"Look through your belongings to see if there's anything else," Rose said. "I'll, uh, think of other things we could use."

After training in the empty courtyard outside, Rose eventually made her way into the library forty minutes before curfew. *Survival, huh?* Stopping in front of the Plants and Animals section, Rose tilted her head to read the titles, picking out two books: *Edible Plants and Animals* and *An Ancient Apothecary's Guidebook,* both relatively thin, recent, and filled with detailed pictures. They'd be useful. After grabbing two or three newest recommendations from Ash, Rose ascended into the flag tower. It was unlikely that the Prince would be there tonight. Most students had actually retired early, forgoing training in the fields for extra rest for the next day. Pushing open the trapdoor, Rose climbed up the rope ladder, humming softly as she closed the trapdoor behind her.

Goddammit.

"And what're you doing here?" Rose asked, placing her books on her desk and opening the trunk in the corner of the room. A few weeks ago, after the Prince had left the study, Rose had found a large collection of dusty blankets within it, likely a gift from some student that had graduated long ago. She had spent the rest of the night carefully dangling them out of the window and shaking them vigorously to get rid of the dust. She smiled to herself, wondering if anyone below had seen. The blankets, all six or seven of them, were now perfectly clean and folded, and Rose yanked them out with joy, creating a nest on the floor onto which she collapsed. Throughout all of this, the Prince watched her with a strange expression on his face.

Cool night air filled the musty study as Rose curled up in the corner and opened the first book and sighed. How had *An Immaculate Conception* gotten here? Putting it aside, Rose opened the next book, *The Letter to the King*, and began reading. It had been so long since she had read a story. Seeing as there would be no homework due in the next couple of days, Rose thought it would be better for her just to relax. A few hours passed in complete silence before the Prince spoke.

"Why are you here? Why don't you just sleep?" the Prince asked, breaking the peaceful silence. Rose glanced up at him, exasperated.

"And why do you care?" Rose noted the Prince's clenched fists and his tense face and shut her book. Their relationship over the past few weeks had been less than pleasant. In order to avoid conflict, they'd stay on opposite ends of the room, each ignoring the existence of the other. It seemed that whenever one opened their mouth, it would escalate into an argument. Rose didn't doubt this would be the same.

"You're so *annoying*," he eventually murmured. It didn't sound grudging, just exhausted. "Always in my brain, not the way Dawn is." He blushed, cutting himself off as if surprised he had said it. "But so familiar. We're too alike."

Staring at him in astonishment, Rose burst into laughter. Them? Alike? The Prince was the absolute pinnacle of perfection, a prodigy in the making from a luxurious, pampered background. Rose was at the very bottom, desperately trying to claw her way to the top, without parents or a family history to speak of. Hell, she didn't even have a real last name. Alike? The only thing they had in common was black hair and insomnia. Oh, Alahna, while it made sense that the Prince knew a Mage's daughter, the fact that he was also smitten with Dawn only made Rose laugh even harder.

"It's not that funny."

"Oh, it is," Rose said. The idea was hilarious, absolutely laughable, but also, somehow, offending. "Trust me, *Prince*, it is. We couldn't be more different, you and I, and I'm not going to complain about it. You and I can't control what you have. I'm going to crush you either way," Rose said. "The difference between us are going to be crystal clear when I do."

Without waiting for a response, Rose descended from the alcove.

Chapter Twelve

"YOUR TASK WILL BE to make it across the forest to your destination on the top of the mountain alive," Master Mekhi explained.

The food Rose had eaten for breakfast sat like a stone in her stomach.

Across a whole mountain. At this moment, Rose wished she had a Fire or Water affinity. Controlling lightning wasn't at all an advantage.

"Luckily for you, you will be receiving other supplies." He pointed toward the servants carrying in the tables which were covered in supplies: tents, compasses, first-aid kits, water purification kits, fire-starting kits, and essential provisions. Everything one would need to survive. "From these tables, you may choose *two*." As quickly as Rose's heart had risen, it fell again. Even with two more supplies from Ash, four wasn't nearly enough to survive in the wilderness.

"Luckily for you, you are allowed to team up in groups. I would like to advise you that the predators who roam these forests are inclined to attack larger groups. To automatically teleport yourself away from fatal attacks or other threats, you may throw down this magical flare," Master Mekhi said, holding up a bright orange, foil-covered ball. "However, doing so will automatically count as a resignation from the Academy."

Silence.

"Get in a line and choose your supplies. Keep in mind that you will be provided with a map and a flare, and those will not be counted within your supplies." As the students immediately rushed toward the tables, pushing and shoving, Ash and Rose eventually secured a spot somewhere near the middle of the line.

"I have bow and arrows, a water bottle, and a backpack," Ash told her. "We have fire too. I can create it."

"Yeah. In that case, we have weapons, and we should be able to find food. I found a book in the library, I'll show you later. We have a compass, map, and first-aid kit. I don't think we need a tent. Do you want—"

"Water purification," Ash interrupted her. Rose nodded.

"Sleeping bags for both of us. It gets cold. We have enough for one more. What else do we need?"

"Some source of light. I couldn't create enough light to travel for more than an hour," Ash said.

"Right," Rose said. "I suspect that fire or torches would be problematic though. They'd attract predators. Let's try to look for an alternative." They were now standing in front of the table, and they each grabbed one of the thin black sleeping bags that reflected body heat. The water purification kit was just a small round glass container filled with tablets, so small for something so important. Just as Rose looked for a reliable source of light, she felt a tap on her shoulder.

"Rose, would this work?" Ash asked. Turning toward Ash, Rose found herself looking at a pair of paper-wrapped glasses. The eyepieces were dark blue, almost like sunglasses, and Rose glanced at Ash quizzically.

"Night vision glasses," she clarified, and Rose grinned.

"Nice job. This is one of our best options, I think," Rose said.

They were one of the first students who were done choosing, and after showing their selections to one of the servants, Rose tore open the paper and handed a pair of goggles to Ash. They split their supplies in case they got separated, careful not to lose a single thing, before leaning against the wall and waiting in silence. The selection took ten more minutes, the most notable event being two highborns getting into a panicked scuffle over a tent.

"Now that you have all chosen your stuff, we can begin," Master Mekhi said. His face was filled with irritation, somehow more so than before. "Please stand in a neat line to be teleported to the testing location. Those who wish to be teleported in groups, please stand side by side." Several mages filed in, and Rose glanced at the Prince and Dawn, both of whom were alone, as well as River, Venus, and Celeste. Emma, the twins, and four other highborns had congregated into one large group, and Rose wondered whether it was because they were stupid or because they were confident enough in their ability to stay alive. Rose and Ash were the sixth group teleported into the forest. The sensation of the lightning hitting her, although strange, wasn't painful.

They were in a forest of tall pines, so close together that they nearly blocked out the sun above, casting a dim but golden light on the soft floor. The hopeful scent in the air was refreshing after a month of the sour scent of sweat and blood, and Rose took a deep breath and swung her backpack onto her shoulders.

The first test had begun.

* * *

The first few hours of this test were monotonous hiking. It was hard exercise, traversing up and down steep slopes, and the pair of girls slowly fell into a rhythm of steady jogging and a brisk walk. By the time they stopped for their first break, the sun was overhead and they had arrived at a small clearing, through which ran a clear, sparkling stream.

"Are we taking a break here?" Ash asked. In response, Rose set her backpack against one of the stones, moving to refill her water bottle before taking out the thin leather book. Flipping it open to the fall section, Rose paused to admire the intricate sketches that covered most of the page, skimming through each plant found in a forest before moving away from the clearing to scout.

"Hey, Ash, if you can, try to shoot something," Rose called. "It's best to just cook some meat now for later, we definitely don't want to attract anything at night."

Eventually, after about half an hour of searching, Rose found a large patch of dandelions, dotted among a large, sunny meadow. After collecting enough to fill her empty leather bag, Rose jogged back to the clearing. Ash had shot a rabbit through its side and was now cleaning it, leaving its head, feet, innards, and fur on the ground. As Ash moved to wash her hands, Rose cleared out the grass from a small circle in the ground before collecting fallen branches and wood from the forest before moving next to Ash and washing the dandelions in the flow of the stream.,

"Where'd you learn to hunt?" Rose asked. The rabbit was cooking on a spit over the crackling fire, emitting a rich, meaty aroma.

"My father participated in hunts with other knights. I started going with him when I was twelve, so I don't have much experience. This was pure luck," Ash explained. "It's not going to taste good without seasoning though." In response, Rose removed the small bottles of salt and pepper, sprinkling them over the meat before turning the spit over. Ash passed Rose a rolled up, pale white sheet of paper, which Rose glanced at quizzically.

"We won't finish the entire rabbit, and we have to wrap the leftovers in something," Ash explained. Rose examined the paper. It was pure white, the inside pale as snow, so Rose ripped her half of the cooked into pieces and wrapped the rabbit tightly inside of them, leaving a hind leg for her to eat. Although it would only stay edible for maybe a day, it was good that they had extra food. They had just stomped out the fire and begun eating the rabbit, which reminded her of chicken with a more earthy taste, when they heard a strange *whomp, whomp* sound from above.

"Hey, Ash, is it just me, or are those wingbeats?" They sat in frozen silence for a few seconds as the sound approached them, getting closer and closer. A rustling sound emanated through the clearing and Rose looked up.

Oh my god.

"RUN!" Rose screamed, snatching the box, bottles, and her backpack up before sprinting toward the vague direction of north, Ash following close behind her. *Don't look behind you, don't look behind you, don't look behind you.* As the wingbeats grew closer, Rose glanced behind her, blanching in fear as the griffin sped up, barreling into Rose with its eagle-talon front legs. Crying out in pain as she smashed into the ground, the griffin pinning her to the ground with its immense weight, Rose summoned lightning from her fingers, thrusting the ball of electricity into its chest. The griffin staggered back, its talons ripping along Rose's chest as it did so, and Rose pushed it off completely, jumping up and away from the griffin before hurling three knives at it. Letting out an angry screech as two of them buried themselves in its side, the griffin lashed out at Ash, barely missing her but cornering her against the tree trunk.

"Hey, stupid, look over here!" Rose shouted. The griffin turned toward her, but as it did so, Ash withdrew her sword and plunged it into its neck. Letting out a screech, it fell to the ground, blood staining the clearing's grass scarlet as it thrashed, twitched, and died, leaving Rose and Ash staring at its body.

"Did we just..." Ash started, then stopped, her mouth open in horror.

"Yeah," Rose replied. Walking forward, Rose bent down, examining the body. A full-grown griffin would have a wingspan of about twenty-four feet and would be seven feet long; this one was smaller, about four feet wide. An adolescent, perhaps.

"Do you think it was attracted by the smell of the meat?" Ash asked, panting as she examined the carcass of the griffin.

"Griffins hunt live prey. They don't eat things that are already dead. It was attracted to us," Rose said, examining her chest. The wound was surprisingly shallow and had already stopped bleeding. The griffin had only just grazed her skin.

"That only makes it worse."

"I know."

"Is your chest okay? Does it need bandages?" Ash asked. Rose shook her head. Taking out a small bottle of antibiotic cream, Rose gingerly dipped her finger inside, carefully spreading a thin layer of the stinging white ointment onto her wound. Her shirt was torn but her cloak from Halt and Blossom had, thankfully, avoided damage.

After settling back down and finishing their meal, Rose and Ash continued in the direction of north, toward their destination, stopping only occasionally to collect edible plants. As the night around them darkened, Rose saw the glimmer of two or three fires around them and sighed.

"We can't stay where there's campfires," Rose said, taking out her glasses and putting them on. "We have to keep going."

"Why?" Ash asked. "Oh, the predators."

"Yeah. If we're too close, we're also in danger."

"I want to see them though! We've already seen an adolescent griffin! What if we meet a full-grown one, or another predator? I'd give anything to see a wyrm—"

"Ash."

Ash sighed, putting on her glasses as she gave Rose an apologetic grin. The sun's light had completely faded now, causing the campfires far in the distance to shine even brighter through the pitch-black forest. The night vision glasses seemed to illuminate the world with a pale blue light. Although Rose couldn't see as clearly as she would during the day, it was light enough so that she could avoid obstacles and continue reading the map, despite the night being thoroughly pitch black. Eventually, after another half hour of walking, the fires had disappeared from their view completely. Rose was sure that there were people ahead of them, but they had had the common sense not to light fires.

"Should we stop for the night?" Ash asked.

"All right. Nearest stream?" Ash nodded. They settled down after just an hour of hiking, Ash laying out her sleeping bags, Rose double and triple checking the food she had foraged with the book before washing it and testing its taste. It was only after she was positive that the food was, indeed, edible that she split it with Ash. There was a small mound of starchy, pale white roots that the book stated had the taste of a potato when roasted, as well as more dandelion and a pale orange berry that was mainly tasteless. Storing away the roots inside the leather bag, Rose finished the berries and most of the dandelions as well as two pieces of rabbit before rolling out her sleeping bag. Just as she was going to crawl inside, Ash spoke.

"We have to keep watch." The idea made Rose want to groan, but she reflected that even if she would've fallen asleep, she'd have woken up not much later.

"I'll take the first watch," Rose butted in.

"Are you sure? You're injured."

"Nah, it's such a small wound that it doesn't really matter."

Soon, with the owls far up in the canopy of trees beginning to softly hoot, Ash was asleep. Her deep breathing was soothing. Even so, Rose found herself becoming twitchy and jumpy. A pair of large possum eyes blinked at her from a bush and Rose jumped, unsheathing her daggers, the motion causing the small animal to leap away into the forest.

It was going to be a long night.

* * *

"Rose! *Wake up!*"

Groaning, Rose screwed up her eyes, turning over inside her sleeping bag, drowsy. It had been three in the morning when her eyelids had gotten too heavy to bear, and she had shaken awake Ash with the instructions to wake her up at seven.

"Wake up, now!"

What was the hurry? Turning over, Rose took a deep breath and began to cough harshly, the scent of smoke filling her nostrils and choking her lungs.

What the hell?

Opening her eyes, Rose felt them water as she stared up at a wall of blinding fire consuming the trees about half a mile away from their location.

"What the hell?" Rose asked, pushing herself to her feet. "Is that a wildfire?" Clumsily rolling up her sleeping bag and forcing it into her backpack, Rose swung it onto her back before following Ash, who was already sprinting north. The wildfire was spreading quickly and Rose could feel its heat, as if it were biting at her heels. *Surrender or run?*

Rose kept running.

Discomfort morphed into distress. Nausea began to sweep through her. The smoke irritated her lungs, each breath sending pain through her throat and chest, and her eyes were swollen and puffy, tears leaking out as she blinked. However, even as Rose acknowledged that this wildfire might be the end, she felt a cool wind stirring, brushing her face, blowing against her as she ran.

Wind.

"Keep on running!" Rose choked out. "Don't stop! There's wind!"

It didn't take long for the wind to get stronger and stronger, pushing against the spreading wildfire, eventually turning its spread south. As the air finally began to smell less like smoke, Rose and Ash slowed to a walk. Collapsing to her knees, Rose coughed and vomited up what little was in her stomach, the taste of smoke and bile in her mouth causing her to nearly retch again as she stood up and wiped her mouth. She allowed herself a small mouthful of water to rinse out her mouth, erasing the taste of smoke before gulping down several mouthfuls of water, sighing as the ache in her throat subsided.

"Who was stupid enough to leave a campfire lit?" Rose asked, gargling a mouthful of water and spitting it out.

"I wonder if it was on purpose," Ash said, only half-joking. They watched, perched on a pair of large boulders, as the wind spread the fire farther and farther away from them. The areas they had run through had been burned until the trees were pitch black and crumbling, and the fire was beginning to abate there. It was by pure luck, Rose realized that they were still in the Academy. If not for the fact that the sudden wind had blown south, Rose and Ash would both be dead.

"Did you get burned at all?"

"Nah. Did you?" Ash shook her head. The sun had completely risen now, and Rose glanced up at it, adrenaline fading from her body, leaving her body feeling heavy and drowsy.

"Is it okay with you if I get some more sleep?" Rose asked. Ash glanced up at the sky and shook her head. "In the meantime, find a stream and some food, all right? I'm just going to... go to sleep." It was still far too hot for a campfire or a sleeping bag, so Rose merely laid it out beneath her drifting into slumber.

* * *

The rest of the day was dead silent. Most of the large animals seemed to have been scared off by the fire, and while Ash had somehow shot a large duck, Rose had barely seen any other animals around. After wasting three hours that morning, Rose and Ash had picked up the pace, leaving them both exhausted.

"We're almost a third of the way there," Rose told Ash, who groaned.

"A third? Only? We're going to have to survive four more days up here?"

"Yeah. Maybe, if we're lucky, we could make it in three more days." The gradual change in altitude was already becoming noticeable, and Rose had spent almost twice as much time foraging for food. After deciding that lighting a fire today was worth the risk, especially because of the silence around them, Rose and Ash roasted the duck over the fire. It was enormous and fatty, but the cooked meat would only last a few days at most. After wrapping up the duck, Rose motioned for Ash to sleep. She was exhausted, eyelids drooping shut even as she ate, and Rose was still mostly awake.

A few hours had passed when Rose first heard movement. There was a rustle and a crack of a branch, and Rose had her daggers out within seconds, her body crouching, tense and ready to spring at the direction of the sound.

"Rose! It's just me!" someone whispered. The familiar, rough voice was hoarser than ever, and Rose only tensed up further as he walked into the circle of firelight. Rose had been perched on a fallen log, and the Prince collapsed to his knees. Illuminated by the firelight, Rose could see his ruined form. His arms were covered in burns and blisters, his sleeves burned on the edges and torn roughly, the corners of his cloak charred black. It seemed that his shirt had caught on fire, his chest area bright red and shiny. Rose sighed as she pulled out her first-aid kit.

"I better get some repayment for helping you," Rose said as she pulled out five or six non-stick pads, medical tape, and antibacterial ointment. "What happened to you, anyway?"

"I was stuck on the other side of the fire and going through it fine, but I found Dawn. She collapsed because of the smoke, and I couldn't just leave her—"

"Yeah, okay, lover boy." Rose interrupted him. The Prince looked away.

"Carrying and protecting both of us from the smoke and flames sucked up my magical endurance pretty badly. I eventually ran out but was near the end, so I pushed on. I was lucky the wind started blowing and I emerged next to a stream, or these burns would be worse." Rose winced as she heard his dry, gravelly voice, and barely hesitated before passing him her water bottle. After rinsing off the wounds, Rose covered his burns with her antibacterial cream, Rose wrapped them loosely in bandages. Through all of this, he was completely silent.

"Take off your shirt," Rose told him. He complied, wincing as the shirt peeled away from the burn, and Rose stopped in utter surprise.

Scars.

They were *everywhere*: burn scars, gashes that were jagged enough that they might have come from a knife. It was easy enough to justify them as numerous training accidents. But the lash marks across his chest and back... Rose knew them all too well. The Prince cleared his throat, and Rose tilted her head back, staring up at him, silently asking for an answer.

"Are you going to help me or not?"

Sighing, Rose silently applied the bandages.

"You should be good now," Rose murmured. "Do you have any spare clothes? This shirt's done." The Prince shook his head, and Rose noticed his lack of supplies. Had he lost them all?

"Uh, do you have any weapons?" He shook his head again. Exasperatedly, Rose dug through her backpack, pulling out her sweater and the extra dagger and tossing them toward him. He fumbled with them, withdrawing the dagger from the sheath with an astonished look in his eyes. Rose watched worriedly as he put the sweater on.

"If you somehow destroy it, I'm killing you. Give them both back." Lowering herself to the grass floor and leaning against the stone, Rose yawned and reassembled her supplies. *Why was he still here?*

"Uh, are you going to stay? Because if you are, you can take the rest of the watch. Either that or you leave." The Prince jerked away, one of his fists clutching the fabric of the sweater, and Rose watched in trepidation as he rolled the sleeves to his shoulders before retreating to the edge of the firelight.

"Why are you being so... kind? After all I've said and done."

Rose rolled her eyes. "Because I'm not a jerk. And you better give me that sweatshirt back," Rose growled. He opened his mouth, likely to make some snide comment, but Rose cut him off. "And if you're going to leave, please do so quickly. Your sacred highborn scent might attract another griffin or something."

He opened his mouth, as if inclined to ask about the griffin or to retort with a comment, but after staring at Rose, he walked away, disappearing like a ghost in the undergrowth. The last thing she saw before he disappeared were those strange eyes. Even after he left, Rose couldn't shake the feeling but felt that she'd *seen* those eyes somewhere else, where everything had been safe and warm. She let the thought linger for a few seconds, trying to remember where else she could've met the Prince before sighing and turning back toward the campfire, resuming her silent vigilance.

* * *

They were traveling the next day, just after a meager lunch, when the next calamity struck.

"Drop your weapons, lowborns!" Emma's voice pierced through the undergrowth and Ash cursed, letting her sword clatter to the ground. Pulling her long sleeves further down to conceal the daggers sheathed on her forearms, Rose made a show of dropping the knives on her belt to the forest floor.

"What do you want?" Rose shouted as seven or eight highborns stepped out of the bushes, some holding bows and arrows pointed in their direction, others with their hands grasping the handles of daggers and swords. Glancing among them, Rose bit her lip and seethed as she saw Dawn and the Prince among them. The twins, though, were nowhere in sight. In fact, none of the highborns were members of Emma's usual group.

"We're eliminating some scum," Emma said. "It's better for you to do it now, so that the Masters can focus on the people with actual talent. Be a good lowborn and throw down that flare, or we'll be forced to treat you like the other ones." Glancing at Ash, who was slowly pulling the flare out of her front pocket, Rose made a minute shake of her head. There had to be a way out of this.

"Scum? Really? I don't think we're scum to you. Maybe you feel *threatened* by us?" Despite the fear flooding through her, Rose forced her voice to remain calm and conversational and her face to show the slightest bit of amusement. Ash glanced at her, and Rose motioned for her to stay quiet. "Feeling threatened by the lowborns, huh? Ganging up on a few of us *scum*, huh? How proud do you think your mom will be?"

Emma's eyes darkened, her hand tightening around her sword's hilt. Rose had hit a sensitive point.

"'How'd you manage to get through the first assessment?' They'd ask, and you'd say, 'oh, yeah, that was scary. Halfway through, we saw a slave. One of them was shorter than us! Me and my seven friends, you see, we were kind of afraid of them, so we ganged up on them. A tough fight, that was.'"

"Why you—"

Rose smirked as Emma hurtled toward her, sword outstretched in a reckless attack driven by anger. She obviously wasn't expecting Rose to fight back, so when Rose ducked underneath her sword, her eyes widened in surprise. Her daggers slipped out of their sheathes, and Rose flipped it in her hand, slamming the pommel into Emma's temple. She went out like a light. As Rose turned around, she felt heat on her back and ducked down, crying out in pain as flames grazed over her arm. There were two people Rose remembered used fire, and the other girl was still holding her bow, staring at Rose, astonished. That left the Prince. Turning toward him, Rose stared at his outstretched hands, trying to keep the betrayal from her face. As the students finally began moving, rushing toward Rose with their weapons, Rose dodged past the first attack, withdrawing one of her throwing knives. *I can't hit him in the chest. That's my sweatshirt.* Two knives sailed toward him, one barely grazing his arm, the other imbedding itself deep in his calf. Crying out in pain, the Prince fell to the dirt, his face filled with astonishment, as if he hadn't expected Rose to fight back. Rose stared impassively down at him, planted a calf on his injury, and dug her heel in, making him cry out in pain. That made them all— Ash, highborns, and Dawn—stop.

Rose knelt down, dragged the Prince up by the collar, and held her dagger against his throat.

"If you make another move toward us," Rose said softly, "I won't kill him. But I'll marr him so badly that he won't be able to speak, let alone rule." Dawn stared at her, mouth open in shock. "Your magic won't be able to make it in time. Now. Step away from Ash. Drop your weapons."

They complied. Rose couldn't help it. The feeling of satisfaction and power that surged through her made her smile.

"Now, to eliminate some *scum*," she spat. "All of you except Dawn, throw your flares down. *Now*." They hesitated, looking at each other and then the Prince. He opened his mouth to speak and Rose dug the dagger in further, letting blood begin to trickle from the wound on his neck. "Well?" Rose asked. Ash moved to stand beside her.

"Rose, maybe... maybe don't hurt him," Ash whispered. Rose didn't respond.

"Do it *now*," Rose said, raising his voice. When the highborns remained still, she lifted her dagger and slashed a shallow wound across his arm. He didn't cry out, but one of the highborns did. Five flares went off in quick succession, leaving Dawn, the Prince, and Emma, unconscious on the ground. The feeling of *utter satisfaction* racing through her veins would scare her if it didn't feel so good.

"Well?" Rose asked Dawn. "Are you gonna attack me?" Dawn merely stared at Rose with this look of utter incredulity, although, Rose noticed, she was smiling.

"No," Dawn eventually said. "And were you *really* going to hurt him?"

"Nah," Rose said, and the Prince let out a huff of incredulity. "Well, maybe just a little." She lowered the Prince to the ground, noting that it was her dagger still strapped on his belt. "Take good care of my dagger!" Rose said cheerfully to the Prince. Dawn stared between them, nonplussed, before turning away and sprinting away, leaving them behind. "C'mon, Ash."

They left with no small amount of glee.

* * *

The second they were out of earshot, Ash turned to Rose with the *biggest grin Rose had ever seen.*

"Oh my *Gods*, Rose, you were *awesome*, I swear you were like Bakha *incarnate*, that was *amazing, five whole highborns—*"

"It wasn't... it wasn't *that* awesome, and definitely not Godly," Rose said, shoving Ash lightly. She was also grinning, though, so widely that it hurt.

"It's too bad Emma was knocked unconscious," Ash said. "We might've been able to make her surrender too. But what was that comment about the dagger?"

"Oh," Rose said. "The Prince turned up last night after the fire on my watch and asked me for help. I treated his burns and gave him a weapon, and, well, we know how that went."

"Oh," Ash said. She paused, brow furrowed as if in deep thought. "Hey, Rose?"

"Yeah?"

"So, I have an idea. What if we, like, screw over the Prince and Emma even more?"

Ash explained in a hushed whisper her plan to Rose, even though no one was around them. She had to admit that it was *amazing*. Risky, but amazing. The Prince and Emma had probably stayed back to tend to their wounds. In fact, the prince was probably slowed down because of his limp. If a wildfire had held them back once, why not do it again? This would be the ultimate, most powerful form of revenge she could think of, and Emma would know it was directed at her. It would be far too risky if not for the howling winds tearing at the branches, still blowing south. Rose was willing to take the bet that it wouldn't change anytime soon. This wildfire wouldn't be a campfire accident.

After refilling their water bottles and gathering up their supplies, Ash and Rose began. Carefully manipulating lightning between her fingers, Rose climbed up a pine tree, watching as the lightning made contact with a large clump of resin. It quickly caught on fire, and Rose quickly climbed down, watching as the tree became engulfed with flame before repeating the process about twenty times. Ash was kneeling on the ground, fire flaring from her fingers as the undergrowth began to burn.

It was glorious, absolute revenge.

"So what do we do now?" Ash asked, watching in wonder as the wildfire traveled away from them, blown by the wind toward the Prince's direction.

"Now? We run."

* * *

It had been five hours, and Rose couldn't wipe the mischievous grin from her face. The fire had indeed been blown south, blocking off entrance from all those stuck behind it. Rose hoped that River's group had made it safely through. The scent of smoke had spread to where Rose and Ash were, even ten miles away, and they could still see the fire burning in the distance, a hand-sized patch of red and orange that Rose would never get tired of watching.

But they had bigger problems than that fire.

With the elevation as high as it was, the weather had become chilly, wind biting at Rose's exposed skin as she dug roots from the dirt ground. The pine trees around them had become short and scrawny and a barely visible blanket of fog had descended upon the air.

"Can you find any food?" Rose asked Ash. She had been foraging for almost an hour and had only found a small handful of starchy, potato-like roots. They were immensely lucky the duck had managed to keep until now, but it would start rotting tomorrow.

"None. I can only find a very small stream. It's just barely trickling."

"Set a bottle against the flow of the stream to collect water," Rose told her. Clenching her fists, Rose felt her fingernails dig into her palms, her brow furrowed with worry. They had only amassed enough water for two bottles that day, and with the hard exercise they were doing, a bottle of water a day wasn't enough. Ash started a fire. Carefully laying out the sleeping bags, Rose huddled next to it, tucking the roots into the wood beneath the fire before taking out the last pieces of duck from her backpack. Their dinner that night was the last of the vegetables they had found the day before and a small helping of meat.

Rose and Ash were covered, head to toe, in grime, soot, and dirt. Even so, as Rose sat down on her sleeping bag to take first watch, the woods around them were subdued. The only sound she could hear was the occasional string of birdsong and a rare, soft rustle in the undergrowth that could only be a small animal. Were predators just less common at higher altitudes, or had the wildfire caused their absence?

The watch was quiet. Peaceful. Almost as if she were stargazing with Halt instead of running for her life.

* * *

Rose woke up with wetness on her face.

Groaning, Rose crawled out of her soaking wet sleeping bag, which luckily had kept most of the water outside. The scent of smoke had vanished, replaced by the fresh scent of rain.

"Seriously?" Ash murmured from within the sleeping bag. Rose glanced toward the wildfire, disappointed. Its red-orange glow had been completely extinguished.

As they had traveled, the trees had grown fewer and fewer in number and were now completely gone. The earth beneath them was rough and dry, supporting only shrubby undergrowth, and jogging grew more difficult. They slowed down to walk more and more frequently, their pace slowing to a snail's crawl. Neither of them had had a full meal at any time in the forest, and it was beginning to show. All signs of the tender edible vegetables were gone. *One more day*, Rose thought as she set up for the night and checked her map.

They had arrived at Emerald Lake.

The day had been quiet. They hadn't seen a single other living creature but for a lone highborn, who had withdrawn when she saw them. The Emerald Lake took after its namesake, shining emerald green under the setting sun. The color was caused by a buildup of algae in its surface, and while it was beautiful, Rose would have traded it with drinkable water in a moment.

"Can you find any food?" Rose asked. Ash shook her head. "We don't have any food left. I can't find any water, can you?" Ash shook her head again, and Rose let out a slew of filthy curses. They had devoured the last of the roots today, and both of them had only had about half a bottle of water to last the entire day. Sighing, Rose curled up into a ball, shivering as the cold, biting wind pierced through the sleeping bag.

They had forgone a watch. The area around them was desolate and empty, void of both predator and prey.

It was pitch black before Rose fell asleep.

* * *

When Rose woke up, she realized that they were in trouble.

There was a dry spot on her tongue that wouldn't moisten, no matter how much she swallowed. Her head pounded with pain. Hunger lanced through her stomach as she walked, step by step, and her fingers and toes felt numb with cold. There was no water, no food, no shelter. Rose was cold, thirsty, and hungry, yet she could still persevere, even with her flagging strength. Ash was a different matter altogether. She was swaying with every step, half-leaning on Rose, who was forced to half-drag her across the ground, both backpacks slung on her other shoulder. They had lightened their loads, abandoning their sleeping bags, and yet the backpacks still felt like a stone on Rose's shoulders as she walked. Every step was a monumental effort. She dragged her feet across the ground, focused on just the next hill, just the next slope, just the next stone.

But in the distance, just as she was going to give up all hope and throw down the flare, she saw a small dot, far in the distance. *An illusion?*

"Do you see that, Ash?" Rose croaked out, lifting a heavy arm to point at the dot in the distance.

"Hmm?" Ash murmured lucidly, her eyes half shut. Rose slapped her across the face, causing her to jerk awake, "What was that for?"

"Look, Ash! You see it too, right? The dot?"

The destination.

"Yeah. I see it. So... we're almost there?" Ash mumbled. Her eyes shut, and before Rose could stop her, she slipped to the ground. "Good... I'll just... sleep first. Okay?"

"Ash! *Ash!* Come on, don't faint on me!"

No response.

Rose didn't dare kneel down. She was afraid she would keel over. Lifting up Ash's body and throwing it over her shoulder, abandoning

Ash's backpack entirely. *Her sword*, Rose realized. *Her sword is important*. She strapped it to her belt. Rose nearly collapsed because of the added weight, but turned back toward the black dot.

She was so close. Rose took one step forward, then another, each sending waves of pain and exhaustion through her body. As she walked, she saw it become bigger and bigger. The first time she collapsed was when she could see its corners. Pushing herself up to her feet, Rose continued walking. She had to.

She could see the lights from the square. It wasn't a square, actually. It was *huge*, a rectangle. A small castle. It was warm, welcoming, glowing golden in the thick fog. There was fog around her? When had that happened?

The door. Windows. She could see it all.

Ash's limp body was slipping off her, but the doorknob was right there. In her hand. Rose couldn't remember grabbing it, but she turned the knob anyway. Took a single step inside. As the warm scent of bread filled her nostrils, black dots swarmed her vision. *I got here. It's enough, right?*

Rose collapsed to the ground and knew no more.

Chapter Thirteen

"WE ATTACK TODAY, MY DARK PRINCE."

"Already? Your Majesty, we might—"

"Prince. Please."

"All right."

* * *

The first thing Rose registered was her pounding head.

Groaning, Rose opened her eyes. She was in a small room, and as she looked to her right, she saw Ash, still and silent on the bed.

"You all right?" The soft, subdued voice of River came from beside her. "Ouch, headache. Here, have some water."

Rose grasped the cold glass of water and gulped it all down, sighing as the headache eased a little. She pushed herself up, sitting up against the pillows. Either someone had given her a thorough bath or they had used magic.

"It was magic," River commented, and Rose glanced at him, brow furrowed. "Uh, yeah. Here, there's food." When Rose looked to the side and saw the plate on the bedside table, all other thoughts left her head. It was covered with rolls, sausages, butter, and sliced cucumbers.

Pushing aside all other thoughts, Rose took the plate and began to wolf down the food, buttering the rolls lavishly and clamping a sausage inside before biting into it eagerly. The sausage was bursting with flavor, salty and spicy with a hint of sweetness, a stark contrast to the bland saltiness of the meat they'd eaten.

"Do you know where the wildfires came from?" River asked. Rose stopped eating and glanced at him guiltily. "We got injured from the first one, but we were in front of the second one. Where do you think that one came from?"

"I... did it?" Rose hesitantly told him. River's mouth dropped open and he stared at her, wide-eyed. Nervously, Rose put down her fork, opening her mouth to apologize. River laughed.

"Why'd you do that?" he asked. Rose looked into his eyes. They were the most brilliant blue she had ever seen in *anything*, even the Prince's eyes, as if someone had placed the essence of water within them. It was no wonder he was a Water user. Grinning, Rose told him the entire story.

"And you sent a knife at him? At the *Prince*? And then *threatened his life*? You do realize he could probably pull some strings and send you to a dungeon for that, right?" River asked, shock in his voice. He was smiling.

"I helped him, and he decided to attack me. He's not the type to pull strings like that," Rose said, accidentally spitting out a piece of chewed sausage as she spoke.

"Shut your mouth. That's disgusting," River told her. Rose laughed.

"Have you seen them? The Prince, I mean? How long have I been out?" Rose asked after a few minutes of silence. She placed the plate back on her nightstand, sighing with satisfaction, her appetite finally sated.

"Yeah, they just arrived a few hours ago. It's nine in the morning," River told her. "The Prince's leg was really badly injured. He was limping. I was actually wondering who did it to him. Dawn, I think, broke off from their group again. Oh, but Emma—" River broke off, snickering. "She was fine, but *mad*. At you, I'm assuming. Very angry that some of her belongings were half-destroyed by the fire."

Rose laughed. "How many students have quit?"

"We have eighty-eight left that haven't quit, counting the thirty or so still in the forest."

Rose sighed and pushed herself off the bed. Her backpack, she noticed, was leaning against her bed, and whoever had switched her into clean clothes had also left her daggers and forearm sheaths on the bedside table.

* * *

The food at the Academy was, all in all, perfectly acceptable fare: nutritional, filling, and not unpleasant to the taste. But this was something altogether different. The students sat at a huge, rectangular table, Mages and Masters sitting toward the front and students sitting behind them. Spread across the table, almost like a feast, sat dozens of different dishes: pasta, six or seven different types of meat, bread, soups, salads, and types of food Rose had never seen or imagined. The aroma of chocolate filled the room, and Rose looked toward the servants staggering in, arms shaking under the weight of enormous chocolate cakes. Frowning, Rose moved toward them, helping them move the dishes onto the table before sitting back down. Rose was leaning back in her chair, satisfied and full, when a single student staggered into the hall.

Something about her was *wrong*.

Rose had never seen her, ever, even when training. Examining her, Rose flinched back when she saw her eyes: their entirety, even the whites, were absolute, midnight black. Hurriedly standing up, Rose unsheathed her daggers, yanking Ash to her feet by her arm.

And then she burst into tendrils of shadow and night.

There was silence, absolute silence, as the tendrils rose into the air and hurtled toward them.

"RUN!" the Prince's voice screamed. "Don't just stand there, run, *run, RUN!* If they touch you, you *die*!"

Rose grabbed Ash's hand and sprinted from the room. The shadows seemed to be alive, a writhing mass of destruction, and adrenaline rushed through her veins as she sprinted up a flight of stairs. Ash whimpered in horror, glancing behind her only to see a splatter of blood arc across the stairs, but Rose yanked her away. They sprinted toward their room, but what good would that do? The tendrils brushed her shoulders, and Rose shivered, pushing herself to sprint faster, yanking Ash with her. Ash stumbled, falling to the floor, and Rose cursed. Turning around, Rose barely had time to process the shadow reaching toward Ash before she threw herself in its way. It wrapped around her ankle and Rose shoved Ash back to her feet, smashing at the tendril with the dagger only for it to go through the darkness.

"Rose!"

"Go get help, you idiot!" Another tendril reached toward Rose, wrapped around her arm, and Rose thrashed away. Just as she felt the shadows consume her, a hand grabbed the back of her shirt and fire flared, tearing her away from them.

"In here!" the Prince shouted, yanking Rose toward another flight of stairs. Rose followed him blindly, stumbling down the stairs, and they entered a large room where a group of six or seven Mages had constructed an orb of protection. *Safety.* Ducking through the shield, Rose watched as the shadows that had been pursuing her bounced harmlessly off the surface. They were safe. Turning around, Rose looked around her.

"Ash?"

She was nowhere in sight.

"Ash. *Ash!*" Rose shouted. When the Prince had yanked her away, what had happened to Ash?

"ASH!"

She was alone. They had been one of the only ones on the staircase. She was *alone*. How would she survive?

"I have to go out for her."

"Lowborn. Calm down. The Mages may be busy with the shield, but more will come soon. They'll help her," the Prince said.

"It might already be too late!" Rose hissed. Shoving the Prince aside, Rose sprinted back through the shield and the shadows followed her. *Blood.* It was all over the staircase that she had left Ash in, covering the walls and floor. How bad had the injury been, to have bled this much? Following the bloodstains, Rose tracked them all the way to an abandoned room. The shadows seemed to pause, writhing in a mass around her, as if encouraging her to open the door.

Ash had been bait. Whoever had attacked wanted Rose.

She pushed open the door. Ash was on the floor, unconscious, blood bleeding out of a gash on her stomach.

"Ash!" Rose shouted, dropping to her knees next to the girl. The gash was deep, gushing blood in arcing spurts, but as she reached for the girl to pick her up and run, she heard deep laughter from the wall.

Turning around, Rose saw the figure and collapsed to her knees.

His voice wasn't what someone would expect from a being of pure, unadulterated darkness. It was soft, warm, smooth and sweet as honey, but unlike Ezra's in that there was no compassion. No warmth. It was that empty shell of saccharine sweetness that left behind an unpleasant, persistent aftertaste.

"I have met you at last, *Rose...*" he hissed. Rose couldn't see anything about him other than pure darkness; his form was consumed by it, almost as if it were the darkness that wielded him and not the other way around. A single name came to her like a bolt of lightning, a dreadful realization that made Rose's heart stop.

The Dark Sorcerer.

"Who are you? How do you know my name?" Rose hissed, moving over Ash's body and shielding her with her body. "I won't let you touch Ash."

"Don't worry. She won't die," the man murmured. "What is relevant now is that *I finally have you.*"

"You're the one responsible for the attack," Rose growled. "What do you *want*?"

"You."

As he said that word, shadows, icy cold and smooth as silk, crept over Rose's skin. She shuddered. The shadows wrapped around her. As she opened her mouth to cry for help, one wrapped around her mouth and dragged her to the wall. She writhed, screamed, and struggled, but the shadows were oblivious to her attempts at escape.

Magic.

Rose let herself go still, pulling out her magic. As the lightning formed on her hand, two shadows wrapped around each of her hands, tips landing on her wrists. Rose flinched as she felt the shadows wrest away the control she had had over the magic, causing the lightning to fade. The shadows on her wrists didn't stop there. They took her magic almost instantaneously. Rose felt her body weaken immediately, as if her magical stamina, carefully built up over the course of months, was nothing.

Her body fell still, her vision was growing black around the edges. *Ash*, Rose thought desperately. She was going to bleed out. *What would she do if Ash also died too?*

The shadows stopped.

Rose forced her eyes open, watching in astonishment as light flooded into the room. Even as her vision blurred, Rose lifted her head and looked at the door. Five figures. Five robes. But instead of the outlined, plain black robes a Mage would wear, they were bright with color, one aqua blue, one silver-white, one white-blue, one verdant green, one scarlet red. They stood in a line, staring at the girls on the ground, the mass of shadows creeping on the wall, the figure of darkness standing in front of them. Crystal, the Water Sorcerer. Aura, the Wind Sorcerer. Erik, the Nature Sorcerer. Aiden, the Fire Sorcerer. Audra, the Lightning Sorcerer. The Five Sorcerers stood, prepared to go head-to-head with the figure of darkness.

We're saved.

With a wave of her hand, Aura surrounded the girls with a shield of hard air. The man of shadows hissed, tendrils staying absolutely still for a tenth of a second before surging at the Five Sorcerers. Audra's hand outstretched and twisted, and in a quarter of a second, lightning crackled through the air; a mass larger than Rose's entire body twisting, morphing into what would undoubtedly be a powerful attack. Even as Rose watched, however, the lightning melted into Audra's body, creating so much static her hair stuck straight up. Lightning morphed, twisted onto her arms and legs, creating enormous gauntlets of lightning that formed five claws on its end.

She vanished.

The Dark Sorcerer was struck so hard he flew into the wall, melting into the shadows. Audra's body was glowing with so much electricity Rose could feel the static from where she knelt. *Wasn't it painful?*

"Behind us," Aura hissed, and as shadow twisted and lunged toward them, Audra brought her arm up, summoning a wall of lightning that melted away the darkness. But as Rose turned toward Ash, she saw a tiny tendril tapping the length of the shield.

Oh.

A scream escaped her throat as the shadow paused, then reared back and cracked the shield open, shattering it completely. As shadows surged toward her, Rose unsteadily shot to her feet, ducking underneath the first attack. The tendrils had sharpened into daggers. *Was he trying to kill Rose? Why?* Knocking aside the second dagger with her own, Rose grunted as a dagger flew into her side. The explosion of pain caused her to loosen her grip on her dagger, which fell to the floor with a clatter, yanked out of her hand by a tendril of shadow. A blade of shadow was coming her way, toward her heart, and Rose cursed as she felt her feet pinned to the floor by shadow. Yanking out the dagger in her side, Rose pressed a hand to her side and deflected the next blade of darkness with her own. The tendril tightened around her ankle, yanking her onto the ground, and she felt it pulling at her leg, yanking it forward, until the bone cracked with a gruesome sound. Rose screamed.

It was over.

As it had been, and as it was now. Rose, on the ground, defenseless, clutching Ash to her chest, praying that she wouldn't die.

I'm still not enough.

And, finally, the Five Sorcerers intervened.

A wave of fire swept aside the daggers, only barely tickling over Rose's skin, and Rose watched as everything stopped. The shadows melted away and the Dark Sorcerer

"Curse you... The Five, once again... curse you." His voice was so soft and deceptively smooth that it hurt. "You of all people to interrupt... I cannot fight you here. There will be far too much destruction."

As he spoke, his shadow grew dimmer and dimmer.

"One day, we will meet again, and that day, the Five Sorcerers will fall. You," he said, turning towards Rose. She flinched back, acutely aware of his gaze on her skin. "You will be joining me soon."

And he disappeared, leaving behind suffocating silence.

Crystal rushed toward Rose, blue healing energy flashing on her hands.

"Ash... first..." Rose murmured. The pain in her leg was overwhelming, but Ash's face was pale and there was *so much blood*. Erik rushed toward her, hands wreathed in beautiful glowing green energy. Hovering over the wound on Ash's stomach, the green energy melted into it, the jagged edges stitching together. He moved his hands over Ash's chest, continuing to heal, and the color returned to her face and skin.

"I'll have to set the bone," Crystal warned, and before Rose nodded, she had twisted her bone back into place, causing Rose to bite down on her lip with pain. However, in a few seconds, as Crystal placed a hand covered in glowing blue energy on the spot of the break, Rose felt the pain ebb away into soft tides of comfort. Slowly, her other wounds stitched together. When Crystal removed her hands, Rose felt like, physically, nothing had happened.

Her hands were still shaking.

"Here, take some water," Erik said, summoning an empty glass that he handed to Crystal. Quickly filling the glass with water, Crystal handed it to Rose, who drank the water eagerly. The Five Sorcerers all watched her as she drank, and Rose examined them from the corner of her eyes. *Crystal*. Porcelain white skin, silvery-white hair that was like moonlight on snow, slender hands, and plain brown eyes that looked gentle, kind. *Aura*. She was blond and fair-skinned, with stunning gray-black eyes, with a stature that seemed more threatening than graceful, muscled limbs contrasting her relatively slim form. *Aidan*. Dark skin, warm brown eyes, he was a large muscled man with chestnut brown hair. He looked like he gave excellent hugs. *Erik*. He was tall, slightly muscled, and stern, with dirty blond hair and brown eyes. *Audra*. She looked like a spirit, her figure reminding Rose slightly of Dawn, and her eyes gleamed like stars in the night as she gazed at the girls on the ground. Eventually, Crystal spoke.

"So, let's talk about—"

"How *stupid* it was to barge into this classroom alone? Why didn't you get help?" Aura shouted at Rose. She winced, pushing herself to her feet, half-expecting splintering pain to shoot through her leg. There was nothing.

"Give the girl a break," Crystal murmured, putting a hand on Rose's shoulder. "I'll take you to the infirmary."

"Take Ash to the infirmary. I don't need to go," Rose insisted. Crystal hesitated, opening her mouth to argue with her, but must've seen the stubborn look in Rose's eyes. She nodded in agreement.

As Aidan picked Ash up and the Five Sorcerers filed out of the room, Rose looked back just once. She didn't know why. Maybe it was to check for a lingering shadow, or just to see the wrecked wall, but what she saw made her pause. On the wall across from her, two jagged words appeared across the wall in a black, jagged script that quickly melted away as soon as she saw it.

I'm Sorry.

* * *

"*Fool!*" he screamed. "You have failed me. You *failed* to kill the Satori in the Academy. You *failed* to keep out the Five Sorcerers long enough for me to take the girl. You *failed me*."

"Your Highness, I'm sorry-"

The Dark Sorcerer laughed. "'I'm sorry' doesn't fix your mistake, *Prince*. Look. I've tolerated your actions for a very, very long time. If you don't stop loving this girl, I do not know how we can continue this."

"Why?"

The Dark Sorcerer sighed. "Love is only used against you. You know this."

"I... understand. I'm sorry. I don't know how to... how to stop. But I will, I swear it."

The Dark Prince melted into shadows. The Dark Sorcerer leaned against the rough wooden wall, briefly scanning the dark-cloaked dirty alley in which he stood in for watchers. Just as he was about to teleport away, something brushed against his leg. Whirling around, darkness already thrashing, the Dark Sorcerer paused in surprise as he met the eyes of two children. Their clothes were torn and tattered and their faces were covered in dirt, and they stared in trepidation at the cracked wooden ball that was now resting against the wall. Sighing, the Dark Sorcerer picked up the ball and smoothed over its worn surface with magic, renewing its perfectly round form and tossing it back, leaving behind a single crack on its surface.

The children shouted and the Dark Sorcerer grimaced in annoyance before melting away into shadows. The sun had disappeared completely, leaving behind only darkness. A few golden coins, pulled from the crack in the wooden ball, glinted in the last rays of light. The children's dirty hands clenched around them, and that light was, too, extinguished.

* * *

By some stroke of luck, no one had died that night. Those who hadn't made it to the destination before the attack had been automatically passed, and the students were teleported back to the safety of the Academy that same night.

Rose didn't care.

She lay in her bed, staring up at the ceiling, her heart filled with dread. That man, wielding darkness with such a honey-sweet voice, was he the Dark Sorcerer? Rose shook her head. That couldn't be possible. The Dark Sorcerer was *dead*, killed by the Five Sorcerers from so long ago. He was *dead*, and even he couldn't come back from the dead. Had someone else figured out how to acquire the powers of darkness? Why would they want to become another Dark Sorcerer?

But then again, there was no other explanation. There was no other individual, she reflected, who had discovered the secret of Dark Magic. For all the world knew, Dark Magic could grant its user immortality. The way he spoke—*The Five, again*—as if he had fought them once before. As if some past Five had defeated him. The Dark Sorcerer—cruel, aloof, heartless evil—was back.

Yet that message. *"I'm sorry."* Who had written it? An unwilling accomplice? Slave? Child? Had they attacked Rose and Ash against their own will?

Ash.

You couldn't protect her.

Rose's fists clenched around her blankets as she took a deep breath, fighting back the panic writhing through her mind. *I couldn't protect her.* Even after all this training, Rose was still weak. Still unable to become the hero of justice she'd envisioned in her mind.

I'll do anything for this power, if only it means I can protect them, Rose thought, staring up at the ceiling. *I'll do anything not to go through something like that again. I'll do anything.*

That night, after curfew, Rose snuck out of the barracks, making her way to the training field outside. It was empty, eerily silent, and Rose saw Dawn on the other side of the field, battering six or seven targets effortlessly with her magic. During normal training sessions, the expensive materials for strength training were being used by the highborns. Now, Rose read through the thin pamphlet teaching students how to effectively train their strength before beginning the exercise. It was late, and she was exhausted.

Anything for power.

She alternated between magic, strength, and endurance, sprinting laps, lifting weights, and pushing her magic to the limit, allowing the strain of the exercise to consume her mind, leaving behind only a comforting emptiness. She finally collapsed as the sun rose.

She woke up in the alcove. Opening her eyes, Rose winced as the sun shone in her eyes, and she looked down and around her to observe herself resting in a nest of blankets.

"I carried you here, or the Masters would've found you," the Prince murmured. "You trained yourself to exhaustion. I saw you collapse."

"Thank you?" Rose hadn't meant for it to come out like a question, but this was unusually kind for him. Standing up and throwing her blanket off herself, Rose wrinkled her nose at the scent of sour sweat and vomit.

"Turn around." The Prince obliged, turning his back as she stripped off her disgusting shirt and yanked on one of her clean sweaters from the closet. It made the smell just a little bit better.

"Are there classes?"

"They're canceled for a few days while the Mages and government tries to figure out what to do," the Prince replied. He was relaxing back in his chair. As Rose watched, he placed a bookmark on the page he was on and closed it gently.

"So. Wanna ask how my leg is?" he asked. "I can't help but wonder where that second wildfire came from. I can't think of two girls with a Lightning and Fire affinity brave enough to start a wildfire that happened to know our exact location. Can you?"

Rose chuckled. "You brought it upon yourself. I knew you'd survive."

"I'm sorry for betraying you."

"You didn't. It was your job. You're a Prince. You can't befriend lowborns."

The Prince stared at her with sadness in his eyes. "A ruler is supposed to be loved and followed by his citizens."

"You are not a ruler. Right now, you're just a student trying to become a Mage."

He paused, his face still torn, before he sighed.

"Prince," Rose asked.

"Yes?"

"What do you know about the Dark Sorcerer? That attack... it was undoubtedly him, right?"

"Yes," the Prince said. He sounded exhausted. "My mother has told me about him. She told me... that everything they say in the history books was true. That he is not only cruel and aloof, but that he doesn't have a *soul*. She told me that the darkness had warped him."

"What?"

"Magic is powerful, Rose. She thinks that he's the way he is not only because of his character, but also because of his magic. He has no ulterior motive beyond *power* because that's all his magic wants. He has no soul, no mercy, no heart, because darkness leaves no room for that."

"That's tragic," Rose said. There was a second of silence in which she remembered the Dark Sorcerer's words. *"I cannot fight you here. There'd be far too much destruction."* Such a sentiment made very little sense from a man without a soul. She must've misheard.

"I suppose I should ask for your name."

"Rose."

The Prince's eyes widened with shock. He sighed, pressing his palms onto his eyes as he sat back. "Rose? The flower?"

"No, I actually know that my mysterious parents who I've never met named me Rose because it's the past tense of rise." When the Prince stared at her, astonished, Rose sighed. "No, I was joking. I don't know why I was named Rose. I'm an orphan. I wouldn't know. Probably the flower, though."

His eyes. They were not brilliantly colored like River's. His left eye was the color of a forest in a heavy fog, dim and faraway, and his right was a blue so pale that under the right light it seemed gray. They were very beautiful.

"What's your name?" she asked. There was a pause that made her think he wouldn't respond.

"Aspen."

Rose and Aspen stayed there for the entire day, Rose only leaving to retrieve enough food for both of them, as well as a bottle of coffee for herself. They weren't friends. Rose doubted the Prince considered anyone as a friend, except maybe Dawn, but Rose had never felt anything like the comfortable, companionable silence Rose found with him.

Maybe not friends, but together nonetheless.

Chapter Fourteen

Citizens of the Lightning Kingdom,
A week ago, the students of the Academy of Magic were attacked by a lethal wave of darkness and shadows that injured four students, commanded by none other than the Dark Sorcerer. We, the Army and Mages of Hikari, are working to apprehend and contain the Dark Sorcerer before his power once more reaches a peak. As an extra measure of protection, guards will be posted around each and every street in the kingdom after 8:00 PM. However, we—the Court, Mages, and I—strongly do not recommend being out after dark.
Her Majesty the Queen, Kireina Mukoto

* * *

ROSE KNEW, somewhere in the back of her mind, that the entire region must be in pandemonium.

People must be panicking, hiring mages, both real and fake, to place wards of protection around their houses, unaware that those wards would be ineffective against the shadows the Dark Sorcerer commanded. There must be an underlying tension in the air everywhere one went: smiles strained and uncertain, people twitchy and easy to startle, pranks that previously amused now capable of causing real fear.

However, the students of the Academy of Magic felt none of it.

They were wrapped up in their own world, absorbed in books and texts and knowledge and memorization. Science, Mathematics, Law, War Tactics, History, and Literacy. Six banes to their existence, difficult for all within the Academy, lowborn and highborn alike. Almost every ounce of the students' concentration were spent on preparing for the midterm finals, the time in which the hundreds of pages of information they had been learning over the past four months would be tested in a cruel test of their mental agility. Their numbers were down to eighty-six, and Rose knew that it would be even smaller after the exams were over.

With the chaos of the exam season, Rose and Aspen had agreed to split the alcove in half, drawing a line across the floorboard in ink. Rose's side was absolute chaos. Books were stacked haphazardly on the bookshelf and tables, carpeting the ground to the left of the desk, thick and thin, though most were so huge that Rose could barely carry more than three of them at once. Loose parchment, quills, pens, and even a huge ink stain from where she'd fallen asleep and knocked over her ink bottle cluttered the desk, as well all six of her massive notebooks, which were entirely filled with notes from her classes, as well as scribbles and an occasional doodle. She had spent the last week of classes taking notes on blank parchment, which she had laid in six stacks, one for each subject, against a wall. They were untidy and one had even tipped over, much to Rose's dismay, but when Aspen had attempted to help her organize it, she'd nearly bit off his head. There were at least four sweaters and two blankets tossed on the ground and over the chairs, and Aspen claimed he could barely walk when he crossed to Rose's side. There was paper *everywhere*, and Rose had even written on a few of the walls as she paced while remembering a math equation.

Aspen's side was a stark contrast, neat and refined, his desk clean and tidy with a single quill and a bottle of ink on a corner and thick notebooks stacked on the other. He stored blank parchment in a drawer, while Rose, as he phrased it, "summoned parchment from thin air." He had a single blanket draped over his chair, and his books were stuck on the shelves in perfect neatness. Either way, they both had forgone the concept of sleep, often finishing their homework, studying and reviewing their notes, and then sneaking out to the training fields to train. It was risky, but worth it.

Faintly, Rose wondered how the actual finals would be if this was just midterms, but she couldn't worry about that now. Beyond the midterms, there was something else also worrying her.

The battles.

These, as the Masters claimed, were "not important," "a check of progress," and a "small warning for slacking students." All of the students knew it was more than that. It was a test to see who had potential, who had actual skill, to predict, early on, who would become an apprentice at the end of the year. Rose and Ash spent the hours after dinner wrapped in careful study of battle in both books and practice. They sparred so often that they knew how the other fought from the inside out. Rose finally began to master swordplay and even began to dabble in more foreign weapons such as the spear and ax. After they had learned how to summon Lightning, Rose had finally cut down the number of attacks she needed to destroy a target from four to two.

The problem was still the versatility of her attacks.

The wild, destructive element of Lightning seemed impossible to bend to her will, and even when she did, there was so little she could do with as little magic as she had. Throughout the past four months of training, Rose had broken three limits in all, each break taking more and more time and effort. Of course, the people Rose truly felt sorry for were those who had seemingly reached their limit, unable to expand their magic further. Celeste hadn't broken a single limit since her first in the beginning of the year, and Venus was beginning to falter.

If it hadn't been bad before, the competition had grown fiercer, cutthroat, even savage. Even the festivities of the Winter Solstice didn't make a dent in the complete concentration and focus of the students. Rose knew she wasn't the only one trying, and she knew that what she was now wasn't enough. Perhaps that was why she pushed on through the mind-numbing exhaustion and the soreness that swept through her muscles every time she moved. It only proved that she was getting stronger.

There were two weeks until the exams started. The schedule had already been released: Math, Science, and Law on the morning of the first day, one battle after. History, War Tactics, and Geography on the morning of the second day, and another battle after.

Two days that would decide their destiny.

"Rose," Aspen snapped. Rose jerked out of her reverie, shifting her shoulders uncomfortably as she sheathed her daggers. The weight of a sword on her back was odd, but she knew she'd need its reach to even have a chance against half the highborns, and she honestly wasn't that bad at it. It was past curfew, and Aspen had followed Rose out when she left to practice. They were both taking a break from magic, and Aspen had agreed to spar with Rose. He was good: destructive, strong, yet nimble-minded and fast.

"Can you help me with my swordplay? I'm good enough with knives," Rose asked, sheathing her daggers and withdrawing her sword from her back. It was from the armory, perfectly plain but finely made. It had a thinner blade compared to standard swords and a smaller one-handed hilt, making it both lighter and faster.

"You should rest. It's late," Aspen said. Rose merely shot him a look, and he sighed and got into position.

"Ready... start!" Aspen said. His eyes, although lacking the wild joy Ash's eyes held when she fought, were filled with thrill. Rose whirled to avoid the first attack thrown by Aspen, a swift slash to her left. Parrying the next blow, Rose and Aspen began a familiar pattern: Aspen attacking, striking like a snake, Rose defending herself with smooth blocks, with Lightning and blade, that eventually failed her. God, he was so fast. It barely took a few minutes for Rose to slip up, overthinking his attacks and making mistakes, until she finally missed the telltale signs of a feint to the left. There was a cool touch of metal to the side of her neck.

She'd lost in three minutes flat, *again*.

Rose sighed, her shoulders slumping with defeat as she dropped her sword in surrender and then frowned at it in anger.

"You're getting better. Your defense is actually pretty sturdy, you just have to stop overthinking. To be honest, I might even give you the advice to rely more on your instincts. The thing is, we've been focusing too much on incorporating your defense into battle. That's all you do. You need to learn how to attack."

Rose's shoulders slumped. "Well, it's hard to focus on both. I've barely had a few months of serious practice with this," Rose said.

"It's said that offense makes the best defense, and defense allows you to create the best attack. You have to stop thinking about defense and offense as two different things." Aspen paused tilting his head up to stare at the sky in contemplation.

"You've drilled through all of the basic and a lot of the more advanced moves with Ash, right?" Aspen asked patiently, sheathing his sword with ease.

"Yeah, obviously. We've spent hours on swordplay."

"You know the drills by heart. All you need to do is incorporate them. So here's what I say: don't be so conscious of what you do."

"Huh?"

Aspen sighed. "Let's do a match of hand-to-hand combat."

"But I don't need to work on that," Rose protested.

"Just do it."

Rose caught Aspen's first fist with the palm of her hand before ducking underneath the next blow, spinning around to sweep her leg toward Aspen's feet, hoping to knock him down. Aspen only jumped up nimbly, using the chance of being in the air to attempt to land a lethal kick. Rose rolled away before nimbly jumping upward and using her left arm to knock away Aspen's incoming fist. Rose seized the chance and ducked underneath his outstretched right arm, bringing her fist up toward Aspen's jaw and a certain victory.

Only for Aspen to duck underneath her blow, grab her arm, and throw her onto the ground behind him. Rose lay prostrate on the ground for a few seconds, pain lancing through her back, before rolling to the side to avoid yet another kick. As she pushed herself to her feet, Aspen paused for a few seconds to allow her to regain her balance before they flew back into motion. Falling into the rhythm of fighting, she didn't think about anything except for the dance, the beautiful, fluid motions of combat. She had been fighting like this for many months now; it was like second nature.

"Stop!" Aspen called, and they came to a halt. "When you're doing hand-to-hand combat, it comes pretty easily for you, right? You aren't thinking about what you should do or would happen, you're reacting to what is happening in front of you. It's almost instinct, because of how much practice you've had with it."

Rose nodded.

"And, to be honest, you've had almost as much practice with a sword. You just need to make it instinct, like hand-to-hand combat is."

"I get it. But it's so *different*."

"I know. It takes practice."

"Can we spar again? So you can show me?"

"No."

Amid the peaceful, friendly training they did together, it was easy to forget who Aspen was. Rose watched in exasperation as he turned away, retreating back to the thirty or so targets he had set in a circle around him. As a plume of fire from his hands morphed into a dragon, tearing off pieces of about twenty targets with jagged, scarlet teeth before melting away, Aspen simultaneously cast a shield of fire that blocked his entire front, fending off imaginary attacks.

He really was amazing.

Rose could barely hold a shield of lightning together on its own, let alone while destroying so many targets at once. The amount of control and strength she needed to improve on to get better was impossible to do before the exams, but there had to be *something* she could do to get better at magic.

Right?

Glancing down at her outstretched swords, Rose examined its dim gleam under the light of the moon. The image of white-blue lightning melting into Audra's skin pervaded Rose's mind, and Rose jerked.

An idea came to her.

It was crazy. Audra must have enormous pain tolerance in order to withstand that much electricity, something Rose couldn't replicate.

But pain wasn't necessarily unfamiliar to her.

Her brows furrowing, Rose began to channel her magic.

* * *

A week running on barely two hours of sleep a day and an all-nighter later, Rose found herself sitting in the alcove, staring down at the enormous pile of parchment and notebooks.

"Aspen?" He was silent, but Rose knew he was listening. "I know this sounds ridiculous, but I think I understand most of my notes."

Upon hearing this, Aspen turned toward her, astonished, and cracked a small smile. "Most of your notes?"

"Yeah, most of them. And the stuff I don't understand is stuff the Masters said wouldn't be on the test. There's a possibility I might pass!" Rose rifled through her notes, pulling out her math workbook and flipping to an extra credit question. She was shocked to see she understood the process to solve it perfectly.

"This is *insane*," Rose breathed. "I knew I was learning a lot, but this feels *great*,"

"Oh, shut up," Aspen growled. Rose decided that he was only joking. "I'm sleeping at midnight and it's already eight, stop wasting time."

Upon hearing those words, Rose sobered. It would be a good idea to get as much sleep as possible tonight, but if she hurried, she could probably go through all of her notes for Math, Science, and Law one last time.

"Your eyes are moving so fast I can barely see them," Aspen commented an hour later. Rose ignored him. Curled up on the floor amid her nest of blankets, she took a gulp from her bottle of coffee before flipping a page. After reciting, out loud, the format of all three types of trials and then the laws of the Lightning Kingdom, Rose sat reading through a few example trials and then the entirety of the list of laws about property, crimes, and magic. Moving on to Science, Rose revisited quantum physics before moving on to magic and then the aspects of advanced biology of animals they had begun to cover. After completing twelve pages of practice equations for Math Rose had found in the library, Rose looked up at the clock. *Twelve.*

Rose stood up wearily, grabbing her notes so she could go over them during breakfast. They descended the ladder together, Rose first, and dropped silently onto the ground.

A movement of black fabric within the darkness was what caught Rose's eye.

Master Mekhi was standing in the flag tower, staring out of the window with what may have been nostalgia in his eyes. It was too dark to be sure. Rose stared at him, waiting for him to register their appearance. There was an unbearable moment of tension before he turned his attention toward Rose and Aspen. She glanced toward Aspen and they exchanged a look.

They were dead.

Absolutely dead.

They were not only up past curfew but suspiciously together. Rose's head spun as she envisioned how much chaos would be caused if news got out that the Prince had been spending time with a girl—a *slave* girl—after curfew. *What a stupid way to get kicked out of the Academy.*

But Master Mekhl didn't look mad. In fact, he didn't say anything, only glancing at Rose's bulging bag, the two notebooks she had in her hands, and the ink smudges covering their hands and faces before sighing.

"So that's why there were two of you there this year. Of course, I'm not surprised the Prince here knows about it, but you?" He directed that last question toward Rose. "Did the Prince tell you?"

"Ah, no. Halt told me," Rose murmured. Master Mekhl's face was suddenly filled with bitter nostalgia, and Rose wondered what Halt had done to make Master Mekhl's face express so much longing.

"I'm going to be lenient on you because you both have promise," Master Mekhl said. Rose's hand jerked. Her, promise? "But get caught again and I'll be obligated to expel you."

The message was clear. Feel free to keep using the alcove, but don't get caught.

Rose nearly ran into the barracks, which were now pitch black but for the glow of a few candles. Sinking into the hot water of the baths, Rose allowed her muscles to relax and her head to clear.

There was only one thought now.

Tomorrow will decide everything.

Win, no matter the cost.

* * *

"Relax, Rose!" River urged.

Rose ignored him. She was rereading her science notes while eating breakfast. Shoving a sausage into her mouth, whole, Rose reached the last few pages and then shut her eyes, slamming the book shut.

"Yeah, I'm screwed."

"Aren't we all?"

Rose opened her eyes, shoving a last spoonful of oatmeal into her mouth before looking around her. Students were standing up, heading toward the library. Rose felt anticipation and fear building up in her chest.

The library was deathly silent.

They had been instructed to bring nothing. Rose left her notes and bag in front of the door and crept into the library with the rest of the students. Looking around her, Rose registered the nervous, utter silence of the library and the empty desks left by those who had already left, a grim reminder of what she could lose today. Rose took her seat. The silence grew, if possible, even tenser as servants passed out two quills and an inkwell to each student.

"A few servants will begin to pass out your Science assessments. We will know if you cheat, and you will be expelled immediately." The test that the servant placed on Rose's desk was concerningly thick. "You have two hours to complete this test. You may turn it over now. Good luck." Master Dara outstretched a hand, and the huge hourglass on her desk flipped over gracefully. The first few grains of sand began to trickle through as Rose picked up her quill and flipped over the paper. Flipping through the pages, Rose regarded with a silent groan the one hundred questions, graphs, charts, and even what looked like a few essays before flipping to the front page and gathering her knowledge into one, honed, sharp knife.

There was no sound in the room but for the scratching of quills and the occasional *drip, drip* of ink.

* * *

"God, I failed that one," Ash moaned, massaging her temples. The students had been allotted a ten-minute break, and Rose was frantically flipping through her notes.

"I messed up one of the rotational motion problems," Rose said lowly, slamming her book shut and tossing it into her bag angrily. "No-slip rotational motion *has* rotational kinetic energy. *Fuck.*"

"I skipped that question," River remarked. Ash laughed nervously.

"I left fourteen questions blank," Venus murmured. He sounded, for once, concerned.

"Ten," Ash said.

"Six," River and Rose said at the same time.

"We can't focus on that right now," Celeste murmured. "We have math. Fifteen minutes."

The Math exam was *brutal*. The one saving grace was that *everyone*, even the top-scoring highborns, were bemoaning its difficulty. The test had asked about a wide range of concepts ranging from vector cross products to implicit derivations, which even Aspen had had trouble with.

"I couldn't solve anything after ninety-three. I didn't have enough time!" By the time she had guessed her way through number ninety-two, time had already been called.

"I got to eighty-nine," Ash told her. Rose wanted to bash her head against a wall. *Oi ciy*. She pushed aside her worries and let out a deep sigh as Master Dara called them back to their seats.

In comparison to Math and Science, Law seemed trivially easy.

After diagramming a trial of a man convicted of theft, stating the first, sixteenth, twentieth, and forty-second laws of public magic use, governmental, and slave-trading laws, and diagramming the entire line of throne heritage in the case of a ruler having no children, Rose laid her quill down after an hour and fifty-two minutes, feeling satisfied with her answers and confident that most of them were correct. Law was so much more comprehensible than Science and Math despite its enormous amount of brute memorization, being that it was an interesting logical process that Rose found came to her naturally.

The students were tired, yet lively as they filed out of the library for lunch. Rose deposited her books in the barracks, grabbing her pair of knives and strapping them to her arms. To her back she strapped the sword from the armory, and to her side three or four extra daggers.

"Rose! Come eat!" Ash shouted, waving at her from the barracks door. Swallowing down her nerves, Rose ate as quickly as she could before heading outside.

Win at any cost. Do anything for power.

* * *

"Aspen and Emma," Sir Percival yelled.

Whispers swept through the crowd. Two prodigies, two highborns, two nearly guaranteed apprenticeships. Rose sighed as she spotted Emma's smug face move into the ten-feet ring, sat back, and prepared for what would undoubtedly be one of the most impressive duels within the Academy. The jewels on Emma's sword could probably feed Rose for months. In contrast to his opponent, Aspen had a light, plain sword that Rose knew was excellently forged, light and sturdy and perfectly balanced. Rose already knew who she was rooting for.

"Begin!" Sir Percival shouted. The students seemed to lean forward simultaneously as the duel began, and even the Five Sorcerers and other mages standing off to the side looked interested. Aspen and Emma seemed to know this. Although Emma seemed to be trying her very best to beat the Prince, the look on his face seemed to tell Rose that he was almost *bored*. It was almost like this battle was not about beating Emma but showing off. His movements were precise, mechanical, and as he seemed to almost watch Emma impassively, weaving between her attacks with boredom painted across her face. After half a minute of this, he withdrew his sword and began to engage. His moments were precise, deadly, cruel, weaving around Emma as their swords met and separated, the clashes of metal-on-metal ringing through the silent crowd of students.

Rose saw his face and shivered.

This was the cruel Aspen, the one that Rose knew had been crafted from darkness and shadows, the one that she had first met that first day. His hand shot out, and the sword in her hand was wrested to the ground with a gust of wind.

Wind?

As a Royal, the Prince could control all five elements. Emma's lips curled into a feral snarl that seemed out of place on her face as she shot forward, gusts of wind on the tips of her fingers, tiny whirlwinds launching toward Aspen, who seemed unperturbed as they were knocked aside with a huge gust of wind. Fire shot out of his hands, and Rose winced as they engulfed Emma, only for the smoke to clear to the sight of Emma shooting down from the sky, spears of wind falling with her. Aspen ducked amongst them like a snake, magic blocking the spears he didn't avoid, and he seemed almost to take pity on Emma as she landed on the ground, chest heaving. Aspen's hands stretched toward Emma as he launched his magic at her, whirlwinds and stones and plumes of fire shooting at her as a singular lightning bolt dropped down from the graying sky. They weren't merely harnessing the elements—they seemed to *embody* them. Where they attacked the magic defended, where a blow about to hit the element blocked, where an opening was seen the magic struck. It was almost like their magic had a mind of its own. A barrage of blades of wind struck against a wall of stone that quickly morphed into spikes that were just as rapidly sliced into tiny cubes by waves of wind. Their duel went on for forty-five minutes, a constant barrage of magic pitted against magic, until a maelstrom of wind finally engulfed Aspen. Rose's eyes narrowed as Emma's face lit up in victory.

She had not won.

Aspen strained for barely two more seconds before he finally wrested control of the whirlwind from Emma. He poured his power into it, lightning and fire flashing through its spinning surface, engulfing Emma completely.

"I surrender!" Emma screamed as the hard shield of wind around her cracked. Aspen's near deadly magic diverted from her, dissipating into streams of air and sparks of static. Burns covered Emma's body, marks of lightning imprinted on her skin, and Rose almost felt bad for her.

Almost.

Aspen barely looked winded. His chest was heaving, likely from how much magic he had used, but he was uninjured but for a single scratch was on his cheek.

There was absolute, dead silence as he bowed at the sorcerers, a tiny stream of blood dripping onto the dirt beneath him as he walked off of the arena.

* * *

Ash was placed against one of the lowborn twin girls. The two girls, both dark-skinned and fair-haired, had been secluded and generally ignored the rest of the students, even the lowborns.

When the battle had started, Ash's opponent knelt down and pressed her hands to the ground, summoning a small storm of rocks that hurled themselves at Ash. In the standard shielding stance, two arms held out and the non-dominant foot slightly behind the other, Ash summoned a shield of fire that deflected the rain of pebbles. While the two's battle was unimpressive compared to the Prince's, both girls were competent. A storm of fire in the shape of a dragon that Rose knew Ash had spent hours honing hurtled at the girl, who yanked a smooth, thin boulder from the ground and sent it crumpling to the ground. Vines curled up from the ground only to be burned to ashes by flames. Finally, after twenty minutes the girl looked up at Ash, chest heaving, magic depleted, she pulled out her knives and rushed at Ash.

Ash grinned, and it was mischievous and foxy.

The battle was over in seconds. The girl found herself pinned onto the floor, sword against her neck, and even the highborns looked impressed. Rose gave her a thumbs up, swelling with pride for her friend, and Ash grinned victoriously back.

"Next up. Rose against River."

The grin was wiped from her face.

* * *

Of all people to be paired against, it had to be *River*.

She stepped into the twenty-foot ring and held out a hand to River. No one else had shook hands, but she felt like she should. He grasped her hand, a steady, firm grip, and they stepped back. Sir Damian called for the battle to begin, and yet they stood still, each hesitating to attack.

"What happens here stays here, all right?" River asked.

Rose nodded, and he smiled.

Rose saw the silver sliver of light rush surge toward her and ducked underneath his sword, daggers flicking out of her forearm as she surged toward River. As she rushed toward him, he darted aside, and Rose stopped out of instinct, just barely avoiding his face. She paid for that lapse in judgement with a cut across her chest, and Rose hissed in pain.

, This isn't training.

They separated, five feet apart, and this time Rose lunged at him, daggers out and slashing. Their weapons crashed against each other, each pressing against the other's blade, and as River pressed closer to her, she channeled lightning through her hands, ignoring the brief pain. He saw the electricity, realized what she wanted to do, and leapt back several feet.

Too late.

As the electricity surged down his blade, it met his skin with an audible sizzling sound. Rose winced as he dropped his blade, body convulsing in pain, and as she neared him cautiously, he dropped to the ground.

"Do you surrender?" Rose asked, her blade outstretched, ready to throw at his body. Her heart ached with guilt as he remained still. She approached him cautiously.

"*No,*" River hissed, and then he was a blur of jerky movements as he surged up from the ground, pulling a knife from his belt, darting behind Rose. She whirled around, fast, but there was already splintering pain in her side as he thrust the knife into her. Rose hissed with pain and lifted a hand, two or three bolts of lightning falling from the sky toward River, each missing as he darted to the side and straightened into a standing position, six feet away from her.

Pulling moisture from the air, River extended his arms using two long strands of water, forming flexible whips on his arms. Rose threw up a shield of lightning as sharp chips of ice flew at Rose, approaching him as she summoned lightning from the sky. It morphed into a small dragon that surged down from the clouds, mostly to test why River had extended his arms using water. She was rewarded with an answer. He froze the water connecting the extension to his hand and then swung onto the air, grabbing onto the back of the dragon and slamming it into the ground.

How do I fight against this?

Pointing toward River, Rose snapped her fingers. An electric charge appeared in the air, barely larger than her finger, and as the entire crowd watched, it began to spin, faster and faster until it looked like a circle of electricity.

Schoolwork hadn't been the only thing she'd investigated in the alcove.

It was a long-forgotten technique, used by one of the few Five Sorcerers with comparatively little magic. By generating a perpendicular magnetic field, Rose could shoot pieces of iron and nickel forward at extremely high velocities, fast enough to pierce through shields of ice. Tossing three pieces of metal from her pouch into the field, Rose shot them at River at a speed so fast she could barely see them hurtling through the air. The first one pierced straight through River's shield of ice, hitting him in the shoulder. The second hit his thigh and the third grazed his arm. Rose grinned in triumph, and River surged toward Rose, bleeding heavily from his shoulder, his extended arms separating from his arms and molding into a mass of water that pinned Rose to the ground, encasing her in ice. Sending electricity currents through the ice, Rose shattered it and threw up a shield of lightning that melted spears of ice. Rose was, she realized, on the defense. River returned with a stream of water that froze her feet to the ground, leaving her still for just enough time for River to manipulate the water into a thin spear of ice that pierced through Rose's body, just below her hip. Crying out in pain, Rose unleashed her electricity, three dragons of lightning hurtling down from the sky. River seized in pain as they struck him, *one, two, three*, and as he did, she approached him, limping heavily, and held a dagger to his chest.

"Surrender?"

In response, within a split-second, River's arms melded into one, rushing toward Rose and pinning her to the ground. As she tried to push herself to her feet, more water was pulled from the air, pinning her to the ground with a mass of moisture.

She was trapped.

"Do you surrender?" River asked, pushing himself to his feet. He had learned from last time, connecting a strand of water to his finger so that he could control her prison easily.

Rose's eyes lingered on the strand of water. She only had a little magic left, enough for two or three more bolts of lightning, but even as she thought that, River formed a shield of ice above him, effectively protecting him from any attacks she could summon.

"No," She hissed, and she let her magic loose.

Usually, a Water user could cut contact from their element almost instantaneously. River, however, hadn't been prepared for this. As the lightning reached his body, his face contorted with pain, and he dropped to his knees, but he didn't let go of the water. In that instant, Rose knew —this was *her friend*. She knew his limits. If he let go, physically, his control over such a large body of magic would disappear and Rose could set herself free. *I can't transmit any more without hurting myself,* Rose realized. The water was still touching *her* as well, and even though she was a Lightning channeler and couldn't feel the relatively tiny amount of voltage she was transmitting, any more would begin to reach her too.

Rose gritted her teeth. There was no other alternative. *Do anything to win.* Lightning, glowing and sparking, surged out of her body and into the water surrounding her. Pain surged through her, spots beginning to appear in the corners of her vision, but she pushed and pushed until the water dropped from her body.

As she pushed herself to shaking feet, she found herself looking down at River, who was kneeling on the ground, head down, hands trembling, the corners of his hair singed and black. He made a move to push himself to his feet, but Rose had already pulled out a dagger, and as he looked up, she pointed it at his head.

"Do you surrender?" Rose asked. She hoped he could see the remorse in her eyes.

He smiled as he nodded. He would have scars from that amount of Lightning, but in that moment, Rose knew he would forgive her.

* * *

"River! You're okay, right?" Rose asked. They had been escorted out of the battlefield by a pair of kind mages, who had restored their magic and healed their wounds. Ash, Rose, and River were sitting at their usual table with the rest of the lowborns, but instead of the ignorance they usually received from the rest of the students, more eyes were turned their way, and there were even a few congratulations. They weren't invisible anymore.

"Rose, I'm *fine*."

"I knew I shouldn't have used as much lightning," Rose fretted. Lightning scars now stretched across one of his arms, and although he claimed he liked them, guilt ate at her every time she saw them.

"He's *fine*," Ash told her from across the table. "If it was someone else, you wouldn't even feel bad."

"Yeah, well, River's definitely nicer than anyone here. And that *includes you*," Rose said, glaring at Venus, causing him to close his mouth and stop any attempt at flirtation.

"Don't worry," Ash hissed into his ear. Flirty Ash was back. "You don't need to be nice. You're already hot enough."

"You would know a lot about that," Venus replied, winking. Rose choked on her food, River sighed, and Ash grinned.

"We have more tests tomorrow," River reminded them. That sobered everyone quickly.

"The Science and Math tests were so hard," Rose groaned. "I hope the next three are easier. Actually, yeah, what am I doing here? I have to study." Without waiting for a response from her friends, Rose surged to her feet, grabbing three or four rolls and her backpack before heading up the stairs.

"Woah there," Aspen's voice called from ahead of her. Rose slowed down, allowing a smile to pass over her face as she mounted the last few steps. He stood on the stairwell, a few books in his hands, and they walked together to the flag tower and it's several tables.

"Nice job on your battle today," Rose responded.

"I can't say the same for you, seeing that you nearly killed yourself."

"I did *not*."

Aspen chuckled, and Rose had to smother a grin.

"How are you so good at what you do, anyway?" Rose asked as she climbed up the rope ladder.

"Practice, Rose. Years and years of practice. I have to be this good in order to survive."

Chapter Fifteen

"HOW DO YOU THINK THAT WENT?" Ash asked.

"It was way better than the last three we had, for sure," Rose murmured. She was secretly very confident in her History exam. It had always been her strong suit, and she had answered all the questions with excess time to spare. Similarly, she hadn't been concerned about her Literature final. They had been assigned three essays to write in two hours. Although Rose's time allocation had been dubious at best, she felt confident in her arguments, though not in the legibility of her handwriting.

"It doesn't matter now! Finals are over!" Venus shouted, tossing a bun at Ash, who caught it with one hand and stuffed it into her mouth, unamused.

"We still have the battles. And you have to win yours. You lost your last one," River reminded him softly. He sobered, looking greatly concerned: Venus had been placed against one of the lowborn twins, and while the match had been close, he had lost to an ice spear to the chest. Rose put down her half-eaten roll, tapping her fingers against the table impatiently.

"Let's go warm up," she said, tapping Ash lightly. Ash jumped at the opportunity, cramming a final bite of eggs into her mouth before grabbing her sword and leaving the atrium with Rose.

* * *

"Rose and Emma."

There were a few derisive snickers from the crowd, and Rose had to restrain herself from visibly frowning. *Emma?*

"Oh, Rose," Ash murmured, moving to squeeze her hand. Rose only looked toward Aspen, who looked away from her pointedly, and then to River, who gave her a thumbs up. He had already won his battle, a one-sided beatdown against a highborn boy. Standing up and descending into the arena, Rose crept into the circle. Emma was already there, giving off a regal air even in the same clothes as Rose. Rose felt her stomach clench.

"Give up, slave, before you embarrass yourself," Emma sneered. Suppressing the anger that came with that word, *slave,* Rose rolled her shoulders and stepped into the arena. Emma hadn't even drawn her sword. Standing there, she radiated an aura of arrogance and superiority. As she saw Rose's face contort in anger, she tilted her head back and laughed.

So Rose moved.

Daggers flicking out of her sheaths into a pair of waiting hands, she lunged toward Emma, opening a cut on her stomach before dodging behind her, ducking and rolling away from the blow of her sword. Although the gash was shallow, it angered Emma.

"Filthy lowborn," she snarled. Her sword, as if it were a silver asp, whipped toward Rose, who just barely dodged. Emma was *good*, very good. Her sword was fast, nimble, on an entirely different level than what Rose was used to. Cursing, Rose ducked underneath another blow. Emma was so fast and fluid that Rose was almost immediately pushed into the defensive.

She couldn't win like this.

It was time to pull out the trick up her sleeve.

Lightning.

It erupted from the sky, six bolts of lightning that merged into a mass, and as Emma stood back and watched it spark with an air of amusement on her face, Rose absorbed it into her body.

It was agony.

Even Aspen, who had watched her train, seemed shocked as he watched from the stands. Rose didn't care. She had experienced enough pain from the whip to endure this. As she fully absorbed the lightning, Rose could *feel* her senses sharpening. She could see the individual grains of sand of the arena and could feel the miniscule movements of the air currents. Rose gripped her daggers lightly, imbuing them with lightning, and *moved*.

Anything to win.

Although she wasn't nearly as fast as Audra, when Rose next moved, she was but a blur. She plunged an electricity-wreathed dagger, a mere whisper of lightning chirping, into Emma's side, and when she turned toward Rose in shock, Rose had disappeared.

It hurt to move.

A human body was not built to sustain such high levels of electricity. By enhancing her nervous system with electricity, Rose was forcing the signals between her neurons to transmit *faster*, which would only last for about fifteen minutes before it would fade away, leaving Rose exhausted and lethargic. She had to finish this quickly. Taking a step forward, Rose broke into a sprint, her sword slashing in a low undercut toward Emma's leg. She was aiming for Emma's tendons. If she could cut through them, she could immobilize her completely.

Her attack bounced off a shield of wind.

Oh god.

"What's wrong, slave? One-trick pony, are you?" Emma smirked. Levitating into the air, her hair billowing with the force of the wind she was summoning, Emma formed dozens of blades that sent ripples through the air, all of them pointed at Rose. Rose narrowed her eyes. As the blades began to surge toward her, Rose reacted with lightning-fast reflexes, literally. She deflected every single blade back at Emma, imbuing them with lightning as her blades made contact. Rose had spent weeks on end training her vision and reflexes in order to have the capacity to react to what she saw on conscious thought rather than instinct. Even so, she had never enhanced her body to this extent. The amount of information she was processing was almost overwhelming. Emma directed her wind into a thick shield that stretched across her front to block the daggers of wind, and Rose seized that moment of distraction. Bare hand sparking with lightning, Rose darted behind Emma, hand moving to plunge the lightning into her chest.

Boom.

Rose let out a choked cry as a mass of wind struck her body, launching her back several feet and sending her rolling across the ground. She got up with immense difficulty, her ribs aching and head pounding. A trickle of blood, warm and wet, had flowed from the back of her head onto her neck. She ignored it, taking a step forward, lightning sparking—

—and fading.

The electricity ceased. When Rose took another step forward, her legs nearly collapsed beneath her, and the world around her spun. She had run out of time.

There was nothing left.

"What's wrong, lowborn? Out of magic?" Emma said, smirking. Despite her bravado, though, Rose could see her slight grimace and tense expression. Rose's blows had *hurt,* but Emma, it seemed, was desperate to maintain the front of *unaffected, superior High Lady.* As Rose thought this, Emma lifted a hand to comb her fingers through her hair, closing her eyes as though she was enjoying the sun.

Rose hurled two throwing knives.

The first flew inches by Emma's head, just barely missing her hand, and the next struck Emma's chest. There was the harsh sound of shattering glass, and Rose watched in astonished horror as two fragments of what must've been a golden necklace fell from Emma's shirt to the ground.

Of course, I had to accidentally hit her jewelry.

But instead of sneering, Emma stopped, looked at her, and fell completely still.

"Hey," Emma said. Her voice was shaking.

What?

"Why the hell did you do that?" Emma took a step forward, her eyes filled with rage, her hand reaching toward the hollow of her neck, as if expecting that the necklace had somehow repaired itself. Staring down at the fragmented golden pieces on the ground, Rose saw the exact moment Emma's body began to trouble.

In an instant, Rose felt herself pinned to the ground by wind.

Blow after blow struck her, hitting her chest, neck, body, beating at her over and over again. Turning her head to the side and spitting out blood, Rose flexed her hands, calling for lightning. *Nothing.*

"You've got to be kidding me, you filthy lowborn," Emma spat. Rose opened her mouth, tried to surrender, but Emma pulled the air from Rose's lungs, robbing her of breath and speech. "You fucking animal. How the hell could you take that from me?"

Take what?

Even as her vision faded and her lungs starved for breath, Rose honed her eyes on the shattered necklace. Even split in half, Rose could see the golden glass symbol easily: a triquetra entwined around a heart.

Her vision faded to black.

* * *

"Rose. Rose!"

Rose opened her eyes, groaning as she pushed herself up to a sitting position. But the expected pain that should've lanced through her limbs was strangely absent. Had someone healed her?

"Seriously?" Crystal's voice asked from beside her. Swinging her legs off the cot and standing up, Rose stared down at herself in astonishment. She was completely healed, even of the minor injuries.

"You were so badly injured that I had to heal everything. Your brain was starved for oxygen. More time and the girl would've killed you."

"I don't know what I did," Rose murmured. "The necklace. I didn't know."

"That's not even the bad part. How could you even *attempt* what Audra does? That requires pain tolerance and training to a level you haven't reached yet. I don't know how you were still moving after pulling such a foolish stunt. This is, what, the third time you've almost killed yourself?"

"Second," Rose muttered. Just as she was about to exit the healing tent, Rose felt a force careen into her from behind, tumbling her to the ground.

"You're okay, thank the Gods!" Ash said. "I thought Emma was going to *kill* you!"

"She nearly did," River said grimly. "She stopped herself. Before you..." Rose shifted, uncomfortable, and River's eyes darted to her quickly. "Anyway, Aspen and Dawn have been paired together. I think you guys will want to see this." Turning toward Crystal, Rose bowed slightly before exiting the tent and running toward the arena.

Aspen and Dawn were standing, perfectly still, facing each other. And, as Rose watched, they approached each other, shook hands, and backed away. A courtesy the Crown Prince hadn't offered even Emma.

Slowly, they withdrew their weapons.

Within Aspen's hands was a battle ax. *Halt's weapon.* Dawn unsheathed her naginata. The front of the blade was sharp, so sharp that a thread would probably be cut in half if laid against it. The back side had four deadly ridges that were smooth, almost like the back of a serrated blade but larger and deadlier.

Would Aspen make the mistake of going easy on Dawn because of his feelings, or would the predator within him rear its head and try harder than ever?

They *moved*.

Aspen's arms strained, the ax undoubtedly heavy and hard to control, as the double-bladed monstrosity executed long, sweeping blows that were heavy and deadly and yet still somehow nimbly dancing. Dawn's naginata twirled and danced, blocking blows effortlessly before stabbing forward. She utilized her superior range effectively, attacking before darting backward even further. Their weapons clashed against each other with sounds that seemed ear-splitting within the dead silence of the audience, who watched on in amazement as they danced an ethereal dance of death, of sharp blades and quick wits.

Suddenly, both of their weapons clattered to the floor.

Their arms raised, weapons forgotten, Aspen sent enormous punches of fire at Dawn that she quickly quenched. Rolling underneath a storm of thorns, Dawn sprinted at Aspen, two twin waves of water rising up and cascading toward Aspen, who crafted a shield of earth that absorbed the water. Aspen sent a wave of wind blades that Dawn nimbly dodged just as Aspen ducked underneath an enormous sharp disk of ice. Elements clashed, water blocking a bolt of lightning that dissipated into nothing, stone deflecting a whip of water, water and fire colliding and forming a curtain of steam. When the arena cleared again, the air was filled with spears of ice that Aspen morphed into gas only to find his feet frozen to the ground. Dawn had propelled herself into the air, floating above him like a goddess, and her arms extended into whips of water not unsimilar to River's. The ends of those arms morphed into claws of ice, and as Aspen freed himself of the ice binding him to the ground, Dawn fell from the sky, ripping marks across his chest, curly black hair billowing back in the wind, knocking him back as Dawn elegantly landed on a patch of water.

Dead, absolute silence. The Prince and Dawn both picked up their weapons, battle ax and naginata, and flew back into action. As their blades met, magic battled around them, spears of ice meeting walls of earth, surges of thorns dissolved into dust as their moisture was stolen, and packs of beautiful water wolves were sliced in half by blades of ice. Throughout the magical battle, the two continued their physical battle, the sound of metal striking metal barely audible through the crackle of fire, whistle of wind, and flow of water as their elements battled around them. It almost seemed like their magic had a mind of its own. It took an entire hour of constant, unending magic for them to display any sign of strain, even then, both parties were only minorly injured.

Amazing. Prodigious, powerful, amazing.

But even the defeat of a prodigy was not always dramatic.

The magic faded from the air as Aspen let out a cry of pain, the tip of Dawn's naginata protruding through the other side of his stomach, and Dawn pulled out her blade with a wet *shick*. Before Aspen could react, he was pinned to the ground by ice, and even as Aspen summoned a bolt of lightning within his bare hands, Dawn froze that too.

A singular spear of ice pressed its point to his exposed neck, pressing down until a single bead of blood bloomed bright red.

"I surrender." Aspen's whisper seemed to emanate throughout the silent arena.

There was a split-second of silence as Dawn stepped away.

Then, the students *exploded* with noise.

* * *

The Prince's defeat was all the Academy talked about. Over dinner and in the barracks, constant chatter pervaded every corner of the Academy. Even the previously appealing topic of what they would do over their week of break had been set aside as the students went over every aspect of the battle, each wondering how the Prince had lost. Dawn was being swarmed by students, lowborns and highborns alike, some congratulating her, others already underestimating her.

The fact that she still sat at Rose's table despite her sudden fame would've warmed Rose's heart if not for the dozens of students fighting over a seat at their table. Eventually, to Rose's relief and Venus' utter disappointment, Dawn chased them off with a well-placed wall of ice. Even so, the eyes of the students looking Dawn's way made Rose's skin crawl with annoyance.

"I'm going to go study. Can't stand the people," Rose murmured to Ash. She congratulated Dawn again before filling her bottle with water and heading up the stairs. As she opened the trapdoor, she heard rapid breathing from within the alcove.

"Aspen? Are you okay?" Rose asked, closing the trapdoor silently behind her. Aspen was hunched over himself, clutching his chest, on the floor next to his chair, and Rose felt her heart stutter when she examined him closely. His eyes were wide, filled with panic as they looked at her, and his breathing only grew faster as Rose approached. *A panic attack.* Although Rose hadn't had one in months, the horrific feeling of suffocation and mindless panic was still fresh and raw in her mind. Approaching him slowly, Rose knelt down next to him.

"I'm going to sit down next to you, okay?" Rose asked, keeping her voice low. He nodded. Sitting down silently beside him, Rose grabbed his hand. He squeezed it tightly.

"Breathe with me, okay?" Rose asked, exaggerating her breathing as she took a deep breath in and out. "I'm here, 'kay? Won't go anywhere. Just breathe."

"Go away," Aspen wheezed. Rose bit her lip.

"I'm not going anywhere. No one else will see this."

"Dawn..."

Rose stayed silent.

It was true that Dawn had defeated Aspen. She tried to imagine what that must've been like, that moment of pain and defeat, of being knocked so suddenly from a throne one had spent years building. But if Rose herself could go from truly helpless to fighting against people like Emma within a few months, Aspen could probably improve at the same rate too. Such a defeat, she reasoned, was not an indicator of a permanent setback. She said so to Aspen in a low and calm tone, repeating trivialities and encouragements until he finally calmed down.

After wrapping him in blankets and passing him her bottle of water, Rose retreated to her chair, flipping through a book and glancing at him occasionally.

"Please don't tell anyone."

Spreading the Prince's moment of vulnerability would only further ruin his reputation, but Rose had no way of proving she wouldn't tell anyone. Unless...

"A few months ago, I was sold to the Salt Mines," Rose murmured. A moment of vulnerability for another. "Someone close to me died there, and I got out. A few days after, I had a nightmare so bad I clawed marks down my front."

Aspen was silent.

"Okay," he finally said. His voice was hoarse, but he sounded steadier. Rose smiled.

"Why did you...?" Rose trailed off, leaving the question behind unsaid. There was a long period of silence, and Rose was afraid that he wouldn't respond.

"My father didn't like it when I lost to anyone," Aspen murmured. "And when I did, he had creative ways to punish me."

The scars on his body flashed before her eyes, vivid and gruesome, and Rose's stomach turned. At that moment, a thought she'd had long ago came back to her—*what would it be like to be a princess?*

Rose wasn't so sure anymore.

* * *

"Rose!" Ash shouted into her ear.

"Mhh?" Rose asked, her voice hoarse and scratchy from a relatively long night of sleep.

"Wake up! C'mon, Rose, the results are already up!" At this, Rose shot up from her bed, her eyes wide, and Ash let out a choked laugh. Scrambling out of her bed, Rose raced to the overwhelmed servant standing near the door, shoving her way to the front and breathlessly giving her name. Her results were handed to Rose on a small piece of parchment, barely larger than her hand. Rose's fingers were trembling so badly she nearly dropped the paper as she unrolled it.

Rose
Midterm Exam Results

Science: 83%
  Math: 79%
  Law: 89%
  History: 98%
  War Tactics: 95%
  Literature: 91%

The relief that flooded her was sweet with victory. She had passed. All those hours in the study, those pained all-nighters and overwhelming stress—

—it had all paid off.

Allowing a smile to work its way onto her face, Rose turned toward Ash, who had just received her results. Rose watched, grinning, as Ash unrolled the parchment, scanned its contents, and whooped excitedly.

"Swap?" Rose asked. They swapped exam results.

Ash Prisca
Midterm Exam Results

Science: 96%
  Math: 84%
  Law: 84%
  History: 81%
  War Tactics: 90%
  Literature: 92%

As Rose and Ash, elated beyond reason, excitedly made their way to the atrium for breakfast, groups of students were being escorted out by guards. Some were crying, some blustering and red-faced, others almost happy, as if they had finally escaped the prison of the Academy. Of the small number of lowborns, Venus had barely passed and one of the twins had failed.

An entire week, Rose realized. A week, entirely to themselves. A week to read whatever she liked, spend as much time eating and reading as she liked, a week in which she didn't have to *study*.

Anything for power.

Rose's gaze hardened, and she stared at her hands in contemplation. Even though she was on break, the weeks wouldn't go by without training.

* * *

Ancient Symbols of the Lightning Kingdom. Sighing, Rose flipped open the inch-wide tome, going through each picture quickly before flipping to the next. Two days into break, although Rose had researched furiously, she couldn't figure out what that symbol had meant to Emma. Flipping past what looked like an idol of a strange-looking bug, Rose stared down at the book in defeat and slammed it shut.

"You might want to try this one," Aspen said from his chair. Walking into his pristine half of the alcove, Rose accepted the book and examined its faded golden title: *A Dissection of Fire Kingdom Symbols.*

"Fire Kingdom?" Rose asked, frowning as she flipped open the book.

"You'd be surprised."

After half an hour of reading through paragraphs about the meaning of certain symbols, Rose flipped to one of the last pages and then stopped. There it was: a heart, entwined with a triquetra. *"Used to embody eternal, everlasting love, this symbol is still commonly used today, traditionally given to young children by a dying parent."*

Rose's heart stopped.

Emma, a High Lady. Perfect in every way.

A dead parent.

"Have you figured it out?" Aspen asked. Rose didn't reply. She hurriedly dug through her stacks of books until she uncovered a book filled with names and descriptions of the Lightning Kingdom's mages, organized by the year they had become apprentices. Emma's last name was *Eneria*, and Rose remembered, vaguely, Halt telling her about his best friend, *Violet Eneria*. Rose stopped at her passage in the book. She felt as though someone had stolen the breath from her lungs.

Halt's friend. Emma's mother. Dead.

"There's no way you can redeem yourself," Aspen murmured. "Don't even bother. Emma has never seen her mother's face. She was from the Fire Kingdom, came here to train at the Academy, and met her father there. Her mother died during childbirth and gave that necklace to Emma as a last gift."

"No photographs? Water Memories? Nothing?"

"No. Trust me, they searched, but everything had either been lost or destroyed."

"There has to be a way," Rose murmured. "I..." Rose swallowed, her throat dry. If someone had a photograph of Rose's parents, she'd treasure it more than her own life.

Halt's best friend.

Realization sparked through her, and Rose let out a little laugh. There was still a chance.

She had to write a letter to him.

* * *

Halt,

It's probably very strange to receive a letter from me. We're on break, and this is important, so a friend is helping me pay. Hopefully you can help me pay her back after? Anyway, we just got through midterms. My results are attached, I told you I'd do well! I even won one of the battles!

So: the important reason I wrote to you. I kind of made a mistake. I destroyed an important necklace from a deceased mother. The person hasn't seen her mother once. We both know how rarely photographs are used. The mother was Violet Eneria. Your best friend. I need a picture of her, any picture, just to redeem myself. Please. You have no idea how important it'd be to her, and to me.

How's Blossom? Tell her I said hi, and give Monte and Cristo an extra sugar cube for me.

Rose.

Staring down at the letter, Rose thanked Ash again before handing it to the post office. He stared down at the short piece of paper, rolled it up and attached it tightly with wax before strapping it onto the dove.

Rose only hoped, now, that he had a picture. Any picture.

* * *

Rose,

Blossom is well. She is very happy to see you still thriving within the Academy. Monte and Cristo appreciated your extra sugar cube.

Your results are passing. Good job. I'm pleasantly surprised. Work more on math.

I have attached a picture below.

Halt.

Short and blunt, as Halt always was. Staring down at the letter, Rose let out a relieved sigh and withdrew the picture of Emma's mother. Photographs were used only very rarely within the Lightning Kingdom, most people preferred to reserve memories within water. Although it was an extremely difficult technique that even some mages couldn't perform, it was an immensely popular practice that involved mirroring memories from people who were nearly dead onto crystal balls of water, which would display them, as if they were a movie. It was far superior to a photograph, explaining their declining use.

The photograph, however, was still beautiful.

The young woman in the photograph had raven hair like Emma's, her arm thrown around a boy's shoulder, laughing and staring at the boy next to her in obvious and utmost adoration.

Guilt swamped over her, and Rose ran back into the Academy, pushing the barrack doors open and approaching Emma. She turned toward Rose and her eyes darkened with hatred.

"What do you want, lowborn?" Emma snarled. "Here to gloat? I never cared about the necklace. You can screw off." When Rose didn't move, Emma just turned away. Her eyes were rimmed red. Rose moved closer, tapping her shoulder and holding out the picture. Looking as though she were ready to murder, Emma turned, her fists clenched, and then saw the picture.

Emma's eyes widened, and she accepted the picture carefully with shaking hands. For a split-second, Rose wondered whether she would believe that the woman in the picture was her mother.

"How....?" Emma whispered. Rose shrugged. Emma looked like she was going to cry. Rose could only turn away in discomfort. As she walked away, though, she heard Emma thank her.

In another world, Rose reflected, they could've been friends.

Chapter Sixteen

"ASH. Oh, no, no, no. Whatever idea you have, it's a horrible one," Rose murmured, shaking her head and snapping her book shut. When Ash had walked into Rose's corner of the library, her face had been filled with a mix of bewilderingly contagious excitement and actual, raw apprehension. Even with Rose's refusal, she still looked hopeful.

"I found something really bad," Ash murmured. This caught Rose's attention. The fact that whatever Ash had found was bad instead of outright exciting was mildly concerning.

"What is it?"

"I was hanging out at the blacksmith's yesterday," Ash said, gesturing toward the sword on her back. "My sword needed some work. So, what happened was, I got lost."

"Oh, no."

"Let me finish! I eventually turned into some dark alley, there were some homeless folks on the ground and stuff. But, in a corner of an alley, I saw this pair of shady-looking guys."

"Ash, this isn't worth it."

"They had a child with them."

"What?" Rose asked, standing up from her seat. "Are you sure it wasn't just their kid?"

"No, she was filthy and her hands were bound. Let me finish. I followed them, they didn't have a Slave Trading Permit or anything, but they each had one kid with them. They led me to a warehouse. There were about ten kids there."

"Oh, shit. Where the fuck are they?"

"No, no, no, here's the problem though," Ash murmured. "There was a lady at a warehouse. She distributed a pair of permits to them, but I'll bet anything they were fake. Apparently, they're taking the kids to the auction blocks in a few days."

"No, we're saving them. I don't care," Rose said. "Where's my sword?"

"In the barracks. No, Rose, listen, we need a plan," Ash said. "Where will we take the kids afterward?"

"I don't–"

"That's my point. Here, I got a map," Ash said. Rose opened it carefully, briefly admiring its detailed drawings before turning her attention to the warehouse, circled in red.

"I don't think we can get away with arresting them based on fake permits."

"Criminal Code UJ122," Rose murmured tiredly. "A Slave Trader accused of a fake permit shall have their permit examined. Only in cases of a faked permit shall the acquisition of slaves be put into question."

"Basically, they'll only check the permits and not whether the traders actually legally obtained the slaves. The problem is, they do have permits, and they won't listen to us, especially if the slave traders are nobles," Ash said. "What we can do, however, is take the slaves."

"Criminal Code UJ123," Rose said. "A Slave Trader claiming their slaves have been taken illegally from them must first present evidence they legally obtained those slaves. If they report a theft but do not have evidence they themselves did not steal the slaves, those who take the slaves will be marked innocent and the Slave Trader marked guilty."

"Exactly. So, what do we do?" Ash said. "We obviously can't raise ten kids, but you know who can?"

"An orphanage."

"Exactly. There's a newly constructed orphanage about a mile away from the warehouse. They're the only ones I've scouted that will accept ten kids."

"So what do we do?"

"I'll fight them off," Ash said. "And you can lead the kids to the orphanage. You have to hurry, though, they both have viscous-looking weapons and both used magic on multiple occasions. I might not be able to hold them off for long."

"Won't you be in danger then? I can fight them off, you can take them."

"I'm not letting you put yourself in danger again. You've already done that too much."

And, even as Rose stared down at the warehouse, marked in red, in disgust, there was a small bloom of warmth within her as she recalled her words. *I'm not letting you put yourself in danger again.*

"Thank you."

* * *

It was hard to get the attention of scared children.

Ash and Rose glanced at each other, both with black cloths covering their faces, and Rose sighed. Snapping her fingers, she formed a small mouse of shining electricity, praying the children's captors wouldn't see it as it scuttled from the floor to one of the children sitting on the floor, bound and gagged. His gaze snagged on the lightning mouse, which danced around his hands in circles before racing back toward Rose's direction. Their eyes met, and Rose made a spreading motion with her hands. The boy's brown eyes widened in understanding. He nudged the girl next to him, tilting his head toward Rose's direction, and she spread the message even further until the entire body of children were looking at Rose expectantly.

Carefully, Rose sent out the lightning mouse once again, commanding it to chew through the ropes on their feet.

"Hey, is that lightning?" one of the men asked. He picked up the lightning mouse with his gloved hands, and Rose glanced toward Ash for confirmation. She nodded. With a cry, Ash burst out of their hiding spot, sword outstretched. She met the weapons of the first trader with a clang, and when the traders turned toward Rose and the fleeing children, Ash created a wall of fire between them.

"Run, Rose! Save the kids!" Ash shouted from behind the fire. The clang of blades rang from behind the flames and Rose hesitated, itching to help Ash. There was a tug at her sleeve and Rose looked down to see a little girl, probably barely younger than six.

"I can't walk. Don't leave me, please," the kid begged, and Rose barely had time to register her twisted, blackened right foot before she scooped her up and ran. The children were slow and had just filed out of the door, but Rose managed to fit the smaller ones in her arms.

"Sprint! Run as fast as you can!" Rose shouted. "I'm taking you somewhere safe. You just have to get there."

It must've been a strange sight, Rose reflected, to see a masked girl wearing the infamous Academy uniform sprinting across the small village, from one end to another, carrying three children in her arms. Ignoring the murmurs and shocked whispers, Rose ran with the children, who were now getting exhausted, switching out the ones in her arms with those who couldn't run anymore. The oldest two children, probably about ten and eleven, were each holding a smaller child in their arms.

They reached the orphanage after a painfully slow twenty-five minutes.

Rose barely had time to spit out a brief explanation to the kindly old lady in the orphanage before she was sprinting in the other direction, as fast as she could, even when she felt like collapsing. Two miles was nothing to her compared to Ash.

A scream echoed from the distant warehouse. It was Ash. Summoning lightning and letting it sink into her flesh, Rose covered the last half-mile within thirty seconds and burst inside, her sword sparking with electricity.

One of the men was already on the ground. Knocked out, Rose realized. There was a bit of blood trickling down from his temple, but otherwise, he was unharmed. *She isn't even killing them.* The second man was standing over Ash, who's beautiful sword was on the ground, the tip of his sword resting against her neck. He didn't even see Rose until he was on the ground, screaming. With her enhanced speed and reflexes, it had taken her barely two seconds to cross the room and draw a dagger across his hamstrings. Screaming, he fell to the floor, immobilized.

"You okay?" Rose asked Ash, allowing the electricity in her body to fade away.

"Yeah, I'm fine. I knew you would come. Do we leave them here, or...?" Ash hesitated. Rose stared down at the men on the ground and her fingers twitched on the hilt of her sword. *Disgusting.*

"Just leave them here," Rose murmured. "I'll see to it that they won't die, I have medical supplies. You go to the orphanage and check on the kids." Ash didn't even question Rose, just nodded and left.

When she was sure Ash was out of earshot, Rose turned toward the two men on the ground. The cold in her eyes must've been clear as fucking day, because the conscious man was trying to drag himself away with his arms.

"I don't think your friend would want you to become a monster," he said, and his voice was steady.

A monster.

Rose nearly dropped her sword.

"I think it'd be worth it, if a few more slave children are saved from your grasps," Rose murmured. "I don't want to become a monster either. But..."

She raised her sword, shutting out her feeling that *this wasn't right.*

There was fear in the man's eyes.

"Are you afraid of me?" Rose murmured, echoing Ezra's words from so long ago.

"Yes."

"Good."

The sword embedded itself an inch from the man's head, and he tilted his head, staring at its shining surface. Delicately yanking out the point, Rose watched the relief flash over the man's face with disgust on her face. Raising the blade once more, she let the blade fall.

Onto the man's wrist.

She sliced through bone and skin, and the man screamed bloody murder. Rose cauterized the wound with a blast of electricity, watching as he stared at the stump where his hand had been in raw, utter horror.

"Never touch another child again," Rose hissed. She wiped the blood from her sword on his tunic and walked out of the warehouse.

* * *

"Ready position... start!" Ash shouted. Rose darted forward, daggers outstretched, meeting Ash's sword with a clang. It didn't take long for Ash to knock Rose to the ground. Both girls paused as Rose got up, brushing powdery snow off her jacket with stiff, leather-gloved hands. Snow crunched beneath her feet. Their breaths were cold mist in the air, and Rose let her blades slip back into their sheaths, rubbing her hands against each other in an effort to regain feeling in her fingers.

"We should go inside," Ash said. "It's cold."

Rose followed her inside, looking backward at the snow-white training fields, dotted with two or three pairs of students sparring or practicing magic. Most students had left the Academy over break, leaving behind only those whose homes were too far away to travel to.

"What do you think Sir Percival is going to be like when he's mad *and* cold?" Ash asked.

"Let's not talk about that," Rose replied, grinning. "Let's head to the library."

They walked up the stairs, shaking snow off their clothes, much to the chagrin of the servants. The library was mostly empty, quiet and peaceful. They seated themselves on armchairs near a fireplace, Rose reading a book about mythical wildlife and Ash playing with some type of puzzle fidget. Just as Rose began to drift off, the library doors burst open with a *bang*.

"Rose!" Aspen shouted, sprinting in. "Do you hear that? There's something in the shadows." Glancing toward Ash, whose face was filled with both bewilderment and amusement, Rose sighed.

"Do you need more sleep?" she asked, trying her best to sound kind.

"No," Aspen snapped. "Listen."

Bewildered, Rose and Ash went silent, straining their ears for something in the shadows. Then, she heard it—a voice of shadows, ringing with indescribable tones of chaos and echoes, and a shiver ran down her back. It was laughing malevolently, and as Rose stared at Aspen, fear in both their eyes, the world around them *shook*.

Ash, Aspen, and Rose turned tail and ran as familiar shadows exploded from the ground.

"Run to the Great Hall!" Aspen shouted, hands outstretched as a shield of wind hardened around them. Shadows, so many that the air around them seemed black with night, struck at the shield, so thick and many that even as they reached the staircase, the shield of air was cracking, shattering. Tucking her body into a ball, Rose let her body fall, rolling down the flight of stairs, ducking between shadows that were suddenly growing fewer and fewer in number.

She looked behind her.

Ash was still running down the stairs, but *Aspen*—

"We have to go back for Aspen!" Rose shouted, her hands sparking with lightning. "Ash, get help. Please."

"Rose, this happened last time, and we both know how that ended."

"Ash, this is the Crown Prince we're talking about. *Go get help.* We have to try to save him," Rose shouted.

Even though her common sense was screaming at her to run away, she sprinted toward the mass of shadows, batting them away with sparks of lightning as she stumbled upstairs. A shadow grasped her ankle, sending bolts of pain shooting through it as Rose wrenched her ankle away—and then she saw it. A cocoon of shadows hardening over a thrashing figure, blood dripping onto the floor from one of the cracks in the cocoon. Crying out, Rose blasted all the magic she had at the ball of shadows, lightning sparking and destroying a large part of the cocoon. A hand thrashed out and Rose grabbed it, summoning more lightning, but even as she did so, shadows yanked her back, restraining her as the ball of shadows began to melt away.

No. Not Aspen.

Summoning a storm, Rose sent a blast of lightning ripping through the ceiling, visible from miles around—a cry for help, a beacon of distress. Aspen was still moving, still alive, still could be saved.

But by the time the Five Sorcerers had rushed into the hallway, the shadows had completely vanished. It was gone.

Aspen was gone.

* * *

No one was killed. The only person that was gone was the Prince.

Aspen.

"All right, you can leave now," one of the healers said to her. They hadn't healed her ankle, merely wrapped with some sort of supportive tape.

"All of us are drained of magic. We can't do more," one of the nearby mages told her, mistaking her look of tentative hesitance for anger.

"I know. This helps a lot, thank you," Rose muttered. She barely registered herself walking out of the atrium into the training field, barely registered the cold biting at her bare hands and arms, barely registered the lightning that sparked and flickered in the air as she absorbed its power.

She barely registered the pain in her body as she trained, honing her vision so that she could see clearly even as she moved as fast as lightning. She barely registered the pain in her legs and hands, the cold biting at her insides, her body begging her to take a break. She barely registered the call of curfew, a blue-robed figure trying to approach her only to back away as Rose turned toward her and snarled.

And even when she collapsed to her knees on the snow, her hands numb with cold and her body still sparking with electricity, Rose still felt nothing within her but grief. *Ezra. Aspen. Ezra. Aspen. Ezra. Aspen.*

No matter how much she tried, no matter how powerful she became, she was still never strong enough to protect them. Any of them.

She needed more.

Tilting her head up to the sky, Rose wept.

Chapter Seventeen

"TWENTY-TWO MINUTES. NOT BAD," Ash said. Rose sighed as the feeling of lightning within her veins faded. Although she had grown some tolerance to its aftereffects, Rose knew that absorbing lightning could only be used as a last-ditch effort in a losing battle, which was why she'd innovated more magic. Rose had trained her magic harder after Aspen's disappearance, pushing her limits at every opportunity—expending enormous blasts of destructive power after meals, sustaining controlled balls of lightning in the empty spaces of the study as she took notes, and incorporating magic into her drills. It was paying off. Rose was improving at an unforeseen rate, having broken two to three limits every month since Aspen had been taken. With practice, she had finally mastered using two spells at once, no matter how complex. Although using three spells still caused her to expend unneeded mana, it was also doable.

"I can still use magic," Rose said. "It takes more stamina than it usually does, but I can still use magic." Ash clenched her fist, suffocating the two pillars of fire that had carefully burned before her before collapsing into a sitting position on the ground. Her destructive power was amazing. She could destroy multiple targets with one blow of fire and her attacks were varied and creative, often tying seamlessly into her elegant swordplay. Stamina was the one thing she lacked. Although Ash had broken many limits, her style of fighting consisted of powerful, draining attacks, causing her stamina to collapse after about twenty minutes.

"Again," Rose murmured.

"You shouldn't exert yourself, Rose. You could seriously injure yourself with this lightning." Rose didn't reply, frowning down at her hands. "I'll work on something else then."

"You should take a break. I don't know when I last saw you relaxing," Ash murmured. Rose snorted.

"The same applies for you. No one's relaxing, Ash, and even if they were, I couldn't. I'm still too far behind." Ash gave Rose a look, and Rose sighed. "It's true. Half of the highborns can triple cast, I can still just barely do it."

"You've developed so much creative stuff though," Ash said. "You're using your magic so much more effectively than most of the highborns. It's actually really cool."

"It still won't be enough to beat someone like Dawn," Rose murmured. Flexing her arms, Rose cast a few more spells before reaching her limit. After drilling against a target with her sword and practicing her archery, Rose and Ash made their way inside just before curfew. The cold March wind gave them one last farewell, beating against their backs as they stepped inside, their cheeks red with cold. Ash turned to the right, heading toward the barracks while Rose ran up the stairs to the study.

The Academy was quieter now than at the beginning of the year. Aspen was gone, and with his absence, there was a struggle for that position as the leader of the highborns. Although the obvious choice was Dawn, but she didn't care to mix with the highborns. Even now, although the only people she talked to there were River and Rose, she still ate quietly at the lowborn table. Even amongst the lowborns, competition had become more cutthroat. The second twin lowborn was still here, though slipping further and further behind. The constant tension of the Academy had only gotten worse when the remaining forty-nine students were told exactly how apprenticeships would work. Fifteen students would be chosen, each given a rank. When you became an apprentice, you would engage in training with both the other apprentices and a mentor. A mentor was ordinarily a fully mature or retired Mage, although there were exceptions, and would teach their apprentice privately. Those who were ranked higher would be chosen by the mentors first, and thus would receive generally better training. As a result, even the most gifted highborns such as Emma or the twins were furiously competitive.

Pushing such thoughts from her head, Rose sat down in the empty study. For the first half of the year, her body had ached for every second of her waking hours. Such efforts had paid off. Now, her arms were toned, her body hard with muscle. Although her height hadn't and probably wouldn't change, she was stronger.

She couldn't say the same for some of the other students.

The lowborns that had made it this far were tenacious and wouldn't be leaving. Now, only River, Ash, and Venus were still here from their original group. Highborns, meanwhile, were drawing out faster than ever. Some had finally realized that their magic simply wasn't enough, others couldn't or wouldn't keep up with studies, others simply didn't want to push themselves anymore. Rose didn't blame them.

Grabbing her backpack, Rose pulled out a large pile of plastic-wrapped rolls, provided kindly by the kitchen staff, and began to eat. In the eyes of the lowborns, time for dinner was a far-forgotten concept. The moment they were released from classes, they were outside training, either until the next class or until they were sent to the barracks, where, through one way or another, lanterns would be smuggled in and homework would be done in the dead of night. River, Venus, Ash, and Rose would take turns sprinting into the dining hall, grabbing enough food to last ordinary children a month but would likely be devoured in the day, and run out again. And so, the lowborns of the Academy, each clutching cold food and a pen in their hands, began to study. They had lasted this far. They wouldn't falter now. Even so, Rose's head was heavy. As she put down her pen and lay her head down on the desk, the last thought she had was that maybe she would tell Ash where the study was, if only to ease her loneliness.

With a sigh, she slipped into a dream.

* * *

"What the hell do you want?" Aspen's voice shouted at the Dark Sorcerer.

Rose's eyes flew open. Everything around her was pitch black, but she heard Aspen's voice. He didn't sound hurt. No, his voice was loud and angry and just as Aspen-like as ever.

"I don't want you," someone else's sickly sweet voice hissed. Rose's delight at hearing Aspen's voice melted away. She could remember this voice, and the sight of a man's shadow against a wall splattered with Ash's blood flashed before her eyes. As if to drive away those sights, the darkness around Rose morphed into something else. She heard the cold wind whistling, although the room she was in wasn't cold, just a little bit chilly. As she waited, the room around her sharpened, and then she heard the clanking of chains to her right. The room was completely dark, and as Rose glanced around, she saw a barred window high up on the wall. The barely-visible mountains outside were dark as night.

"Aspen!" Rose shouted, lunging to his figure. His wrists were chained to a stone wall, his ankles to the ground, his body forced into a kneeling position as he glared up at someone behind them. As Rose neared him, though, her fingers passed right through him, hitting the cold, stone wall behind his body.

Of course. This was a dream.

Rose turned around, and, along with Aspen, stared into the masked face of the Dark Sorcerer.

"What do you want, then? If it isn't me?"

"Don't you worry, my little Prince. Nothing will happen to you, for now. But unfortunately, if they don't try to rescue you soon, something will."

And then the Dark Sorcerer turned around and stared straight at her. Rose sucked her breath in, backing away from him until her back hit the wall. Could the Dark Sorcerer see her? He walked toward her, but passed directly through her. He was pacing.

And then, a door opened. Someone walked in, completely cloaked in darkness.

"Prince," the Dark Sorcerer snapped. Aspen's head shot up. *"Not you,"* he spat at him. *The figure walked toward the Dark Sorcerer and bowed.*

"What is it that you require?"

Rose jolted.

That voice. Smooth and beautiful, not as luring as the Dark Sorcerer's, but familiar to her ears. Where had she heard it before?

"Keep watch over him. If he tries to do anything, subdue him. If he speaks, subdue him."

"Understood."

* * *

Rose awoke abruptly, her eyes wide, breath ragged. Shooting up from her chair, Rose kicked open the trapdoor, nearly falling out of the study in her hurry as she sprinted down the flight of stairs and banged on the headmaster's door.

"What the hell is this racket?" Master Mekhi shouted, opening the door. "It's you. The girl who was with the Prince. What happened?" Good. He knew that, if a student dared do something like this at night, it was serious.

"I need you… to call the Queen and the Five Sorcerers… I had a dream," Rose told him between harsh breaths.

"You had a dream? You're kidding me. Go back to sleep before I expel you."

"No, this wasn't just a dream. This was real. It was about Aspen. It was real, I'm telling you. Just call the Five Sorcerers."

* * *

"Explain," Aura barked. Rose sighed.

The library windows showed just a hint of light as Rose stared at the people before her. Crystal and Aura, who looked just as deadly as ever. Erik and Aidan, who looked tired but were listening, and Audra, who's hair was wild and whose eyes were irritable.

"I heard their voices first. Aspen… He asked the Dark Sorcerer what he wanted. That's when I actually saw them. They were in a room, completely dark. There was a window. Outside, all I could see were towering mountains, and it was dark. Unnaturally dark, and windy."

"Mountains?" Erik interrupted her. "Did you see any vegetation? Any animals?"

"The window was small, and no, not from what I saw. The mountain's summits were about equal to my point of view, so I'd have to assume we were on the top of one too. But there wasn't any snow, or trees. It was silent. Absolutely silent. Then, I heard him. The Dark Sorcerer."

"You heard him? Saw his form?"

"Yes. It was completely cloaked in darkness."

As Rose explained her dream to the Five Sorcerers, they became more and more worried.

"And then, a second figure walked in."

"A second figure?" Aura interrupted, standing up from her chair abruptly. "An accomplice?"

"He had control over darkness," Rose told her.

"What did they do to him? Is he okay?" Erik asked.

"I saw no injuries, but it was dark, I couldn't see clearly. They didn't do anything to him, but the Dark Sorcerer said something would happen to Aspen if we... if we didn't save him."

"He's trying to bait us," Crystal hissed.

"Will you rescue him?" Rose asked. They ignored her.

"This has to be real," Aura murmured. "Rose, have you heard of the Ken'o Mountains?"

"Only in name, while reading. I don't know anything about it. Why?"

"Because you described what is known about it perfectly."

"The question is, are we going to fall for the bait? This is the Prince we're talking about," Audra hissed. It was the first thing she had said throughout the entire conversation.

"No," Erik said.

"What?" Rose shouted. They ignored her.

"He's baiting us. We'll be killed if we walk straight into whatever trap he has set up," Crystal agreed.

"You're kidding me. Didn't you hear what I said?" Rose shouted.

"I know, and there's nothing *we* can do about it. I will inform the Queen, and we'll be resorting to more subtle means. Take the girl back to class," Aura hissed. Rose looked at the Five Sorcerers. Their faces were set, united in this decision, but Audra's eyes were gleaming with rage as she glared at Crystal.

"Rose, if you have any more dreams, notify Master Mekhl immediately," Crystal told her. Rose sighed as the servant put a hand on her shoulder and steered her out of the library.

They knew where Aspen was. They weren't rescuing him.

The only thing Rose could do about it was shut her mind down as she grabbed her weapons and book bag, weaving among highborns in the atrium and walking outside to the training field.

* * *

The next dream came two weeks later. Rose had decided to take, for the first time in a month, a day off. She had finished all her homework for that day last night, and, for the first time in what seemed like forever, sank into bed as curfew was called for a good night's sleep.

"You can't touch her," Aspen's voice murmured. Even as quiet as he was, his voice was hoarse.

"Oh, really?" the Dark Sorcerer murmured. This time, the scene around her was already here, already in place.

"You're wrong about everything. She's better than you, always will be."

"We'll see."

* * *

When she woke up, Rose had the distinct feeling they were talking about her.

* * *

Even as the dreams continued, Rose found herself caring less and less. She was numb to the Dark Sorcerer's words, numb to the Dark Prince's presence, numb to the guilt she felt. Each time she had another one, though, she'd inform Master Mekhl, who'd inform her in turn that *"rescue missions are being executed. I can't tell you anything else."* It had frustrated her until she realized that she couldn't change anything.

There was something far more important happening.

It was already May. Forty-two students remained. The wind outside had morphed from biting to pleasant, ruffling her hair and cool against the sheen of sweat across her forehead as Rose sparred with Ash outside. The final examinations were in three weeks.

Three weeks until the days that would decide her future.

The servants and Masters had given up on enforcing any semblance of order. Rose hadn't actually sat down for a meal in weeks and hadn't slept in at least thirty-six hours. Even the highborns, usually preoccupied with making sure they were clean and well-rested, had stopped being so inane. Reinforcement of curfew had fallen apart. The student body, lowborns and highborns united, had simultaneously decided not to follow it, and the servants couldn't do anything about it.

The atmosphere of the classroom in the library every day was nearly identical to that of midterm exams. Instead of classes, the students reviewed the material learned over the past year, occasionally assisted by the Masters. Some students were beyond help, Venus included, while others like Ash and Rose were just barely hanging on. Over the course of the year, Rose had composed enormous notebooks with everything they had learned: two for each subject, although Law had overflowed into Literature.

"This is ridiculous," Rose groaned, shaking her head and slamming down her Science notebook. If anything, Science was proving to be the hardest among all of the subjects aside from Math. Much of it was pure memorization, but Rose was having the most trouble with Physics—which, she thought, was unsurprising, seeing as it was *a lot* of applied math.

"I know," Ash muttered. A snore echoed from the library floor, and Rose turned her head, irked, and punched Venus lightly in the shoulder. River looked up at her, met her eyes, and grinned.

"This is ridiculous," Rose muttered again. Stretching and easing her aching back, Rose lay down on the floor, her head pounding as she stared up at the ceiling.

"Rose, you can't sleep," River reminded her. When Rose didn't move, River moved toward her. Ash and Venus stepped aside, watching them curiously. It was only midnight—if only she could fall asleep now. But on the library floor?

"She's been awake for nearly two days," Venus muttered. "Let her sleep."

* * *

Two weeks until finals.

Rose had finished memorizing what was needed for Science, Math, and Law. Hell, she had even reread their curriculum books to prepare for Literature. The hard subjects were over. She prayed now that she could remember everything in History and War Tactics.

* * *

One week until finals.

Rose was tired. She rubbed her eyes and put down her math workbook. She might sleep early again tonight.

* * *

One day until finals.

The air around her was tense and filled with static. No one talked. Not even Emma had opened her mouth the entire night. There was only peaceful silence as Rose stared across the empty beds, most of which had been occupied the first night she had stayed here. That night seemed like it had happened a lifetime ago. A chuckle escaped her as she viewed the twenty or so girls that were left – Emma's small group of three or four highborns, another ten or so nobles' daughters, and then a group of girls who Rose knew were daughters of merchants and knights. Although Rose still hated them all for how they treated her, she had to respect them.

When she woke up in the morning, there was only a brief tightness in her chest. She had slept through the entire night unscathed. An invaluable blessing from the Gods up above.

The examination day had come.

* * *

"I feel less nervous now," Venus muttered.

The rest of the table didn't respond.

The examinations had been brutal. Absolutely, completely brutal. They had been tested on all six subjects today. Two hours, one hundred and fifty questions for every subject but Literature, and a ten-minute break between each subject's exam. *Thirteen hours* of testing. Her head was pounding.

"That was impossible," River murmured. His voice, normally soft and steady, was shaking.

"River, are you okay?" Ash asked.

"I was just thinking... even after all our work, will the highborns beat us?" River said, staring up at the ceiling of the library.

"No. I don't think so. We have a fighting chance," Rose insisted. "We do, River, trust me."

The doubt in their faces told Rose that they thought otherwise. Ash looked down at the floor, River scratched his head and looked sideways, and even the normally bravado-filled Venus had his head between his legs.

You can't let the unfairness get to you now. Not after all we've gone through.

"You're all idiots. You've gotten this far, why are you sad and mopey now? The mere fact that you've survived until now is an affirmation of your strength. So stop whining."

Stunned silence. River's hands, which had been shaking, steadied. Venus lifted his head, smirking. Ash grinned. They would be okay. Sometimes, she couldn't stand her friends, but they were her precious people nonetheless.

* * *

"First of all, students, *congratulations*," Master Mekhi shouted.

Rose was stunned.

"You've made it this far. You've survived. You haven't quit. Now, the real question is, who amongst you will become an apprentice?"

Everyone was silent.

"Now, I know that none of you are aware of how you will be assessed fighting-wise. Even if you do, you've kept quiet about it, am I right?" Master Mekhi said, glaring at the highborns. They nodded.

"You will be fighting in an arena-style battle. In a relatively large arena, you will all fight each other until one victor is left. You will all be supplied with a first-aid kit and will bring weapons of your own choice. If you feel that you need other weapons besides the ones you own, you may take weapons from the armory."

Rose sighed with relief.

"You will be checked before you enter the arena, because all you will bring into the arena will be your weapons and your first aid kit. Even if the battle lasts longer than a day, which it has on a few occasions, it will be proof of your mental fortitude to survive without food. Rankings will not only be based on who lasted the longest, although that is the largest factor. You will also be judged on how many enemies you fought as well as how you fought them, your strategy, and your humanity. Furthermore, alliances are not allowed."

Rose's eyes widened as she glanced at Ash.

"If we see you making an alliance, you will be disqualified immediately. If you kill someone, you will be disqualified immediately. That is all. The competition will start the day after tomorrow and will be held in an arena specially built for this near the Royal Palace. You will spend tomorrow traveling to the location. You may do whatever you want for the rest of the night. After your arena-style battle, you all may be required to fight in one-on-ones. They, too, will decide your ranking and apprenticeships."

With that, Master Mekhi walked off.

The student body exploded.

"We can't do alliances, huh?" Ash murmured. "That's not good. We stand much less of a chance."

"If we see each other, we're not fighting," Rose murmured. Her friends nodded in agreement. Staring into the face of each of her friends, Rose reflected that she whole-heartedly wanted every single one to pass. They were her precious friends, and even though they were sometimes annoying and painfully naive, she loved them nonetheless.

Chapter Eighteen

THE ARENA WAS MASSIVE. With a diameter stretching three hundred square feet, it consisted of an open, hard-packed dirt field in the center surrounded by a forest of thick oak trees. The sides of the huge arena were covered in doors, each about twenty feet apart, designed so that as soon as they exited, a student would be surrounded by enemies.

Rose snapped back to attention, staring at the servant who was demonstrating proper use of the flare. They were behind one of the doors right now in a small chamber, twenty minutes until the bell would ring, opening the doors and beginning the battle. Even their entrance into the arena was a test, an assessment of their strategic mindset. The door would remain open for a total of five minutes, giving students options regarding when to exit. Rose had decided to enter the arena as soon as the bell rang. That way, she could see and hear enemies approaching. If she hid in her chamber, there were no rules stating that someone couldn't burst in and take her by surprise.

"I have to pat you down for anything you shouldn't have. Is that okay?" the servant said. Rose nodded.

"I have a small carving of a crow. Is that okay?" Rose asked.

"Why?"

"It's a keepsake."

The servant nodded, and Rose sighed in relief. After she pat her down, Rose opened the large first-aid kit, examining the various bandages, antibiotic pills and cream, and needle and thread within before shoving them into a leather pouch by her side. The first-aid kit would only be extra weight. Otherwise, Rose was covered in weapons: a small dagger was tucked inside her boot, a belt of throwing knives, her pair of daggers strapped onto forearm sheaths, and a sword and bow, both strapped onto her back. No arrows.

From inside a cloak pocket, Rose withdrew Halt's pair of leather gloves. A good luck charm, maybe. She was patted down, and then asked to wait on a couch in the corner.

As she picked at her nails, a light lit up on the wall across from her.

One minute.

Rose stood up, flexing her hands, and then walked toward the door, carefully stroking her fingers along the familiar, smoothed carvings of the crow.

Forty-five seconds.

This was *everything*. Over the past nine months, this had been what she had been preparing for. This moment, this gut-wrenching battle that would decide her future. This would decide her future. If she won here, if she succeeded, she would finally *be someone*. Finally have something to call her own. Finally be free.

And maybe, just *maybe*, finally be *enough* to exact her justice onto the world.

Thirty seconds.

The irony was unavoidable. If it hadn't been for Master selling her, she would still be a servant. Powerless, unable to protect herself and chained to him like a pathetic dog.

Fifteen seconds.

If it hadn't been for Ezra's death, the rage that she had felt, the magic that she had awakened... she might not be here at all. The universe had a strange sense of humor, it seemed.

Ten seconds.

What had Aspen's disappearance done to her, then?

Five.

Aspen's disappearance had made her even stronger. But what did that mean? Was she descending or ascending?

Four.

But that didn't matter now. She had a battle to win.

Three.

She was a servant, a slave, a salt miner.

Two.

She was Rose.

One.

And she would not be afraid.

With a gong, the bell rang. The door in front of her opened. Without fear in her heart, Rose: orphan, slave, salt miner, servant, the lowest of the low, stepped into the battlefield.

Win at any cost.

As she looked around her, Rose saw at the corner of her vision, two doors away on her left, Ash stepped out. Their eyes met, and they grinned. One door away on Rose's right, a highborn entered the arena.

Before he could react, Rose lunged. A throwing knife from her belt went flying toward his head as she lunged at him, lightning sparking. As he ducked underneath it—*perfect*—he was met with a barrage of lightning that he was forced to roll to avoid, only to look up and see Rose descending down upon him, daggers outstretched. Rose pinned him down to the ground, a dagger pressed to his neck.

"Surrender," she hissed. Rose freed a hand, allowing the boy to draw the flare from his cloak pocket and smash it down.

Rose grinned. She felt the tiniest twinge of guilt, but this was the most effective way to win the attention of the mentors watching above. To win *Audra's* attention.

Because, as Rose had read last night, this had been exactly how she had taken out her right-hand opponent in her arena battle. Indeed, Rose had essentially stolen from the library the accounts of the last ten arena battles and spent the better part of the journey to the castle reading them over. To win, she had to be aggressive. To run away would be deadly in such an enemy-packed arena. The more enemies she took out, the better.

The student on her left still hadn't exited the chamber. They weren't one of her friends, then. They had all agreed to leave their chambers immediately and avoid combat. Rose glanced around, checking for any signs of nearby enemies and finding none. Footsteps as soft as a lynx's, Rose stalked toward the open door, her hands sparking with lightning. *Not too much*, she reminded herself. She allowed it to fly into the room, bouncing from wall to wall.

There was no cry of pain.

"I have you," an ice-cold voice murmured from behind her. Rose froze. He was a knight's son, powerful and skilled in swordplay.

Rose was a fool.

He pressed the ice-cold point of a dagger against Rose's neck, and her muscles tensed.

"Surrender now, please," he muttered. "I really don't want to hurt you." He was being honest. While he was pompous, he wasn't cruel. He was different from Emma in that regard.

That was also his weakness.

Twisting to her side, Rose ignored the slash of pain across her throat as she burst free from his hold. She knew she couldn't beat him. He was far more powerful both physically and magically.

So she ran straight toward a flat dirt plateau.

This led to the second part of her strategy. Rose was a *lowborn*, fundamentally underestimated by her opponents. Any sane opponent would rather root out this knight's son, and that could be used to her advantage. The flat dirt plateau was covered in complete bloodshed. Five or six highborns, Emma included, were sparring viciously.

So she threw a dagger at Emma.

It grazed her leg, and she cried out in pain, looking in Rose's direction, but when she looked, she saw both Rose and the dark-skinned boy in pursuit. One powerful opponent and one lowborn, both of whom she could take down. Lips curving into a smile, Emma broke free of her current opponent to lunge toward him. Rose's mouth lifted in a smirk as she set foot into the shade of the forest. She was safe. Just as she relaxed, a dagger flew past her, missing her by inches. Rose cursed, whirling around to see a highborn girl running toward her.

Fight or flight?

This highborn girl wasn't very physically strong, but her magic was stronger than Rose's. Flicking her wrists, Rose imbued her daggers with lightning, lunging toward the highborn girl with the taste of electricity on her tongue. The girl was an Earth user. Spikes of stone shot up from underneath Rose and she cursed, sprinting away, the trail of spikes barely missing her as she ran. Jumping into the air, Rose summoned lightning, letting it arc across the spikes rising beneath her. It destroyed all but one spike, which was heading directly toward her legs.

Oh, shit.

Twisting in midair, Rose kicked off of the side of the spike, launching herself farther into the air, directly above the highborn girl. Lightning fell from the gray sky above her, twisting into the form of an aerodynamic, arm-length spear. Hurriedly, the girl constructed a sphere of hard-packed dirt that surrounded her, protecting her from all attacks.

Rose surrounded her leg with lightning, kicking the sphere and landing in a roll as it collapsed. Daggers outstretched, Rose surged toward her feet, ready to force the girl to surrender.

But she was nowhere in sight.

Rose cursed as vines began to sprout from the ground, admonishing herself for her carelessness as she spotted the human-sized hole in the ground. The girl rose from the earth two feet away from Rose, sword outstretched. Before she could hold it to Rose's throat, Rose let her body spark with electricity, dissolving the vines, allowing her to duck underneath the girl's slash. Withdrawing her own sword, Rose brought it down on the highborn girl's blade, pushing her back with an onslaught of ruthless attacks, each weaving into the next as smoothly as silk, again and again until the girl was disarmed. Her blade clattered to the ground and Rose pressed a sword to her neck.

"Surrender."

The tears in the girl's eyes as she stared down at the sword almost made Rose feel bad. She threw down the flare and vanished. As Rose made to sheath her sword, she heard the metallic clang of blades meeting approaching her. The opponents were a pair of highborns, both of whom Rose didn't want to fight on equal ground, and she cursed, turning toward the trees. Could she climb them?

The bottom half of the trees were devoid of branches, but as Rose examined the wood, she found that the wood beneath was soft. Withdrawing two of her extra daggers from her belt, Rose jumped up several feet, clinging to the trunk as she drove her daggers into the wood, praying that the metal would hold. Using only her arms and scrabbling for footholds, Rose quickly climbed, driving the daggers deep into the wood and pulling herself up.

She hoisted herself into one of the branches, fifteen feet above the ground, just as the two highborns emerged in the clearing she had just been in, and Rose held her breath as they both came to a standstill. Not even the highborn facing her saw her. She was invisible unless someone looked closely, relatively shrouded by the leaves that hung above her.

This was perfect.

Withdrawing her bow from behind her sword, Rose grinned as she beheld the smooth metal, icy-cold in her gloved hands.

The highborns flew back into action and Rose held a palm upward, allowing lighting to spark into life as she shaped it carefully into the form of an arrow. It had taken days to learn how to manipulate lightning into such a condensed shape, even within her hands; she'd spent weeks on end trying to make the form aerodynamic and sufficiently compact so that it wouldn't dissolve in midair. It had taken at least a month to perfect. The design of the lightning arrow was to immobilize the opponent for at least thirty seconds. When it was buried in someone's flesh, the lightning that formed it would, very slowly, melt away, electrocuting the person and directly targeting their muscles. To pull out the lightning arrow would, admittedly, cause the immobilization to stop; however, Rose theorized that most people wouldn't willingly touch an arrow of lightning.

Now, Rose just prayed it would work.

Below her, the highborn girl had been ruthlessly felled by the boy, who was now standing over her bleeding form, demanding for surrender. *It's time.*

Lips curling into a grin, Rose nocked the arrow, pulled back the bow, took aim, and shot. It struck his side and he keeled over in pain. Rose threw herself off her tree, rolling as she hit the ground and ignoring the shockwaves of pain as she stumbled to her feet, lunging toward the boy prostrate on the ground.

"Surrender," Rose growled, withdrawing her sword pointing it at the boy's neck. The boy, who Rose now realized was a noble's son, looked up at her with a mix of hatred and surprise in his eyes. "Now," Rose growled.

Instead of surrendering, the boy lunged up at her, a dagger in his left hand that she'd carelessly missed grazing her side. Rose grimaced as blood began to flow, turning to see the boy rising from the ground even as tremors caused by electricity made his limbs tremble. Dropping her sword and allowing both her daggers to pop free, Rose lunged at the boy, causing him to tumble to the ground. Within a few seconds, she had disarmed him, knocking his shaky dagger to the ground and pressing her blade to his throat. With her other hand, Rose searched his cloak pockets, searching for his flare. She didn't trust this boy to surrender peacefully. Smashing his flare beneath her feet, Rose picked up her sword and stood up, side twinging with pain, and approached the bleeding girl on the ground.

"Surrender."

She obliged and Rose grinned with success. Watching the two highborns teleport away, Rose ran deeper into the depths of the forest.

As the adrenaline left her system, she began feeling pain. This wasn't good. Being injured this early was never optimal, and given how much the wound had bled, the gash was problematic. Cursing, Rose fell into a sitting position on the ground, hands trembling as she yanked open her hip satchel and pulled out a needle and thread. The wound had stopped bleeding, the blood staining a large circle half a foot in diameter on her shirt. Sighing, Rose threaded the needle, dousing it in the tiny bottle of alcohol in the satchel as she held it above the wound and inserted it into her skin. God, that hurt. Gritting her teeth, Rose stitched the wound shut before dousing the needle in her remaining alcohol and putting it back in her pack.

This wasn't good. She couldn't move without pain lancing through her. Rose knew if she moved too quickly and suddenly, the wound would reopen. Cursing, Rose pushed herself to her feet. She had five daggers left, her sword and bow still on her back.

She would be okay. She had to be okay. No matter what it took, she had to be one of the top fifteen.

* * *

After resting for ten minutes, Rose moved farther away from the center of the arena. Eventually, she reached the wall and sank down into a sitting position with her back against the wall. She was relatively safe here, with only three directions to watch.

After another twenty minutes, Rose heard a twig crack. Snapping her fingers, Rose summoned six small electromagnetic fields and stood up. A familiar figure was running in the other direction. River. But even as she sighed in relief, she looked in the other direction, saw a boy nocking an arrow, and threw herself flat onto the ground.

The arrow that the boy sent at her missed her by a hair's breadth and Rose pressed a hand against her aching side—by some miracle, the wound hadn't reopened. Throwing two small pieces of metal into each electromagnetic field, Rose watched in mild satisfaction for a split-second as they rocketed themselves in the boy's direction. He threw up a shield of fire, burning hot, that melted through the metal as it approached him. Nonetheless, when his fire dissolved into wisps of flame, Rose was standing behind him, daggers outstretched, darting toward him like an asp. *Garrett. A knight's son and fire element.* He leapt backward, drawing his sword, and Rose's next stab was parried with a resounding *crash*. Even as they continued to battle with only blades, magic began to spark around them: lightning from the sky, reforming into shields and spears and dragons of lightning as soon as they fell past him. Meanwhile, plumes of fire punctuated the boy's every move. A slash of the sword sent out a blade of flame and each parry summoned a burst of fire. Rose was lucky she had experience dealing with Ash, who had a similar battle style. Even so, by the time both parties leapt back several feet, stuck in a standstill, Rose had been burned several times on her forearms.

Both students stared at each other, and their magic flared. They began with brute force, a single wave of lightning and fire that collided with a brutal explosion. A storm of lightning spears was blocked by a shield of fire, erratically flying, tiny wyrms of fire were struck through by tiny darts of lightning, two dragons clashed with each other, biting and tearing at the other's ethereal flesh until they both dissipated.

But was he *playing* with her?

"It's really been fun," Garrett murmured. "Honest. You're good. But I gotta go. I don't want to waste too much magic."

"You think I'm just gonna let you—"

Garrett cut her off with the crackling of fire. Rose watched in amazement as the fire gathering around him grew higher and higher until it towered above them, forming a mass twenty feet high and fifteen feet wide in the shape of a tiger's head.

What the fuck?

"How in the name of…"

And then it made sense. He was a prodigy, a natural-born Mage with a higher mana reserve than nearly all of the population. Superstition would call him Bakha-blessed. If he had trained harder, he could've been on par with the Prince.

There has to be a way I can get out of this.

Turning, Rose sprinted toward the nearest tree. She had *never* seen him on the training fields, and even for a prodigy, gaining full control over such a large body of magic would require more time than Garrett had spent. She had a minute, maybe two, to find a way out.

"You can't run. If this attack lands, you might die. Just surrender now," Garret said. Rose ignored him, scrambling up the tree as high as she could go, and when she saw the tiger rear its head and pull back, she surrounded herself with a cocoon of lightning—an ultimate, impregnable defense that cost her *enormous* amounts of mana. It was enough. It *had* to be enough because Rose felt her mana draining at an alarming pace.

Above them, the sky darkened.

It wasn't Rose's doing. No, the fire that streamed past her, uncontrollable and wild, flew toward the sky and disappeared into the clouds. His magic—as strong and potent as it was—was creating so much excess heat that it was creating a thunderstorm. There it was.

With a deafening *roar*, lightning fell.

The rest of the ray of fire was dispersed by an explosion of electricity.

Straightening up and ignoring the pain sparking along her body, Rose stared down into Garrett's eyes.

Within them, she saw terror. Rose's control over Lightning—her ability to create tiny magnetic fields and sustain her control from over fifty feet away—was undeniably excellent. With access to such an enormous body of Lightning, she was undefeatable.

Rose raised her arm, and the lightning around her formed the shape of dozens of enormous spears. She didn't need twenty-foot tigers to win.

"Do you surrender?"

Garrett's mouth mouthed no, and Rose lowered her hand. As she did, she spoke. "A waste. You're a waste." His head jerked up, and Rose could almost read his thoughts. *How could you say that? I'm a prodigy.*

"You could've become a force of nature. Almost as good as the Prince. But you never stepped foot within the training grounds, no, not even once. You were too lazy, too self-assured."

His face whitened.

"If you had trained more, done the same as the rest of us, you could be standing toe-to-toe with Dawn. The battle between you two would have destroyed the arena. And here you are." He shook his head slowly, his mouth opening and closing.

Rose was jealous. His magical power wasn't even close to his limit, but he couldn't defend against Rose's lightning like she did against his fire. Such utter defenses required experience and control.

"This is what it's like," Rose said, softly. "This is what it's like to taste *despair*."

An orange flare flew into the air, and Rose watched as he was teleported away. Rose turned her gaze to the dirt turf in the middle, lowered her hand, and sent her spears flying. Even as thunder continued to sound above, Rose gave it up, falling heavily into a sitting position on the branch. The adrenaline faded from her veins. Everything hurt. Her arms and shoulders had taken the brute force of the burns. The sleeves of her shirt had been burned off, leaving behind shiny red skin and blisters, and her side wound had reopened, further staining her tunic with blood. Rose, gritting her teeth, cauterized the wound with a spark of lightning. She was so high that the branches were precariously thin. A single wrong move could send her tumbling to the ground. But from here, she could see the fire-emblazoned board on her left hand, set on a towering pair of pillars so that the audience could see. Atop the board were the digits: *eighteen.*

Cursing, Rose sighed as she settled in the branches, high enough that she didn't care whether she was hidden or not. As she watched, a fire mage changed the number from eighteen to seventeen.

She was so close she could taste victory on her tongue. She only had to survive until two more people surrendered. Two more people. *Two.*

Then, as she looked down in alarm, the trunk of the tree she was in burst into flames. *I'm having shitty luck with fire mages today.* Beneath her, a highborn looked up at her as if he was looking at trapped prey. The fire rapidly grew, eating at the branches beneath her, and Rose cursed, adrenaline pumping through her. A jump from this height would kill her. She couldn't climb down, and she couldn't shoot the boy from this height.

She was trapped, and had thirty seconds to surrender or burn alive.

Could she somehow fly?

And then it hit her. The tree next to her was more than three meters away. If she dared, she could jump, but if she missed, she would fall to her death.

Fear. For the first time since the competition started, she tasted fear. From within her cloak pocket, Rose withdrew the orange flare, then looked at the count of students still remaining. Sixteen.

Anything to win.

Muscles tensing, Rose prepared to jump. The boy beneath her, sensing her purpose, shouted something that Rose couldn't hear through the adrenaline pumping through her, turning everything around her into a roaring silence.

She leapt.

The feeling of falling was sickening, and Rose watched as the tree grew closer and closer. She was falling too fast.

Far too fast.

As she neared the tree, Rose scrabbled for a branch, fingertips grazing and missing it by inches as she hit the trunk and fell, the ground swelling up beneath her.

There were no branches for her to grab.

Was she going to die?

Flicking her wrists, Rose freed her daggers. The ground beneath her was so close, so close, but Rose ignored it, grasping both daggers in her left hand and plunging them deep into the trunk of the tree. Pain exploded across her left wrist, sending bright white flashing across her vision. The force of gravity combined with how fast she had been falling forced her sweaty, slippery hands off the handles after a few seconds, but it was enough to save her life.

Rose hit the ground rolling, ignoring the concerning crack in her ribs as she leapt to her feet, forming a spear within her right hand and hurling it at him.

It hit him, and he shouted in pain. Rose lunged toward his prone figure, yanking his flare from his pocket and crushing it beneath his feet.

The crowd began to shout.

Fifteen students.

I did it.

The adrenaline rush faded, and Rose felt pain lance through her. So much of it. And her left wrist—oh god, her left wrist—she couldn't move it. She had almost definitely torn a tendon. Spots flashed across her eyes, and she felt her legs weakening. *I can't stop here. No, no, no.*

With a thud, Rose slumped to the ground and knew no more.

* * *

"Rose? Are you there?" Aspen's voice said.

"Aspen? Can you hear me?" Rose asked. Rose watched as the familiar scenery around her formed.

"Rose, what's the date? What time is it? How long have I been here?"

"How can you see me?"

"Rose, should you be here right now? What time is it?"

"It's the date of the arena battle. June sixth. I don't know what time it is."

"Arena battle? Why are you here? Rose, why are you here?"

"Aspen, it doesn't matter. I'm here now. We can talk. We have to find a way to get it out."

"Rose, you have to go back."

"Aspen, I don't. It's fine. I don't even remember what happened."

"Rose, you have to go back."
Rose stayed silent.
"Rose, go back, now! You can't give up on the arena battle now. Go back."
"No."
"Please, Rose. Go."

* * *

Rose's eyes flew open. She sat up and had to bite back a cry of pain. Okay. Okay. Something had definitely gotten fucked up in her ribs, and her left wrist was completely unusable, but she could still fight with a sword. Rose assessed her magic next. She had been nearly completely drained by Garrett, but blacking out seemed to have let her regain some amount of mana.

For a split-second, Rose considered surrendering.

Her entire body was aching in pain. Burns covered her bare arms and shoulders, her wrist hurt with the slightest movement, breathing sent spikes of pain through her ribs, and her side was badly burned by her clumsy cauterization.

Aspen. I have to keep going for him.

Tilting her head up to the sky, Rose began to wait.

"Rose, are you okay?" Ash's voice shouted from the forest. An hour had passed in peace.

"I'm pretty badly injured, but I can still move. There're fewer than fifteen students left."

There wasn't a reply, and Rose knew Ash had moved on. The forest around her was silent, the sun had begun to set. As she sat in solitude, staring at the sky, she saw five more flares go off. *Ten students left.*

But just as she sighed and leaned back, she looked behind her and saw a wall of flame. *Another one?*

But it didn't target her.

Someone was burning the forest to the ground. The only safe space left was the center, the dirt plateau, a stage for the final ten students to battle in. Rose, at her limit, badly injured and barely able to move, would be one of the first students to fall.

"Hey, Ash? Are you there?" Rose murmured.

"Yeah."

"It's time for *it*, don't you think?"

Silence. Ash knew what Rose meant.

"Yeah. Go wreck them, Rose."

Summoning the last of her lightning, Rose watched as eleven lightning bolts fell from the sky. The last of her magic, the final stretch. Rose seized with pain as it melted into her body, imbuing her body with power. Rose's first rendition of Audra's magic had been clumsy, an increase in her reaction time and speed that allowed her to move faster, react quickly.

This was different.

She had spent hours researching anatomy in the study, studying the works of the nervous system. The basis of power was rooted in knowledge.

As lightning surged through her, Rose couldn't help but smile.

She had never used this form of electricity in battle before this moment. It was risky and could result in permanent damage, but Rose knew she would be healed after this. She could take risks. The fact was that a human was much stronger than they seemed—that strength, however, was locked behind a mental barrier to prevent damage to the body. By using electricity to force her muscles to contract at the speed Rose wished, she could increase the very capacity of her body, not just her senses or speed, but her very reflexes and strength as well. According to her research, going too far could kill her.

Even so, Rose continued. She balanced on that thin edge between life and death, slowly walking along its knife-sharp surface, and when she was finally balanced, Rose turned her gaze toward the plateau and laid her sword carefully on the ground. Its duty was finished.

Rose moved so quickly that those around her saw her only as a spark of electricity.

The first highborn she punched was sent flying so far away he crashed into the arena wall twenty feet away. Sprinting toward him, Rose ripped out his flare and crushed it beneath his feet. Her vision had never been clearer. She could see the individual fibers on the boy's shirt and the ripples in the air from his slightest movements. She could smell the scent of his blood in his veins. Someone hurled a dagger at her and Rose could hear it whistling through the air. She turned, caught it by its handle, and hurled it back at such a high speed that it pierced through the highborn girl's thigh and *kept flying*. Rose crushed her flare, and now her Godliness was fading. Her vision was blurring. She had only a few seconds left.

Rose turned, searching for a final victim, and then saw Dawn. She was pinned to the floor by three highborns, and Emma was standing above her. *What happened to no alliances?*

In a split-second, as Rose felt her magic begin to fade, Rose made a decision.

Lightning flashed and the three highborns were launched thirty feet away. Rose knocked Emma to the ground, kicking her away, and the lightning left her veins. She was, once again, human. But it was enough. Dawn scrambled to her feet as Rose collapsed to the floor.

"Hey, Dawn?" Rose murmured. Dawn surrounded them with a shield of water, her hands shining with gentle, healing light, but Rose shook her head.

"I've done... enough. Too much damage." Dawn surveyed Rose's injuries. Her eyes, Rose noticed, were brighter than usual.

"Over and over," Dawn said. "Over and over, you've saved and spared me. Why?"

"You better get first place," Rose said. Dawn nodded. "Crush the flare."

The pain overwhelmed her. Everything faded away.

* * *

Rose's eyes opened.

The arena.

"What was I? What rank?" Rose asked, pushing herself into a sitting position. It took a second for her to recognize that her injured wrist could move again.

"You were seventh," a voice said from beside her, and Rose's eyes widened.

It wasn't Ash.

"Halt?" Rose asked, her eyes wide and disbelieving. "You're... you're here?"

"No, in fact, I'm an illusion brought on by your grievous injuries." Just like always, Rose couldn't tell whether or not he was joking.

"Did you... did you see?"

"Yes."

"I—"

"You were amazing."

Rose's throat tightened.

"Against all odds." Rose tilted her head to look toward Halt, and she stopped in surprise. She had seen him smile before, but, looking back, it now seemed so long ago. A distant memory.

"I don't think ... I don't think I could've gotten this far without you," Rose murmured.

"No," Halt said. "You did this. You worked for this. Against all odds, from slave to *seventh*. Even I only placed eleventh, Rose. You're unprecedented."

Rose, though she didn't know why, almost wanted to cry.

"There's a duel tomorrow, right?" Rose asked, ignoring the lump in her throat. Halt nodded, and then he was coaching her through flaws in her strategy, inefficiencies in her magic use. This was familiar. By the end of the evening, Rose's cheeks hurt from smiling.

* * *

"The first-year duals will commence," Master Mekhl shouted. The audience quieted. Rose, any exhaustion erased by nerves, stared at the rising sun. "And the first match... Emma and Rose."

Rose's body jerked as she stared at Emma, who was avoiding her gaze. Clenching her fists, Rose stood up from the row of students sitting on the edge of the field and walked into the arena from the day before. Without the trees, it was even larger than it had appeared. The entire field was empty, sand coating the floor. The audience would be watching closely, the Five Sorcerers looking on from above. This was a final judgment.

Rose stepped into the arena and bowed at Emma, and to Rose's utter surprise, she bowed back.

Respect.

"If you surrender or black out, you lose the battle. You may not use any medical materials or potions. Do you both understand?" Rose nodded.

"Begin."

Both girls didn't move. There was a reluctance in the air.

"An honorable duel?" Rose asked, her voice carrying into the audience. Emma hesitated, and the crowd was silent.

She nodded.

Swallowing her shock, Rose flew into action.

Everyone knew the base rules of an honorable duel. Although the handbook Rose had read had covered and explained over *sixty* rules, there were two essential rules that even those who weren't knights followed. One, never drop your weapon unless to cast magic. Two, precede any clash of magic with either a verbal warning or clash between blades.

Rose flicked her wrists, the movement now intimately familiar, and she lunged at Emma, who dodged to the side, unsheathing her sword. This time, there was no talk between the two, no condescending words. While Emma was still assured in her victory, Rose could tell she held just the smallest bit of respect for Rose. After all, she had agreed to an honorable duel. Rose was ferocious, attacking at every turn, and Emma responded in kind. The audience was silent besides the clang of sword against blade, and Rose found herself sinking deeper into a peaceful serenity that she had never experienced. Was this how Ash felt? Was this the joy she found in battle?

Her eyes only saw the blades and Emma, examining every detail of Emma's movements, and it was Rose that drew first blood, a tiny cut along Emma's cheek. They came to a standstill, Rose's daggers meeting Emma's sword with a *clang,* and they pressed against each other, fighting for leverage.

They stared at each other, and Rose smiled.

"Magic?" Rose murmured, soft enough so that the crowd wouldn't hear. An honorable duel. Emma's gaze held a hint of that old contempt, even so, she nodded. They jumped away from each other, retreating until they were twenty feet away, and as if in some invisible agreement, both built up power. Twenty seconds passed in total, absolute silence.

Armageddon.

A maelstrom of lightning fell from the sky, and Emma responded in kind with a whirling body of sharp, slicing wind. Their storm stirred up bursts of sand from the ground and electricity sparked and danced, so thick and bright that Rose was sure the crowd had been blinded. Each girl shielded, surrounding themselves with their element. When the dust cleared, both summoned their power. Lightning writhed above Rose, ripe with potential, and both girls paused, registering the loaded electromagnetic fields and blades of wind floating in the air.

Their blades met with a resounding *clash*. Slave and High Lady both shouted as their magic arced through the air, Rose's arrows of electricity sent hurtling toward the ground by gusts of wind, falcons of swirling gray fog pierce through by bolts of lightning, tiny darts of electricity meeting those of wind within the air, all simultaneously, all while their blades crossed.

Rose's magic seemed endless.

Battle was an art, a dance. When Rose's eyes met Emma's, she saw that the same light within her own eyes shone within them. Magic met magic with beautiful flashes of light and sparks flew as their blades met.

Rose saw the split-second of an opening before Emma realized it was there.

She had surrounded her sword with electricity and Emma had retaliated with a shield of wind, but Rose felt before seeing the slight weak point. Stabbing toward it, Rose expected to meet flesh only to be stabbed through her left shoulder by a spear of wind protruding from the shield.

Baited again.

"You've got to stop falling for that," Emma murmured, and Rose backed away, pulling herself off the spear of wind. Ignoring the pain, Rose allowed lightning to arc across her skin, burning the wound shut on both sides.

They flew back into battle, Rose increasing her intensity further. It only took ten more minutes for Rose to bypass Emma's defense with a cleverly placed feint, allowing her to plunge her dagger into Emma's side before backing away. They were both panting, Emma's shirt now streaked with blood and Rose's shoulder aching with pain. Tiny scratches covered Rose's face and arms from tiny blades of wind, and Emma sported a second-degree burn on her left cheek from a stray bolt of lightning.

Emma was, truly, amazing.

She didn't hold the same prodigious power as Dawn or the Prince. Her power had been achieved through pure, absolute hard work.

"I respect you," Rose said. She bowed her head. There was a split second of silence, and then—

Pain.

Rose was barreled back by an explosion of wind. She crashed into the wall and cried out, stunned by the pain lancing across her back. Invisible chains wrapped around her wrists, chaining her to the wall, and Rose bit her tongue to stop from crying out again as blades of wind pierced through her body. *Emma had broken the rules.* Rose wasn't entitled to an honorable duel, but Emma had *promised her one.* Had it all been an elaborate trick? Had Rose simply imagined the respect in Emma's eyes? The crowd was murmuring, even the highborns, and Rose knew that Emma had crossed the line. An honorable duel was an honorable duel—to break those laws was to break an invisible code of honor

"I don't dual honorably with a slave," Emma snarled, and Rose's heart fell.

I was a fool to believe her.

"What are those murmurs for? I'm merely putting her back in her place. Look closely at the scars on her wrist, and you'll see why my chains fit around her so well."

Silence.

Rose felt hot tears sliding down her cheeks.

"A slave? Become a mage?" Emma laughed, and Rose thrashed against her chains. Blunt force crashed into her and Rose cried out in pain—then stopped.

The crow.

Rose went perfectly, absolutely still as small splinters of wood fell from her pocket to the ground.

The crow.

The chains around her wrists shattered, and Rose touched the ground gently, ethereally silent. Rage incarnate.

The crow.

"How dare you," Rose murmured. When Emma saw the fragments of wood on the ground, her face whitened for just a split-second before lightning descended from the sky. The lightning cleared to reveal Emma straightening from a crouch, wind dissolving around her as she smiled.

"I'm glad to see you still have fight in you."

"This isn't an honorable duel anymore."

Lightning and wind met with a clap of thunder, and the crowd gasped as one. There was no more polite tact, no more blades meeting, just one burst of power after another, each sending sprays of sand and dust across the battlefield. *If she's going to play dirty, so will I.*

Emma couldn't, *wouldn't* know that Rose could cast three spells at the same time.

As a dragon of lightning reared its head back and struck Emma's shield of wind again and again, Rose created a shield of lightning in front of her. Emma's eyes latched onto it and Rose felt blunt force strike the shield, but her own eyes were focused on the space behind Emma. A small portion of the lightning from the dragon broke off, forming a spear behind Emma. It rocketed toward Emma, aiming directly toward her hand, and Emma cried out as it pierced her hand, breaking through skin and bone. Yanking out the paralyzing lightning spear, Emma let her hand hang limply to the side, covered in blood and fragments of bone.

"I didn't know you could cast three at once, slave," Emma murmured. She snapped her unbroken fingers and Rose felt the wind blow as spikes of wind pressed against her back.

Rose realized this with a jolt. If Emma still had mana, she would've staunched the bleeding in her hand using a barrier of wind and would've put up a second skin of hard air as a precaution. This was the last of her mana, a last-ditch attack.

Rose raised a hand, furrowing her brows, and then feigned magic exhaustion. She collapsed to the floor and held her stomach.

"It's time to surrender, Rose. You're out of mana, there's a spear against your back. Admit your defeat," Emma said. Rose pretended to try again, clenching her fist and then seizing in pain.

"Stop trying, you *insignificant thing*," Emma spat. She turned toward the crowd, her back to Rose, and Rose couldn't repress her grin of triumph. "Look at her. This is the fate of the lowborns. It was set in the stars from her birth. There is *nothing* she can do to fight against it."

Electricity rained from the sky as Rose ripped out a final piece of magic. It struck Emma with the sound of thunder clapping and the scent of burning flesh.

Emma collapsed to her knees, her eyes rolling to the back of the head, and Rose felt the spears around her dissipate.

I won.

Even as blood from her wounds dripped onto the floor, Rose stumbled toward Emma one shuffling step after another and planted her foot on her head. The crowd murmured, some even shouted: this was unforeseen, unheard of, a slave with her foot planted on an unconscious High Lady's head.

It's time to let go of me, Rose.

Jerking her head up, Rose wondered whether she had imagined Ezra's honey sweet voice or whether some spectral force had allowed her to hear those words. And, either way, those words were true.

Ezra was dead.

But Rose—she was still here. Still living, still fighting, seeking a better life for herself – and justice for others like him.

Rose took one last glance at the shattered figurine of the crow before turning away. *It's time to move on.*

Tilting her head up, Rose dropped to her knees and roared her victory to the skies.

* * *

"You fucking idiot," Halt snarled from beside her. Rose opened her eyes and immediately grinned.

"C'mon, Halt, that was *awesome* right? C'mon, admit it, I was *awesome*. Did you see me control three bodies of Lightning at once? And faking being exhausted at the end—"

"That was reckless," Halt admonished, but he was smiling nonetheless – wide and unabashed, filled with joy.

"It was! I won! I won against the second-best girl in our *year*, Halt!"

"She's a High Lady, no?"

"Yeah! *Let's fucking go!*" Rose jumped up from her bed, barely sparing her magical exhaustion a thought.

"Kid," Halt said. Rose turned to him, grinning widely. "You did amazing."

This time, Rose did cry. Happy tears. They were unbelievably joyful tears.

* * *

Rose was healed just in time for Ash's match.

She was paired with another knight's daughter, the only other one still present. They agreed to an honorable duel and stuck to it until the very end, shaking hands, backing away until they were six feet away, bowing, waiting ten seconds, and then diving into battle. Their swordplay was terrific, at a pace so terrifyingly fast that Rose could barely discern what was happening. Finally, with a *clang* and the flying of sparks, both backed twenty feet away. Magic sparked.

Rose loved watching Ash battle.

Fire sprang to life on her blade and flame sparked to life around it in flowing, beautiful arcs. When they next flew into battle, fire sparked and flew as if it had a mind of its own. The arcs around Ash's sword spread into the air, surrounding the battling pair of knights, and the crowd gasped as it suddenly formed a spear of flame that plunged into battle. Upon seeing a shield suddenly materialize where the flame was heading, it melted away back, back into the arcs of fire. It morphed into a shield when Ash missed a step in swordplay and just as quickly found openings in her opponents defense, flashing fluidly between attacks and defenses. Most importantly, it was based entirely on Ash's instincts. Built over a decade of battle, Ash's instincts were always accurate, always on point. It was impossible for her fire to miss an attack that wasn't shielded or create a flawed defense, because Ash's instincts were nearly perfect. It was often her own mind and overthinking that brought her down.

But her opponent was good.

She had extremely fine control and seemed to focus her magic defensively. Her lightning shield was permanent, infallible in its defense, and morphing from place to place within milliseconds. Their battle, Rose realized, was not a show of power but of skill, showing not brutality but elegance.

Even so, their battle barely lasted twenty minutes before a quick defeat. Ash's four-pronged attack struck the girl's lightning shield, and as fire and lightning flared, the shield cracked with an audible *snap*. The fire pierced through her shield, surrounding the girl within seconds.

She surrendered gracefully and the fire melted away, leaving both parties relatively unharmed. They bowed at each other and the crowd cheered: an ordinary battle, free of drama, presenting amazing skill and strategy.

River, a rare long-distance fighter, presented a rare, refreshing change to the increasing monotony of weapons-focused, close-ranged fighting with magic battling around them. After hours spent on increasing his stamina and speed and receiving training from one of the Masters in private, River had honed his speed until he could sprint at an uncontrollable but shocking pace, marking the crux of his battle strategy. After sprinting away from an opponent, he'd stop for barely a split-second before firing an arrow with shocking, deadly precision. This was entwined with the most important strategy of all: his magic. Silent and invisible, River channeled water from within the earth, allowing it to creep through the ground until it was positioned beneath an opponent, freezing their feet to the ground and giving him the chance to perfectly land an arrow. Even with his deadly power from a distance and impressive stamina, River still possessed a crucial disadvantage: by sacrificing most of his training time on speed, magic, and the bow, River was below average in close-range battles. The single time he faltered with his water magic and allowed his fire-wielding opponent to reach him, River was decimated by a barrage of slashes before he could get away. Even so, his opponent, a fire-wielding merchant's daughter, was at a severe disadvantage due to fire being a mid-to-close range element. She was eventually knocked out by a sixth arrow to her side, leaving River standing fifty feet away from her, chest heaving, face flushed with victory.

Dawn—well, her battle had been a one-sided beatdown. Her physical strength alone had overwhelmed her opponent, and she had drawn it out only to display her skill.

"Rose, do you know what this means?" Ash asked her. Rose snapped out of her reverie, tearing her gaze away from the ceiling, and glanced at her.

"Hmm?"

"We're apprentices now. *Apprentices*. We won our battles, we were in the top fifteen, we're *apprentices*."

"Not if we don't do well on the examinations. Remember, if we fail more than two subjects, we get kicked out even if you were the winner of the whole arena battle." Ash's expression didn't even change, she looked so absolutely thrilled that Rose smiled as well. She was right to be happy.

"I call first bath!" Rose said. Ignoring Ash's indignant shout, Rose stepped into the empty bathrooms and sighed in contentment. Many highborns who had homes within the city had returned there, but Rose, Ash, and a few others thought that staying at the Academy would be more convenient. Filling a tub with steaming hot water, Rose realized that she couldn't remember the last time she'd relaxed in a bath. Stepping into the bathroom, Rose stripped and stared at the mirror, her eyes widening with astonishment. Despite her daily exhaustion, she had visibly grown. Her skin was smooth and taut with muscle, and her hair had grown to her ribs, which were now only barely visible.

Most importantly, however, scars dotted her skin, like individual marks of glory. Physical proof of what she had survived.

The ones on her wrists weren't even severe compared to those she had collected during the Academy. There was the scar on her side from the arena, an array of smaller scars on her arms and legs from training incidents, as well as several burn scars from cauterization. As Rose turned around and examined her back, she winced—lash scars, despite it all, were still present.

Rose sank into the bath, allowing its warmth to relax muscles.

Apprenticeship was no longer a faraway dream. It was within arm's reach, barely in her grasp, and Rose could finally allow herself to rest. The final stretch was over, her future was set in stone.

* * *

Rose stood in the corner of the atrium, rubbing one arm with another, watching families and students reunite with tears and joy. Rose could see Ash in the distance, hugging a younger kid who had to be her brother, and Venus explaining something animatedly to his father. Just as she was ready to leave for the barracks, she heard a distant voice cry her name.

"Rose!"

"Oh, thank god," Rose said, turning around. Halt and Blossom. A smile spread over Rose's face, and she sprinted toward her, barreling into her and hugging her tightly. Rose had missed her.

"I saw your battles," Blossom murmured, and Rose drew back hurriedly.

"Hey, no, I'm okay, look!" Rose said, gesturing toward herself. "The healers are really good."

"Yeah. Trust me, I've seen Halt have it worse." Faintly, Rose wondered when Blossom had met him. "Rose, when I saw you were put up against the High Lady, I wasn't happy."

"I don't know why they did that, either," Rose admitted. "It wasn't a good match-up for me."

"I knew you would win," Halt said. Rose blinked, surprised, and smiled. "I'm impressed by your performance in the arena. You forced six people to surrender and disabled two more people," Halt told her. "You're lucky that Master Mekhl finally put in a no-alliance rule. The highborns loved to gang up on the lowborns."

"The results are being announced soon," Blossom said, and Rose's heart clenched with nerves. Her stomach felt like it was trying to escape from her mouth. The atrium's tables had been cleared and a stage had been erected in the front with Earth Magic, and mounted on one of the walls was an enormous metal board. *The results.* Rose's heart nearly stopped as Master Mekhl and the Queen approached the stage. The Queen. Aspen's mother.

"I would like to request the parents leave the atrium. The results are for the students to view and interpret. Students, please take a seat and quiet down!" Master Mekhl shouted. The parents filed out of the atrium, leaving a tense, absolutely silent group of students behind. Rose, seated in between River and Ash, had to clench her fist to keep from shaking.

"First of all, I would like to congratulate every one of you that has made it this far. The fact that you have endured until the end makes you a warrior in itself." It was the nicest thing Master Mekhl had said all year, and yet it meant nothing in the face of what was going to be revealed.

"I know you all are anticipating the results. I will not dally longer. We will now reveal the ranks."

And then, without warning, with a flourish of fire and lightning, the wall behind Master Mekhl burst into flame. Rose's heart beat faster and faster as the writing began to form, from first to last, and Rose began to scan the list for her name, beginning from number fifteen.

Ten. there wasn't a sign of her name. Ash was number ten, she grabbed Rose's hand and screamed with joy, but Rose continued scanning. Her heart fell as she saw River in number eight. It wasn't plausible for Rose to have ranked above him.

Right?

"Rose! Look! You're number six!"

Rose stood up so quickly that the chair behind her tipped over.

Number six: Rose.

Against all odds, against all hope, Rose's name was on that wall.

She was an apprentice.

"Oh my god," Rose whispered, and when she touched her face, she found that she was crying tears of joy. Someone knocked into her and Rose tumbled down, breaking out in sobbing laughter as River apologized. Turning toward the door behind which Halt and Blossom were doubtlessly waiting, Rose ran toward it, shoved it open, and dove into Halt's arms. As Rose looked around herself, tears of joy streaming down her face, surrounded by her family and the people she loved, she was happy.

* * *

Rose spent the rest of the day telling Halt about the Academy.

Her first encounter with Ash, Dawn's rescue, and the survival test. When she told Halt about the wildfire, he'd actually chuckled and clapped Rose proudly on the back. She told them about the first attack, the midterms and Emma's parents, rescuing the orphan children, and Aspen's kidnapping. Rose didn't know why, but under the guise of retrieving a few of her belongings from her barracks, she had wandered back up to the flag room study.

Aspen's notes were still on his table.

What he could've become if he had stayed, what another battle between him and Dawn would've looked like... Rose turned away and stared out of the window.

Do I deserve to be this happy?

The question shot through her like a bolt of lightning and Rose jerked back, her eyes widening. Aspen was *gone*, and even though she had promised herself she'd let go of Ezra, his death was also her fault. Her mistake. Her own weakness. Sure, she had grown, but was she enough?

Was she allowed to be this happy, even after she had failed so many people?

The trapdoor opened.

"I thought I'd find you here," Halt murmured. He didn't even look surprised when he saw her face, streaked with tears. "What's wrong?"

"Do I deserve to be happy?" Rose looked back toward Halt, a strained smile on her face.

Her words were cut off by Halt embracing her. Rose buried her face in his shoulder, allowing herself to sink into his warm hug.

"You do, Rose," Halt murmured. "It wasn't your fault. None of it was your fault, Rose, *none of it.*"

"Really?"

"Yes."

***

The food was spectacular.

Shoving a piece of roast duck into her mouth, Rose groaned as it melted on her tongue, buttery and salty and perfect.

"It's not *that* good," Ash said, watching her incredulously.

"It's a feast prepared in our honor by the cooks from the palace. It *is* that good," Rose replied. She looked up from her meal, wiping her mouth with the back of her hand, winced at the stain of grease, then reached down and wiped it inconspicuously on the corner of her dark gray robe. Standing up, she examined the many nobles and few students dancing on the dance floor, Halt and Blossom included, and grinned wider.

"I'm going to the table again," Rose told Ash, who looked at her and sighed.

"Isn't this your third helping?" Ash asked.

"No, fourth."

Ash snorted in incredulity.

As Rose approached the enormous table of food, she turned around, nearly bumped into a person who was standing behind her.

"I'm sorry," she said as she looked up. Upon seeing who it was, she stumbled backward and nearly dropped her plate. "Your Majesty!" she said. She quickly dropped to a kneel, one knee on the ground and hands clasped behind her back, as was customary for a slave.

"Stand up, Rose."

The queen knows my name.

"You're the one who's been having dreams about Aspen, right?" the Queen asked. She had midnight black hair, like Aspen's, and held herself impressively, her stare regal and yet not condescending. Despite how intimidating she was, Rose lifted her chin up slightly and made eye contact.

Rose's eyes widened.

The queen's eyes. They were like her own, *exactly* like Rose's, stormy gray, almost alive. The queen jerked back as if slapped, staring at Rose as if she was an alien. There was a tense silence as they stared at each other.

And then, as Rose began to back away, someone screamed.

Shadows, oh so familiar shadows, burst from the walls and floor. They were coming toward them, toward the *Queen*. The Five Sorcerers were beside the Queen in an instant, surrounding her and lifting her into the air, but the shadows didn't follow them.

No.

They kept on rushing in Rose's direction. Toward Rose.

Rose's eyes widened as the shadows reached her, her mouth opening in a scream as they surrounded her. They didn't hurt. They didn't kill. They wrapped around her, forming a cocoon. Sound around her melted into a vague buzz in her ears as and the shadows shut off all light. The only thing she could see, surrounding her, was pure darkness. Rose thrashed, fought against the cold prison, but a sweet fog wafted through her nose, and Rose felt her eyelids droop and her conscious melt away.

The last thing she felt before she blacked out was a cold hand soothingly brushing over her brow.

* * *

"Save her!" the Queen screamed. She broke free of the Five Sorcerers, who watched as the Queen lunged toward the cocoon of shadows, magic of all elements bursting from her hands and hitting the cocoon with a thud. The cocoon, just as suddenly as the shadows had appeared, melted away into nothingness.

The Queen dropped to her knees on the ground.

"Your Majesty?" Crystal asked, her voice filled with confusion. The entire hall was staring at their Queen in confused astonishment.

"Rose. That's what the Dark Sorcerer named my daughter."

Crystal's eyes widened.

"Halt told me... she was a slave. With no last name. He'd found her in the desert, unconscious, and she'd told him nothing about her past. And at first, I wasn't sure... but... her eyes. They're like mine, like a storm cloud. Her element is Lightning, the masters told me she's been steadily increasing her mana reserves at a shocking pace, even when the highborns were beginning to slow."

"Rose would have Five Elements if she were—"

"It was locked away," the Queen whispered. "By the Dark Sorcerer. He locked her power away to make sure she wouldn't get away as a kid, then reawakened it with trauma. That's how she was a Null before."

Silence. Absolute silence as the entire Great Hall stared at her. They couldn't hear what she was saying, but everyone knew that the girl that had been taken meant much more to the Queen than they had imagined.

"Rose is my daughter."

Chapter Nineteen

ROSE OPENED HER EYES.

She knew this place.

It was the cell. She could see the familiar, black, desolate mountain outside, could hear the whistling of wind and could smell the faint scent of irony blood. *Another dream.* But when she tried to stand up and move around, she couldn't. Instead, she heard the clanking of chains.

Rose was on her knees, wrists chained to the wall and feet chained to the floor.

Ah.

The memory of the cocoon of shadows returned to her, and Rose slumped in her chains. Across from her, she saw Aspen's unconscious, slumped over figure. Even in the darkness, Rose knew something was wrong. He was painfully thin, his wrists bony and face pale, his black hair matted with dried blood.

As she fell back against the chains, her mind racing with panic, a third figure she hadn't seen before emerged from the corner of the room, as if unfolding from the darkness. He was cloaked in shadows but was shorter than the Dark Sorcerer. Strangest of all, he held himself differently: he shrank back against the shadows when Rose stared at him, his shoulders were slumped, and his posture was horrible.

"Who are you? What do you... what do you want?" Rose's voice was hoarse and dry, and she shrank back against the wall. He picked something up from what seemed to be a table. Rose winced as he approached her, but he merely held a cup of water to her lips. Parting her lips, Rose drank, sighing as the icy cold water soothed her throat.

"Who are you?" Rose asked again. He hesitated before he spoke, a second of silence that enveloped Rose with despair. This person was not an ally.

"I am the Prince of Darkness. The Dark Sorcerer's creation"

Rose's heart stopped.

"Thank you... for everything."

She would never forget that voice, not for as long as she lived.

Staring up at the dark figure before her, Rose's body fell limp against her chains, shock and fear pumping through her veins as she stared at the boy who had haunted her dreams for months.

The Prince of Darkness. The Dark Sorcerer's accomplice.

Ezra.

"You... you're alive?" Rose whispered, and in that singular moment, everything was all right. *Ezra's okay. Ezra's okay. Ezra's okay.*

"I..." Ezra's voice was like honey to her tongue, but something told her this was wrong. "I'm alive. I..." The realization came to her like a lightning bolt.

A hero of justice.

"It was all for you," Rose murmured, and he drew back, confused. She was crying again. "All of it. It was for you. If it wasn't for you, I'd still be with Halt and Blossom. I wouldn't care about becoming some hero, I wouldn't care about becoming an apprentice, I wouldn't have had to do any of it." Ezra didn't respond. "I would be happy with Blossom and Halt. I wouldn't *be here right now.*"

"Rose, I'm sorry-"

"You *bastard*!" Rose shouted. The cup of water he had placed beside her spilled as Rose lunged at him, stopped by the chains on the wall. "You fucking bastard! I fucking hate you, I fucking *hate you.* You — How *could you?* Do you have *any idea* how badly your death affected me? You could've told me something. *Anything.*"

"I didn't have a choice!" Ezra shouted, and Rose would've jerked back if not for the burning anger surging through her.

"There is *always* a choice," Rose snarled.

"Not for me. I am a Homunculus, the Dark Sorcerer's creation. I do what he commands, what he wills."

"Then you kill yourself, or kill him, or become anything but what you are now. You've killed people, Ezra, and for what?"

"I want to live!"

"If I were you, I wouldn't," Rose snarled back. Ezra paused. If she could see them, she was sure there would be hurt in his eyes.

He deserved it.

There was only silence as Ezra walked across the room and opened the door. He was just about to step outside when Rose spoke.

"I was wrong." He paused, looking back at her. "I was wrong. You're a monster."

* * *

"This will be more deadly than anything we have attempted to do," Crystal told the four other sorcerers. They didn't reply.

"We know, Crystal," Aura finally replied. Erik nodded.

"If..." Crystal paused. "If you feel you must leave, I would not blame you." No one moved, no one spoke. The Five Sorcerers merely stared at each other, eyes hardened and determined.

"Come on, then," Crystal said, swinging herself onto her horse. "Let's go. Audra. Teleport us."

With a flash of lightning, the Five Sorcerers disappeared. They reappeared in the Ken'o Mountains, a land of utter darkness, even during midday.

"Scout for buildings. Search for Rose and the Crown Prince. We'll rescue both of them, no matter what it takes."

* * *

The Dark Sorcerer walked into their cell without warning.

Rose jumped back as he burst inside, her mind suddenly overwhelmed with fear as she stared at that non-human figure of darkness.

"Rose," he hissed.

"Dark Sorcerer," she replied. They contemplated each other.

"I have waited a long, long time for this moment," the Dark Sorcerer murmured. He approached her and Rose shrunk back. "I've been searching for your power since you escaped those despicable mines."

"Why *my* powers? Aspen's more powerful," Rose said, nonplussed.

The Dark Sorcerer tilted his head.

"I thought you'd have figured it out by now."

"Figured what out?"

"Ah. Well, I won't tell you. Just know that, Rose, you are much more powerful than you may first think. Your power is endless. It has been sustaining me for your entire childhood."

"*Sustained* you? How?" Rose asked. She was growing more confused by the minute.

"Well, you may have known me as Master?"

Rose jolted back. Shocked. The Dark Sorcerer had been *Master?*

"Then why did you let me go?" Rose asked. "Why not take my powers as soon as I developed them?"

"We both know how magic works, Rose. When you first develop it as a child, it keeps on growing until late adolescence. After I placed that seal on your magic, there wasn't a way to reawaken that magic of yours unless you went through extreme emotional pain. My plan was to have the Dark Prince force you to trust him, then break your heart. He ended up faking his death instead. The grief that his death caused was so powerful that it released more of your power than I expected. You escaped. Either way, you are here now, and that seal is still present. With it, I can still take your power—and with your power, I will create a better world."

"What about *this* is a better world?" Rose asked softly. "What about this death and suffering and pain is a better world?"

The Dark Sorcerer stared at her.

"Pain? Death? Suffering?" the Dark Sorcerer laughed. "Naive child. Those things will never be worse than what I, and many others, have gone through because of the traditions of these kingdoms."

Without speaking, he motioned to Ezra. Together, the two left the room, leaving Rose to rot in grief and confusion.

* * *

Aspen and Rose both looked up as the Dark Sorcerer strode into their cell.

"She's awake," a voice said from behind him. Ezra.

"Good. Grab her."

Ezra avoided her glare as she was unchained slowly. Reluctantly. As soon as her limbs were free, Rose lunged at Ezra, only to be restrained by darkness.

"Hey! *Hey!* Where are you taking her?" Aspen yelled from behind her. He was ignored. Rose thrashed in Ezra's tight grasp to no avail. Rose was carried roughly into a room, where the door was locked shut behind them.

"Chain her to the ground."

Rose was slammed into the ground with a roughness that jarred her teeth. She was pressed to the ground, lying face-up, wrists and ankles were attached to the ground with manacles of iron.

"What are you *doing*?" Rose shouted. The Dark Sorcerer ignored her. He picked up a piece of chalk, pushing Ezra out of the way as he began a strange circular design on the floor.

"Insert the serum," the Dark Sorcerer ordered, drawing a syringe from his pocket and throwing it at Ezra. He walked toward her, and, without hesitation, plunged the needle into one of Rose's arms, pushing the cool liquid in without hesitation.

Almost immediately, Rose's vision went black.

* * *

She was in a realm of light and beauty.

Although she was standing on solid ground, she could see nothing but light, light of all colors, shining and twisting and moving in the air.

Suddenly, before her, a figure emerged. In sharp contrast to all that light, the Dark Sorcerer looked like a black hole.

As he stared right at Rose, she felt a familiar feeling of light erupt within her. Whirling around, Rose saw before her gates of darkness, the very same that had cracked open when Ezra had died.

"I thought those were broken," Rose murmured to herself.

"Do you know why I want you?" the Dark Sorcerer asked her.

"Why?"

"Because you have power."

"Aspen. Why not have him instead?"

"Because you have more."

Slowly, as the Dark Sorcerer commanded, the gates gently opened.

As it has been, and as it was again.

A gate that hid light and writhing, beautiful power. There had been more power within her then she had ever imagined, trapped behind those pitch-black gates.

With an exhale, Rose felt it begin to flow from within the gates, from within *her*. Beginning and end and eternity, conscious and oblivion and wonder, good and evil and chaos that flowed from her in a pure stream of power. It pooled in front of her in a glowing ball of life and light and beauty. Rose almost instinctively knew that if this power was taken by someone else or lost to the never-ending ether that they stood in, she would never get it back. The loss of this magic would be permanent.

This was her magic, in its purest form.

And still he took more. It hurt.

He ripped the light, the life, the beauty of her magic from her. Oblivion and consciousness. Creation and destruction. It swirled in front of her, taking a shape that she knew had lay within her, a shape swirling with lapis and scarlet and emerald and silver-white.

Four elements.

Flexing her fingers, Rose watched as lightning formed on her fingers.

When she had opened those gates the first time, she had gained lightning. Had the other four elements been hidden behind those gates too? Imprisoned and unused until now?

And still, he took more.

It was agony. *Pure agony.* She could feel the power she had never known ripped from her like a candle's fragile flames blown out by a gust of wind.

She screamed.

The magic that had flowed in her bones after she had first gained that power disappeared. Her power was disappearing.

Her power.

Her power.

After all those months spent honing it and shaping it with her blood and tears, it was being taken from her.

With a piercing scream, Rose took the power that poured from her. She took the tether connecting the ball of power to her and *snapped* it. She could feel the disconnection resounding in her body, in her soul, in every inch and pore of her body.

The flow of energy trickled to a stop.

She collapsed to the floor, panting through clenched teeth, then looked up at the Dark Sorcerer. She was empty. Completely empty.

Her magic was gone. The Dark Sorcerer stepped toward the glowing ball of energy, hand outstretched.

"No!" Rose screamed. A tendril of darkness from his hand extended toward the ball. The Dark Sorcerer stared at it reverently, a hand on either side of the ball of energy, and darkness formed on his fingertips.

He was preparing to absorb the pure energy. Her magic.

No. Please, Rose begged. *Stop. Stop.*

"Stop."

As the Dark Sorcerer whirled around, fire careened into him, sending him to the ground. Rose surged toward her power, clenching her fist as the energy flowed slowly, *achingly slowly,* into her. The Dark Sorcerer let out a shout of rage, but it was too late.

It was hers.

So much power. Within her, now, sparked not just lightning, but all five of the elements. As one, Rose and the Dark Sorcerer looked toward the two figures who were now standing before them.

One of darkness and one of light. Shoulder-to-shoulder, they were two polars, two extremes, two opposites.

Two Princes.

Aspen and Ezra stepped into the ether, and the Dark Sorcerer laughed.

"Little boy. My Dark Prince. Step away from the boy beside you."

Even though Ezra's muscles rippled with tension, he obeyed, nearing the Dark Sorcerer, who summoned a blade of darkness.

"Come closer, little one. Closer. Closer."

"Ezra," Rose whispered. The ones around her seemed to be mute to her cries as Ezra stepped closer and closer to the Dark Sorcerer, until his chest was pressed up against the tip of the blade of darkness.

"Run yourself upon my blade," the Dark Sorcerer ordered.

And then Ezra spoke.

"Sometimes, when you stare into the darkness long enough, Father, you'll find that the darkness may stare back."

Everyone seemed to go completely still as the shadows around Ezra slid to the floor.

"And the darkness didn't just stare. It whispered, coaxed, telling me that if I took one tiny step within, everything would be okay."

Standing in the Dark Prince's place was the Ezra Rose knew. The one with a soft smile, silver hair, and golden eyes.

The lost boy, terrified of becoming a monster.

"But one day, I met someone else. A light. And even though she was submerged in the darkest of shadows around her, she shone with such intensity that I saw her. I *saw* her, even through the darkness."

Ezra turned and stared at her, intensity glowing in those stunning golden eyes. He was still staring at Rose when he spoke.

"And that's why I'll never listen to you or the Blood Oath again, Father. I don't need Darkness anymore."

The Dark Sorcerer stared at him.

He laughed.

"A light?" the Dark Sorcerer's laugh was horrendous, high and cold, the sound glitching in the air, wavering in and out of existence. "A light? My dear prince, I'm afraid you're entirely mistaken."

"How?"

"That light isn't going to save you."

"How do you know?"

"Because I've had that light too. The thing is, that light is never permanent. Light can be extinguished. And what happens to you then, Prince?"

Before any of them could object, the Dark Sorcerer continued talking.

"Do you know how I got my powers?"

Rose shook her head.

"I was a twin of a queen. The one who was born second. They couldn't kill me, nor did I belong among those of the living. So I was cast into shadow. Forever the second. Forever ignored by my doting mother and forever hated by my own kingdom.

At first, I didn't mind. I was powerful, magically, and a quiet child. I liked being left alone so that I could practice my magic and practice fighting. I liked being powerful, but only so that I could help others. Sometimes I'd disguise myself and go out into the streets, healing the sick and impoverished in the slums.

But everything changed. On my sixteenth birthday—on my sister's sixteenth birthday, my mother organized a duel. My sister against me. The beautiful against the ugly. No one had taught me. No one had helped me. They all expected me to lose.

But then, when we started, a single blow of my sword disarmed hers. A single blast of my magic destroyed her shields. She was inferior, far inferior, and I was the more powerful. There was silence when I won with her on the ground beneath me, and then everyone looked at me with... awe.

From then on, I was the most important. I was better. I was named the next heir to the throne, even as a second-born, for my power was so much more potent than my sister's that it was unquestionable who was the better. My sister was cast aside, and I was to become the King of the Light Realm, the first second born to take the throne. But I was a quiet child. I disliked the crowds, I disliked ruling and had never been trained for it. I preferred fighting, being a warrior instead of a scholar. So I cast away my crown to my sister, who accepted. I chose to become her guard. She had always treated me with kindness. She was my light.

But when she was crowned, she turned on me. The first thing she did was *destroy* me. She stripped me of my powers and positions, framing me of treason, and threw me into prison. I fought hard, but I was subdued. My magic was stifled. I was chained to the ground with barely enough food and water to live. But of course, I could not die. I was a Prince, I was still powerful, to send me to death would be a near crime.

So one day, as I sat there, emaciated and weak, my sister opened the door. She handed me a fresh set of clothes and unlocked my chains. I could barely stand. I wobbled toward her, and she looked at me, before saying that I could go free. Exiled out of my kingdom, never to come back, but free.

I, foolish and naive and hoping that she had changed, stepped out of the castle and experienced sunshine for the first time in years. My magic was slow and weak, but as I began taking the closest route out of the kingdom, it grew stronger. It was thanks to my magic that I survived the twenty assassins that were sent after me. By my sister.

All of them were disabled, out cold on the ground but one. We stared at each other. I knew the girl who stood before me. She was a girl I had healed, younger than me by five years. When I was eleven, I had removed a dangerous tumor from her lungs that would have killed her.

'You.' She had stared at me, then acknowledged, 'you were the one that healed me.'

'I'm not a bad person,' I begged in response. 'Just let me go free, I beg you. Think of it as repayment for saving your life.'

The girl had stood there and stared at me. Contemplating. I thought she would say yes.

'You aren't. But you're the second-born. Your sister is the firstborn. No matter what, you'll never be as good as her. I'll never listen to someone like you.'

I wasn't prepared for the knife she plunged into my back.

When I woke up, my light had turned to darkness. At first, I was disgusted. At first, I hated my powers. I had loved my light, just as I had always tried to love my sister. But as I explored my powers alone in the edges of the territories. I came to know this... with love comes the risk of hate, but with hate? There is no risk."

"Rhysand," Aspen whispered. The Dark Sorcerer jerked backward, as if that name had physically hurt him.

"How do you know my name?" he hissed at Aspen. Aspen didn't reply, his eyes beseeching.

"None of us have a choice," Aspen said. His voice, previously a hoarse whisper, was stronger now. Confident. "You can't choose whether or not you get hurt. It's inevitable. It's a part of the human condition."

"Aspen," Rose whispered.

"You can't choose whether or not to get hurt," Aspen repeated. "But you *can* choose whether to hurt others. I like my choices. Do you?"

Silence.

The Dark Sorcerer's shadows were melting away. For just a second, Rose saw the man underneath. He had golden eyes, even more vivid and beautiful than Ezra's.

"No more hurt. No more betrayal," Aspen whispered. "You can change."

And then his darkness raged.

"Did I choose who *hurt* me?" the Dark Sorcerer screamed. "Did Rose?"

And then the Dark Sorcerer turned to Rose.

"There is another who has experienced the same story as me, but on another magnitude of horror."

He was looking at Rose. Talking to Rose.

"Rose."

"No," Rose breathed. "I'm a slave. I'm an orphan."

She was a slave. No one. Devoid of magic, parentless, *no one*.

Rose held out her hands, summoning her magic. Instead of lightning, a plume of fire burst before her. Rose stumbled back, landing on her hands and knees as she held out her hands again. Lightning.

"Rose. How...?" Aspen asked, his face white.

The Queen's eyes. They were the same as hers.

Rose summoned wind next. Then water. Earth. The magic came as naturally as breathing for her. The five elements burst from her fingers, dancing and weaving among themselves like five ethereal dancers.

"I'm sure you've guessed already," the Dark Sorcerer sneered from above. "You're not just a slave. You have parents. You have power, more so than Aspen. See how easily the power flows through you? See how you're not confined to one element? *You could've been a Princess.* You see Aspen? His royalty, his privilege, his wealth? That could've been you."

Rose shook her head, staring at her hands, the world that she had known crashing down around her as she stared up at Aspen.

"You're Aspen's sister. His twin. His *younger* sister."

Rose's eyes widened.

"How... how am I a slave, then?" Rose stammered.

"Your mother made a deal with me."

"What?"

"Your mother's ancestor made a deal with me. The Five Sorcerers from long ago, after defeating me and draining me of power, were on the verge of death. As I was being led away by guards, your mother begged me to save the Five Sorcerers with the last of my power. She was afraid of what would happen if the cornerstone of her ruling power, the Five Sorcerers, died so soon after a revolution that had torn apart her country. She wanted power. In return, she would give me her child and allow what was left of me to go free. I don't think she expected that I would survive at all. I was covered in wounds and drained of power."

Rose stared at him with wide, disbelieving eyes.

"I agreed. I used the last of my power to save the Five Sorcerers, and went free. However, when I returned to this bloodline as soon as I had regained power, your mother given birth to her first children. She had two. One girl and one boy."

Rose shook her head mutely.

"Even though the girl was obviously more powerful and the boy a born scholar, the Queen did not hesitate when she chose which one to give to me for a life of eternal suffering."

Tears slipped down Rose's cheeks, dripping onto the floor of light as she stared at Aspen.

"She chose you. The second-born."

Silence.

It can't be true.

Rose wept.

"I will conquer the world," the Dark Sorcerer murmured. "And then create a new one, in which all is equal. In which the second-born can rule. In which rank does not exist. Commoner, peasant, noble, and slave, all equal. A world in which power is all that matters. Long ago, when I took the throne, people viewed me as barbaric. I enforced a system of battle in which a second-born had a chance to become a ruler. I slaughtered the Light Kingdom in revenge. Because of that, I was overthrown. But this time, when I rule, I will be successful. I will create a world in which Rose's story will never be retold."

Rose stared up at him, and for one horrible second, she believed him.

"And yet Rose has become an apprentice," Aspen growled. Rose looked up at him, surprised. "My mom has told me about Rose, my long-lost twin. Do you know why she chose you, Rose?"

Rose shook her head.

"Because she *knew* you were stronger! She *knew* you could survive, knew you were powerful, knew you would find a way back to where you belonged. And she *has*. She is an apprentice, a mage in training, and she is where she belongs. She is a warrior. Rhysand, if you come back, if you *change*, you can go back to where you belong too."

Everyone stared with bated breath at the Dark Sorcerer. At Rhysand.

"You looked just like her," Rhysand whispered. He looked, almost, human as he stared at Aspen. "Beautiful blue-green eyes. Both of you had eyes that were strange, unlike those of your family. Royals of the Lightning Kingdom have stormy gray eyes. Royals of the Light Kingdom had golden eyes. You are both different."

"I'm not her. I'm different. *You're* different," Aspen whispered. He outstretched his hand, as if offering it to the Dark Sorcerer. He stared at it.

"She said the same thing. 'You're different from before. You used to be worse than me, *Rhysand*. Why are you powerful now, *Rhysand*? Why am I jealous of you, *Rhysand*?* She said the exact same thing, boy. Everyone does."

The dark aura around him deepened as his face became covered in shadows, his eyes black pits of stygian, his body contorting into his figure of darkness and shadows and nightmares. Yet behind him, very faintly, Rose could see the outline of the human he used to be, glitching in and out of vision like a ghost, a look of frenzied fear and anger on its face, stuck in grotesque configurations as the Dark Sorcerer opened his mouth to let out a bone-chilling scream.

"*You are all weak,*" the Dark Sorcerer hissed. "Just like the past me was, burdened by the ideas of love and peace and mercy and kindness. You are all weak and worthless. Look at you all, sitting here, watching me. If you were stronger, you would *kill me,*" the Dark Sorcerer snarled. He pointed at Ezra, who's eyes grew wide. His body stiffened. "Kill her. Kill them both," the Dark Sorcerer hissed at him.

Ezra's body moved in twitchy, unsteady motions, an arrow of darkness forming in his hands as he moved to launch it at Rose.

"Ezra, please," Rose whispered. "Don't do it. *Don't do it!*"

Ezra let the arrow fly.

* * *

She shot awake, the bonds around her disintegrating as she opened her eyes.

"Rose!" Ezra's voice hoarsely yelled as Rose whirled around. She ducked, the ball of darkness hitting the wall across from her with a crack and a burst of dust. Rose shot to her feet and then leapt sideways as another wave of black from Ezra's fingers writhed toward her. A dark laugh echoed from the shadows as Ezra sent wave after wave of shadows at her, shooting past her and hitting the walls around them.

"Don't touch my sister!" Aspen screamed. He barreled into Ezra, magic curling in his fingers, fire and lightning preparing to strike. Ezra outstretched a fist and a tendril of darkness ensnaring Aspen's magic and knocking him out effortlessly.

"Ezra, please. No," Rose begged.

Ezra shook his head, a jerky movement that opposed the smooth movements of his hands as, from his fingertips shot a *net* of shadows. Rose was pinned down, writhing beneath the cold darkness, and the Dark Sorcerer let out another laugh.

"So. *Love.* What has it done for you, *Dark Prince?* What has it done for you, *Princess?*" he hissed, voice filled with maniacal glee.

Ezra approached her, hand outstretched, every muscle in his body tensed as if preparing to strike a death blow. Preparing to strike *her* death blow.

And there, in that figure of darkness, akin to the Dark Sorcerer's form, there were tears gleaming, trails of glowing silver on his face.

"What are you waiting for? *Kill her.*"

But Ezra didn't.

The trembling in his limbs stopped. His body straightened, and his other hand rose from the side of his body.

"*No.*"

* * *

This feeling, what was it?

This feeling of power, this feeling of flame, this feeling of rage and destruction and carnal anger.

He would not kill Rose.

Even though every cell in his body was itching to obey his father's orders, he would not, *could not* kill Rose.

But he had to.

Splintering pain shot through him with every second he resisted—never this long, never this strongly. He had to kill her. But he couldn't. He *couldn't*.

So Ezra tilted his head to the sky—to the light and the stars and the night and the clouds that he would never see—and let out a guttural roar. A roar of rage, of pain, of anger erupted from him as the force of a thousand dying stars shot from his fingertips.

As the walls of that mighty fortress came down around him, Ezra's last memory was the Dark Sorcerer howling in derisive, insane laughter as something inside him snapped.

* * *

Rose could only watch as the Dark Sorcerer laughed and Ezra crumpled to the floor.

She could only watch as the Dark Sorcerer raised a hand covered in darkness and thrust it at Ezra.

Not again.

But before the Dark Sorcerer struck his death blow, a blur of light knocked him to the ground.

"Rose. Aspen. Are you okay?" Crystal's voice shouted. "Audra, get them out of here. The boy too."

"The boy? Are you sure?"

"*Do it!*" Crystal commanded.

Rose felt lightning envelop her. As she blinked her eyes, clearing them from the sudden burst of light, she found herself staring at the ruins of the fortress. Audra had teleported them about fifty feet away, on top of a pile of boulders. Aspen and Ezra were beside her. Both were unconscious.

"Ezra. *Aspen!*" Rose shouted, shaking their shoulders. No response. In the dim light of the mountains around her, Rose could see Aspen's body. His clothes were torn, his back covered with dried blood, and bruises forming on his face. She looked back at the ruined fortress, where the Dark Sorcerer was floating slightly in the air, facing the Five Sorcerers. They stood shoulder-to-shoulder, weapons outstretched.

"I didn't think you would show up," the Dark Sorcerer shouted. His voice was so loud that even Rose could hear it. "I never thought I would see the day when Five Sorcerers stood before me again.

"Our ancestors have defeated you once, we can do it again," Crystal snarled back. The Dark Sorcerer blinked out of sight, appearing a foot away from Crystal, leaning forward and whispering in her ear. He said something Rose couldn't hear, but Crystal's face whitened.

Then, he blinked out of sight. Erik whipped around, the sword in his hand clanging against the Dark Sorcerer's blade of darkness with a resounding clash as he darted away. Audra lunged in from behind, and in her hands she held a staff. Rose watched, eyes squinted, as the two engaged the Dark Sorcerer in physical combat.

Crystal, standing off to the side, pointed at the Dark Sorcerer. His eyes widened and his movements slowed to a halt as his limbs were suddenly dragged down, his blade of darkness dissipating as his limbs trembled. *She's increasing the density of the water in his body, but the Dark Sorcerer is resisting the magic, so she can't kill him*, Rose observed. The Dark Sorcerer surrounded himself with a ribcage of darkness, and

Crystal looked up to see Aura and Aidan descending down from the sky. Aidan had been lifted to an impossible height, his fists coated with flames, and as Crystal pointed at him, he began to fall at a blinding speed. His density was also being increased, so that he could fall faster, and he hit the ribcage with a crack resounding through the air as the darkness fractured into pieces.

Before the Dark Sorcerer could retaliate, lightning teleported Aidan away, and vines began to sprout from the lifeless ground, binding the Dark Sorcerer in place as a storm of bright blue assaulted him. The Five Sorcerers all softly landed on the ground, standing shoulder to shoulder again as the dust from where the Dark Sorcerer had been cleared.

"Behind you!" Rose screamed. Crystal whipped around, a wall of water blocking the storm of miniscule, barely-visible darts of darkness that the Dark Sorcerer had sent at them. The Dark Sorcerer flashed from one position to another, moving through the shadows at an impossible speed, launching one attack after another at the Five Sorcerers, who retaliated with their own. Rose watched in awe as the clouds parted, revealing a dragon of lightning whose head was as large as the fortress that lunged down at the Dark Sorcerer. A maelstrom of wind and fire, formed within *seconds*, flew toward the Dark Sorcerer, who laughed as he darted between attacks, his shadows manipulating and blocking and attacking back.

He retaliated with his own enormous dragon of darkness that Crystal and Erik quickly suffocated within a wall of earth and water, forks of lightning so numerous Rose counted thirty before she lost count raining from the sky as Audra and Aura began to form a pack of wolves, each as large as a horse. As they roared at the Dark Sorcerer, they sent blasts of wind from their mouths so strong that the loose boulders and stones around them cracked as they lunged at the Dark Sorcerer, who weaved between their deadly attacks, gleefully laughing as his shadows writhed and twisted around the wolves. They became beings of pure darkness, and although they still had lightning at the tips of their claws and wind at their beck and call, they lunged at Aura and Audra instead, only to be wrapped in an orb of water and thrown into the great beyond.

The Five Sorcerers quickly established a system. While Aura, Audra, and Aidan threw attacks at the Dark Sorcerer with everything they had, Crystal and Erik supported from behind, batting away and disabling attacks that targeted the offensive, allowing them to push forward without worry for their own safety. If the Dark Sorcerer tried to target Crystal and Erik, Audra would teleport them away and the three attackers to the Dark Sorcerer.

However, despite their overwhelming power, the Dark Sorcerer seemed almost to be *toying* with them. He copied their own attacks, dodged seemingly impossibly powerful attacks effortlessly, and never attacked.

"Enough of this," the Dark Sorcerer hissed. "This is child's play. If this is all you have to offer, I may as well kill you here and now."

And then he launched into motion.

"*Rite of the Wicked Angel!*" he shouted. *No one uses incantations for magic.* Magic was all around them, in the air and in their blood. It didn't need to be summoned.

This wasn't magic.

From within the ground rose hundreds, *thousands* of shadows. There were hundreds of variants of colors, all tinged with the same darkness that seemed to swirl around them, more chaotic than the darkness the Dark Sorcerer usually wielded. As he continued summoning magic, thousands of what could only be described as *beasts* appeared. All walking on four legs, they seemed to take thousands of shapes and sizes, some small and agile with deadly horns and claws, other blundering and enormous with a blow that could crush someone's skull within seconds.

"Your armies are no more powerful than ours. *Descend, Cursed Fae!*" Audra shouted. She slammed her staff onto the ground, and the crystal that topped the twisted wood suddenly shone with the force of a thousand stars. Rose winced, looking away, and when she could open her eyes again, the skies cracked open.

The skies revealed lightning so fierce and beautiful that Rose could only stare as thousands of beings of lightning descended from the skies. They touched down on the floor, beings of lightning that had riders on their backs, and then Audra's arm fell and they rushed forward at the dark creatures. The two sorcerers had both summoned an army, and they clashed together with the sound of the earth cracking beneath them. Audra barely looked winded. As the two armies battled, the Dark Sorcerer gazed at Audra and laughed.

"Perhaps this will be fun after all," the Dark Sorcerer sneered, and as the sound of animals screaming and battle ripped through the air, the Five Sorcerers launched themselves at the Dark Sorcerer.

And then, to Rose's horror, she heard Audra's voice cry out in pain. In a split-second, Audra had teleported herself away from the battle with Erik, and as Rose squinted her eyes, she saw scarlet blood *everywhere*. The Dark Sorcerer teleported toward them, eyes wild and crazed as he sought to strike Audra's death blow, but before he could reach her, Crystal barreled into him.

Green energy flashed as Audra's wound healed.

Crystal let out a choking sound as the Dark Sorcerer lifted her up by her throat. Aidan rushed in from behind, sending them both tumbling to the floor, and the Five Sorcerers scrambled away from the Dark Sorcerer, eyes wide, Crystal massaging her throat as she coughed and spluttered.

Something was wrong.

When the Dark Sorcerer next moved, his form was a blur of speed. Crystal's eyes widened as he appeared behind her, and she barely dodged his next blow. He was *fast*, and Crystal was barely saved from a dagger to her chest as she was teleported away by Audra.

"Audra!" Aura shouted. Audra snarled at her, but lightning erupted from her fingers, rushing at not the Dark Sorcerer but at the Five Sorcerers. Lightning coated them in a bright blue cloak of magic, and then Crystal's hands moved in a circular motion.

When the Five Sorcerers next moved, they were as fast as the Dark Sorcerer.

For every devastating blow the Five Sorcerers struck, the Dark Sorcerer retaliated. The earth beneath them shook, the dirt cracking in rivets as power and magic flowed through the air, clashing with each other as the two superpowers battled. The army of dark and lightning were fading away, driving each other to non-existence.

As the attacks and magic the Five Sorcerers and the Dark Sorcerer threw at each other grew stronger and more numerous, Rose began to see the strain on the Five Sorcerer's faces. They were now dripping with sweat, covered in insignificant wounds, and while the Dark Sorcerer's face was masked, his movements were now slower, his magic less showy and more conservative. And still the battle continued. Blow after blow shot through the air until, finally, the Five Sorcerers pulled away.

"So it has come to this," Crystal murmured. She looked tired, as did all the other Sorcerers, and the Dark Sorcerer remained silent. Even as Aura wiped a stream of blood from a cut on her forehead, she grinned ferally at Crystal.

What were they going to do it?

Realization hit Rose as the Five Sorcerers, standing in a line, began to glow with pure power. Their Last Stands. A manifestation of years of training, the Last Stand was a Mage's last resort, only usable in moments of desperation and utter exhaustion.

This is it.

If they kill him, I'll finally be free.

"Last Stand: Rise of the Raiju!" Audra shouted.

The skies above her raged and storm with the force of the gods. The lightning hit Audra with a crackle, and she glowed with power as the lightning around her took form and manifested into the shape of the legendary Raiju. It was made of pure lightning, so massive that it stretched far above the destroyed fortress, and within its forehead stood Audra.

"Last Stand: Gaia's Wrath!" Erik shouted. The Dark Sorcerer lunged forward at him; however, Crystal lunged forward and cut him off with a shield of water. Even in the barren land around them, plants began to sprout from the ground. As Rose watched in fascination and horror, they sprouted from Erik. He screamed, whether from pain or joy as the wood devoured him completely. After a few seconds, standing in his place was a giant woman of wood and stone. Her eyes glowed with the essence of nature, and as Rose watched in fascination, the giant bowed to the Raiju.

In response, the Raiju kneeled down. The Dark Sorcerer's eyes widened, but he remained still as the giant mounted the Raiju's back.

"Last Stand: Sword of Fire!" Aidan shouted. From somewhere deep within him, he emitted purple and blue flames. They burned so fiercely that the stone beneath him was charred to a crisp, and as it continued to flow from him, it formed the shape of a sword. Finally, the sword's form was complete, and Aidan, levitating it in his hands, knelt as he presented it to the giant. She took it in her giant hands, and Rose watched as the Raiju scooped Aidan up with a paw, throwing him into her forehead next to Audra.

And there were still two more Last Stands left.

"Last Stand: Tenshi's Protection!"

"Last Stand: Wings of Gods!"

The two sorcerer's powers exploded in tandem as the sky above them darkened and rain began to fall. As Crystal clenched her fist, the water turned into solid armor, wrapping itself around the Giant and Raiju's figure. Meanwhile, a gust built up, and as Rose watched, the Giant and the Raiju both sprouted bright white wings.

Before the Dark Sorcerer stood a creature that Gods could not hope to defy.

Yet, to Rose's shock, the Dark Sorcerer began to laugh.

"Last Stand: Fallen Angel!"

It was fitting, Rose decided. The Dark Sorcerer had turned from light to dark, from a Prince to an enemy of all six realms. In all eyes, *he himself* was a fallen angel.

And so, when he took the form of a being of pure darkness, Rose felt not anger, not fear, but grief. In that moment, Rose mourned Rhysand, mourned the man that he used to be and could have become.

He was enormous, stretching easily as tall as the combined height of the giant and the Raiju. From his back stretched wings, akin to an angel's but pure black. His form was that of pure darkness covered in dull silver armor and the edges of his form were tinged with scarlet red. Within his hands were two enormous axes.

His eyes were piercing, beautiful gold.

"It is impressive that you have forced me to use my Last Stand," the Dark Sorcerer said. "But this ends here."

And the Five Sorcerers rushed forward. The earth rumbled, shaking so violently that Rose's teeth chattered as the sword of violet fire met the axes of pure darkness.

The battle between the two forces was so potent that Rose could taste destruction upon her tongue. Lightning and violet fire raged and cast light upon the darkness of the Ken'o mountains. The giant and the Raiju moved as one as they battled the fallen angel, and the armor of water was unyielding even when the mighty axes of darkness struck.

Then, very suddenly, it was all over.

The demon of darkness's axes were by his side one moment, and the next, the giant's head was severed. It fell to the floor with a thud, and the rest of the giant toppled off the magnificent Raiju. Its body began to dissolve, the wondrous body of wood and stone melting away into nothing. The Raiju snarled at the demon, crouching and jumping into the air, jaws outstretched as it leapt toward the demon's neck.

The demon grabbed the Raiju by its face. Ignoring its flailing claws that struck and tore, the demon squeezed its fist.

Lightning sparked as the wondrous beast of lightning melted into nothing.

To the ground fell the Five Sorcerers. They were conscious, Crystal rising to her feet, legs shaking and hands trembling.

The cost of the Last Stand: once the user's magic was completely depleted, the Last Stand would melt away. The user would face a complete and absolute drain of the user's magic for a great amount of time. The Dark Sorcerer's demon melted away as he strode toward the Five Sorcerers.

Magic sprung from steady fingers as he stared at Audra. She pushed herself up on shaking arms, then collapsed back down.

Rose moved.

"Rose, no!" Crystal shouted, but Rose ignored her. Lightning flashed down from the sky as Rose drew from that huge, bountiful magic within her, summoning lightning that struck at the Dark Sorcerer. He backed away, his eyes widened, and smiled.

"Rose, what are you doing?" Aura shouted. Rose lunged at him, fists covered in fire, but he batted her away with a tendril of darkness as if she was nothing. Lightning flashed down from the sky, but the Dark Sorcerer shielded, a dagger of darkness outstretched as he cast it toward Crystal.

Crystal squeezed her eyes shut. Rose cast water, straining as she tried to form a shield to protect Crystal, but she was too slow, *too slow.*

The dagger hit home with a thud and a spray of scarlet.

Rose fell to her knees, tears leaking from as she shut her eyes as the Dark Sorcerer yanked out his blade of darkness and aimed it toward the next person. Audra. Fierce anger shone in her eyes as she rose up on shaking feet, but tendrils of darkness shot up from the ground, binding her in place.

But before the dagger hit Audra, it melted away into a wisp of nothing.

A cold hand clenched Rose's as she opened her eyes and met his eyes.

"No more," Ezra whispered. "No more death."

Rose unleashed her magic.

*　*　*

Rose's magic was stardust and beauty and light.

Ezra and Rose stood together, hands entangled. The Dark Sorcerer's eyes widened as he backed away from the glowing pair.

"I will *destroy you*!" he shouted. He cast a wave of darkness at them, but it melted away at the cusp of their wave of power. The Five Sorcerers stared as the pair glowed brighter and brighter, their bodies overflowing with pure magic. It was as if duality itself had presented its existence. From the boy flowed pure darkness, from the girl flowed pure light.

And then they exploded.

Light and dark, stars and black holes, destruction and creation hand in hand. Their magic exploded, and the Dark Sorcerer staggered back, his eyes widening as the magic they formed ate away at him. At his darkness.

As the very magic he used to cloak himself vanished.

The light glowed so bright that the darkness of the Dark Sorcerer was but a shadow in the corner as they glowed and glowed and glowed.

They found him. The *darkness* inside of him, his magic, dark and black as night. They ate away, tearing away at his power as the Dark Sorcerer begged and pleaded.

As more and more vanished, his human body formed.

Darkness melted away from him, revealing black hair. Golden eyes. Pale skin.

And then they met his core. Within him lay beautiful light, so deeply buried within darkness that it had nearly gone out. But not anymore. Rose and Ezra, hands entangled, tore at the darkness until the light was all that remained.

They stretched out toward the light, like beckoning to like as the light looked up. Saw that the darkness around it had been vanquished. Strained and stretched out, slowly expanded, as if searching for a way to reclaim the body that had been filled with shadows.

As quickly as the light had exploded across the battlefield, it melted away into nothing. The Dark Sorcerer was kneeling on the ground, clutching his head, his mouth forming the words *no no no no no*. The battlefield was still as Rose and Ezra, devoid of power, sank to their knees. Rose's breath was harsh in her lungs, and as she stared at the Five Sorcerers, she suddenly realized that they were also slowly getting to their feet. Their wounds were gone. Healed.

They all stared, breath bated, at the Dark Sorcerer. There was no sign of that dark power within him. He stood up. Golden eyes pierced Ezra and Rose as he stared at them. Rose started, staring at him as he approached them. A cool, pale hand smoothed over her jaw as the Dark Sorcerer stared at them and began to weep.

Everyone watched in silence as his shoulders shook, the force of his tears overwhelming him as he put his head in his hands. For a single minute, he was wholly human.

Darkness erupted.

Rose felt herself yanked within darkness as she thrashed and screamed, but when she could see again, she was in the air, floating above the Five Sorcerers, and when she looked to her right, she saw *Aspen*. He was conscious, eyes wide as he met Rose's gaze.

"Choose one," the Dark Sorcerer snarled. The Five Sorcerers stared at each other, wide-eyed. "Choose one and leave."

Aura stepped forward. She had steel in her gaze and ice in her soul as she stared at the Dark Sorcerer. She flexed her hands, trying to summon magic, but nothing came out.

They were completely drained.

"Who are you going to choose?" Aspen asked.

Aura's eyes darted between Rose and Aspen – and fixated on the scars on Rose's wrists. In that horrible moment, as Rose looked into Aura's eyes, she saw their answer.

"Please," Rose begged. "Please. *Please.* I saved your lives. I'm more powerful than Aspen. *Please, please,* I worked so hard. I'm an apprentice. Please." Tears rolled down her face as she stared at the sorcerers, who looked impassive, uncaring. *"Let me have my life, just this once."*

"Choose Rose," Aspen rasped. She jolted in surprise, stared at him, wide-eyed. "She deserves it"

Silence.

"Give us Aspen," Aura growled.

Rose felt her heart fracture into a thousand tiny pieces.

The Dark Sorcerer laughed. The tendrils of darkness melted away from around Aspen, and he dropped to the ground. Aidan walked up to him, hoisting Aspen up in his muscular arms.

"Please," Rose begged. Her voice was hoarse, desperate. Aspen was thrashing in Aidan's arms, screaming something she couldn't hear through the roaring in her ears. "Please. Take me. *Don't leave me!*"

"Rose! *Rose!*" Aspen screamed. Aidan hoisted him over his back, and all of the sorcerers placed a hand on Audra's shoulder. "Take Rose instead! Don't leave her!"

"Please," Rose whispered.

With a flash of lightning, they vanished. The last thing Rose saw was Aspen staring back at her, hand outstretched, a scream escaping from his mouth as

Rose stared at the place they had been as she felt her dreams fracture within her. She had found something akin to a family. She had been an *apprentice.*

Ash. River. Halt. Blossom.

They're gone.

It began to rain. The Dark Sorcerer looked faintly surprised as he lowered Rose to the ground. Even though there were no restraints binding her, Rose didn't run. Didn't fight.

She sank to her knees. Tilted her head up to the sky. The rain now covered her face, mixing with her tears.

Love. Mercy. Family. Peace. Kindness.

Rose felt something within her shatter as she screamed.

***

"Are you awake?" the Dark Sorcerer's voice asked her.

Rose ignored him.

Slave. Slave. Slave.

"I'm sorry. I really am," the Dark Sorcerer murmured. His voice was softer than she had ever heard it.

Second-born. Second-born. Second-born.

They were in a new hideout now. Ezra was still unconscious. Rose's legs and arms were free.

"You can leave any time you want," the Dark Sorcerer told her. "Your powers are no longer mine to take. I cannot restrain them. I cannot make you take a Blood Oath either. You are of no use to me. You may leave. We're too far away from the kingdoms. You'll die off in a few days."

Second-born. Slave. Second-born. Slave. Second-born. Slave.

Rose didn't move as he stood up and left the room.

She didn't move when he brought back a tray of food six hours later.

The words kept on repeating within her.

Second-born. Slave. Second-born. Slave. Second-born. Slave.

Other words, too.

Firstborn. Magic. Love. Peace. Happiness. Ash. River. Loyalty.

But they began to fracture.

There was only two words in her mind.

Second-born. Slave. Second-born. Slave. Second-born. Slave.

***

"Did you rescue my daughter?" the Queens asked.

In response, Audra collapsed to the ground.

"You bastards!" Aspen screamed. "They didn't save *anyone*. The Dark Sorcerer gave them a choice, and they saved me instead of Rose."

The Queen's eyes were filled with unquestionable grief as she sank to her knees.

"You chose Aspen again?" she asked Aura, the only Sorcerer still standing. Palace guards had already brought the rest of the unconscious sorcerers to the medical wing.

"She was raised a *slave*, Your Majesty. Aspen's the firstborn," Aura whispered. "I didn't have a choice."

"You have no idea what you've done," Aspen snarled at Aura. His eyes were gleaming with hatred and fear. "Do you know what she's gone through? How hard she has worked?"

"I know. But you're the firstborn," Aura repeated. "Saving you was the right choice. It was the right choice," she repeated, as if trying to convince herself. Devastation reared its ugly head, settling into her eyes as she shook her head.

"And she's the stronger child. The better one. The one with more scars, the kinder one, the one who used to love and give freely," Aspen screamed. "Do you know what you've done?"

The Queen and Aura were both silent.

"*She* was the one who worked so hard to become an apprentice. *She* was the one with more power. *She* was the one who *saved your life!*" Aspen said. "The Dark Sorcerer was also a second-born. Just like her. Just like her, he suffered because he was a second-born. And now, Rose must loath us just as much as the Dark Sorcerer does. More."

Aura's face went white.

"I'll never forgive you," Aspen snarled.

Aura's face crumpled.

"And neither will she."

Epilogue

HATRED.

As she sat in the dark room, the only thing she could feel was hatred.

A hero of justice.

"Ezra?"

"Yeah?"

"I wanted to become a hero of justice because you died. I saw your tragic, beautiful lie of a life and thought to myself, *'If I could stop even one person from reliving it, it'd be worth it.'*"

"Yeah."

"And, even now, I still wish that. I wish that no one would ever have to go through any of this. Born a second-born, born as a slave, born into suffering and a life that could never be changed."

"Yeah."

"A hero of justice. Do you think that's realistic, Ezra?" Rose asked. His silence said enough. "After everything I've been through, after everything I've done, after everything I've sacrificed, I'm still the one who's here. I was the one who became a slave. I was the one who was sent to the Salt Mines. I was the one who had to work without sleep every single night just to achieve *half* what Aspen already had since birth. It's an interesting thing, really," Rose murmured. "And, to be honest, if life was fairer, if I had actually made it, it would've been worth it."

"I—"

"And after *years* of abuse, I finally succeeded. I became an apprentice. And *still*, after all I've gone through, I'm the one who's here. Imprisoned by one of the most demonic people in the world."

She laughed, then. It was dry, devoid of humor, a twisted shadow of what it used to be.

"Rose, are you—"

"Being a hero of justice isn't going to work."

"What?"

"That's what the Dark Sorcerer finally realized, right? There are no heroes. There is no justice without a cost."

"Rose."

"You understand, don't you?" Rose whispered. "This is the only way."

The door opened, and the Dark Sorcerer stepped inside.

"You've refused to leave us," the Dark Sorcerer said. Rose noticed that his figure, cloaked with darkness, wasn't as tragic as she had remembered.

It was powerful, world-changing.

"I have to kill you."

It was what Rose needed to become.

"Goodbye, Princess," he said. Ezra stepped forward, but Rose motioned for him to stop. He obeyed. Darkness sprung up from around the Dark Sorcerer, and Rose felt herself lifted in the air. As she stared at the Dark Sorcerer, stared into those shining golden eyes, Rose noticed that they seemed to be gleaming a little brighter than usual. A blade of darkness pressed against her neck.

"Don't."

"I think I've made my intentions cle—"

"Hear me out, *Rhysand*," Rose said. There wasn't any panic in her voice, nor fear in her face. The Dark Sorcerer stared at her, surprised. She was dropped to the ground. Rose gathered her nerves, balled her fear into a tiny little orb.

Fear makes you weak.

Rose stared into the face of death and smiled.

He didn't move.

"Be honest. You did it all for your end goal, right?" Rose asked.

"Yes. A world where everyone is equal, where becoming powerful is a choice and not a matter of when you were born."

"What about the nobles, those born with more magic? What about the slaves, the Nulls?"

"They're all a part of it, aren't they? A Null can become as powerful as an average magic-user, they merely have to work harder. You and I both know this. With the basic assistance of magic, Nulls can attain physical capabilities that could decimate any Mage. You've read the history books."

"How do you plan to accomplish any of this?" Rose asked. "How do you plan to create this beautiful world?"

"I'm not telling you that," the Dark Sorcerer responded. "I'm not stupid."

Turning her back on him, Rose stared up at the stone wall.

There had been no hero of justice in his story.

Only a broken man, cursed and beaten by the world around him, a reflection of what she had become. Broken, weary, toiling through the trials society provided only to have their efforts torn into pieces by forces beyond their control.

"I hate you," Rose murmured. He didn't reply. "I hate you. For everything that you've done to me, when you had the chance."

"I'm sorry."

A broken man, but stronger than any prince she had met.

"But you wanna know who I hate more, now?" Rose asked. He cocked his head, waiting for a response. "I hate the people who gave you the chance to hurt me more."

"What are you implying?"

"I have nowhere to go," Rose murmured. "How could I face Aspen and the Five Sorcerers after what they've done? How could I face my friends after what I've learned?"

The Dark Sorcerer stared at her.

"The world is not what I've believed it to be," Rose said. She stood up. Approached the Dark Sorcerer. "There are no heroes of justice, nor champions of glory. There are only those born higher, and those born lesser."

The Dark Sorcerer smiled as Rose, less than a foot away from the Dark Sorcerer, outstretched her hands. Magic erupted from them, and she watched the Five Elements dance among her fingers impassively.

"So what do I do now? What do I do with all this power I've never had the chance to use?" Rose murmured. She clenched her fists, suffocating her magic. Her eyes were devoid of joy.

"So what will you do?" the Dark Sorcerer asked.

Rose turned her eyes toward the Dark Sorcerer, and the man who lived and breathed the darkness shivered. Those beautiful gray eyes had darkened into a stormy black, a thundercloud about to erupt. Ripe potential. Raw rage. Rose's lips curled into a feral smirk as she walked past him, toward the door, toward the dark future that awaited her.

"I'm going to help you. Together, we'll create a new world."

Made in United States
North Haven, CT
08 October 2022